Lord Brocktree

A Tale of Redwall

Tales of Redwall

- Lord Brocktree
- Martin the Warrior
- Mossflower
- The Legend of Luke
- Outcast of Redwall
- Mariel of Redwall
- The Bellmaker
- Salamandastron
- Redwall
- Mattimeo
- The Pearls of Lutra
- The Long Patrol
- Marlfox
- The Taggerung

Click onto the Redwall website - and discover more about the legendary world of Redwall and its creator, Brian Jacques!
http://www.redwall.org

BRIAN JACQUES

LORD BROCKTREE

A Tale of Redwall

Illustrated by Fangorn

RED FOX

A Red Fox Book

Published by Random House Children's Books
20 Vauxhall Bridge Road, London SW1V 2SA

A division of The Random House Group Ltd
London Melbourne Sydney Auckland
Johannesburg and agencies throughout the world

3 5 7 9 10 8 6 4

First published in Great Britain by
Hutchinson Children's Books 2000

Red Fox edition 2001

Printed and bound in Great Britain
by Bookmarque Ltd, Croydon, Surrey

Papers used by The Random House Group Limited are natural, recyclable products made from wood grown in sustainable forests. The manufacturing processes conform to the environmental regulations of the country of origin.

THE RANDOM HOUSE GROUP Limited Reg. No. 954009

www.randomhouse.co.uk

ISBN 0 09 941119 9

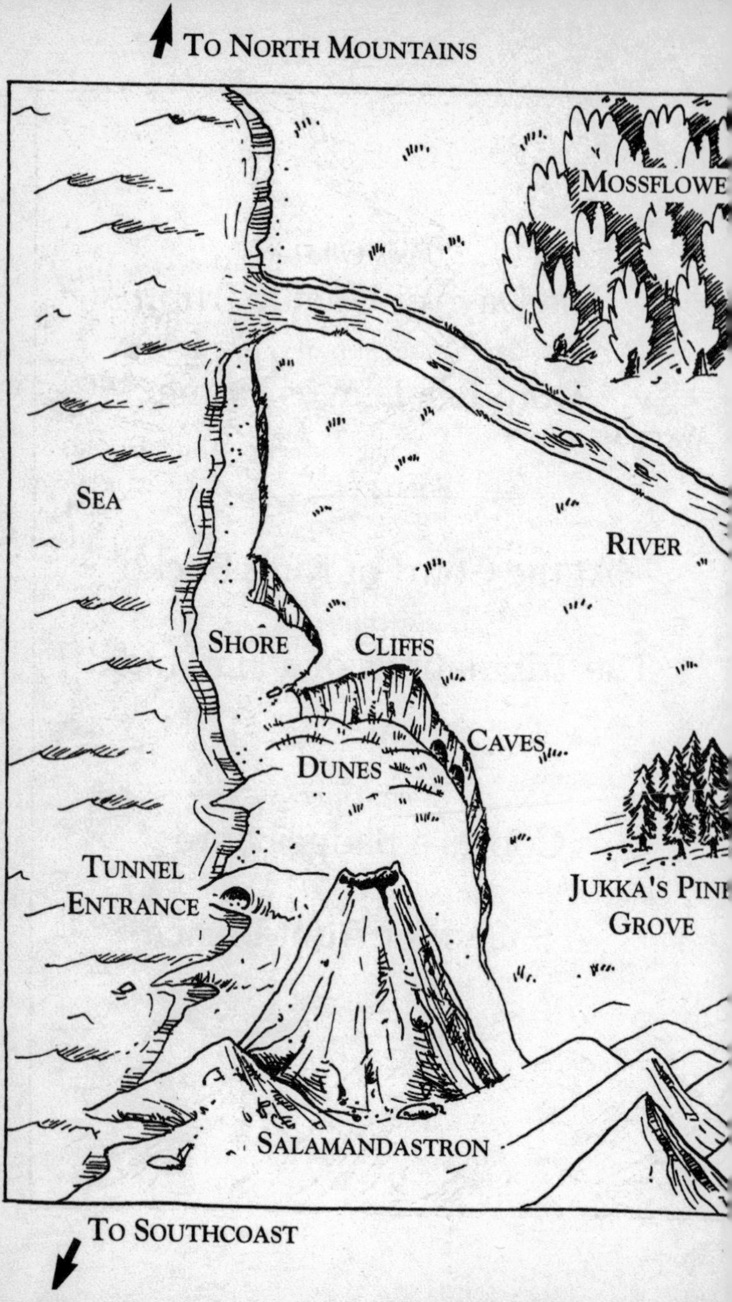
To North Mountains
Mossflowe
Sea
River
Shore
Cliffs
Caves
Dunes
Tunnel
Entrance
Jukka's Pin
Grove
Salamandastron
To Southcoast

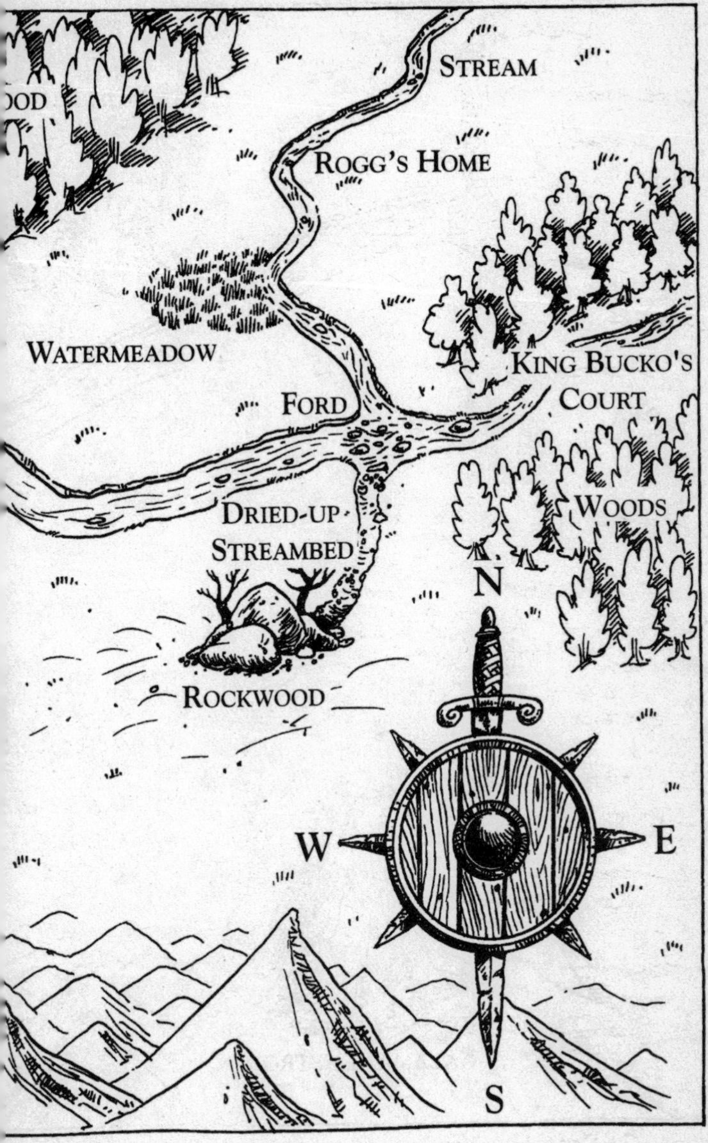
OOD
STREAM
ROGG'S HOME
WATERMEADOW
KING BUCKO'S
COURT
FORD
WOODS
DRIED-UP
STREAMBED
N
ROCKWOOD
W
E
S

I am the Teller of Tales,
Gaze into the fire with me,
For I know of the Badger Lords,
And their mountain, by the sea.
'Tis of a fearsome warrior,
Full of fate and destiny,
Who followed dreams, along strange paths,
Unknown to such as we.
This Badger Lord was fearless,
As all who followed him knew,
And the haremaid he befriended,
Why, she was as young as you!
But no less bold or courageous,
Full of valour and strong of heart,
Aye, young 'uns like you, good and true,
May stand to take their part.
So here is my story, may it bring
Some smiles, and a tear or so,
It happened, once upon a time,
Far away, and long ago.
Outside the night wind keens and wails,
Come listen to me, the Teller of Tales!

Prologue

Lord Russano of Salamandastron put aside his quill and capped a tiny gourd of ink with a wooden stopper. Leaving his study, the badger went downstairs, clutching a wooden pail full of parchment scrolls. He was met at the bottom by his wife, Lady Rosalaun, who shook her head reprovingly at him.

'So, that's where my pail went. I've been looking everywhere for it. Aren't you ashamed of yourself, pinching pails!'

However, Russano looked anything but ashamed. He held up the pail and shook it triumphantly. 'Look, Rosalaun, I've finished it, my history of Lord Brocktree's journey and conquest of our mountain!'

Rosalaun smiled at her husband. He was the kindest and wisest badger Salamandastron had ever known, though when he was enthusiastic about his pet projects he behaved like a cheerful eager youngster. She took hold of his inkstained paw as they walked to the dining hall. 'They're all waiting, you know. Remember, you promised to read them the story once you'd completed it.'

Russano chuckled. 'I don't suppose Snowstripe,

Melanius and the leverets would wait a day or two until I tidy this manuscript up a bit?'

Rosalaun stopped Russano in his tracks. 'There's not just our son and daughter and some young leverets waiting to hear you read the tale. Word has got round. Every hare on the mountain wants to hear it too!'

Russano turned and made for the stairs, but his wife held on to his paw. The Badger Lord appeared rather flustered. 'Every hare, you say? You mean all of them? But . . . but . . . I only meant this as something for the young 'uns, to teach them a little of our mountain's history!'

Rosalaun squeezed his paw affectionately. 'That's not fair. What about us older ones, the parents and grandkin, aren't we entitled to know our mountain's history? I for one would love to hear it. Besides, you have a wonderful storytelling voice. Oh, say you'll read it to us all, Russano, please!'

The Badger Lord allowed himself to be led off again towards the dining hall. 'Oh, all right, but it'll take a few days. This is a big work. I've been two seasons now, reading through dusty old parchments, interviewing creatures for stories about their ancestors, and studying carvings in the forge. I've sat on the shore, listening to sea otters, stood beneath trees recording squirrels - huh, I've even had to crouch for four days in a mole dwelling. Had to keep waking those two fat old moles up so I could hear their story. Do you know, it was told to them by their great-grandma, who had it from her old aunt's cousin, twice removed on the uncle's side, or so they said?'

Rosalaun stood with her hand on the doorlatch. 'Yes, yes, I know all that, Russano. It won't matter how long you take to read the thing. You can space it out, a bit every evening. Nothing nicer on a winter's night than a good story. Now, the fire's banked up, supper's on the table, and everybeast is waiting. So in you go!'

The dining hall was packed to capacity, mainly with

hares, though there was a scattering of moles, squirrels, hedgehogs, mice, and some visiting otters. Lord Russano was immediately captured by his two young offspring, Melanius and Snowstripe, who tugged him up the three broad steps to where his chair had been placed next to a supper-laden table.

'Papa Papa, read the story to us, please please!'

'Are me an' Snowstripe in the story, Papa?'

Russano chuckled as he sat them down on the cushioned chair arms on either side of him. 'Great seasons, you'd have to be many many seasons old to be in this tale. Now sit still and be quiet, my dears.'

Silence fell over the hall, broken only by the door's opening as the duty cooks came hurrying in. Everybeast turned round and shushed them loudly, and quiet was restored once more. Russano split open a small loaf, cut a thick chunk of cheese and jammed it in the bread, making himself a rough sandwich. Every eye was upon him as he took a few good bites and washed them down with a half-tankard of October Ale. The still atmosphere was broken by a small hedgehog squeaking aloud.

'When's a Badgelord goin' t'get on wiv it?'

Russano left off eating and looked quizzically at the hogbabe. 'Get on with what?'

A deafening roar rang out from the crowded hall. 'The story!'

Russano looked up in mock surprise. 'Oh, did you want me to read you my story?'

He clapped paws to his ears as the noise hit him like a tidal wave. 'Yeeeeeeessssss!'

The small polished hardwood stick that Russano always carried with him was lying on the table. Lady Rosalaun picked it up and waved it warningly under his nose. 'Lord Russano, will you please stop teasing and read the story. Either that, or straight off to bed with you!'

Everybeast, especially the little ones, laughed at the idea of a Badger Lord being sent to bed for being naughty. Russano pulled the first scroll from the pail. Unrolling it across the tabletop, he placed his tankard on the top edge to stop it folding back. His kind brown eyes roamed the hall, a smile hovering upon his lips as he spoke.

'Friends, I will read to you for a few hours each evening. Salamandastron's history goes back further into the mists of time than even I would dare to guess. But the mountain as we know it today, with its leveret school, Long Patrol and laws set down for all to live in peace by, is due mainly to the work of one creature: Lord Brocktree of Brockhall. It was he who was responsible for the life we enjoy here – the outer gardens and terraces, the orchards and crop-growing areas, and the wonderful chambers, so full of comfort. Other badgers were here before him, and they were all good Lords in their own fashion, but not until the time of Lord Brocktree of Brockhall did the mountain really come into its own. I have recorded the history of his early years as faithfully as I could.

'So, then, here it is. I hope you learn lessons from it, take heed of its value, and most of all I hope you enjoy it as a mighty tale of great warriors.'

BOOK ONE

The Days of Ungatt Trunn

also entitled

Dorothea Leaves Home

1

Loneliness was everywhere. Hopelessness and an air of foreboding had settled over the western shores, casting their pall over land, sea and the mountain of Salamandastron. Yet nobeast knew the cause of it.

A pale moon of early spring cast its wan light down upon the face of the mighty deeps, touching each wind-driven wavetop with flecks of cold silver. Soughing breakers crashed endlessly upon the strand, weary after their journey from the corners of the earth. Above the tideline, gales chased dry sand against the rocks, forcing each particle to sing part of the keening dirge that blended with the sounds of the dark ocean.

In his chamber overlooking the scene, Lord Stonepaw sat in his great chair, feeling as ancient as the mountain he ruled. In one corner, his bed stood neatly made, unused now for a score of seasons. He was far too old; the ritual of lying down each night and rising next day had become painful for his bones. Drawing his cloak tight against vagrant night chills, the once mighty Badger Lord squinted rheumily out to sea, worrying constantly about his domain.

Without bothering to knock, a venerable hare creaked his way into the chamber, leaning heavily upon a small serving cart which he was pushing before him. Stonepaw's efforts to ignore him were of no avail. He fussed hither and thither, like a broody hen with only one chick, chunnering constantly as he went about his chores. 'Mmmm, no fire lit again, eh, m'lud? Catch your death o' cold one night y'will, mark m'words!'

Sparks from the flint he was striking against a blade, coupled with his wheezy blowing, soon had a flame from dry moss crackling against pine twigs.

'Hmmm, that's better, wot? C'mon, get this supper down. You've got to blinkin' well eat to live, y'know!'

Stonepaw shook his head at the sight of the food his servant was laying out on the small table at his side. 'Leave me alone, Fleetscut. I'll have it later.'

'No y'won't, sire, you'll flippin' well have it now! I ain't goin' t'the bother o' luggin' vittles from the kitchen to watch you let 'em go cold. Hot veggible soup an' fresh bread, that'll do you the world o' good, wot!'

The ancient badger sighed with resignation. 'Oh, give your tongue a rest. I'll take the soup. Bread's no good t'me, though. Too crusty – hurts my gums.'

Fleetscut brooked no arguments. Drawing his dagger, he trimmed the crusts from the still oven-warm loaf. 'No crusts now, wot? Dip it in your soup, m'lud.' The hare perched on the chair arm, helping himself to soup and bread, in the hope that it might encourage his master's appetite. Stonepaw snorted mirthlessly.

'Huh, look at us. Me, Stonepaw, hardly able to hold a spoon with the same paws that used to lift huge boulders, and you, Fleetscut, doddering round with a trolley!'

The hare nudged his old friend and cackled. 'Heh heh heh! Mebbe so, but I can still remember the days when I could leap three times as high as that trolley, aye, an' run from dawn to dusk without stoppin' to draw breath. Wasn't a bally hare on the mountain could even stay with my dust trail! Those were the seasons, wot! You too, Stonepaw. I saw you lift boulders bigger'n yourself when we were young, you could break spears an' bend swords with your bare paws . . .'

Stonepaw gazed at the paws in question. 'That may have been, my old messmate, but look at my paws now, silver-furred, battered, scarred and so full of aches and pains that they're no good for anything!'

Fleetscut hauled himself from the chair arm and went to lean at the long window overlooking the sea. 'So what's the blinkin' problem? Everybeast has t'grow old, nothin' can stop that. We've had a long an' good life, you'n'me, fought our battles, protected the western coast against all comers, an' never once backed off from any fight. There's been peace now for as long as any creature on the mountain can remember. What're you worryin' about, sire?'

With a grunt, Stonepaw rose slowly from his chair and joined his companion at the window. He stared out at the darkened waters as he replied. 'Peace has gone on too long. Something inside me says that trouble such as these shores have never known is headed our way. I wished that we could live our days out without having to take up arms again, Fleetscut, but deep down I'm stone cold certain it won't happen. Worst part of it is that I can't even guess what the future holds.'

Fleetscut looked strangely at the Badger Lord, then shuddered and went to warm himself by the fire. 'Sire, I know exactly how you feel. Matter o' fact I was thinkin' those very thoughts this afternoon, when old Blench the cook said to me: "Looks like evil comin' soon." She says: "See for yourself, there ain't a sight or sound of a single bird anywhere on land or sea!"'

Lord Stonepaw stroked his long silver beard thoughtfully. 'Blench was right, too, now you come to mention it. Where do you suppose all the birds have gone? The skies are usually thick with gulls, cormorants, petrels and shearwaters in late spring.'

Fleetscut shrugged expressively. 'Who knows what

goes on in the mind of a seabird? Maybe they know things we don't. Stands t'reason, though, sire, why should they hang about if they know somethin' bad is due to come here?'

The badger smiled at his faithful old friend. 'Why indeed? They have no duty to protect this coast and they can always build nests elsewhere. Leave me now, I'll talk to you on the morrow. There are things I must do.'

Fleetscut had never questioned his Badger Lord's authority, and was not about to do so now. Bobbing a stiff bow he left the chamber, pushing his trolley.

Lord Stonepaw made his way to the secret chamber where countless other Badger Rulers of Salamandastron had gone to dream mysterious dreams. It was a place that would have made the hairs on any other creature's back stand stiff. Ranged around the walls of the inner chamber were lines of little carvings, telling of the mountain's history. Guarding it in fearsome armoured array stood the mummified bodies of past Badger Warriors: Urthrun the Gripper, Spearlady Gorse, Bluestripe the Wild, Ceteruler the Just and many other legendary figures.

From his own lantern, Stonepaw lit three others. Then, taking a pawful of herbs from a shelf, he sprinkled them into the lantern vents. As the sweet-smelling incense of smoke wreathed him, he sat down upon a carved rock throne. Closing both eyes, he breathed in deeply and let his mind take flight. After a while he began speaking.

'If the gates of Dark Forest lie open for me soon, if the shadow of evil darkens our western shores, who will serve in my stead? My hares are scattered far and wide. Peacetime makes young warriors restless; they are gone questing afar for adventure. Only the old guard are left here with me on this mountain, dim of eye and feeble of limb, the seasons of their strength long flown.'

Lord Stonepaw's eyes began flickering, and the herbal smoke swirled about his great silver head as he sat up straight, his voice echoing around the rockbound cavern.

'Where is the strongest of the strong? Who can be so perilous that a force of fighting hares will rise and follow that creature? Is there a badger roaming the earth brave and mighty enough to become Lord of Salamandastron?'

Outside on the strand, the gale increased, waves crashed widespread on the tideline in their effort to conquer the land, like a maddened beast the ocean roared. Sand swept upward into winding columns, driving, spiralling, crazily across the shore. Yet still was there no sound of birds or any other living thing to be heard.

A foreboding of great evil lay over the land and sea. But nobeast knew the cause of it.

. . . Yet.

2

In the northeast reaches of Mossflower Wood a traveller had walked straight into trouble. Drigg Slopmouth and his brood numbered thirteen in all, nasty, vicious stoats every one. Drigg's family loved to cheat, lie, steal, bully or murder, even among themselves; their chief hatred was honest toil. The only work they had done that day was to lie in wait for an unsuspecting wayfarer, a lanky carefree young hare known to her friends as Dotti. She was reckless and impatient and not over-fond of studying, but what she lacked in scholarly achievement she made up for in impudence, courage and a sharp wit. The realisation that she was surrounded by Drigg and his band of robbers did not seem to upset her unduly.

She nodded amiably at them. 'Good mornin', chaps an' chappesses. Not a bad old sort o' day for the time of season, wot!'

A snigger arose from the stoats.

'Lookit wot we caught, Drigg – a posh rabbit!'

Dotti rounded on the speaker, a fat frowsy female. 'Specifically incorrect, doncha know, my old stoatess. I'm a hare, not a rabbit. Now say it correctly after me. Lookit wot we caught, Drigg – a posh hare.'

Drigg stepped between them, pointing to the travelling

haversack, which resembled an outsized handbag, swinging from the young hare's paw. 'Empty yer bag on the ground!'

Dotti smiled sweetly at him. 'Oh, I'd rather not, sir. It'd take me half the day to get the jolly old thing repacked, wot!'

A large, dim-looking stoat, Drigg's eldest son, pushed forward. 'Then tell us wot you got in yer bag, an' don't say it isn't nothin'.'

Dotti clucked reprovingly. 'You mean don't say it isn't anything. Dearie me, I'll bet you never attended woodland school.'

The big stoat snarled, pawing at a long dagger he wore hanging from his belt. 'Just show us wot's in the bag, rabbit!'

The haremaid wagged a paw at him. 'There you go again with that rabbit error. Did I call you a stoat? Of course I didn't. It's obvious to anybeast you're an oversized toad. Oh, sorry, the bag. Here, you take it!'

Dotti swung the bag, hard. There was a cracking noise as it struck the stoat's head, laying him out flat. She whirled upon the others, a perilous glint in her eyes. 'I can forgive bad grammar and insults, but that was a good flagon of old cider, a gift for my aunt Blench, an' that oaf has just broken it with his head. Unforgivable! Ah well, there's only one thing I've got left to say to you lot . . . Eulaaaliiiaaaaaa!'

The time-honoured war cry of fighting hares rang out as Dotti hurled herself upon the would-be robbers, laying about her with her bag left and right, leaping and kicking out fiercely with powerful rangy footpaws.

From the shelter of a broad beech nearby, another traveller watched the mêlée. He chuckled quietly. The young hare seemed to be doing fine, despite the number of vermin she was facing. Dotti had accounted for three more stoats and was in the process of depriving the fat frowsy one of her remaining snaggle teeth when Drigg caught her footpaws in a noose. The haremaid was yanked off balance and floored as three stoats leapt upon her back. Drigg Slopmouth drew a sharp double-edged dagger and circled his fallen victim, calling to those who had piled in on her: 'Get 'er on 'er back an' stretch 'er neck, so's I can get a stab in. 'Old 'er still, ye blitherin' oafs!'

From his position behind the beech tree, the watcher decided it was time to step in and help the beleaguered hare. Drigg screeched in terror as he was lifted into the air and used as a swatter to knock the other stoats willy-nilly. His flailing paws swept vermin left and right, the wind was knocked from him as his stomach connected with the back of another, and stars exploded when his head cracked against the jaw of a hefty young stoat. Dotti scrambled upright swinging her bag, but there was nobeast to strike. Vermin lay everywhere, those still conscious moaning aloud, nursing their injuries. Drigg still hung, half dazed, from the paw of a mighty male badger. The huge creature looked like one who would brook no nonsense from anybeast, from his wild dark eyes and rough bearded muzzle to the homespun tunic and traveller's cloak he wore. An immense double-hilted battle sword hung at his back. He tossed Drigg aside like a discarded washrag and nodded sternly at the haremaid.

'I've been watching you awhile from behind yon beech. For a young 'un you were doing well, until they came at you from behind. Remember, if there's more than one enemy always get your back against a rock or a tree.'

The haremaid kicked over a stoat who was struggling to rise. She addressed the badger none too cordially. 'Well you've got a bally nerve I must say, tellin' a gel how t'conduct her battles, whilst you sit hidden on the blinkin' sidelines watchin'. Are you sure it wasn't too much bother, havin' to jolly well get off your bottom an' help me out?'

The badger shrugged non-committally. 'As I said, I

thought you were doing quite well. If I'd thought you could have taken them single-pawed I wouldn't have stepped in.'

Dotti was subject to instant mood changes. She smiled, scratching ruefully at her long ears. 'Hmm, suppose you're right. I lost my head a bit when that flagon of rare old cider got broken. Confounded stoat must have a noggin like a boulder. Never lose one's temper, that's what my old mum used t'say.'

The badger nodded sagely, carelessly stepping on Drigg's tail as the stoat tried to crawl away. 'She sounds like a wise creature to me. Pity you never heeded her words. By the way, my name's Lord Brocktree.'

The haremaid clapped a paw to her cheek. 'Oh my giddy aunt! I do apologise for speakin' to you in that sharp manner, sah. I didn't know you were a Badger Lord!'

A ghost of a smile hovered round Brocktree's stern face. 'No matter. You were upset at the time. What do they call you, miss?'

The haremaid did an elegant leg, half bow, half curtsy. 'Dorothea Duckfontein Dillworthy at y'service, sah, but I'm generally called Dotti, though my papa always said you could call me anything as long as you didn't call me late for lunch. 'Scuse me a tick . . .'

The fat frowsy female stoat had risen and was preparing to make a run for it. Dotti reflattened her with a well-placed swing of her bag. She gestured at Drigg's band. 'What do we do with this covey of curmudgeons, m'lord?'

With a fearsome swish, Lord Brocktree drew his great battle sword. It was almost as tall as himself, with a blade wide as two dock leaves. A moan of fear arose from the stoats. Holding it single-pawed between the double hilt, Brocktree swung the huge weapon, making the air thrum like a swan taking off into flight.

Whump!

He buried the point deep in the earth, and his voice dropped to a dangerous growl as he addressed the cowed vermin.

'I save my sword for proper combat with real warriors. Scum such as you would only dishonour its blade. But I will make exceptions if any of you are still within my sight by the time I have counted to three. Remember, I always keep my word . . . One!'

Dotti was bowled over in the mad scramble. Before the Badger Lord had counted further, Drigg Slopmouth and his wicked brood had vanished. Dotti chuckled. 'By gum, that's what I should've done in the first place. Pity I didn't have a sword like this one. What a smashin' old destroyer it is!'

She tugged with both paws, unearthing the blade, then fell over backward under its colossal weight. 'Flamin' sunsets, sah! How d'you handle a weapon like this?'

For answer, the badger picked up his sword, twirled it in a warrior's salute and stowed it one-pawed across his broad back, nodding seriously at her. 'Strength, I suppose. They say I was born even stronger than my father, Lord Stonepaw.'

Dotti flopped her ears understandingly. 'I know what y'mean. Beauty's always been my curse – they say I was born more beautiful than the jolly old settin' sun at solstice. That's prob'ly what made those blinkin' stoats attack me – somebeasts take beauty as a sign o' weakness, y'know. I say, did you mention that old Lord Stonepaw was your pater?'

Brocktree retrieved his travelling bag from behind the beech and shouldered it. 'I did. Why, do you know of him?'

Dotti pulled a face and scuffed the dust with her footpaw. 'I should bally well say so. I'm bein' sent to his blinkin' old mountain, Sallawotjacallit . . .'

'Salamandastron?'

'Aye, that's the place. My aunt Blench is the chief cook

there. I believe she's a right old battleaxe.'

Lord Brocktree sensed a story behind Dotti's remarks. Seating himself with his back against the beech tree, he unpacked provisions from his bulky haversack. 'Sit down here by me, Dotti. D'you like oatcakes, cheese and elderflower cordial?'

The haremaid plonked herself willingly on the grass. 'Rather! I haven't eaten for absolute ages – almost an hour, I think. Mmmm, that cheese looks good!'

Lord Brocktree could not help but smile at the hungry youngster. 'Well there's plenty for two, miss. Help yourself and we'll exchange our stories, you first. Tell me, why are you being sent to Salamandastron?'

3

It was an hour past dawn. The gale had passed on and the winds subsided; mist from the seas cloaked the western shoreline. Stiffener Medick, an old boxing hare, was just completing his daily exercise on the sands above the tide-line. Though he was well on in seasons, Stiffener never neglected his daily routine. He had finished his dawn run, lifted stone and log weights, and was on to the final part of his duck and weave drill. Throwing a final few combination jabs into the mist, he retrieved his champion's belt from a rock and began fastening it about his hard-muscled waist.

Stiffener's scarred ears picked up an unfamiliar sound on the ebbing tide. Batting at his nose with a loose-clenched paw, he jogged down to the water. A narrow sailing boat, with its sail furled, was being rowed in by a dozen big rats, their fur dyed dark blue. A cloaked figure stood at its prow as it cut through the sea mist. The hare stood his ground, ready for trouble. Its keel scraping on the sand, the craft nosed up on to the beach. Shipping their oars, the rats silently piled out and threw themselves prone upon the wet sand. Without a glance at them, the gowned and cowled figure used them as a bridge to reach dry land without wetting its elegantly shod footpaws, treading carelessly upon their upturned backs.

Stiffener nodded towards the newcomer aggressively. 'Ahoy there, mate, who are ye an' what do ye want 'ere?'

One of the rats arose and walked over to face Stiffener. He was a big, evil-looking creature, clad in armour under a tabard embroidered with a sickle hook insignia. The rat's voice was heavy with contempt as he addressed the old boxing hare.

'Koyah! Creatures of the lower orders are not allowed to speak with the Grand Fragorl. Kneel before her and stay silent until I address ye further!'

Stiffener smiled dangerously at the armoured rat. 'I think you'd better kneel t'me, laddie buck. A lesson in good manners wouldn't go amiss in your case.'

A smart whack to the jaw caused the rat to totter groggily. Stiffener clubbed down with his left paw on the rat's shoulder, forcing him into a kneeling position. Suddenly the boxing hare found himself hemmed in on all sides by the swords of the other rats. One of them looked towards the hooded figure, who made a few gestures with its shrouded paws. The rat turned back to Stiffener and spoke.

'Nobeast ever raises paw to the Chosen Ones and lives. You are fortunate that the Grand Fragorl has spared your miserable life, for she wishes to deliver a message to your chief, he who rules the mountain. You will take us to him.'

Stiffener was not about to argue with twelve blades. He nodded to the cloaked figure, speaking as he turned to go. 'Y'best foller me, marm. I'll take ye to Lord Stonepaw, though I doubt he'll offer yer breakfast if'n yore bound to keep actin' all 'igh an' mighty.'

Stonepaw was back in his living quarters when Fleetscut ambled in without knocking, as usual. Turning from the fogbound view at his window, the old badger raised his hoary eyebrows at the absence of a trolley. 'No breakfast today? Has Blench overslept?'

Grave-faced, the ancient servant bowed stiffly. 'I think the trouble we were talkin' about has finally arrived, m'lud. Somebeast t'see you down at the shore entrance. You'd best get dressed for company.'

Wordlessly, Stonepaw allowed his retainer to select a flowing green robe from the closet. When the Badger Lord had shrugged out of his nightgown, Fleetscut climbed on a chair and assisted his master to get into the robe.

'Hmm. I'll get your red belt to go with that, an' maybe a war helmet an' javelin.'

Stonepaw ignored Fleetscut's selection. 'Bring my white cord girdle. No helmet, it keeps slipping over my eyes. There's no need of a javelin, either.' Picking up a long ceremonial mace, the badger surveyed himself in a long copper mirror. 'Get Stiffener, Bungworthy, Sailears and Trobee. They can accompany me.'

Now that dawnlight was clearer and the mist had begun to disperse, one or two of the old hares watching from vantage windows in the mountain remarked on the curious appearance of the rats and their cloaked leader below, at the mountain's main entrance.

'Stap m'whiskers, they're blue!'

'Must be somethin' wrong with your eyes, old chap. Whoever heard o' blue rats?'

'No, he's right, see, their fur is a sort o' darkish blue. Can't tell what the dickens colour that one with the cloak on is. Sinister-lookin' bod, wot?'

Blench the cook took a final look before going off to supervise breakfast with her kitchen helpers. 'Pink, blue or rainbow-coloured, that lot down there look like trouble, you mark my words!'

The heavily robed figure of the Grand Fragorl stood immobile and mysterious, but the rat who had challenged Stiffener paced up and down impatiently. He was obviously some type of officer. After a lengthy while

Lord Stonepaw and his retinue of four hares, all carrying javelins, appeared. The spokesrat swaggered forward. Toying arrogantly with his sword hilt, he looked Stonepaw up and down.

'Are you the one in charge here? Speak!'

Lord Stonepaw brushed past him as if he were not there, and pointed a great gnarled paw at the cloaked one. 'Who are you and why do you trespass upon the western shore with armed soldiers?'

Removing the cowl of her cloak the hooded one revealed herself. She was a blue-furred ferret wearing a nose ring, from which hung a gold sickle hook amulet. Her voice carried with it the haughty tone of one used to being obeyed.

'I am Grand Fragorl to Ungatt Trunn, Ruler of the Earth. You are one of the inferior species, but he has given me permission to deliver his message to you.'

Feeling his hackles begin to rise, the Badger Lord growled, 'Inferior species, eh? Stand here talking like that to me, vermin, and you'll be crabmeat before the mist lifts fully. Aye, and your rats too. If you have something to say then spit it out and begone whilst I'm still in a reasonable mood. So, speak your piece now!'

Drawing a scroll from her robe the ferret read aloud: 'Be it known to all creatures of lowly order, the days of Ungatt Trunn are here. All of these lands and the seas that skirt them are from hereonin his property. You have until nightfall to vacate this place. You must take nothing with you, neither victuals nor weapons. You will also leave behind you any serving beasts who are of use. This is the will and the law of Ungatt Trunn, he who holds the power to make the stars fall from the sky and the earth to tremble. Obey or die!'

Stiffener Medick raised his javelin. 'Just say the word, m'lud, an' we'll give 'em blood'n'vinegar. Us lower orders are pretty good at things like that, y'know!'

Stonepaw touched Stiffener's javelin so that it pointed

down to the sand. He heaved a sigh of resignation as he replied to the Grand Fragorl.

'Deliver this message back to whatever lunatic scum you serve. Tell him that Lord Stonepaw of Salamandastron is accustomed to the blowing of windbags, as your master will find to his cost if he dares to land here. Now get out of my sight and take those blue-painted idiots with you!'

Wordlessly the ferret and her soldiers retreated to their boat and rowed off into the mists.

Sailears, a garrulous old female warrior, twirled her lance nonchalantly. 'Nice little parlay, wot. Well, is that it?'

Shaking his grizzled old head, Stonepaw turned and stumped back into his beloved mountain. 'I wish it was, friend. I wish it was!'

4

Lord Brocktree listened with amusement as Dotti unfolded her story.

'Well, sah, what with one bally thing or another, I was always in trouble back home in the mid-eastern hills. If a confounded pie went missin' from a window sill, or somebeast had bin at the cider store, guess who got the blinkin' blame? Me! Troublecauser, rabblerouser, scoff-swiper – I've been called all of those, y'know. Not t'mention frogwalloper an' butter wouldn't melt in me mouth. Fiddle de dee, I say, 'twas all because of my fatal beauty. They always pick on the pretty ones, I've already told you that. Anyhow, just after Grandpa's whiskers went afire an' some villain tore the seat out of Uncle Septimus's britches, my dear old parents made a decision. Here, cast your lordly peepers over this little scrawl!'

Dotti dug a tattered barkcloth letter from her armbag. Brocktree's dark eyes twinkled as he read it.

Dear Sister Blench,

Cramsy and I can no longer put up with Dorothea, so I am sending her to you. Your Badger Lord has our permission to deal with the wretch as he sees fit, short of slaying her; you also may do likewise. Please keep her captive upon your mountain until such time as she is civilised enough to live among decent creatures. Teach her to cook and other domestic skills. I know it is too much to ask that she be taught etiquette, deportment and other maidenly pursuits – she is a fiend in hare's fur, believe me. Sister dear, I implore you to take her off our paws whilst we still have a roof over our heads, which are grey with care and worry. I would be fibbing if I said Dorothea does not eat much. She is an empty sack with legs – her appetite would frighten a flock of seagulls. Grant her father and me this one favour, and you will have our heartfelt thanks, plus the beaded shawl Mother passed down to me and a flagon of palest old cider from Cramsy's drinks cabinet. Please write to let me know she has arrived safely, and if she does not return by winter I will take it that she has settled down to her new life. Cramsy sends his love to you, Blench. I remain your devoted sister.

Signed, Daphne Duckfontein Dillworthy.

Brocktree had to turn his head aside and wipe his eyes on a spotted kerchief, to keep from laughing. Dotti, surmising that he was wiping away tears, nodded sympathetically.

'Sad, ain't it, sah, the woeful tale of a fatal beauty. I say, did you get chucked out by your parents too? You'll forgive me sayin', but a chap of your size must've taken some bally chuckin', wot wot?'

The Badger Lord patted his young friend's paw. 'No no, 'twas nothing like that, Dotti. I was restless, just like all Badger Lords before me. It grieved me to leave behind my young son. Boar the Fighter I named him. A badger's son is his pride and joy, when he is a babe. But he must grow up, and it is a fact that two male badgers cannot live together in peace, especially Badger Lords, for that is what Boar will grow to be one day. So I had to observe the unwritten law. I left Brockhall and began roaming, to follow my dream.'

Dotti carefully stowed the letter back in her bag. 'Beg pardon, sah, but what dream is that?'

Brocktree unshouldered his battle blade and began whetting its edge on a smooth rock, even though it looked as keen as a razor. 'A vision I see in my mind's eye, sometimes when I'm awake, or other times when I sleep. It must have been the same picture that other badgers have dreamed. A mountain that once shot forth flames and molten rock, older than time itself, its fires now gone. Waiting, always waiting for me on the shores of a great ocean. I could not describe the way to Salamandastron, for that is what I know the mountain is called, nor could I draw a map of the route. But something in my brain, my very heart, is guiding me there.'

Dotti interrupted perkily. 'Oh, sooper dooper, sah! I'm glad you know the flippin' way. I haven't got a confounded clue, only that it's someplace down on the western shores. Oh, beg pardon, sah. Didn't mean to butt in on you. Bad form, wot?'

Brocktree smiled at his young companion and ruffled her ears indulgently. 'We'll find it together, young 'un. You're right, 'tis on the western shores. In my dreams I've seen the sun setting in the seas beyond the mountain. But my feelings tell me that the place for which we are bound will have great need of a Badger Lord. One who will not shrink from evil and cruelty, a warrior ready to stand and fight!'

Dotti chuckled, cutting once more into Brocktree's speech. 'Well, your jolly old feelin's have no further to look than yourself, sah. You look like the very badger t'do the job, an' y'come ready equipped with that bloomin' great monstrosity y'call a sword!'

Squinting one eye, Brocktree peered down the mighty blade, its deadly double edge keener than midwinter. 'Aye, methinks it will have its work well cut out when the time comes. That face, the one which visits and disturbs my slumbers . . . I have seen nothing like it, the face that turns dreams to haunting nightmares!'

The tone of Brocktree's voice caused Dotti to shudder. 'Great seasons, what face is that, sah?'

'Nothing I want to talk more about, young 'un. Now, no more questions, please. We'll make camp here. There's a brook beyond that tall elm yonder – you go and fill this bowl with water while I get a small fire going. Come on now, Dotti, stir your stumps. You'll have to shape up if you want to travel with me!'

The haremaid sprang up, grabbing the bowl from Brocktree's big paws and saluting smartly in a comical manner. 'Brook beyond tall elm! Fill bowl with water! Yes sah! Three bags full sah! Goin' right away sah! About turn, quick march! One two hup!'

Brocktree grinned as he watched her strut off, trip, send the bowl flying, and catch it clumsily. She grinned back at him sheepishly.

'Good wheeze, sendin' me for water, wot? If you'd told me to light a fire I'd have prob'ly sent the whole forest up in flames. Not too clever at fires, doncha know!'

Brocktree took out his tinderbox, murmuring to himself, 'At least she can't flood the forest with a single bowlful o' water, but who knows? Ah well, at least she's company for a lone traveller.'

Flickering shadows from the fire hovered about the woodland glade; somewhere close by a nightjar warbled in the branches of a sycamore. Dotti scraped a wooden ladle round the empty bowl and licked it. 'Confounded good soup that was, sah. Can all Badger Lords cook as well as you do? Mebbe you'd best fire my aunt Blench an' promote y'self to head cook when we get to Salamathingee, wot?'

Brocktree hooded his eyes in mock ferocity. 'If I do become head cook I'll make sure that you get lots of sticky greasy pots to wash, young miss!'

Dotti began rummaging in her bag. 'If the scoff tastes as good as that I'll lick 'em all shinin' clean. Least I can do is to render you a little ditty to aid your digestion, sah.'

The badger folded his paws across his stomach. 'Aye, that'd be nice. Carry on.'

Dotti peered into the bag as she rooted around in its interior. 'Oh corks, half the beads have fallen off this blinkin' shawl the mater gave me for Aunt Blench. It's absolutely soaked with cider, too. Aha! Here's me faithful old harecordion. A few of the keys'n'reeds are stickin', but that cider may have loosened 'em up a touch. Right, here goes, pin y'ears back and get ready for a treat. Wot?'

To describe the haremaid's voice as being akin to a frog trapped beneath a hot stone would have been a great injustice, to both frog and stone. Moreover, the instrument she was playing on sounded like ten chattering squirrels swinging on a rusty gate. However, Dotti played and sang on blithely.

Brocktree squinched both eyes shut, fervently hoping that the song did not contain too many verses.

'I am but a broken-hearted maid,
My tale I'll tell to you,
As I sit alone in this woodland glade,
Yearnin' for a pudden or two.
I hi hi hi, si hi hi hi hi hiiiiiing!
Whack folly doodle ho, whoops cum whang,
The greatest song my grandma sang,
Was to her fam'ly of twenty-three,
Ho dish up the pudden, save some for me!
'Twas made from fruit an' arrowroot,
Hard pears an' apples too,
Some honey that the bees chucked out,
That set as hard as glue,
Some comfrey leaf an' bulrush sheaf,
An' damsons sour as ever,

She stirred the lot in a big old pot
While we sang "Fail me never".
When all of a sudden Grandma's pudden,
Burst right out the pot,
Round as a boulder, not much older,
Fifty times as hot!
It shot down the road, laid out a toad,
An' knocked two hedgehogs flat,
Splashed in the lake an' slew a snake,
An' the frogs cried "Wot was that?"
Oh deary me calamity, oh woe an' lack a day,
Without a pudden to my name
I'll sit an' pine away . . . awaaaaaay
Whack foholly doohoohoodelll daaaayeeeeeee!'

Dotti made her ears stand rigid on the last note to add effect. Fluttering her eyelids dramatically, she was squeezing the harecordion finally shut when its bellows shot forth a stream of old pale cider, right up her nose. She sneezed and curtsied awkwardly.

'Whoo! That cleared my head. Shall I sing you another of my ditties, sah?'

The Badger Lord demurred, hoping she would not insist. 'No, Dotti, please. You must save your voice for another evening. Now you should get some rest. Here, take my cloak.'

The haremaid settled down with the cloak swathed round her like a huge collapsed tent. She sighed. 'Funny thing, y'know, my voice has that effect on many creatures. You should thank the stars that you were born just a plain old Badger Lord. That's the trouble with bein' a fatal beauty with a voice that's too fine t'be heard more than once a night. Hmm, it affected my dad so much that he said once in a lifetime was sufficient for him. Good job you ain't like him, sah. At least I can sing to you once every night, wot!'

Turning his back to her Brocktree winced. 'Well,

perhaps not every single night. Don't want to strain a beautiful voice, do we?'

Dotti closed her eyes, snuggling down in the cloak. 'Let's just say I'll sing to you whenever I feel up to it. Goodnight, Brocktree sah. I say, can I call you Brockers?'

The tone of the Badger Lord's reply stifled any argument. 'You certainly can not, miss. Huh, the very idea of it! Brockers! Good night!'

Morning sun broke cheerfully down upon the little camp, the twittering of birdsong causing Dotti to poke her head out of the cloak folds. Blue smoke rose in a thin column amid the dappled sunshadows cast by trees in full spring leaf. Brocktree was turning oatcakes over on a flat stone, which was laid upon the fire he had rekindled. His great striped head shook reprovingly. 'Dawn has been up two hours, miss. Are you going to lie there all day?'

Yawning and stretching, the haremaid lolloped over to the fire, muttering as she helped herself to hot oatcakes and mint tea sweetened with honey. 'It's the confounded beauty sleep, that's what 'tis. My mater was always sayin' to me when I came down late for breakfast, "Been takin' your beauty sleep again, m'gel." I say, these oatcakes are spiffin' when they're hot. Well, sah, which way do your voices say we go today, wot?'

Brocktree recovered his cloak and bundled it into his haversack. 'I think we should follow the course of that brook, where you got the water from. Sooner or later it'll bring us to a stream.'

Dotti rescued the oatcakes just in time as Brocktree doused the fire and broke camp. Stuffing items in her bag she hopskipped behind him, slopping mint tea about and bolting oatcakes as she breakfasted on the move.

'Question, sah, why are we lookin' for a stream?'

The Badger Lord replied without looking back. 'Streams always run to rivers, rivers run to the sea. That way we find the shoreline and follow it south. Sooner or later we'll come to the mountain on the west shore. Save your breath for marching, young 'un.'

By mid-morning Dotti was hungry, pawsore and had nearly talked herself out, though to no effect. All she saw was the badger's broad cloaked back with the great sword slung across it in front of her. All her observations and complaints were met with either silence or a deep grunt. Lord Brocktree was not one for lengthy conversations when he was on the march. Dotti stumbled, barking her footpaw upon a willow root as they followed the meandering brook.

'Yowowch! Ohh, I've gone an' broke a limb. The pain's shootin' right up to my bally eartips!'

There was no reply, either sympathetic or otherwise, from Brocktree, who merely trudged onward. Dotti continued her lament to a ladybird that had lighted on her shoulder.

'Might have to borrow that big sword an' chop off me blinkin' footpaw. If I find the right piece o' wood I should be able to carve another to hop along on. Breakfast was ages ago, ages an' ages an' ages! I'll bet lots of poor beasts die of starvation, havin' to walk along for days'n'days behind big rotten ole badgers who never say a flippin' word!'

Brocktree bit his lip hard to keep from chuckling.

'Now if I was a badger I'd talk all the time, in fact I'd make it me duty to talk to nice friendly haremaids. Oh dearie me, I'd say, hurt your footpaw, Dotti? Here, let me cut it off with my sword. You can ride up on my back until I find a log to chop up an' make you a new one.'

Brocktree halted without warning, and Dotti walked straight into his back, still chunnering to herself. He turned. 'There's the stream up ahead, missie. You can sit on the bank an' cool your paw in the water. That'll make it feel a lot better, and whilst you do that I'll get lunch ready for us.'

With a deft motion he produced his great battle blade.

'But I can always oblige by doing as you wish. Here, hold out your footpaw an' I'll chop it off!'

Dotti shot past him for the streambank, yelling: 'Yah, I'd chop both your bloomin' great footpaws off if I could lift that sword. At least it'd slow you down a bit. Lord Paw-whacker they should've called you!'

The haremaid's mood softened as she sat cooling her footpaws in the shade of a tree, letting the soothing stream work its magic as she ate lunch. Brocktree had gathered some early berries and mixed them with chopped apple and hazelnuts from his pack, which made a delicious fruit salad with a syrup of honey and streamwater poured over them. Then the badger gave her dock leaves and waterweed he had collected along the streambank.

'If your paw's still sore, bind it with these. That will fix it up.'

Taking the badger's face in both paws, Dotti murmured, 'Look straight at me, sah, pretend I'm thankin' you. Now don't look over, but there's a willow overhangin' the water the other side o' the stream. Don't look! There's somebeast in there watchin' us!'

Brocktree straightened up, winking swiftly at her. 'Oh, right. I'll look further down the bank, see if I can find you some bigger dock leaves. Sit an' rest, I'll not be long.' He strode off down the bank, disappearing round a bend.

Dotti could feel the watcher's eyes on her from the willow shade on the far bank. Taking care not to stare back she acted as though she were completely unaware of the presence of an eavesdropper. Taking the harecordion out of her bag, she placed it in the warm sunlight to dry out. Then, dangling her footpaws in the clear cool current, the haremaid hummed a little tune to herself, flicking the odd secret glance across the stream. She reflected that had she been completely alone, a tranquil setting such as this would have been the ideal place to while away the sunny spring midday. However, the peace was short-lived.

Amid sudden howls and roars the overhanging willow seemed to explode in a shower of leaves and twigs. Foliage scattered across the stream surface as two burly forms smashed through the tree cover and crashed heavily into the water. Dotti hurled herself into the stream, whirling her bag aloft.

'Hang on, sah, I'm comin'! Eulaliiiiaaaa!'

5

Off the western shores a heavy fog persisted. The afternoon had not fulfilled the morning's promise. Beneath a dirty white sky, layers of mist sat unmoved on a still sea, its oily waveless swell lapping tiredly against the hull of a large barnacle-crusted ship, whose single sail hung furled. A small boat hove alongside, and the Grand Fragorl climbed into a canvas sling which had been lowered from the ship. She nodded and was hoisted swiftly aboard. An aisle appeared amidst the blue-furred rats who crowded the deck, and silently she climbed out and made her way through to the stern cabin.

The interior of Ungatt Trunn's stateroom resembled the stuff of which nightmares are made. Dangling from thick chains, deep copper bowls contained fire that burned blue and gave off a heavy lilac-coloured smoke. Oppressive heat enveloped the cabin, heightening the nauseous stench of rotting flesh. Huge cobwebs festooned every corner, spreading up over the deckheads, set aquiver by fat hairy forms which scuttled back and forth after the flies that buzzed everywhere. Carefully avoiding the webs, the Grand Fragorl made her way to the cabin's centre and prostrated herself, face down, with one paw raised in the air. Two other creatures sat in silence watching her, one a small silver-furred fox, its growth stunted by some terrible accident, giving it a shrivelled appearance. The fox, a quill pen held awkwardly in its crabbed paw, was seated at a table where it had been peering through thick crystal-lensed eyeglasses at various scrolls piled upon the tabletop. This was Groddil, High Magician to Ungatt Trunn. Now, turning his eyes from the Grand Fragorl, he sat watching his master for a sign.

Only the tail of the wildcat moved. Black-ringed and yellowish grey with a thick rounded tip, it seemed to possess a life of its own, swishing back and forth behind Ungatt's chair. The fiercest of warriors, Ungatt Trunn had no time for personal fripperies, but dressed like any plain fighter: chain mail tunic, two iron bracelets and a mail-fringed steel helmet surmounted by a spike. Yet anybeast only had to look at him to see that here was a ruthless conqueror. Beneath the striped brow, permanently creased in a frown, the wildcat's fearsome black and gold eyes remained hooded and unblinking, his stiff white whiskers overhanging two sharp amber fangs, which showed even when his mouth was shut.

He stared at the prone ferret stretched on his cabin floor, then, turning his gaze aside, he nodded briefly to his magician. Groddil spoke in a thin reedy voice, starting with his master's praises.

'Know ye that ye are in the presence of the mighty Ungatt Trunn, son of the Highland King Mortspear and brother to Verdauga Greeneye. Ungatt Trunn who makes the stars fall and the earth shake so that the lesser orders will fear him. Ungatt Trunn whose Blue Hordes are as many as leaves of the forest or sands of the shores. Ungatt Trunn who drinks wine from the skulls of his enemies. This is Ungatt Trunn the Fearsome Beast and these are his days!'

The Grand Fragorl, still face down on the floor, called aloud the ritual answer required of her. 'Though I dare not look upon his face, I know that Ungatt Trunn is here and these are his days!'

Ungatt replied in his coarse rasping voice, 'So be it! Did you see my mountain? What took place there? Tell me all and speak true, or flies will be born from your carcass to feed my Webmakers.'

The Fragorl allowed herself a fleeting glimpse of the dead rat, mouldering in the corner, knowing all too well what happened to anybeast foolish enough to displease Ungatt Trunn. Though the heat in the cabin was stifling, the ferret felt cold sweat break out beneath her long robes. She spoke, fighting to stop her voice trembling.

'O Fearsome One, I saw your mountain, though not all of it, only what the mists would allow. I was not invited inside. It is called Salamandastron, just as you said. The place is defended by inferior species, rabbit things, who all appear to be well on in seasons. They are ruled by a stripedog called Lord Stonepaw who is even older than they. He said many insulting things, which I fear to repeat, but mainly he said it would be to your cost if you dared to land upon his shores. I followed your orders, O Ungatt Trunn, and not stopping to bandy words with the stripedog or his creatures I returned to you immediately.'

Only the flies could be heard as they buzzed around the Conqueror's stateroom. Neither Fragorl nor Groddil moved. A fly swooped across Ungatt's vision and his paw shot out like greased lightning and caught it. Holding it to his ear he listened to its anguished hum, then tossed it swiftly upward, where it lodged in a cobweb. In a flash two voracious Webmakers were upon the trapped insect. Ungatt never looked up, his hooded eyes fixed on the ferret sprawled near his footpaws.

'You did well, my Fragorl, you may rise and go now.'

When the ferret had departed, Ungatt poured wine into a goblet fashioned from the bleached skull of a long-dead otter. 'Read me the prophecy again, Groddil.'

Hastily sorting out a scroll the fox unrolled it.

'No highland willed from kin deceased,
Or quest for castles, vague, unknown,
For Ungatt Trunn the Fearsome Beast
Will carve a fortune of his own!
Find the mountain, slay its lord,
Put his creatures to the sword!
When the stars fall from the sky,
Red the blood flows 'neath the sun,
Then let mothers wail and cry,
These are the days of Ungatt Trunn!
Hark, no bird sings in the air!
The earth is shaking everywhere!
His reign of terror has begun!
For these are the days of Ungatt Trunn!'

A fat spider fell from its web, landing on the wildcat's shoulder. He let it run down on to his paw, turning the paw over and back again as the spider scurried to escape. 'Now explain it to me!'

As he had done several times, Groddil translated. 'It says that you are too fierce and strong to accept the Highland Kingdom when your father dies. Nor are you a wandering robber, dreaming of conquering some castle, as your young brother Verdauga says he will do someday. You will establish your own realm, ruling it from a mountain that is greater than any other. Nobeast has an army to command as large as your Blue Hordes. I am your magician, and I say that tonight you will see the stars fall from the sky. At tomorrow's dawn you will feel the earth shake beneath you.'

The wildcat stared levelly at the undersized fox. 'You have many clever tricks, Groddil. But if you fail me then you will feel the earth shake from above you. Because I will be dancing on your grave! What about the Badger Lord? Tell me.'

Groddil knew the wildcat would not slay him – he was far too valuable a creature for any warlord to kill. The magician fox merely shrugged and went back to studying his scrolls.

'The stripedog is as your Fragorl described, an old one. He should be no trouble to the mighty Ungatt Trunn.'

The wildcat leaned on the desk, bringing his face close to the fox. 'My dreams do not contain any doddering ancient stripedog. The one who disturbs my slumbers is a badger of middle seasons with the mark of a warrior stamped on him. So, my withered friend, explain that to me?'

Groddil removed his eyeglasses and began wiping them. 'I cannot dream your dreams for you all the time. This badger you see might be just that, a dream!'

Ungatt returned to his chair, stroking his fangs. 'You'd better hope for your sake that he is, Groddil!'

Lord Stonepaw had been staring from his window at the masses of fog shrouding the seas. He was beginning to see phantom shapes looming in the mists, as one is apt to after gazing awhile. He rubbed at his tired old eyes and lumbered over to his bed, where he sat down to brood over the troubles that beset him.

Stiffener Medick knocked on the door and entered. 'Sire, every harejack in the place is waitin' on you t'come an' talk to 'em. They're gathered in the main chamber, armed t'the ears an' primed for action!'

With a weary sigh the Badger Lord rose. 'The old, the weak and the feeble. I wish we were all as fit as you, Stiffener. Huh, if wishes were fishes. Ah well, fetch me my armour and javelin. Least I can do is to go down there looking like a Mountain Lord!'

Main chamber was just short of half filled with hares. Two of them, Bungworthy and Trobee, assisted the armoured badger up on to a rock platform. Stonepaw shook his head sadly as he assessed his army. Holding up his javelin, he waited until silence fell, then he spoke up loudly, for the benefit of those hard of hearing.

'Good creatures, faithful comrades, you know I have always spoken truly to you, so I am not going to lie about our present situation. I see before me many brave warriors – alas, none of them young and sprightly any more. Like you, I too can remember the seasons gone, when this chamber and the passages outside would be packed solid with young fighting hares. Now we are but a pitiful few. But that does not mean we cannot fight!'

A ragged cheer rose from the old guard, accompanied by warlike comments.

'Eulaliaaa!'

'Aye, we'll give 'em blood'n'vinegar, sire!'

'We're with you to the last beast, lord!'

'We ain't called Stonepaw's Stalwarts for nothin', wot?'

'Send 'em on an' let's begin the game!'

A tear trickled from Stonepaw's eye. Hastily, he brushed it aside and swelled his chest out proudly. 'I am honoured to lead ye! We know not the number of our foes or how skilled they be at weaponry, but let's give them a hot old time in true Salamandastron fashion!'

Amid the cheering, orders were shouted out.

'Bar all entrances!'

'Archers at the high window slits!'

'Long pikes at the low windows!'

'Stone-slingers on the second level!'

'Sailears, take your crew up on to the high ledges where the boulder heaps are ready!'

As the hares dispersed to their places, Lord Stonepaw held two of them back. 'Blench, marm, they'll need feeding. I know you've only got a few kitchen helpers left, but can you see to it?'

The head cook saluted with an iron ladle. 'H'ain't seen the day I couldn't, m'lud. There'll be nobeast fightin' on a h'empty belly whilst I'm around!' She whirled off, yelling at her helpers. 'Check the larders an' bring the list t'me. Gather in h'anythin' that's a-growin' up on those ledge gardens, fruits, salad veggibles, h'anythin'!'

Stonepaw turned to the one hare left, his faithful retainer. 'Fleetscut, have you still got the ability and wind to be called a runner?'

The ancient hare laughed mirthlessly. 'S'pose I could still kick up a bit o' dust, m'lud. Why?'

Stonepaw lowered his voice to a whisper. 'Good creature! I want you to draw field rations and leave this mountain within the hour. Go where you will but use your wits. Search out our young wandering warriors and any bands of hares about the countryside. Young ones with a touch of warriors' blood in their eye. We need help as we've never needed it. Find them and bring them back to Salamandastron, as fast as you can!'

Fleetscut bowed dutifully as he flexed his paws. 'I'll give it a jolly good try, sire!'

Lord Stonepaw hugged his old friend briefly. 'I know you will, you old grasswalloper. Good luck!'

When Fleetscut had left, the Badger Lord retired to his secret chamber. When he had sprinkled herbs into the burning lanterns he sat back, closing his eyes and breathing deeply. Concentrating hard, he willed the face of his successor to appear in his mind.

'Where are you, strong one? Come to me – I need you now. Feel the call of the mountain and hurry to it!'

Stonepaw finally drifted into slumber, rewarded by no sight of any badger's face, just a worrying puzzlement of troubles as yet unborn.

6

Lord Brocktree felt himself borne underwater by an adversary of tremendous strength, which seemed to increase on contact with the stream. The beast was built of muscle and steely sinew, wrapping itself about the badger's head, neck and shoulders, blocking off air and light in a skilful deathlock. As soon as he felt his paws touch bottom, Brocktree used his formidable strength, thrusting upward to the surface with a powerful shove.

As both beasts broke the surface, the badger managed to gasp in a breath of air. Then he was aware of thudding blows raining on his opponent as Dotti yelled: 'Gerroff! I'll pound your blinkin' head to a jelly if you don't let him go an' jolly well fight fair!'

The beast wrapped about Brocktree's head roared aloud. 'Fair? Y'call two to one fair? Yowch ouch! Watch that bag, ye doodlepawed fool, y'near put me eye out. Owww!'

The Badger Lord seized his chance. Clamping his paws round his assailant's tail and jaws he tore the creature from him and lifted it above his head. It was kicking and wriggling as he hurled it forcefully into the far shallows. Then, diving down, he grabbed his battle blade, which had fallen from his back in the struggle. Dotti gasped with fright as the massive Badger Lord surfaced in a cascade of streamwater, whirling his sword aloft.

'Brocktree of Brockhall! Bones'n'bloooood!'

The otter, for it was a fully grown male of that species, stood up dripping in the shallows. 'Aye aye, steady on there, matey, there ain't no need t'go swingin' swords around. Wot's yore trouble?'

Brocktree waded towards him, sword still upraised. 'You were trying to drown me back there, murderer!'

The otter threw back his head and chortled. 'Hohoho, murderer is it, cully? Shame on ye! Yore the one who sneaked up an' started all this. Ambusher!'

Dotti thought about this for a moment, then wading over she placed herself between both creatures. 'Stap me if he ain't right, sah. It was you who attacked him first, y'know.'

Brocktree dropped his sword in bewilderment. 'Hi there, miss, whose side are you on, mine or his?'

The otter sat down in the shallows, chuckling merrily. 'Now now, youse two, stop all yore argifyin'. Tell ye wot, d'yer like watershrimp an' 'otroot soup? I've got a pan of it on the go – should be plenty for three.'

At the mention of food Dotti felt immediately friendly. 'I've never tasted it, but I'm sure I'll like it, sah!'

The otter waded over, paw outstretched. 'Hah! Don't sir me, young 'un, I goes by the name o' Ruffgar Brookback. Y'can call me Ruff, though. Ruff by name, rough by nature, that's wot my ole grandma used t'say when I wrestled 'er!'

Dotti looked at him in surprise. 'You used to wrestle with your old grandma?'

Ruff grinned. 'Aye, but she always beat the daylights out o' me. C'mon, hearties, foller me.'

Further upstream they came upon Ruff's camp, merely a blanket made into a lean-to. There was a slow-burning turf fire on the bank edge and a long flat elm trunk floating in the water. Ruff attended to a cauldron of soup bubbling on the fire, dipping in a wooden ladle and sampling it gingerly.

'Haharr, all right'n'ready. This is the stuff t'put a shine on yore fur an' a glint in yore eye, good ole 'otroot!'

He scrambled aboard the log, which was obviously his boat, and retrieved a battered travelling bag. From this he dug three enormous scallop shells, tossing one apiece to Dotti and Brocktree.

'Dig in now, I ain't yore mother. Serve yerselves, mates!'

Dotti filled her shell and went at it like a gannet in a ten-season famine.

'Yah! Whoo! Mother help me I'm on fire! Oh! Oohaaah!'

Ruff, who had been watching in amusement, took pity on her and scooped up some cold streamwater in his shell. 'Cool yore gob on this, missie!'

She drained the water in a single gulp, blinked the tears from her eyes and sniffed. 'Good stuff this, wot? A little warm an' spicy, but first-class soup. I like it!' Ruff and Brocktree sat gaping as she refilled her shell and tucked in with a will.

The badger winked at the otter. 'She's a hare, you see.'

Ruff nodded sagely. 'Aye, that explains it, mate!'

After the meal they lay about on the bank, and Dotti and Brocktree told Ruff their stories. Ruff explained to them how he came to be in those parts.

'I'm a bit like you, young Dotti, I left 'ome when I was young, just afore they decided to sling me out. Wild an' mischievous? Haharr, I was more trouble than a bag o' bumblebees. Me pore ole grandma was sorry t'see me go, but the rest of me family breathed a sigh of relief. Any'ow, I been a loner most o' the time. It ain't so bad. Nobeast to keep shoutin', Ruff stop that! Or, Ruff don't you dare! Nowadays I can do wot I likes, without anybeast hollerin' at me.'

Brocktree nodded. 'And what are you doing at present, Ruff?'

'Oh, a bit of this an' a bit o' that, nothin' really. Why?'

The Badger Lord's eyes twinkled. 'Dotti and I need to get down to the shores of the great sea. Best way to do that is to follow waterways, as you well know. It would be nice if we could go by boat, instead of all that trekking by paw. Suppose you came with us?'

Ruff's rudderlike tail thwacked down upon the bank, propelling him upright, grinning from ear to ear. 'No sooner said than done, Brock me hearty. Can you two paddle?'

Dotti replied for them both. 'Well, if we can't I bet you'll soon teach us, wot. I'm no Badger Lord, but I'm jolly well strong of paw!'

Ruff touched the swelling around his eye. 'You already proved that by the way you swing yore bag!'

Floating down the broad sunlit stream was a very pleasurable experience. Dotti and Brocktree soon picked up the knack of wielding a paddle. Passing beneath overhanging trees the young haremaid sighed with joy, watching the dappled patterns of sunshine and shade drifting by on the smooth dark green water.

'Oh, whoopsy doo an' fiddley dee! This is the life, eh, sah? I say there, Ruff my old streambasher, d'you know any jolly songs that creatures sing when they're out boating?'

The otter flicked water at her with his paddle. 'Bless yer 'eart, Dotti, course I do, but they're called shanties or water ballads. 'Ere's one y'can both join in with. The chorus is very simple – 'elps t'keep the rhythm o' the paddles goin', y'see. It goes like this.'

Ruff sang the chorus once, then launched into a deep-throated old boatsong.

'Hey ho ahoy we go.
Row, me hearties. Row row row!

Chucklin' bubblin' life's a dream,
I'm the brook that finds the stream.
Hey ho ahoy we go.
Row, me hearties. Row row row!

Sun an' shade an' fish aquiver,
This ole stream flows to the river.
Hey ho ahoy we go.
Row, me hearties. Row row row!

Down mates down an' foller me,
I'm the river bound to the sea.
Hey ho ahoy we go.
Row, me hearties. Row row row!'

Ruff's elm tree fairly skimmed the water, with him singing the verses and his two friends roaring out the chorus like two seasoned old riverbeasts. The otter signalled them to stop rowing. 'Ship yore paddles, mates, let 'er run with the current!'

Normally a staid creature, as befits a Badger Lord, Brocktree was exhilarated, grinning like a Dibbun. 'My my, Ruff, I can see why you love the freedom of the waterways. It certainly is a pleasant experience.'

Guiding his elm log boat with the odd paddle stroke, Ruff watched the stream ahead knowingly. 'Oh, it ain't so bad most seasons, but don't go gettin' too taken up with it, Brock. You gets the ice in winter, snow, hail, rainstorms, dry creeks, rocks, driftwood an' gales. Once y'gets used to that lot then you got to face rapids, sandbanks, cross-currents an' waterfalls. Aside from that there's savage pike an' eel shoals an' all manner o' bad-minded vermin watchin' the water an' huntin' their prey both sides o' the banks.'

Dotti waved a paw dismissively. 'Oh, pish tush, sah. It doesn't seem t'bother you!'

Ruff pulled a tangle of line from his pack. Checking the

hook and weight on it, he baited up with a few water-shrimp left over from the hotroot soup. 'Fish for supper, shipmates. Look 'ere at this fat shoal o' dace!'

Through the deep fast-flowing stream they glimpsed the dace, cruising through the trailing moss and weed, their olive-green backs and silver flanks shining wherever rays of sunlight pierced the water. They were fine, plump fish. Ruff trailed the line as they followed the log, keeping in its shadow.

'I'll just snag two o' the beauties, that should do us. Hearken t'me, Dotti. If'n yore bound to take the life of a livin' thing for food, then take only wot you need. Life's too precious a thing t'be wasted, ain't that right, Brock?'

The badger nodded solemnly. 'Aye, that's so. A lesson every creature should learn.'

That evening they camped at the mouth of a small inlet and Ruff cooked the fish for them. After the long day on the stream it was a delicious meal.

Lord Brocktree sat back, cleaning his teeth with a twig. 'I've tasted trout and grayling, but never anything like that dace before. You must tell me how you prepared it, Ruff.'

Looking furtively about, the otter managed a gruff whisper. 'My grandma's secret recipe 'tis, an' if'n she was 'ere now she'd skelp me tail with a birch rod for tellin' ye. You needs tender new dannylion shoots, wild onions an' hedge parsley, oh, an' two fat leeks. Chop 'em all up an' set 'em o'er the fire in a liddle water, but don't boil 'em. Then when you've topped'n'tailed yore two dace, you lays them fishes flat on a thin rock. Mix cornflour an' oats with a drop o' water from yore veggibles an' spread it o'er the fishes, so they bakes with a good crunchy crust. Drain off the veggibles whilst they're still firm, spread 'em in a bed an' top the lot off with your dace. But don't you two ever breathe a word to any otter that 'twas me wot told ye the recipe. Alive or dead, ole Grandma'd either hunt or haunt me!'

Dotti began reaching for her harecordion. 'Time for a jolly old ditty, eh, chaps?'

Nobeast was more relieved than Brocktree when Ruff put the blocks on the haremaid's warbling. 'Best not, missymate. This ain't too friendly a part o' the woodlands – you'd prob'ly attract unwelcome visitors. Best sleep now. We've got an early start in the morn.'

Dotti yawned. 'You're right, of course. My beauty sleep.'

When the fire had burned to white embers, Ruff checked that Dotti was sound asleep. He shook the badger gently, cautioning him to silence. 'Lissen, Brock, we could've sailed further today, but I chose to berth in this spot because I feel there'll be trouble further downstream. No sense in upsettin' young pretty features there. Look, I've got a plan. 'Ere's wot we'll do. I'll wake ye at the crack o' dawn an' the pair of us will rise nice an' quiet. Then . . .'

When Ruff had outlined his scheme Lord Brocktree nodded agreement. Then he lay down again and stared at the canopy of stars twinkling through the trees, his paw clasping the battle blade at the ready, noting every noise of flora or fauna in the forest night.

7

The night that fell over the three companions on the streambank also lowered its shades over Salamandastron and the western shores. Silently, with furled sails, ships drifted in on the flood tide. Out of the thinning mists they slid, headed for the shore on the quiet swell. Ships upon ships upon ships . . . craft of every description from single- to four-masted, flat-bottomed, deep-keeled, bulky and sleek, large and small. Any creature could have walked the length of the sea, a league from north to south, by stepping from ship to ship without once wetting a paw.

Then came the Blue Hordes of Ungatt Trunn from north and south, marching along the shores, the sounds of their footpaws muffled in the soft sands, in columns fifty deep and fifty long, following their commanders. No war drums were seen, nor trumpets, nor any other instrument, flute, cymbal or horn, to aid the marching. Starlight glinted dully off armour, speartip, blade and arrowhead as they came, closing in on Salamandastron like the jaws of a giant pincer. Inscrutable masses, perfectly drilled, the ultimate machine of destruction.

Flanked by twoscore soldiers Ungatt Trunn strode up to the rocky fortress, his only illumination a torch held in the paws of Groddil. The wildcat's keen eyes flicked up to the long open rectangle of Stonepaw's room. There stood the Badger Lord of Salamandastron, clad in war armour, holding an enormous javelin.

'So, you are still here, stripedog?' Ungatt Trunn called up in his savage guttural growl.

The reply was immediate. 'Aye, to the death, stripecat!'

The wildcat's fangs showed in a sneer of derision. 'So be it. 'Twill be your death, not mine!'

'Big words,' Stonepaw retorted mockingly. 'I've already heard big words from the bad-mannered scum you sent here earlier today. They mean nought to me, the ravings of fools and idiots. Your messenger said you would make the stars fall from the sky. Look up, braggart. They are still there and always will be!'

The badger's words stung the wildcat. His voice quivered with rage as he detected the laughter of hares all around. 'I have no more words for you, stripedog. Tell them, Fragorl!'

Like a ghost, the hooded figure materialised out of the night. 'These are the days of Ungatt Trunn the Fearsome Beast. Know you that he always speaks truth. If he says the stars will fall from the sky, then even they must obey. Look!'

Groddil flung a pawful of powder on his palely burning torch. With a whoosh it shot up a bolt of brilliant blue flame. This was the signal. Every beast of the horde onshore and every creature crowding the decks of the hovering ships immediately lighted, each one, a torch they carried specially for the purpose. In the awesome scene that was revealed, land and sea, as far as the eye could gaze, was ablaze. Stiffener Medick peered up at the sky. Because of the intensity of light below, not a single star could be seen, just a wide black void. Any creature on the reaches of Salamandastron's heights could look out and see countless myriad lights ranging out to the horizon.

At another signal from Groddil, the twoscore guards nearest the mountain roared out aloud: 'Mighty Ungatt Trunn has made the stars fall from the sky!'

Every hare on the mountain was stunned with shock. The seas and the whole shore were ablaze with light; it was like having day below and night above, the stars made invisible in the sky due to the powerful lights radiating upward.

Groddil held a whispered conference with Ungatt, and the wildcat nodded before speaking out. His voice echoed off the mountain in the awestruck silence.

'I see you have no scornful comments to make, stripe-dog. You have witnessed the power of Ungatt Trunn. My Blue Hordes will camp here on your doorstep. When dawn comes you will feel the earth shake. You have left it too late to retreat from the mountain as I commanded you to do. Now you must reap the penalty.' Then, turning his back on Lord Stonepaw, the wildcat marched off, back to his ship.

The Badger Lord watched as the torches turned into campfires. Bramwil, the oldest hare on the mountain, came shakily forward to clutch the badger's paw, his voice trembling like a reed in the wind.

'Lord, I would not have believed it, had I not seen it with these old eyes. What can we do against one who is truly magic?'

Stonepaw patted Bramwil's stooped back gently. 'That was no magic, my friend, 'twas only a very clever trick, an illusion. But the reality of all those lights is a fearful thing, for it shows the extent of Trunn's army. Trobee, your eyes are still useful. Could you have counted the number of torches out there?'

Trobee shook his head vigorously. 'You must be jestin', sah. Nobeast alive could do that!'

Stiffener's comment confirmed Stonepaw's worst fears. 'Aye, an' every one o' those torches was held by a vermin soldier. 'Tis hard to imagine such an army!'

Stonepaw stared out at the campfires burning holes into the night, both near and far. 'No doubt you all heard what the wildcat had to say – we've left it too late to retreat.'

Silently the hares pondered the enormity of what their lord had said, but the feeling of doom was broken when Stiffener Medick spoke out boldly. 'So what do we do? Stand around here waitin' t'be conquered an' slain? Not this hare, no sah! Chin in, chest out, stiffen the ole lip an' stand firm! Mebbe that scum can make stars fall an' earth tremble. But let's see him crack a mountain with us to defend it!'

Lord Stonepaw's eyes lit up with the flame of battle. 'Stiffener, gather my hares at every ledge and window. Let's show the vermin what we think of them!'

Ungatt Trunn came hurrying from his stateroom cabin as defiant roaring from Salamandastron ripped through the night stillness.

'Eulaliaaa! Eulaliaaa! Eulaliaaaaaaaa!'

Groddil hobbled behind his master, and spat contemptuously into the sea. 'Fools! Do they think they can scare us with their battle cries?'

Ungatt Trunn did not even deign to look at the shrunken fox. 'No, they don't mean to scare us, but they're letting us know that they aren't scared either. That's called courage, Groddil, but you wouldn't understand it. If those hares were enough in number to match us one to one, then I'd be scared.'

Dawn arrived pale-washed, though in less than an hour it had blossomed into a beautiful late spring day, showing the promise of a good summer. Lord Stonepaw had witnessed the day's arrival; he had scarcely slept throughout the night. Now, sitting on the edge of his bed in a warm shaft of sunlight, he fell into a doze.

Blench the cook shook him gently. 'Wake up, sire, those villains are waiting t'see you outside on the shore. I brought ye a bite o' brekkist.'

Stonepaw opened his eyes slowly and winced. 'Ooh! Don't ever fall asleep wearing armour, Blench, it feels like waking up in a cooking pot. I suppose that wildcat villain is showing off his army at our gates?'

Blench placed the tray of food at his side. 'Aye, there's all manner o' blue-dyed vermin paradin' up an' down on the beach, in full fig too. Mercy me, they're a strange lot. D'ye think they're about to start the war?'

The Badger Lord chose a warm damson muffin and poured himself a beaker of dandelion and rosehip tea. 'More than likely, Blench, more than likely. Hmm, I feel peckish this morning. Let them wait until I've broken my fast. Did you bring any honey?'

'Right there under yore muzzle, lord.'

Stonepaw spread honey on his muffin. 'You run along now, marm, an' see that my hares get fed.'

As she withdrew, Blench chuckled. 'Fat chance of any Salamandastron hare a-goin' into battle on an empty belly. Did y'ever hear of such a thing?'

Ungatt Trunn stood on a rock, Groddil and his Grand Fragorl alongside him, and looked around the western shores. Nodding his satisfaction, he turned to the fox and the ferret.

'Can you see the sand?'

Fragorl shook her hooded head. 'No, Mightiness, only the Blue Hordes. They are in such great numbers that nobeast could see the sand they stand upon. They are even shoulder to shoulder in the shallows.'

Ungatt fixed his stern eye upon the shrunken fox. 'Another trick you've missed, eh, Groddil?'

The magician cringed as he shook his head in bewilderment. 'Sire?'

Ungatt Trunn's paw swept across, indicating the scene. 'Not only can I make the stars fall, but I can also cause the land to disappear. Use your head, stupid!'

Thinking to divert his master's wrath, Groddil pointed to the mountain. 'But the stripedog shows his insolence by not bothering to appear and witness your power, O Exalted One.'

'That is a mere ploy which the commanders of armies use upon one another,' Ungatt Trunn replied scornfully. 'He thinks to fray my temper by keeping me waiting. Have you no brains at all? I should have slain you with the rest of your family, eh, Groddil?'

Lowering his head, the fox mumbled humbly, 'I thank you for sparing my life every day since, sire!'

Ungatt smiled dispassionately at the fox's bowed head. 'I think I must have damaged your brain when I crippled your back. Hah! There's the stripedog at his window.' Turning his attention to the mountain, the wildcat did not see the hate-laden glance which Groddil shot at him.

Lord Stonepaw and a dozen archers looked down from the window, showing no surprise at the masses of vermin crowding the shores.

'A fine day to die, eh, stripedog?' Ungatt Trunn called.

The badger smiled down in a patronising way. 'So soon, cat? I thought you were going to make the earth tremble. Could you not spare us long enough to see your next trick?'

At a nod from Ungatt, the Fragorl held a red banner high and announced aloud: 'Let the enemies of Ungatt Trunn feel the earth tremble!'

The entire army began to jump up and down in perfect unison, chanting as they did, 'Ungatt Trunn! Ungatt Trunn! Ungatt Trunn!'

As Fragorl waved her banner they increased their speed, jumping in the air and landing hard on the sand, their chant becoming a roar, the noise of countless footpaws stamping down becoming greater. Water splashed high on the tideline and clouds of sand began rising as they continued their relentless pounding.

Though he could scarcely be heard above the din, the hare named Bungworthy funnelled both paws around his mouth and shouted at Stonepaw, 'Look, lord! The earth is shaking! See! Great ripples are spreading seaward! The shore is shaking where they jump! Great seasons, the earth is shaking. It's shaking!'

As suddenly as it had started the demonstration stopped. Ungatt Trunn stood smiling grimly up at Stonepaw as the sand clouds settled and the ripples receded.

'Well, stripedog, did you feel the earth shake? Did I not speak truly? Throw down your arms and come out!' Ungatt climbed down from his rock perch and stood at the head of his army, confident he had made his point.

Lord Stonepaw merely grunted. 'Hah! You might have felt the earth tremble, cat, but Salamandastron remained rock-firm – we didn't feel a thing. Now let me show you something!'

Stonepaw hurled his big war javelin right at his foe. The ranks closed around the wildcat. A rat, transfixed, fell dead, another behind him sorely wounded. No matter how fearsome the foe, or how great their numbers, when it came to fighting, Badger Lords were renowned. Old as he was, the present ruler was no exception. Lord Stonepaw of Salamandastron had begun the war.

Fleetscut was close to total exhaustion. The old hare had not stopped since he left the mountain. Ranging east to begin with, then sweeping back west in a great arc, he searched hills, flatlands, valleys and clifftops, finally arriving back on the shores, somewhere north of Salamandastron. Slumping down on the beach, he waited until his breathing calmed a bit before unslinging a small pack and drinking some cold mint tea.

Like an angry wasp, a barbed arrow buzzed by the hare, nicking his ear and burying itself in the sand. A small patrol, ten rats, from the great Blue Hordes emerged from the dunes behind Fleetscut.

'Stop there. Move an' you die!' their officer shouted.

With blood trickling from his ear on to his jaw, Fleetscut took off as only a hare can, galvanised back to his former self as he sought to lose his pursuers. But the rats were hard on his paws as he led them on a twisting course round the shore and back into the dunes. With his footpaws sinking deep into the soft sandhills, Fleetscut panted raggedly, strong sunlight beating down on him as he breasted one dune and rolled down it to face another. He wished with all his heart that he were many seasons younger – he could have drawn circles round the rat patrol when he was a leveret. Every so often arrows zipped into the sand alongside him; once a spear almost pierced his footpaw. Fleetscut kept going. He knew that a moving target was the hardest to hit. Now, as he turned inland, the dunes gave way to hummocks and hillocks, coated with sharp, long-bladed grass. He tripped over a blackberry creeper, leaping up as best he could, ignoring the scratches the thorns had inflicted on him. But he could hear the laboured breathing of the ten rats getting closer.

'Fan out an' circle him. Lame him if y'can!' their leader rasped out.

Straining as though his lungs would burst, Fleetscut managed an extra turn of speed, dashing headlong to outdistance the flanking manoeuvre. A small grove of pines appeared up ahead, seeming to offer a hiding place. But one rat, faster than the rest, detached himself from the flankers and went directly after the hare. No matter how hard he ran, Fleetscut could not prevent the rat closing up on him. Now he was not more than ten paces behind. Chancing a backward glance, Fleetscut saw the rat preparing his spear for a throw. Then his footpaws hit thick beds of pine needles as he dived headlong into the grove, the spear thudding into a pine trunk a fraction to his side. Next moment there was the sound of a meaty thud. The rat fell poleaxed, his scream cut short by a slingshot.

'Up with thy paws, old 'un, quick!'

Without thinking Fleetscut rolled over and threw up his paws. A thick woven net enveloped him, and he grabbed tight as he was swung off his back into the branches above.

A big, rough-looking female squirrel, with a loaded sling dangling from one paw, winked at him. 'Don't thee say a word now, longears, be still!' Sighting the rats entering the fir grove, she glared fiercely about her at forty-odd squirrels, similarly armed, concealed in the upper branches. 'Take no prisoners. T'the Dark Forest with 'em all!'

Whock! Thwack! Thock! Thud!

In less time than it took to draw breath the rat column was slain to a beast, strewn about the bottom of the pines, some of them with their eyes still wide open in surprise. Leaving Fleetscut still caught up in the net, the squirrel and her band leapt down on to the corpses, stripping every scrap of armour and every weapon from them. Squabbles broke out over the ownership of possessions, and there was much tooth-baring.

'I sighted yon sword first. Give it 'ere!'

'Nah, 'tis mine, not thine. I slew the longtail!'

The big female squirrel was among them like a whirlwind, sending argumentative ones winded to the earth as she clubbed their stomachs savagely with her loaded sling.

'I say who gets what! Up on thy paws, Beddle, or I'll give ye more'n just a love tap next time!'

One young male muttered something, and she laid him flat with a tremendous smack. 'Thee've been told about usin' language like that, Grood! Can ye not see we've got company? Behave now, all a' ye!'

Fleetscut strove to disentangle himself from the net. 'Stap me, any bloomin' chance o' gettin' out o' this, you chaps? Lend a paw here!' he called down.

The female squirrel and two equally big males

bounded up and lowered the net expertly to the earth, where the others soon had Fleetscut free. Somersaulting neatly out of the tree, the big female landed lightly on her footpaws.

Fleetscut bowed gravely to her. 'Thanks for savin' my life, marm.'

She examined a dead rat's bow and arrows. ''Twasn't to save thy life we dropped 'em. Weapons an' plunder, that's why we slew the longtails. I'm called Jukka the Sling, and these are my tribe. Be you from the mountain south o' here?'

The hare nodded. 'Aye. My name's Fleetscut.'

Jukka sat, her tailbrush against a pine trunk. 'Ye've got big trouble o'er there, Fleetscut. We been watchin' blue vermin marchin' downcoast for days, all headed for thy mountain.'

Fleetscut crouched down facing her. 'That's only a third o' them, Jukka marm. There's as many must've come up from the south an' another horde from the sea, great fleet o' the blighters.'

Jukka watched her band dragging the rats off for burial. 'Old badger'll have his paws full. They'll massacre him. Hares on yon mount be as old as thee – thy young 'uns are long gone from there.'

Fleetscut was mildly surprised at Jukka's intelligence. 'You seem t'know rather a lot about Salamandastron?'

The squirrel wound her sling around her tailtip. ''Tis my business to know what goes on hither an' yon. Only a fool would live a lifetime in these parts an' know nought of them. Did ye escape the mountain, Fleetscut?'

The old hare shook his head sadly. 'No, I was sent out by Lord Stonepaw to scout up reinforcements, but there ain't a bally hare round here any more. Don't suppose you'd fancy helpin' us out, marm?'

Jukka tossed a slingstone deftly from one paw to the other. 'Nay, not I, nor my tribe, e'en though I pity thy plight, friend. Other creatures' troubles are their own, not ours. But that doesn't mean we don't show hospitality to guests. Thee must be weary and hungered too. Come rest awhile an' sup with us. Thou art too tired to go further, friend.'

Fleetscut heaved a sigh as he rose stiffly. 'Sorry, marm, but I have to travel on, wot. Can't let the jolly old side down by takin' time off.'

He accepted Jukka's paw, and she smiled wryly at him. 'Fare thee well, old 'un. Fortune attend thy search.'

'Aye, an' good luck to you, Jukka the Sling. Let me know if you change your mind. You've got a perilous tribe there, good warriors all!'

Jukka watched Fleetscut lope off through the pine grove. 'Huh, brave an' foolish, like all hares. What say you, Grood?' The young squirrel muttered half to himself, half to Jukka. She whacked him soundly across both ears. 'Thee've been told about that language. I'll scrub thy mouth out with sand an' ramsons if there be any more of it!'

8

At the inlet camp, dawn was already well advanced, and dewdrops glistened on the blossoms of hemlock, marshwort and angelica. From upstream the constant call of a cuckoo roused Dotti from sleep. She lay there for a moment, expecting her nostrils to be assailed by the odours of woodsmoke and cooking. However, the haremaid was disappointed. Apart from the monotonous cuckoo noise, the little camp was quiet and ominously still. Rising cautiously, she checked around. The elm tree trunk lay moored in the shallows, but of her two friends there was no sign. Taking care not to raise her voice too much, Dotti hailed her companions.

'I say, Brocktree sah, Ruff, are you there?'

A rustle from some bushes caused her to turn, smiling. 'Come on out, you chaps. I know you— Yeek!'

As she leaned into the shrubbery, a big blackbird burst from it, the bird's wing striking her face as it flew off. Dotti decided then to be stern with her fellow travellers.

'Now see here, you two, a joke's a joke an' all that, but I've had about enough. Show yourselves front'n'centre please, right now!'

But the only answer she received was the cuckoo calling, 'Cuckoo cuckoo cuckoo!'

Dotti flung a twig irately in its direction. 'Oh, shut your blisterin' beak, y'bally nuisance!'

She decided that Brocktree and Ruff had gone out foraging for breakfast. Muttering darkly to herself, the haremaid sat on the bank, munching a stale barleyscone and an apple she had dug from her bag. The warming sunlight did nothing to raise her spirits. She felt deserted and alone.

'Huh, rotten ole Brocko an' slyboots Ruff, sneakin' off just 'cos a gel's got to have her beauty sleep, wot! Bet they've found a patch of juicy berries or somethin', prob'ly sittin' there stuffin' their great fat faces!'

She pictured the otter and the badger doing just that and began imitating their voices in conversation. 'Haharr, stap me rudder an' swoggle me barnacles, matey, these berries is prime vittles. Shall we save some an' take 'em back t'camp for the young 'un?

'Hah, don't talk silly, Ruff. Let the lazy whippersnapper find her own berries. That's the trouble with young 'uns these days, want everything doing for 'em!' She was working herself up into a fine old temper, when she noticed something on the flat top of the elm boat.

It was a crude sketch, done with a piece of burnt wood from last night's fire. There was an arrow pointing downstream and a depiction of herself sitting on the boat. By a sharp bend in the stream, Ruff and Brocktree were drawn, apparently waiting for her. Also there was some sketchy writing, obviously Ruff's: 'See U att noone.'

The haremaid studied it, still chunnering to herself. 'See me at noon where the stream bends, eh? Well how flippin' nice to let a body know, blinkin' deserters! Tchah! Is that supposed t'be a picture of me? Just look at those miserable ears. Mine are a jolly sight prettier than that, wot! Hmph! No wonder that otter's folks chucked him out – his spellin's dreadful!'

She found the burnt stick and corrected it all to her satisfaction, drawing a huge stomach on Ruff and an ugly drooping snout on the Badger Lord. Finally, after adding many touches to make the likeness of herself more beautiful, Dotti gave Ruff a black mark for his spelling. Feeling much better, she tossed the charcoal away.

'Righto, young hare m'gel, time you commanded your own vessel, wot wot!'

After one or two minor setbacks Dotti found the going fairly simple. The stream was straight and smooth enough, and she soon got the knack of keeping the log in midstream and sailing on course. The haremaid never tired of holding conversations with herself, for who better was there to talk with, she reasoned.

'I say, I've just thought of a wheeze. I'll paddle right past those two, leave 'em on the blinkin' bank. Wot ho! I'll shout to them, keep the jolly old paws poundin', the exercise'll do you the world o' good, chaps. Put yourselves about a bit, that's the ticket, find lots of super grub an' I may consider lettin' you back aboard. Bye bye now!'

She giggled aloud at the picture she conjured up and continued her conversation. 'Yes, I think I'd make a good captain, or a captainess mebbe. Wish I could play my harecordion awhile – pity I've got to keep hold o' this confounded paddle. Never mind, I'll just have to sing unaccompanied. Think I'll compose one of those shanty type things, like these watery types are always caterwaulin' as they sail along. Here goes!'

She broke out into a ditty which caused nearby birds to abandon their nests, chicks and all.

'Whompin' along with a woffle de ho,
As down the stream I jolly well go,
Shoutin' "Lower yore rudder an' furl that log",
There's nothin' on land like a seagoin' frog.
So oar that paddle an' paddle that oar,
Listen, me hearties, I'll sing ye some more!

I'm a beautiful hare wot lives on the river,

In winter I sweat an' in summer I shiver,
I don't need no badger or otter for crew,
I'm cook an' I'm paddler an' captainess too!
So mainsail me gizzards until we reach shore,
Listen, me hearties, I'll sing ye some more!

Ye don't mess with Dotti that ole riverbeast,
I'm grizzled an' fearsome an' that ain't the least,
So swoggle me scuppers ten dozen I've slew,
I'm a jolly young creature an' quite pretty too!
So mizzen me muzzle an' mop the boat's floor,
I'm sorry, me hearties, I don't know no more!

'Beg pardon about the grammar, of course,' she commented to a waterbeetle swimming alongside. 'Dreadful terms us nautical types use, y'know. I'll work on it, I promise, wot! Er, let's see, strangle me binnacle? No, that doesn't sound right. How about boggle me bowsprit? Rather! That sounds much better!'

Away down the stream Dotti paddled, composing more horrible lyrics from her store of seagoing knowledge.

'So boggle me bowsprit, mate, just one word more,
An' I'll give ye a whack with the back o' me paw!'

She backed water with her paddle to slow the log down, for a creature had appeared on the bank. He was an enormously fat, scruffy weasel with a runny snout and the better part of that morning's breakfast evident on the filthy tunic he wore. He was hanging on to a thick vine rope which trailed upwards and was lost among the trees above. Spitting into the stream, he eyed Dotti nastily and uttered one word. 'More!'

The haremaid smiled politely at him. 'Beg pardon, what was that you said, old chap?'

He thrust his chin out belligerently at her. 'More. I said

more! So then, are yew gonna give me a whack wid the back o' yer paw? Jus' you try it, rabbit!'

The haremaid sighed, rolling her eyes upward as if for help. 'If you washed your face this morning then you missed out cleaning your eyes, sah. I am not a rabbit, I'm a hare, y'know. As for swiping chaps with paws, it didn't apply to you, it was merely a ditty I was singing.'

The weasel spat into the stream again. 'You said that if'n I said one word more you'd gimme a whack wid the back o' yer paw. So I said one word more. More!'

Dotti eyed him disdainfully. Her mother had warned her about creatures who used aggressive language and spat a lot. There was only one way to treat such beasts: with disdain. Accordingly, she stared regally down her nose at him.

'Disgusting habit, spitting. And let me tell you, my good vermin, this stream level won't rise a fraction, no matter how much you continue to spit in it. Good day!'

As she sailed by him, the weasel roared out, 'Boat ahoy!'

She waggled her ears at him, a sign of contempt often used by well-bred haremaids. 'Of course it's a boat, you benighted buffoon. What did you suppose it was, a tea trolley?'

The weasel signalled to the opposite bank, where another similarly fat and untidy weasel appeared. He too was hanging on to a vine rope and was in the habit of spitting into the stream. He leered at Dotti as she sailed by. 'Fink yer tough, don'tcher? We'll see!'

Both weasels let go their ropes and a log came crashing out of the trees above. It splashed sideways into the water, blocking off the stream behind Dotti's boat.

The haremaid knew she was in trouble, and paddled furiously to get away from the revolting pair. Unfortunately she had not gone more than a dozen boatlengths when another log came hurtling downward into the stream. Now she was blocked in fore and aft.

Dotti controlled her craft as the prow bucked slightly on the bow wave set up by the falling trunk. She watched in apprehension while two more weasels emerged from the bushes. These were females, even bigger, fatter and more repulsive than the two males who came shambling up to join them. Dotti sat primly on her vessel. She knew that reasoning with such blaggards was likely to be useless, but she decided to give it a try.

'Good morning to you, ladies. I trust I find you well, wot?'

One of the females spat in the stream. 'Oo, lissen to 'er, willyer? She called us ladies, la di dah!'

Her male companion scratched his head with a grimy claw. 'I ain't no lady – she wuz gonna whack me wid the back of 'er paw!'

Immediately things got nasty. The other female produced a rusty woodsaw and began wading out towards Dotti. 'Ho, did she now? Well I'll leave me mark on 'er fer that!'

Dotti stood up, wielding her paddle warningly. 'Stay away from me, marm, I'm beautiful but I'm dangerous!'

Lunging forward, the weasel grabbed her victim's footpaw. 'Hah, yer won't be pretty no more when I'm done wid yer!'

Whock!

The haremaid brought the paddle down hard between her opponent's ears. Making a horrendous din, the weasel flopped back to the bank.

'Owowowow! Murder! I'm killed, me pore skull's splitted in twenny places! Yaaaaargh! There's blood everywhere, I'm killed, murdered, slayed I tell yer! Yeeeegh!'

Dotti could see she had raised a bump on the weasel's head, but there was no sign of blood. 'Oh, stop moanin', you great fat fraud, there's nothing wrong with you apart from a bump on the noggin. I wasn't about to let you come at me with that big rusty woodsaw!'

The other weasel, who was hauling his injured comrade out of the water, let her fall back in with a splash. He clapped both paws over his mouth. 'Oh! Oh! Did yew 'ear that? She called Ermy fat! She's an insulter as well as a murderer!'

The other male sniffed and wiped a paw across his eyes, looking ready to burst into tears. 'Yew 'ad no need to 'it Ermy like that, an' you got no right to call 'er fat. We'll punish yer when y'come ashore.'

Dotti brandished her weapon. 'Not while I've got this paddle you won't. Now pull that log out the way and let me by!'

The weasel stuck out his bottom lip and scuffed the soil with a footpaw. 'Won't!'

Dotti splashed the water with her paddle and glared fiercely. 'Oh yes you will!'

'Won't!'

The female Ermy set up a fresh wail. 'Yaaaahahagh! I tole youse we shoulda sneaked up jus' after dawn an' killed 'er after the badger'n'otter runned away. Now lookit me. Dyin' away. Waaahaaahaaagh!'

Brocktree and Ruff stepped out of the woodlands, both trying hard not to smile. The badger pointed a warning paw across at Ermy. 'Stop that blubbering before I give you something to cry for!'

She lapsed into instant silence. Ruff shook his head at her. 'Good job you never tried to ambush Dotti after dawn – we were watchin' ye from the trees.'

Brocktree pointed to the log barrier blocking the way downstream. 'Haul on your ropes and raise that thing' – he unsheathed his battle blade – 'now!'

Dotti had never seen four overweight weasels move so fast. Puffing and blowing in between sobs of distress they hauled the log back up, whining continuously.

'Oh, spare us, sire, we never meant 'er no 'arm!'

'No, you never mean harm to any creature brave enough to stand up to you. I never liked bullies. Now, hang on tight to those ropes and hold out your left footpaws. Be quick about it!'

'Waaahagh, you ain't gonna chop 'em off, are yer, sire? We won't never bully no more travellers. Don't 'urt us!'

Ruff knotted the free end of their rope tight around the footpaws of the nearest pair, then swam across to perform the same office for Ermy and her companion. 'Bless yore filthy 'earts, course we won't hurt ye . . . left, left the beast said, that's yore right!'

When they were securely tied Brocktree barked out an order. 'Let go of those ropes now!'

As the four weasels released their hold, the log started to fall back towards the stream, jerking the vermin off their footpaws and slowing suddenly as it was counter-balanced by their weight. With yelps of alarm they were raised upside down with their left footpaws bound securely to the ropes. Equilibrium found all four dangling alongside the log, in midstream, just above Dotti's head. The haremaid winced as Ermy's wailing rang out close to her ear.

'Yaaaahahahaaagh! Don't leave me 'ere 'anging upside down with a big lump on me 'ead, I beg yer. Waaahaaagh!'

Placing her wet paddle blade over the lump, Dotti soothed the unhappy vermin. 'Hush now, m'dear, cryin' won't make it better. Here, I'll flatten it for you. Hold still, please.'

Dotti whacked the paddle forcefully with her paw and flattened the bump completely. She also stunned Ermy, much to everybeast's relief.

Brocktree and Ruff had climbed aboard, and now they sailed on downstream, with Dotti admonishing them. 'I'm surprised at you, Ruff, deserting me like that, wot. But as for you, sah, it comes as no surprise, let me tell you. I was beset by villains once before, as I recall, while you hid behind a tree until I was overcome. This is the second time you've left me to it now. Bad form, sah, bad form! I thought you Brocktree types were made of sterner stuff. Seems I was wrong though, wot, wot?'

Brocktree dangled his footpaws in the streamflow, nodding. 'I can understand how you feel, miss, but we had our reasons. We didn't want to confront them until you learned a little object lesson, which you did wonderfully, what d'you think, Ruff?'

The big otter saluted Dotti with a swirl of his tail. 'I was proud o' ye, missymate, y'never showed any fear, you stood up to 'em. That's the only way t'deal with bullies!'

Inwardly Dotti glowed happily at her friends' remarks, but she was still a bit peeved, and she let them know.

'Yes, all very nice thank you, but that's not the point. What if those weasels had rushed me? I wouldn't have stood much blinkin' chance against four of 'em, not t'mention that awful rusty saw. I shudder t'think what they might've done to me if anything had gone wrong with your timing!'

Ruff winked roguishly at his indignant young companion. 'Haharr, you 'ad no cause to worry. We were watchin' you every bit o' the way; there was never any real danger. Y'see I knows this stream, an' those vermin too. They're nought but fat ole blusterers – I've seen 'em back off from a bad-tempered frog. But if'n you didn't know that an' you were a bit faint-'earted, the looks an' the size o' those four nasty lumps might've scared you into surrenderin' to 'em. But you taught those baddies a lesson, Dotti.'

Brocktree chuckled drily. 'I'll say you did, young 'un, a born perilous hare you are!'

Dotti was about to make some frosty rebuke when Ruff caught sight of the sketch and message he had so painstakingly written out on the log.

'Oi, that ain't the way I drew it.'

Dotti fluttered her sweetest smile at him. 'It was far too crude. I altered it a teensy bit.'

Suddenly it was the otter's turn for indignation. 'You

cheeky liddle tailwag! Lookit the great fat belly you've drawn on me! I look like a stuffed stoat!'

Brocktree's booming laughter echoed off the banks. 'Hohohoho! Well done, miss, hahaha, a stuffed stoat, eh? Oh, come on, Ruff, where's your sense of humour?'

The otter looked him straight in the eye. 'Same place as yores'll be when y'see wot she's done to yore picture, milord!'

The badger put aside his paddle and leaned across to view Dotti's artwork. She covered both ears as he exploded.

'You foul little fur-covered grubscoffer! I haven't got a wobbly fat drooping nose like that! How dare you, miss!'

For answer Dotti leapt to her paws, waving her paddle about. 'Back I say, back, droopynose and fattygut! You know that I'm a blisterin' perilous beast an' know no fear!'

Ruff went into a pretty fair imitation of the weasel Ermy. 'Owowow, I beg yer, don't 'arm us, miss floppyears!'

The situation was so funny that the three friends fell about laughing until tears streamed from their eyes.

A deep gruff voice hailed them from the south bank. 'Yurr, oi do loiks to 'ear 'arpy creeturs, pertickly in ee springtoim. Wot be you'm larfin' abowt, zurr Ruffo?'

Wiping moisture from her eyes, Dotti saw the mole more clearly. He was a stout, dapper-looking creature, wearing a green smock embroidered with daisies and buttercups, and sporting a bright orange kingfisher feather in his tall mushroom-shaped cap. Clutched in his paw was a ladle, almost as long as a travelling staff. He had the friendliest of smiles, exposing lots of milky white teeth.

Ruff evidently knew the mole. He waved his tail at him as he steered the log to shore. 'Sink me rudder, 'tis Rogg Longladle. How's yore snout twitchin', mate? It must be four seasons since I clapped eyes on ye. Well, this is an 'appy day!' Bounding ashore, Ruff embraced Rogg's stout form heartily.

Still smiling, the mole protested. 'Hurr, let oi go, ee gurt lump, you'm creasin' moi smock!'

The otter called his friends on to the bank. 'Brock, Dotti, come 'ere, mates. I want ye t'meet my pal Rogg, the best cook on this or any other stream an' the smartest turned out mole on or under the earth!'

Rogg doffed his hat gallantly, bowing his velvety head. 'Gudd day to ee, zurr an' miz, noice t'meet ee oi'm sure!'

Dotti leapt lightly ashore and curtsied nicely. 'Bo urr, gudd day to ee, zurr Rogg. Stan' on moi tunnel, but you'm an 'ansome gurt beast, hurr aye!'

Rogg threw up his big digging claws in surprise. 'Burr! You'm spake ee molespeak vurry gudd, miz. Whurr did ee lurn et?'

Dotti answered in the quaint mole dialect. 'Moi ole mum's molechum, Blossum Bunn, she'm taughten et to oi when oi wurr a h'infant, bo urr aye.'

Ruff shrugged helplessly at Brocktree. 'Just lissen to those two goin' at it? I could always unnerstand mole-speak, though I never learned t'speak it.'

'Me neither,' Brocktree said as they followed in the wake of the chattering haremaid and mole.

'Urr, Blossum Bunn, do ee say, miz? She'm be's moi h'auntie, twoice removed on moi granmum's soide. 'Ow she'm a-doin'?'

'Burr, ole Blossum be's brisker'n a bumblybee an' loively as ee bukkit o' froggers, zurr!'

Rogg Longladle's dwelling was a marvellous cavern beneath the roots of a great beech. Lord Brocktree gazed about wistfully.

'This place puts me in mind of my old home Brockhall, very much so. Hmm, don't suppose I'll ever see it again.'

Ruff patted the badger's broad back. 'Same as

me'n'Dotti. Don't be sad, mate, we're good friends an' both with ye!'

Amid the alcoves of thick downgrowing roots, Dotti sat herself in a comfortable old armchair. Moles kept scurrying by to introduce themselves to the hare who could speak their dialect.

'Oi be Granfer Clubb, miz, an' thiz yurr's moi ole dearie Granma Dumbrel. Ee'll stay an' take vittles with us'n's, oi 'opes, miz?'

Dotti shook all the outstretched paws as more came by. 'Thankee, zurr Clubb, oi'd be gurtly pleased to, hurr aye!'

Ruff and Brocktree seated themselves on a thickly mossgrown ledge, where they were inspected by some tiny young moles. The smallest of them had a voice like a bass foghorn.

'Gudd day to ee, zurrs. Moi name be's Trubble.'

'I can see that – you look like trouble!'

'Hurr hurr, moi mum allus sez that. Wot sort o' mole be's you, zurr? Oi bain't never see'd one wi' a gurt stroipy 'ead loik yourn.'

'Oh, I'm called a badgermole and Ruff's an ottermole.'

'Humm, ee must be h'eatin' gurt bowlfuls o' pudden t'grow oop big loik ee are. 'Ow did ee get so gurt?'

Ruff winked at the badger and replied, 'Keepin' clean, me liddle mate, that's 'ow. We gets scrubbed five times every day, an' that's why we growed big.'

Trubble wrinkled his baby snout at the other small moles. 'Whurrrgh! Reckerns oi'll stay likkle then!'

Rogg appeared, dabbing at his brow with a dock leaf which he used to shoo the moles off with. 'Gurr, be off'n with ee, Trubble. Gurlo, Burkle, Plugg, you 'uns leave ee gennelbeasts t'rest awhoile. Cumm an' 'elp oi in ee kitchun if'n ee wants vittles t'be ready sooner. Hurr, an' be washen ee paws furst!'

Left to themselves, the three travellers took their ease, Brocktree and Ruff stretching out on the mossy ledge. Dotti sprawled comfortably in the armchair, letting tempting aromas from the kitchen hover about her. Through half-closed eyes she took in the homely cavern. Lanterns of varying hues hung everywhere, shelves and cupboards were carved neatly into the rocks and heavy tree roots, the floors were strewn with woven rush mats, and two black and orange banded sexton beetles dozed close to the embers on the hearth, household pets, used by the moles to keep the cavern free of crumbs and other morsels which the babes left about. Before Dotti's eyes finally closed, she sighed. What a pleasant place. A real home.

9

It was sometime in the late evening when Fleetscut collapsed. A combination of overwhelming fatigue, thirst and hours of strong sunlight, together with the fact that the old hare had run without stopping for almost two days, brought him down. Head hanging, paws dragging, he tottered about on the open flatlands like a beast driven crazy. He did not realise he had fallen at first. Fleetscut lay on the rough ground, the tongue hanging dry from his mouth, footpaws still moving in a running action, kicking up small dustclouds. In his delirium he squinted at a rock, imagining it was Lord Stonepaw gazing sternly at him.

'Sire, there ain't a hare nowheres t'be found,' he croaked feebly. 'I tried, I did my best for you, but alas, lord, the young hares are gone from the land . . .'

Fleetscut's eyes glazed over and he fell back senseless.

From a rocky outcrop a crow had been watching the old hare, waiting. Now it flew forward, cautiously at first, using rocks as cover. On reaching the fallen hare it pecked lightly at his ear; he did not stir. Emboldened by this, the crow swaggered and strutted round Fleetscut, weighing up its prey. At the very moment the crow decided to start pecking at the hare's eyes, a slingstone knocked the talons from under it. Squawking angrily, the hefty black bird took awkwardly to the air and flapped off, sent on its way by another stone narrowly missing its wingtip.

The young squirrel Beddle and five companions hurried to Fleetscut's side and ministered to him.

'Just drip the water on his tongue, not too fast.'

'Poor fool, Jukka said he'd not get far. Look at his paws!'

'Aye, they be torn badly. Hast any herbs in thy bag, Ruro?'

The squirrel Ruro emptied out the bag. 'Sanicle, dock leaves and moss. Here, let me attend him.' Pouring water on the ingredients, she made compresses. 'He be lucky Jukka sent us after him. Beddle, can thee make up a stretcher?'

Beddle set about removing his tunic. He slotted two spears down the sleeves, calling out to the youngest of the party, 'Grood, I'll need thy tunic, give it here!'

Reluctantly Grood removed the garment. Beddle eyed him fiercely. 'Watch thy tongue, young 'un, or thine ears'll get boxed twice, once by me an' once by Jukka Sling!'

Moonlight shafted pale through the pines; a small fire encased within a rock oven sent out a welcome ruddy glow. Fleetscut became aware of creatures hovering over him, squirrels. One of them called out softly, 'Ye be right, Jukka, he lives!'

Jukka the Sling's tough features hove into view. 'Most creatures of long seasons would be dead after putting themselves through such a trial.'

Fleetscut's tongue moistened his lips, his voice when it came sounding cracked and hoarse. 'When I go it'll be with a weapon in me paw, fightin'. 'Til then I'll just hang about and annoy you, friend.'

Jukka chuckled. 'What's that they say on yon mountain,

thou art a perilous creature. Rest now, longears, drink some soup an' sleep. We'll talk on the morrow.'

Rest was the last thought on Fleetscut's mind, but no sooner had he drunk half a beaker of mushroom soup than the vessel slipped from his paws and he went into a deep slumber.

Morning and noontide came and passed, and it was evening when Fleetscut wakened.

'How do thy paws feel? Sore, I'll wager?'

The old hare struggled to a sitting position, allowing Ruro to change the dressings.

'Just bandage 'em tight, so I can run on 'em, marm!'

Ruro shook her head at the defiant old hare. 'Nay, thou art going nowhere. Jukka Sling would have words with thee. Rest and eat something.'

Fleetscut tried to get up on to his paws, but collapsed wincing from the pain. 'Where is Jukka?'

Beddle brought food and placed it before the hare. 'She'll be back by dark o' night. You must wait. Jukka will have news of thy mountain, what has taken place there. Come, be not foolish, ye must eat to live.'

Fleetscut picked up a potato and hazelnut pasty. 'So be it, old lad, but 'tis you who are foolish, inviting a hare to eat. Is that a carrot flan I see?'

When he had satisfied his hunger and thirst, Fleetscut lay back and fell into a doze. Beddle sat wide-eyed. 'Strewth! Did ye ever see a creature eat like that in all thy born days?'

Ruro removed the empty platters, shaking her head. 'And still he be skinny as a willow withe. Would that I could pack away vittles like that an' stay lean as he!'

Midnight had long gone when Jukka the Sling arrived back at the pines. She sat panting and sipping at a flask of elderberry wine. 'Our hare sleeps yet, eh?'

Ruro fed the fire with a dead pine log. 'He wakened earlier, ate like a madbeast and fell asleep again. Shall I wake him?'

The squirrel leader put aside her wine. 'Nay, let him sleep on. There's nought but bad news to hear when he wakens.'

'The mountain of Salamandastron has fallen, then?'

Jukka warmed her paws by the fire; a chill breeze was blowing in from the seas. 'Aye, 'tis conquered by the Blue Ones. I could not get too near, but I saw from a distance some vermin scaling the slopes. They carried large new banners to put up there. 'Tis a sad day for these western coasts, Ruro.'

Beddle crouched nearby, preparing Jukka's meal. 'Mayhap we should have helped the old one, Jukka.'

'Thou art a fool if that's what thee think, Beddle. We'd be nought but slain carcasses rolling in the tide shallows now, had we gone up against such a force. Yon Badger Lord an' his hares were brave, mad beasts, they did what they had to. But 'twas a foregone conclusion.'

Spots of rain that had found their way through the pine canopy roused Fleetscut in the dawn hour. Jukka was awake also, sitting watching him, cloaked in a blanket. Turning her back on the old hare, she raked ash from the fire embers and brought it to crackling life by feeding broken pine branches into the rock oven. Fleetscut's voice hit her back like a whip.

'Tell me what has happened at my mountain. Speak!'

Jukka did not turn, but she gave him his answer.

By the time the entire squirrel camp was up and about, Fleetscut had hauled himself upright and stood supporting himself against a pine trunk, a plate of food lying at his footpaw, untouched. Jukka still sat watching him.

'There was nought anybeast could have done, Fleetscut. Come now, eat. I hear tell that thou art a beast with great appetite.'

A kick from the hare's footpaw sent the plate flying. His eyes were like stone, his voice dripping contempt. 'I don't eat with cowards!'

Jukka sprang up, a loaded sling automatically in her paw. 'Nobeast calls Jukka the Sling a coward!'

The old hare tore his tunic open, exposing his scrawny chest. 'Then kill me, Jukka, go on, kill me! One old hare shouldn't be too difficult for a warrior like you, wot? Slay me an' see how long you an' your band can hide out in this pine grove until Ungatt Trunn's Blue Hordes find you all. Then you'll wish you'd helped t'fight against him an' save Salamandastron!'

Thrrrakk!

Jukka's slingstone clipped off a branch a hair's breadth from Fleetscut's head and whirred off among the trees. The squirrel stood before him, her wild eyes blazing. 'Any other beast would have been dead by now, hare. But I'll prove to thee that me and mine aren't cowards. We'll go with thee on thy search – aye, an' carry ye if needs be. I'll help ye build an army – hares, or any creature crazy enough to go against the hordes on yonder mountain. Then we'll fight them, us for the taking of weapons which we value so highly, an' thou for thy vengeance on the foes who slew thy brothers. I, Jukka the Sling, do not do this out of comradeship for ye. War is a business. I do it for profit, for all the weapons my tribe may plunder if victory is ours!'

Hare and squirrel stood face to face, their wrathful eyes searing one another. Fleetscut curled his lip scornfully. 'Do it for whatever reason y'like, brushtail. But do it!'

Jukka was trembling all over with rage. 'Oho, I'll do it, never fret about that, longears,' she growled. 'Once Jukka the Sling gives her word, thou canst stake thy life on it!'

Fleetscut turned his back on the squirrel and began hobbling off, calling back over his shoulder, 'Well y'won't get it done standin' round makin' bloomin' speeches all day. Actions speak louder'n words, doncha know!'

In total, Jukka's tribe numbered fifty able-bodied creatures and a dozen who were either too young or too old to serve her purpose. She left eight of the warriors with these twelve, and the other forty-three, counting herself, were ready to march within the hour, each of them armed and provisioned.

Ruro caught up with Fleetscut, who was limping ahead near the pine grove's edge. 'Hold up, friend, my tribe will be with thee shortly. Here, take these. 'Twill make the going easier.'

Fleetscut allowed her to loop a small bag over his shoulder. Then he took the short, thick-handled spear and hefted it. The weapon had a sharp double-edged blade, shaped like a grey willow leaf, with a crosstree where it joined the shaft.

'Strange spear, wot? Wouldn't be very accurate to throw. Rations in this bag, I s'pose, though by the feel of it there's not more'n a couple o' days' supply.'

Ruro showed him her spear, which was the same type as his. 'Useful things, these. Jukka designed them for close combat, not for throwing. See, the blade is as good as a sword, the crosstree can ward off blade thrusts and the thick shaft makes a fine long club. Our food is good for long treks. 'Tis made of dried fruit an' berries stuffed into a farl of oat an' rye bread which has been well soaked in honey. A creature can march all day on just a few mouthfuls, providing there's water to drink. Here come the others now. Lean down on thy spear, Fleetscut, grasp the cross hilt, but keep thy paw clear o' the blade. Makes a good walking stick, eh?'

The old hare was forced to agree: the going was much easier with the spear to aid him. Jukka strode by them in high bad humour, remarking to Ruro as she passed, 'Tell me if the ancient one falls behind, we can carry him trussed to a long pike like a carcass!'

Fleetscut's voice rang out after her. 'You've got a good fast stride there, marm, stap me but y'have! Must be with havin' to retreat from all your foes, wot?'

Jukka kept marching, but her ears and tail shot up rigid

with anger at the insult. Ruro shook her head sadly. 'Do not provoke Jukka Sling overmuch, my friend. She has never been bested in a fight. No matter how much thou thinkest she hath wronged thee, remember, she was only doing what was best for her tribe. I would have done the same in her place.'

Fleetscut had come to like Ruro a lot, so he did not argue with her, but changed the subject. 'I wonder where she's takin' us?'

His friend pointed to the northeast. 'To the Rockwood. We should be there by nightfall, methinks. Jukka will want words with Udara Groundslay.'

'An' who in the name o' seasons is Udara Groundslay?'

Ruro quickened her pace as other squirrels went by. 'Enough talk now, friend, we're starting to lag behind. Save thy breath for travelling, or mayhap Jukka will carry out her threat an' have ye slung on a pike.'

Fleetscut stumped along faster on his makeshift stick. 'Huh, if she ever tries it she'll find out what the term perilous hare really means!'

Jukka marched them ruthlessly all through that day, taking it out on Fleetscut for his ill-chosen remarks to her. Out on the flatlands there was no water. The sun beat down without respite, and not a breeze stirred the brownish scrub grass, which would be withered before the advent of summer. Grasshoppers chirruped dryly, larks could be heard high overhead. Like the squirrels, the old hare sucked on a flat pebble to retain the moisture in his mouth. His paw ached abominably from holding and leaning upon the metal crosstree of the spear, even though he had tried to cushion it with clumps of grass. Jukka remained silent and angry, but her tribe sang a marching song to keep up their spirits. The old hare had never heard the tune before, so he too kept quiet as they tramped wearily across the scorched acres of open land, though like any old soldier he kept pace with the beat.

'Down goes the paw an' up rises dust,
Keep thy courage, hold thy trust,
Come to our journey's end we must,
Marching the high road together.

Tramp tramp tramp! Can we make camp?
Not whilst there's light, not 'til tonight!
One two! One two! Beneath a sky o' blue,
Sing out, comrades. Tramp tramp tramp!

On goes the trail, for ever more,
Weary of limb, and sore of paw,
Keep on moving, that's our law,
Marching the high road together.

Tramp tramp tramp! Can we make camp?
I'll tell ye when, don't stop 'til then!
One two! One two! Daylight hours growing few,
Sing out, comrades. Tramp tramp tramp!'

In the late afternoon Fleetscut stumbled and fell. Before anybeast had noticed, Ruro heaved him up, set him back on his stick and supported his other side. The old hare gritted his teeth as he stumbled onward at the rear of the tribe. 'How far is it now, Ruro?'

She indicated with a nod of her head. 'Yonder, see, there's the Rockwood. We made good time – methinks we'll be there before evening. Can ye carry on, friend? 'Twould not hurt to take a rest, now that Rockwood be in sight.'

Fleetscut wiped dust from his eyes with a free paw. 'If a squirrel can do it I'm sure a Salamandastron hare can. I'll blinkin' well make it, m'gel, just you watch!'

Rockwood turned out to be a huge stone outcrop, dotted with gnarled trees and stunted bush. Beddle had been sent ahead to scout it out, and he came dogtrotting back to report as the tribe arrived at its base.

'I spotted Udara, but he vanished 'mid the shrubbery. Good news, though – the little lake hasn't dried up. Plenty o' water there!'

Jukka held up a paw for order as a ragged cheer went up. 'Hearken, all of ye, we be on the domain of Udara Groundslay. Give no offence, mind thy manners. That goes for thee too, longears. Wait you all here 'til I return.'

She scrambled up into the rocks and was lost to sight amid the foliage. Fleetscut sat down with the tribe, glad of the rest, but still very curious.

'So then, Ruro, who is this Udara Groundslay? Tell me.'

The squirrel lay back, shading both eyes with her tail. 'Ye'll find out soon enough, friend.'

Jukka returned after a short while. 'Udara will see us after sundown. Ye may drink of his water, but not swim in it, nor wash. I will deal with anybeast that does. There be small apples an' pears on some of the trees. Take only the high ones, leave those in the lower branches. Ye will do as I say, understand?'

A weary rumble of assent came from the squirrels. As they moved off into the rocks, Grood could be heard muttering under his breath.

Jukka caught the youngster by his ear and tweaked it, none too gently. 'I heard that mouthful ye came out with, wretch. See this strip o' bark? I'll gag ye with it if I hear one more word from ye whilst we're guests upon Rockwood!'

Fleetscut patted his stomach. It made a swilling noise from all the cool, sweet water he had drunk from the little shaded pool. He gnawed upon a pear which felt as hard as the rocks surrounding him and lay still whilst Ruro changed his dressings.

The good squirrel soaked dock leaves, sanicle and rockmoss in water and pounded them into a soothing poultice before applying them to the old hare's footpaws. He sighed.

'Aaaahhh! My thanks, friend. D'y'know, my paws are startin' to feel wonderful, wot. I feel like a young leveret again.'

Ruro put the final touches to her dressings. 'Then rest thee an' try not to go dashin' about – 'twould ruin all my work. Lay up in the shade here where 'tis cool.'

Fleetscut did as she instructed. He took a few bites from the heavy honey-soaked farl of trekking bread, a couple more swigs of water to counteract the sticky sweetness, and lay back.

All around him others were doing likewise. Some distance away he glimpsed Jukka, sitting alone and waiting for evening shades to fall. That would be when their mysterious host might put in an appearance. Fleetscut dozed off, wondering just what sort of creature Udara Groundslay would turn out to be.

10

Ungatt Trunn sat closeted in his humid stateroom while his officers led his Blue Hordes against Salamandastron. He watched the spiders scuttling across their silky gossamer webs, pursuing flies, trapping them, and finally sucking the life from their victims' bodies. Spiders were savage, independent and deadly; Ungatt liked them. He had learned many lessons by lying back in his cabin and watching them. One thing, however, was troubling his mind. The stripedog, not the old one who ruled the mountain, but he who bestrode his dreams, big, strong and forbidding, with his face always wreathed in a blur of mist. The wildcat would have given much to see the features of his foe. For foe he surely was, and coming closer each day. Now when Ungatt's eyes closed he saw the phantom badger looming larger, surrounded by an ever-growing presence. The signs were there: this stripedog was gathering an army about him.

Ungatt Trunn had never been a superstitious creature, until he first heard of the mountain called Salamandastron. Prior to that he had been a conqueror, a warrior, with little regard for omens and dreams. Now he found himself listening to the riddles of a crippled fox, simply because, being neither wizard nor magician, he could not construe what went on in the land of visions. It angered him. He closed his eyes tightly and spoke aloud, trying his utmost to concentrate his thoughts on the big stripedog who haunted the corridors of his mind.

'Come, show your face to me, come to my mountain and meet with your fate. I am Ungatt Trunn the Fearsome Beast; you will die by my paw the day you look upon my face!'

Outside on the afterdeck, Groddil and the Grand Fragorl were leaning on the stern rail, watching Salamandastron fall to the Blue Hordes, who broke upon it like the never-ending waves of the sea. Both creatures heard the wildcat's raised voice from the cabin beneath. They could not hear his exact words, so, fearing that they might be absent when he was calling for them, Groddil and Fragorl hastened down to the stateroom door. The magician fox tapped respectfully and called, 'Mightiness, do you wish us to attend you?'

Ungatt Trunn prowled sinuously out on to the deck, his plain war armour accentuating the strength and size of a fully grown male wildcat. His slitted eyes flicked shorewards before turning to the pair. 'How goes the conquest of my mountain?'

Grand Fragorl replied in her usual monotone. 'You will be enthroned within it by nightfall, O Shaker of the Earth. Already they are battering down its gates.'

The wildcat strode to the rail, both creatures following in his wake. 'Bring a boat. We will go ashore!'

One of the Hordes' most respected captains, a female rat named Mirefleck, stood awaiting them on the tideline. With her were two newcomers, big, sturdy young rats, one carrying bow and arrows, the other with a cutlass thrust in his belt. Ungatt silently sized them up: searats both. He stood to one side, allowing Mirefleck and his Fragorl to do the speaking.

Mirefleck saluted with her spear. 'These are two rats

from the seas. They heard of the master's fame and wish to join his Blue Hordes.'

Fragorl nodded and turned to address the pair. 'Know ye that ye can serve no other master than Ungatt Trunn, son of King Mortspear. Swear this under pain of death!'

The rats looked at one another, and then the one with the cutlass bowed his head slightly, answering for them both.

'I'm Ripfang, and this is my brother Doomeye. We swear we will serve Ungatt Trunn.'

Fragorl held a small whispered conference with the wildcat before turning her attention back to the brothers. 'His Mightiness looks upon you both with favour. Beasts who are skilled with arms and useful in battle are ever welcome to the Blue Hordes. Put aside your weapons and come.'

Ripfang and Doomeye carried out the orders issued by Groddil. First, they immersed themselves completely from ears to tails in a rock pool; then, climbing out, they both knelt in front of him. Groddil bade them close their eyes as he shook the contents of a large bag containing dark blue powder over them. Meanwhile, Fragorl intoned the initiation words.

'Blue is the sea, blue is the sky,
Mightiest under the sun,
Blue are you, the same as I,
Servants of Ungatt Trunn.
Let him see what you are worth,
Make lesser creatures see why
The Chosen Ones can shake the earth,
Whilst the foes of their master die!'

Turning on his heel, the wildcat headed for the mountain with Fragorl in his wake. Groddil stayed momentarily, to acquaint the new recruits with their duties.

'Rub the powder into your fur, all over, and stay away from water until the sun has risen three times. By then the blue colour will be permanent, and you can report to Captain Mirefleck and join her horde section.'

The din of battle rang out from the mountain. Both rats opened their eyes, wiping away blue powder residue from their eyelids as they watched the three retreating figures. The one called Doomeye retrieved his bow and arrows, rubbing the powder into his fur as he did so. 'Well, it looks like we're Blue Hordebeasts now, eh, brother?'

Ripfang suited his name. Some quirk of nature had left him with one great curved tooth growing out of the centre of his top jaw, so that now his smile appeared as a ghastly grimace. 'Aye, fer as long as we gain more plunder an' vittles than we did at piratin'!'

Lord Stonepaw knew defeat was inevitable. Against frighteningly overwhelming odds his hares had put up a gallant battle, but to no avail. Stiffener Medick had fought his way up to the high-level chambers, where the Badger Lord and his remaining warriors had retreated. Black oily smoke swirled around them as it rose from the lower mountain passages and chambers. Ignoring a deep slash in his paw, the fighting hare threw a salute to Stonepaw.

'We're cut off from the rest, sah. Bungworthy's command were cut t'pieces tryin' to hold the main gate – those vermin burned an' battered it down. Ole Bungworthy was standin' up to his scut in slain blue 'uns, yellin' Eulalias an' hackin' at wave after wave of the scum, but they kept on comin'. He went down just as I made it t'the main stairs. Seasons rest his brave memory!'

Stonepaw's shattered lance fell to the floor. 'Did you see any of Sailears's command on the second level?'

Stiffener wiped tears from his eyes. 'They was taken, lord, surrounded an' beaten. 'Twas full o' foebeasts, packed tight – Sailears an' the rest didn't even get a chance to fight! I got a smack o'er the ears an' fell down stunned. One of 'em thought he'd stuck me with a blade, but I only got cut on me paw an' side. They dashed off then, carryin' torches to search the chambers for more prisoners. That's when I escaped an' made it up here, sire. We'd best do somethin' quick afore they come!'

Ever gallant, the hare called Trobee drew his blade. 'We'll hold 'em at the stairhead. Mebbe we won't last long, but we'll take a tidy few o' the villains with us. Who's with me? Eulaliaaa!'

Stonepaw plucked the blade from Trobee's grasp. 'No! Listen to me. I know you're all perilous beasts, but if we're dead then Salamandastron's completely lost. There are secret passages that lead down to the cellar caves – we'd never be found down there. At least we'd be alive until help arrives in one form or another. Come on!'

Eighteen hares, the pitiful remainder of the mountain's old guard, were left to follow Lord Stonepaw. They filed after him, with his final words ringing in their ears.

'At least where there's life there's hope, my friends!'

Evening skies rimmed the western horizon with fiery scarlet as the sun dipped to the winedark seas, and still no birds were heard or seen. Warm from the day's heat, the sand was crowded with fresh Blue Hordebeasts, none of whom had seen action that day. Ungatt Trunn had the Badger Lord's great chair brought out from the dining hall on to the beach, where he sat watching black smoke wreathe from the rock-carved windows whilst his officers made their reports.

The first, Captain Fraul, a sombre-looking stoat, bowed his head. 'Losses in the first wave amounted to—'

'Silence!' Groddil interrupted in a squeaky shout. 'His Mightiness does not want to know about losses, fool! Report the victory, you great oaf!'

'Our victory was complete, O Great One!'

The Grand Fragorl took her place at Ungatt Trunn's

right paw. 'What other outcome could there be for Ungatt Trunn, son of King Mortspear? Captain Swinch, you were in the second wave. How many foebeasts do you report slain?'

Ungatt held up a paw, halting Swinch. The wildcat's other paw circled the Fragorl's neck, in what appeared a friendly embrace. However, it was anything but friendly as Ungatt tightened his grip into a stranglehold. Pulling the Fragorl close he growled low and harsh into her ear.

'I am Ungatt Trunn, I carve my own path, I conquer for myself. Call me son of Mortspear again and I'll see to it that you die slowly over a fire. Erase Mortspear's name from my list of titles – I never want to hear it again!' He released the ferret and she staggered back holding her throat. Ungatt signalled Captain Swinch to continue.

'Threescore and twelve of the lesser orders lie dead, Mighty One. Their unworthy carcasses will be fed to the waters of the seas at ebb tide.'

Groddil did some hasty figuring before pursuing the matter. 'And how many were taken captive?'

Captain Fraul answered. 'My Hordebeasts have threescore captives awaiting your judgement, Mightiness!'

The stunted fox cocked his head on one side, pacing a circle around the stoat officer. 'Hmm. Seventy-two dead and sixty captured. I make that one hundred and thirty-two in all, captain. Surely there were more hares defending the mountain than that?'

Fraul swallowed and stood to attention, looking straight ahead. 'Sire, I do not know the exact number we fought against. I can only report on the ones we have, dead or alive, sire.'

Ungatt Trunn stepped down from his great chair then, right on to the fox's bushy tail. Groddil winced, but stayed still, fearing to move. Like a knife, the wildcat's voice pierced his back.

'Our scouts who watched the mountain reported at least a hundred and a half of those old hares. Then there's another matter, my malformed magician. Where's the Badger Lord Stonepaw?'

Groddil jumped as Ungatt shouted the last words, though he knew better than to try to give an answer. Ungatt kicked him, sending him sprawling as his master ranted.

'Old Stonepaw the stripedog must still be alive inside that mountain, with a faithful few around him. Did nobeast have the sense to think of that? I want that badger here, flat on his muzzle in front of me, and the last of his hares, alive or dead. Find him, Groddil! Take some Hordebeasts with you, search every crack or hiding place inside that mountain, but find him. Now get out of my sight!'

The fox signalled to Captain Swinch to bring his soldiers and scrambled off through Salamandastron's broken gates.

Stonepaw and his hares encountered nobeast on their journey down to the cellars. Without even torches, they felt their way through dark unused corridors and silent forgotten chambers. Down, down to the network of caverns beneath Salamandastron. Holding tight to the ancient Bramwil, Blench the cook waved her ladle in the Stygian blackness, so that she would not bump into any unseen rocks. Her voice echoed spectrally.

'Are you sure y'know where we're goin', lord?'

The badger's weighty paw descended lightly on her shoulder. 'Hush, marm! Sound carries down here. Don't fret, I know this place like the back o' my paw. I've been Lord of Salamandastron more seasons than I care to recall, longer than any other badger. Stay to your left now, keep the rocks close to your backs, everybeast.'

There was a slight splash, followed by a muffled groan. Stonepaw's voice sounded out a whisper of reprimand. 'Left, I said, Blench – the paw you wear that shell bracelet on. Keep close now – not far to go!'

Blench heard her ladle clicking on rock both sides of her, and guessed that they were passing through a narrow tunnel. Wisely, she ducked her head.

'Wait here, all of you, I'll be back in a moment.'

The hares obeyed their lord's command, speculating in low voices as they huddled together in the dark.

'Where's he gone? Wish he'd jolly well hurry up!'

'What's that plip-ploppin' sound up ahead, Trobee?'

'Don't ask me, I'm as much in the dark as anybeast!'

'As much in the dark. Heehee, that's a good 'un!'

'Keep your blinkin' voice down, Bramwil, y'sound like a frog in a barrel. I say, what's that?'

Sparks flew up ahead, and there was a chinking sound of steel striking flint. In an instant the area was flooded with light and waving shadows.

Lord Stonepaw loomed up, a blazing torch creating a redgold aura around him. 'This way, friends. Follow me!'

Gratefully, they shuffled along in the badger's wake until he halted, holding the torch up against what appeared to be a solid rock face.

'Through here. 'Twas a bit of a squeeze for me, but you hares shouldn't find it too difficult.'

There was a fissure in the rock wall, barely detectable. Stiffener looked at it incredulously. 'You got through there, m'lud? 'Tain't nought but a sort o' sideways crack!'

Emerging one by one from the narrow gap, the hares greeted the sight that met their eyes with gasps of surprise. They were in a medium-sized cavern, with a pool at its centre, which threw off a pale luminescent green aura. Water dripping from white limestone stalactites plopped gently into the pool, rippling it constantly and causing a shimmering effect in the light. Smooth, worn stone ledges bordered the cave walls, with knobbly stalagmites looking as if they had popped up from the floor.

Stonepaw busied himself filling four big lanterns from a barrel of vegetable oil near the entrance. He lit them with his torch. 'Here, place these about midway on the ledges.'

When this was done the added light had quite a cheering effect. The Badger Lord called them all to sit in a semicircle around him.

'First, a few words for our dear comrades who are slain or captured by the foebeast. Bramwil, would you say it?'

Faint eerie echoes rebounded from the walls as the ancient hare intoned in a husky whisper to the bowed heads before him.

'When sunlight tinges the dawn of the day,
Remember those brave ones now gone.
We who recall them to mind, let us say,
They were perilous beasts every one!
For those who live, but are not free,
May we see their dear faces again,
Mother Fortune grant them sweet liberty,
And cause slaves not to suffer in pain.'

A moment's silence followed, the only sound the measured cadence of droplets hitting the pool surface.

Lord Stonepaw coughed gruffly and wiped his eyes, blinking as he surveyed the pitiful remnants of one hundred and fifty loyal hares.

'Right, council of war. First, we've no food down here, but as you see there's lots of cold clear water. Now, let's take a vote by show of paws. What do we do next? Shall we sit here and wait to be rescued, or do we search for a way out to freedom?'

Every paw was raised for finding a way out of Salamandastron. The Badger Lord nodded approvingly. 'Well, at least there'll be no arguments. Down to business, then. What weapons have we, Stiffener?'

The boxing hare had his estimate ready. 'Four light rapiers, bows'n'arrers, eight, full quivers too. No more'n 'alf a dozen javelins, but everybeast carries a sling an' there ain't a shortage of stones 'ereabouts. Oh, eight daggers an' Blench's ladle. That's the lot, sah!'

Stonepaw mused over the situation before speaking. 'Hmm. If we're going to get out we'd best make it soon. I'll guarantee that Ungatt Trunn is having the mountain searched stone by stone for me right now. If we linger down here we'll have to face three things: discovery, and a fight to the death, or capture and slavery. Our final option is that we remain hidden here and die of starvation. Not a pleasant thought, eh?'

Blench dipped her ladle in the pool and drank. 'So, lord, let's get goin' right away. D'you know the way out?'

Stonepaw shook his massive striped head. 'I haven't got a single clue. Have any of you? Maybe an old ballad or poem might hold the answer. Let's put our thinking caps on. Hark, what was that? Listen!'

Sound carried far in all directions beneath Salamandastron, and now faint echoes reached them. Voices.

'Huh, 'slike searchin' for a grain o' salt on a seashore down 'ere. Jus' think, we could all get lost ourselves!'

There followed a screech of pain and the voice of Captain Swinch threatening the speaker. 'Jus' think, eh? You ain't down 'ere t'think, Rotface, yore down 'ere to obey orders. Now git searchin' or next time I won't be usin' only the flat o' me blade on yer!'

'We need more torches, Swinch. Send somebeast back for them.'

'Hah! Couldn't yer magic us some, Groddil? Yore supposed t'be Ungatt Trunn's magician. I think it'll be a great piece o' magic if'n we finds anythin' but rock down 'ere.'

'Oh, do you indeed? Well let me tell you, Swinch, if we return empty-pawed we could end up paying for it with our lives. You know how His Mightiness must be obeyed.'

'Aye, yore right there, fox. Hoi, Rotface, you'n'Grinak go back an' get more torches – an' fetch some vittles back with ye, too. We might be some time gettin' the job done. Well, don't stand there gawpin'. Get goin'!'

The voices faded as the search direction changed, and soon there was silence again.

'Whew! That was close. Where d'you reckon they were, wot?'

Stonepaw gestured for Trobee to lower his voice. 'These caves do strange things to sound; they could have been anywhere. One thing you can count on, though – they'll be back. The wildcat won't give up until he's found me.'

Old Bramwil's stomach gurgled. He rubbed it hungrily. 'I could eat a mushroom'n'cheese pastie right now, one with a soft-baked crust – mebbe a salad, too.'

Blench patted the old one's paw. 'If'n I was in me kitchens I'd bake ye one – aye, an' a deep apple pudden with lots o' fresh meadowcream on it.'

Stiffener Medick licked his lips. 'You could throw in a cob o' cheese too, marm, the yellow one with sage'n'onion herbs in it. My favourite!' Then he wilted under Lord Stonepaw's stare. 'Thinkin' o' vittles when we should be rackin' our brains for a way out? My fault, sah. Sorry, sah!'

The Badger Lord softened to his faithful creatures. 'I'm hungry too, but 'tis easier for a badger to forget food than 'tis for a hare. Never mind, friends. Let's get back to figuring our way out.'

Hours passed, interspersed by the dropping of water and the odd sigh from a hare who could see no answer to the problem. Lord Stonepaw kept his silence, knowing there was no solution available. They were imprisoned inside their own mountain, and likely to perish miserably down in its cellars.

11

Food! Dotti vowed to herself that she could not touch another morsel that night. Then she relented and set about nibbling candied lilac buds from the edges of an almond cake. Rogg Longladle was surely a master of victuals, unequalled at baking, boiling, grilling or cooking any edible his moles could find. The haremaid watched Lord Brocktree digging into a huge bowl with a wooden ladle, his cheeks bulging as he ate.

'Well, pickle me ears, sah, y'look pleased enough with that!'

The badger grinned wolfishly over another ladleful. 'Scrumptious, miss. The moles call it deeper'n ever turnip'n'tater'n'beetroot pie. I could eat it all night!'

Ruff took his nose out of a foaming tankard still half filled with chestnut and buttercup beer, and chortled as he blew froth from his upper lip. 'Haharr, ain't it true, though? I'd 'ave never left 'ome if'n I'd got vittles o' this quality. Rogg, ye ole ovendog, give us another o' yore kitchen ditties!'

Brandishing his oversized ladle and smiling from ear to ear, the good mole beckoned the little Dibbuns to take their dancing places. Brisk as bumblebees and plump as robins, the tiny molebabes formed two facing lines. Dotti marvelled at the fact that they could eat so much and still be eager to dance. The infant molemaids grabbed their pinafores and curtsied comically as their partners licked paws and dabbed them on their snouts in reply. Rogg's wife scraped out the opening bars on an old fiddle and all the watchers started tapping their paws in time. Rogg's rotund body bobbed up and down with the rhythm until he found the appropriate moment to join in with his tuneful bass voice.

'Ho berries'n'pickles an' corjul wot tickles,
Gudd apples'n'pears from ee h'orchard do cumm,
Gurt taters'n'beets an' ee redcurrinks sweet,
Get ee owt o' thy tunnel an' go fetch oi summ!
Urr rowtle dee tootle dee, spring be a-born,
Ee fields be all full o' roip barley'n'corn!

Ho turnips'n'dannyloin, damsing an' plumm,
Yon loaf's in ee uvven an' crispin' oop noice,
Carrots'n'onions an' chesknutters cumm,
Get owt'n ee tunnel oi woan't tell ee twoice!
Urr gollybee gullybee wudd for ee foire,
Oi luvvs ee moi dearie moi ole 'eart's desoire!

Ho radish'n'celery, custidd'n'cake,
An' ee sweetest of hunny from bumbledy bee,
Thurr's beer in ee cellar, cumm naow moi owd feller,
You'm fill up'n thoi tummy wi' wot pleasures ee!
Urr trucklebee rucklebee larks oop abuvv,
Cumm darnce ee moi petal an' 'old moi paw luvv!'

Amid the applause Rogg skipped swiftly to one side, giving way to the little ones, who danced furiously, twirling and whirling, smocks, tunics and aprons billowing. It was the funniest sight, all those tiny Dibbuns, bowing, leaping, touching noses, kicking up their paws, whooping in their gruff small voices.

Rogg sat down next to Dotti, rattling his digging claws on the tabletop as he watched the antics of the molebabes. 'They'm loively likkle darncers sure 'nuff, miz!'

'Ho aye, zurr Rogg, them'll sleep loik 'ogs in ee beds arter all ee whurlygiggin'.'

The mole clasped Dotti's paw, immensely pleased that she spoke his own odd dialect. 'You'm a gudd hurrbeast, miz Dott!'

In truth the Dibbins did sleep well, though they snored uproariously, which moles consider a virtue among their babes, reckoning that snoring improves the gruffness and depth of voice. Dotti found herself a nice moss-strewn arbour close to the ledge where Ruff and Brocktree chose to lay their heads for the night. It must have been sometime before the dawn hours when the entire mole household was roused by Brocktree.

It was a nightmare, but clear as day; a swaying room, decked with cobwebs and spiders, and flies buzzing everywhere. Tossing and turning in his sleep, the Badger Lord tried to rid his mind of the unbidden vision. Then suddenly a great evil-looking wildcat appeared, its voice grating through him like a rusty blade.

'Come, show your face to me, come to my mountain and meet with your fate. I am Ungatt Trunn the Fearsome Beast; you will die by my paw the day you look upon my face!'

Still in the grip of nightmare, the Badger Lord sprang up. Seizing his battle blade he roared out in a thunderous voice, 'It is *my* mountain! I am the Lord Brocktree of Brockhall! My sword will look into your mind and touch your heart on the day we meet, Ungatt Trunn! Eulaliiiiaaaaa!'

Dotti and Ruff leapt up in shock. The haremaid was knocked to one side as her otter friend hurled himself at her, shoving her out of danger in the nick of time. Brocktree's great battle blade whooshed past them a hair's breadth away, cleaving a rock ledge in two and ploughing a furrow in the floor like a small trench.

'Back, mates! Get back, all of ye!' The otter was up and waving paws and rudder at moles scurrying about in their nightshirts, wanting to see what all the disturbance was about. Rogg Longladle acted swiftly. Taking a jug of cold mint tea from the banqueting table nearby, he sloshed it accurately in Brocktree's face. The Badger Lord staggered back and slumped on the ledge. Freeing a paw from his sword handle, he wiped the liquid from his eyes. Then he looked at the creatures all about him in bewilderment.

'The room, it was moving from side to side, spiders, webs, flies, everywhere . . . every—'

Without warning the double-hilted sword was in his paws again. He swung it up in a fighting stance, glaring at everybeast with dangerous eyes. 'Where's the wildcat? Did any of you see him? Tell me!'

With great courage, Ruff stepped forward, placing himself in the path of the monstrous blade. 'Put up yore weapon, mate. 'Twas only a dream.'

With a dazed look Brocktree lowered the sword and sat down. 'I don't understand it, Ruff. He was here, his name is Ungatt Trunn, and he wanted to do battle with me.'

Rogg dispersed the moles with a wave of his long ladle. 'Goo on naow, back abed, all of ee. Leave us'n's be!'

Rogg listened as Dotti told him of their quest for Salamandastron and Brocktree's reasons for needing to be there. When the Badger Lord recounted the scenes of his nightmare, Rogg had something to say.

'Wait ee, zurr. Bide yurr ee h'instant!'

He trundled off, returning shortly with another mole, a full-grown male, very sturdy, with a look of Rogg about him. 'This'n yurr be moi sunn Gurth. Ee'm a foine big 'un, bain't ee? Uz calls 'im Gurt Gurth. Ee'm a born wunderer an' fond o' travellern. Tell um wot ee see'd, Gurth!'

Rogg's son touched his snout politely to the guests. 'Pleasured t'meet ee, zurrs, miz. Hurr naow, 'bowt three moons back oi wurr roamin', south an' west o' yurr. Oi waked wun morn an' see'd ee gurt h'army o' vurmints, all a-painted blue, trampin' west'ard to ee sandshores. Them wuz a-chantin', loik this. Ee chief vurmint, ee showts . . . Ungatt! An' t'others showt back three toims . . . Trunn! Trunn! Trunn! Oi watched 'til 'em varnished in ee distance, trampin' an' a-shouten all ee way. Ungatt! . . . Trunn! Trunn! Trunn! Jus' loik that, zurr! Bo urr, sez oi to moiself, thurr be a thing to tell ee molefolk back 'ome. But moi ole dad, ee sez t'keep soilent abowt et. So oi did 'til naow.'

In the light of Gurth's tale, it took a lot of persuading to stop Brocktree following the vermin instantly. In the end he agreed to wait until dawn. They would set off immediately after breakfast.

Daylight had barely cracked when Lord Brocktree levered himself away from one of Rogg's epic spreads and shouldered his sword.

'Come on, you two, or are you going to sit there feeding your famine-stricken faces all day?'

Dotti wiped her lips ruefully on an embroidered napkin. 'I bally well wish we could, I've never tasted honeyed oatmeal like that in m'life. I say, Rogg, how the dickens d'you make it taste so jolly good, wot?'

Rogg chuckled at Dotti's momentary lapse from mole-speech. 'Hurr hurr, young miz, oi chops in lots o' chesknutters an' hazelnutters too, cover ee lot wi' sprinkles o' candied h'apple'n'pear flakers an' bakes et slow in ee uvven.'

Ruff twitched his rudder in admiration of Rogg's skill. 'Haharr. I can't tell one nutter from another, but ole Rogg there makes it sound wunnerful!'

The friendly mole dumped four packs on the table. 'Thurr be vittles for ee journey, guddbeasts.'

Brocktree had noted the number of packs. 'There's four lots here and we're only three?'

Rogg twiddled his digging claws, as moles do when they are confronted with a tricky situation. 'Urr urr, wudd ee grant oi a boon, zurr?'

Dotti translated. 'He wants a favour from you, sah.'

Brocktree spread his paws magnanimously. 'I would be churlish if I refused, after such hospitality. Ask away, Rogg my friend!'

The mole hummed and hahed a bit before coming out with it. 'Cudd ee taken moi sunn Gurth along with ee? Oi'd be allus h'obliged. Ee'm gudd company, deadly with ee slinger an' stronger'n any mole aloive. Oi be gurtly wurried when ee goes off a-roamin' alone, zurr, but moi 'eart'd be easier if'n moi Gurth wurr with gennelbeasts like you 'uns.'

Lord Brocktree shook Rogg's paw warmly. 'Gurth will be a welcome addition to our little band – and if his cooking is anything like yours, I beg you to let him come along with us!'

Gurth appeared out of nowhere and swept up his ration pack. 'Oi been teached ee cookin' trick or two boi moi ole dad, zurr. Thankee koindly furr lettin' oi join ee!'

At the river bend the four friends boarded their log and paddled off along the sun-flecked stream, with Rogg and his family calling farewells.

'Goombye. 'Twere ee pleasure 'avin' ee t'visit!'

'Miz Dott, goombye. Pity ee wurr too fulled t'sing furr us'n's larst noight. Mebbe nex' toim!'

'They don't know 'ow lucky they were not to hear our Dotti warblin',' Ruff muttered under his breath to Brocktree.

Gurth was receiving instructions from his kin, to all of whom he replied with the same phrase: 'Thankee, oi'll amember that!'

'You'm keep a clean 'ankycheef with ee allus, Gurth!'

'Moind ee manners an' doan't scoff ee too much!'

'Pay 'tenshun to wot gurt Badger Lord tells ee, Gurth!'

'Bringen a pressink back for ee ole mum!'

'Be guarden ee young hurrmaid well naow, sunn!'

Gurth's gruff bass voice echoed back along the stream: 'Thankee, oi'll amember that!'

The moles stood in the shallows, waving until the log was out of sight. Gurth's mother wiped a kerchief about her eyes. 'Burrhoo, oi do 'opes ee'll be safe!'

Rogg placed a paw about her shoulders. 'Ee surpintly will, marm. Ee be a rock o' sense, that 'un!'

12

Udara Groundslay was a short-eared owl. Unfortunately he had been born without the gift of flight, but this did not seem to worry him one little bit. He had made his birthplace, the Rockwood, and its surrounding moors his domain. Nothing moved or went on there that he did not know about. Udara was immensely wise and very fierce. He protected his territory jealously and made his own rules for any creature venturing within its boundaries. These rules he enforced by his own natural ferocity.

Fleetscut sat with the squirrels around a small fire. It was almost twilight when the owl arrived.

Jukka rose to greet him. 'Thou art looking hale an' fine of feather, Groundslay!'

Ruffling his brown and umber barred feathers, the big owl stared solemnly at the squirrels with huge golden eyes which shone in the reflected firelight. 'Rukkudooh! What brings bushtails to my lands?'

Fleetscut had never heard a creature speaking so slow and deliberately. Moreover, the murderous curved beak of Udara scarcely moved when he spoke.

Jukka politely let a moment elapse before replying. 'We have brought a longears with us. He seeks news of his kind, or any other beasts seen hereabouts.'

The owl closed both eyes and twitched his ear feathers gently. Fleetscut thought he had gone to sleep, but then the big golden orbs opened again.

'Hurrukooh! Udara sees all, even in the moondark. Longears have passed through here, young ones, noisy and frivolous creatures. Spikedogs, also. I like not the spikedogs – they are rough, ill-mannered beasts.'

Fleetscut stood up from the fire. 'How many longears went through here, and when?'

Udara's body did not move, but his head turned as if it were a separate part of him, in a great half-circle. He regarded the old hare like a piece of mud stuck to his talon, his eyes anything but friendly.

'Hoorokkuh! You have lessons in courtesy to learn, longears. Speak only when you are spoken to. Your seasons have not made you any more sensible than the young ones of your kind.'

The head turned in leisurely fashion until Udara was facing Jukka once more. 'Nothing in this life is free, believe my words. If the old longears wants information he must pay me.'

Jukka shot an enquiring glance at Fleetscut, who nodded his head vigorously. The squirrel spoke for him. 'The longears wants to know what you require as payment?'

'Hooooooh!' Udara let out the long slow noise as if he were considering. 'The sweet heavy bread you carry, Udara likes that, it is good.'

Fleetscut tossed his ration pack to Jukka, who placed it on the ground, close to the owl's talons. Udara Groundslay looked down at it. His eyes closed, then reopened.

'Uhkuhkuhk! More. I want more than just one!'

The old hare stared around the fire at the other squirrels. None seemed ready to give up their rations. Fleetscut shrugged and held his paws wide.

Jukka stared at him impassively. 'Udara says one is not enough. Thou wilt have to find more.'

Ruro tossed her ration alongside that of Fleetscut. Silence seemed to stretch out into the growing darkness before Udara deigned to reply to the offer.

'Rukkudooh! One more!'

'You hear him, longears. Hast thou any more?'

Fleetscut shook his head. Udara kicked the packs lightly. 'Hootooh! Then you wasted your time coming here, longears.'

Fleetscut had put up with enough. 'Just a tick there, featherbag, I think you're the one needs a lesson in courtesy. It's no blinkin' wonder that other creatures avoid comin' here, wot, y'bad-mannered old swindler. I wouldn't give you the dust off me paws after the way you've treated me!'

A gasp arose from the squirrels. Udara stalked slowly round the fire until his beak was level with the hare's eye. 'Kurruhum! Two it is then, longears. You are a perilous beast – I have slain many for less than what you said to me. But mind, two only buys the information that two merits!'

Thud!

Jukka's pack landed with the other two. 'There, now thou hast three. Give the longears all your information, Udara. All!'

Hooking the three packs with his talons, the owl slung them up over his useless wings, calling as he stalked off, 'Be here at dawn light. I'll tell you all then. Koohumhum!'

When Udara had gone, Fleetscut slumped down angrily by the fire. 'Great feathered buffoon, wot?'

Jukka squatted in front of him, shaking her head knowingly. ''Tis ye who art the buffoon, hare. Hadst thou not given up thy pack so quick I could have bargained and got thine information for one pack. An' thee, Ruro, what were ye thinking of, adding thy pack to his so quickly? I only gave up my ration to Udara when the situation became hopeless. Udara was insulted by thee, longears. Hadst thou walked away with the pack, he'd have hunted an' killed thee. That bird is not named Udara Groundslay for nothing. Now put a latch on thy tongue an' get some sleep!'

Feeling rather foolish and properly chastened, Fleetscut lay down. However, before he closed his eyes, the old hare patted Ruro's shoulder. 'You're a jolly good pal, Ruro. I won't forget the way you offered up your pack to get my information. Thanks!'

Ruro lay staring into the fire as she replied, 'Jukka Sling was right, we be nought but two fools. Aye, an' we'll find that out soon enough, methinks, when we have to march on empty bellies. Good night to thee.'

Udara returned in the dawn hour, when most of the squirrels were still sleeping, thanks to the previous day's marching. Jukka and Fleetscut hastily got a fire going and made mint and dandelion tea, sweetening it with lots of honey to suit the owl's taste. Sunlight was beginning to flood gold into the aquamarine skies of the eastern horizon before Udara deemed it fit to begin his narrative, which he did with much deliberation.

'Humrumrum! There is a certain longears, a hare, not of the mountain from which you come. They say he is a March hare, wild and perilous. I have not met him – I do not know. Many longears are gathering to him at a secret place. I have heard them whisper his name, King Bucko Bigbones!'

Fleetscut could not help cutting in. 'King?'

Udara's huge golden eyes blinked reprovingly. 'I did not ask you to interrupt me. If you want to talk, then carry on, and I will hold my silence, longears!'

Jukka apologised for Fleetscut hastily. 'Forgive him. It is the manner of longears to be excited. I will vouch for his silence. Please, the floor is thine.' She shot a warning glance at the old hare.

Udara continued: 'Whoohum! One of the longears dropped a piece of bark scroll. Reading is not part of my wisdom and of no interest to me. That is all I have to say. You will begone from my land before noontide. Here is the writing – you may keep it.'

Lifting his left wing slightly, with great effort, Udara allowed a small folded scroll to drop near the fire. Fleetscut pounced upon it before it rolled into the flames. Without a backward glance, Udara Groundslay, the flightless owl, ambled off to pursue his solitary existence.

'Read thee aloud. I wouldst hear this longear message!'

Jukka's arrogant words got the better of Fleetscut's temper. 'Now just a bloomin' moment, bushtail. Hah! I see y'don't like me callin' you that, do you? Well, I'm sick an' fed up o' bein' called longears, see! I'll call you Jukka, you call me Fleetscut, I'll call your blinkin' lot squirrels, an' you call my flippin' lot hares, wot, wot?'

Jukka feigned an air of indifference. 'As thou pleasest.'

'You can bet your jolly life I pleasest!'

'Then calm thee down an' read, lon— Fleetscut.'

Jukka's tribe were awake by this time. They gathered round to hear what was on the scroll as the old hare read aloud.

'Two points north of dawn,
Find stone and shade and drink,
Follow where no water runs,
March on through two moons and suns,
My sign you'll see, I think.
Discover then a streamwolf's ford,
Tug thrice upon the royal cord,
Then my honour guard will bring,
Loyal subjects to their king!'

Fleetscut's paw thwacked against the parchment. 'Tchah, the very idea of it, a hare promotin' himself to king, the pollywoggle, an' doubtless lurin' our young

Salamandastron warriors to his side. Who does he think he is, wot wot?'

Jukka could not help smiling at Fleetscut's indignation. 'For sure, he thinks he's king. Canst thou solve any of this riddle poem, hare?'

Fleetscut snorted. 'Of course I canst . . . squirrel! Us chaps from Salamandastron eat lots o' salad – good for the old brain, doncha know. We try not to scoff large amounts o' nuts – makes the tail bushy an' next thing y'know you want to go climbin' trees!' He paused to note the look on Jukka's face, then continued, 'Ahem, now let me see. Ah yes, the place where stone an' shade an' drink can be found is right here. Hmm, the directions are clear enough, but two points north o' dawn, er, that's a bit of a poser, ain't it?'

Ruro provided the answer. 'Dawn is in the east where the sun rises; two points north of that is northeast. We must go northeast, methinks.'

Fleetscut sniffed. 'I knew that, just testin' you chaps. But what about a spot o' brekkers first? I've only had a drop of tea so far today. Chap can't go far on that, wot!'

Ruro thrust two hard green apples at him. 'Remember, friend, thou hast no rations, nor have I or Jukka. Come now, we'll travel o'er the top of this Rockwood, and mayhap we'll find our way with a view from there.'

A wearying and difficult climb brought them to Rockwood's peak by mid-morning. As they sat down in the tree shade, breathing hard, a solemn call hailed them from one of Udara's hiding places.

'Kuwhoohuuuh! You are still on my land and the morn is half gone. Beware if you are still here at noon!'

Fleetscut was trying to climb an old gnarled rowan to scout out the countryside. When the owl called he slipped and barked his shin. Biting his lip, he shouted back, 'Yah! Go an' boil your beak, mattressbottom.'

Ruro helped him down to earth before bounding easily up into the branches, saying to the old hare, who was wincing and rubbing his shin, 'Bide there, friend. After all, I've scoffed large amounts of nuts!'

She was back down to report, almost as swiftly as she had gone up, pointing northeast. 'A dried-up streambed that way, going off into the distance.'

Fleetscut was up and about, feeling much better. 'Strewth, just like the poem said: "Follow where no water runs." Solved that pretty smart, wot wot, Jukka?'

Jukka led off the march, informing the old hare, 'I had already figured that much, O thou who art fleet of scut.'

Ruro took up the rear, with her friend muttering by her side. 'Huh, fleet o' scut, indeed! Can't even pronounce a bally chap's name right. How'd she like it if I called her Sling the Jukka? I say, that's a good idea, why don't we sling her?'

It is never a good thing to be hungry, and Fleetscut felt the pangs on that day's march. Single file they went, through a twisting, turning, long dried-out streambed, with the hare plodding along in the rear, coughing and sniffling from the dust of others tramping ahead. He had neither food nor drink, having bolted the two little sour apples the moment Ruro gave them to him earlier on. First he tried sucking on a pebble to allay his thirst, but when moisture came to his mouth it formed a nasty paste with the dust he was inhaling. Next he began grabbing at pawfuls of grass as he passed, but when he chomped on the first clump he gave a muffled yelp and spat it out, glaring at the yellow and black banded body humming angrily amid the dust.

'Confounded bloomin' wasp, loungin' about in the middle of a chap's tuck. Oh, it ain't fair! I'm starvin'!'

Ruro turned and tugged his paw to make him keep up. 'Carry on trying to feed thyself and thou wilt be left behind. No time for stopping when we're on the march!'

Late that evening Jukka called a halt. Fleetscut flopped exhausted alongside Ruro in the dry watercourse, gazing longingly at the other squirrels. Opening their packs, they sipped from little flasks and ate sparingly of the honey-soaked, fruit-filled farls. With a face the picture of misery and despair he begged them, 'I say, chaps, how about sharin' supper with a pal, wot?'

Ignoring Fleetscut, they carried on eating and drinking. The old hare tried a different approach.

'Aha, this is the life, mates – comrades together, wot! Marchin', sleepin', singin', firm friends on life's jolly old highway, wot. I say there, old pal, old chum, throw your messmate a cob of that stuff over, an' a drop t'drink, ye good old treewalloper!'

The squirrel in question stowed his food away carefully, glaring hatred at Fleetscut. 'Give thy foolish gob a rest, longears. 'Tweren't for thee we'd be snug in our pine grove, instead of tramping about on some wild goose chase because of thy bad-mouthing our leader. Put a gag on thy tongue – aye, an' eat that!'

Fleetscut slumped back and sulked a bit, watching an ant crawl over his footpaw. He was about to reach for it and try his first taste of insect when a fresh idea struck him. Scooting over on his tail, he got closer to Jukka. She wondered what he was about until he winked, smiled at her and whispered, 'Bet you're rather peckish too, old gel, wot. Rotten bunch o' cads this lot, aren't they? Look at that bounder over yonder, stuffin' his face like a frog at a fry-up. Listen, you're the leader, ain't you? I've got a rippin' idea – now how does this sound t'you? Suppose you issue a stern order for one or two of 'em to give you half their rations. I mean, they daren't refuse Jukka the Sling, the old boss tailkicker, could they? Then we just divvy the grub between us, half for my clever wheeze, half for your position as chief. Heeheehee. Spiffin' scheme, ain't it, wot?'

The look Jukka gave him would have split a solid rock.

Fleetscut scooted hastily back, resigned to a night of hunger and thirst. He lay down, closed his eyes and shouted, 'G'night, you grubgrabbin' foul perishin' mob o' skinflints. Hope the noise me tummy's makin' keeps you awake all bloomin' night. Hope you dream of me starvin' to death of hunger. Tailtwitchin' nut-eatin' bark-wallopers!'

Morning brought Fleetscut no relief. As soon as he opened his eyes he was complaining.

'Yaaagh! Ooh, the famine cramps, me paws've gone dead, I can't see, it's the Scoffless Lurgy, I've been struck down with the Witherin' Ear Fever. Food! Somebeast save me!'

Whump!

Jukka landed slam in his middle, bringing him down flat and stifling his mouth with both paws as she hissed angrily, 'Fool, shoutin' and wailin' across the country. Didn't thou hear Beddle calling for all to keep low, there be vermin abroad? Lie still and silent or I'll slay thee myself!'

She peeped over the top of the dried streambank. Ruro and Grood scuttled up to join her.

'Something be moving o'er there, Ruro, see!'

'Aye, I see it well enough. The grass is long out there, and 'tis moving the opposite way to the breeze.'

'I wonder how many of them there be?'

Young Grood was about to make an estimate when Jukka cuffed his ear lightly. 'Curb thy language, Grood! Stay low, everybeast, and mayhap they'll pass us by. No sense inviting trouble.'

Rubbing his stomach, Fleetscut popped his head up, took a quick glimpse of the waving grass and called out, 'Wot ho there, show yourselves, we're friends!'

Immediately the spiked heads of two hedgehogs rose above the grass as they strode towards the streambed.

Jukka fixed the old hare with her gimlet eye. 'How didst thou know they were hedgedogs?'

Fleetscut waggled his ears in cavalier fashion. 'I'm a

Salamandastron hare, y'see. We can scent vermin a day away, or at least we used to in the old days. Well now, you chaps, whom have we the honour of addressin', wot?'

The two burly male beasts rolled awkwardly into the ditch.

'G'day to yer. I'm Grassum an' this 'ere's my brother Reedum. You ain't by any chance spotted an 'ogbabe wand'rin' loose in these parts, 'ave yer?'

The hare shook their paws, carefully avoiding the spikes. 'Can't say we have, really. Give us a description an' we'll keep a weather eye out for the little tyke.'

Grassum did all the talking, his brother merely nodding and saying aye to emphasise the case.

'Skittles be 'is given name. We took 'im off'n some foxes last season. Doesn't know who 'is mum'n'dad are, or where they be, ain't that right, Reedum?'

'Aye!'

'A right liddle pawful 'e is if'n you ask me, talks very h'educated, very imperdent, very cheeky. An old 'ead on young shoulders, that's wot 'e is, right, Reedum?'

'Aye!'

'Calls us 'is two wicked uncles, jus' 'cos we makes 'im go t'bed early an' wash reg'lar, eh, Reedum?'

'Aye!'

'Enny'ow, Skittles done a bunk on us an' got hisself lost. We been a-searchin' for 'im two days now, me'n'Reedum.'

'Aye!'

'Enny'ow, if'n yew goodbeasts finds 'im an' we ain't about, y'd best leave 'im wid the first 'edge'og fambly or tribe y'come across. That's best, ain't it, Reedum?'

'Aye!'

Laboriously they began climbing out of the streambed. Fleetscut called hopefully after them, 'I say, you chaps haven't got the odd morsel of grub about you – a leftover apple pie or some unwanted salad, wot?'

Grassum looked down on him from the banktop. 'We ain't got a crust t'spare atween us, 'ave we, Reedum?'

'Nay!'

The old hare smiled ruefully. 'Good day, sirs. Thanks for the information, Grassum. Oh, and thanks for your scintillating conversation, Reedum. I actually got quite excited when you switched from aye to nay. Dashed clever trick that, wot?'

Jukka cast a jaundiced eye over Fleetscut as she marched off. 'I wish thou wert as talkative as yon Reedum!'

The day passed uneventfully, hot, dusty and tiring, wearying on both paws and spirits of the trekkers. Fleetscut became convinced his end was near from starvation. Jukka and Ruro bore their hunger steadfastly, neither asking nor taking sustenance from the sparse rations of their tribal comrades. At evening the dried streambed petered out, and they made camp for the night on the open moor, squatting around a fire they had kindled in the lee of a boulder. Fleetscut's moods had ranged from outrage and name-calling to silent high dudgeon and finally a fatalistic resignation. He lay apart from the others, quiet for a while, then began to moan his thoughts aloud.

'Oh dearie dearie me, 'tis a hard life an' a jolly old sad death, wot. Perishin' out here on the grassy plains without anybeast to mourn over me benighted bones. Hunger, thirst, the Scoffless Lurgy, Witherin' Ear Fever an' the Dreaded Numb Deadpaw. That's besides Tummyshrink Ague an' Fearsome Red Scutrot. Oho yes, mates, you name it an' old Fleetscut's suffered it! A walkin' bonebag, courageous t'the last, too proud to beg a crust from me messmates. Fadin' away sad an' slow. Wonder if they'll strike a medal for me, wot? A skinny hare with a brave smile, that'd be about right. Oh, an' in the background, lots of fat wobbly squirrels, grinnin' like stuffed toads. Eh, wozzat?'

A slingstone bounced off the ground close to his head. Jukka was whirling her sling, fully loaded with a rock, and she had a wild determined glint in her eye.

'We've stood enough o' thy ceaseless whimperin' an' whining, longears. Speak one more word an' this rock will find thee!'

Fleetscut turned quickly over and shut his eyes tight. 'Oh, right y'are, marm. Nighty night now!'

As a new day dawned, Fleetscut, unable to sleep because of hunger pangs, leapt up roaring: 'Aha! I think I see his sign, chaps. There 'tis!'

13

Silence reigned in the hidden cavern beneath Salamandastron, broken only by the dripping of water and the snores of Lord Stonepaw and his hares. Not knowing the time of day or night, they had succumbed to their natural urge to sleep.

'Where in the name o' fang'n'fur have they got to?'

Stiffener Medick came awake at the sound of voices outside the cave. It was the two Blue Horderats Rotface and Grinak, returning with the food and drink they had been sent for. The boxing hare listened to their conversation; they were obviously lost.

'Huh, don't ask me. Y'd think they'd 'ave left us some sign for direction, or jus' sat an' waited fer us!'

'Well, wot d'y'say we jus' sit down an' wait for them?'

'Can't do that. They might be miles away. We could be down 'ere for ever!'

'Aha, but they won't last long, will they? We've got the food. Heeheehee, d'yer fancy some o' this plum pudden from the Lord Badger's kitchens, eh, Grinak?'

'You must be jokin', Rotface. Cap'n Swinch'd 'ave the hide off'n our backs fer stealin' vittles!'

The voices receded down the passage. Stiffener slipped through the rift and went after them, silent as a shadow.

Before long he could see the flicker of their torch up ahead. He followed, hoping they would soon stop to rest, but the rats wandered on, willy nilly, from chamber to corridor and cavern to tunnel, for what seemed an age. Finally Stiffener's hopes were rewarded. Grinak found a low rock shelf and plonked himself down on it.

'This is 'opeless. We're lost, aye, an' by the looks of it they are too. We've not 'ad sound nor sight of 'em yet!'

Rotface sat down next to his companion. 'Yer right there, Grin. These flasks of ale are weighin' me down – me paws are killin' me. Wot say we swap, you carry the drink awhile, I'll carry the food, eh?'

Grinak snorted. 'No chance, mate. You thought they'd be lighter – that's why you ran t'pick 'em up.'

'Over here, idiots, over here!' A voice was calling them. Both rats jumped up, scared of being caught sitting down. Rotface peered into the darkness behind them.

'Sounds like they're down there, wot d'you think, Grin?'

'Sounds go different ways down 'ere. Mebbe they're up yonder.'

'Wot'll we do, then?'

'Give me the torch. I'll go an' look where you reckon they are. Stay 'ere an' wait fer me.'

'Oh no, slyboots, yore not leavin' me alone wid no light!'

'Well, you go. I'm not scared, I'll wait 'ere. Go on!'

Grinak went cautiously, holding the torch high, calling out softly, so it would not echo, 'Cap'n Swinch, Magician Groddil, is that you, sirs?'

A voice called from round a bend in the passage: 'Who d'you think it is, addlebrain? We're here!'

Grinak hurried round the bend, his face illuminated by the torch. 'We been lookin' all over for y—'

His words were cut short by a swift powerful right and a left uppercut which battered him flat with lightning speed. Stiffener even caught the torch before it fell.

Rotface peered down the passage and saw the light of the torch wave from side to side.

'Wot is it, mate? 'Ave yer found 'em?'

A passable imitation of Grinak's harsh voice answered, 'We're goin'. 'Urry up!'

The rat scuttled down the passage dragging the food and drink behind him, afraid of being lost and alone. 'Wait, 'ang on, I'm comin'!'

As he rounded the bend Stiffener struck. Unfortunately, the boxing hare had not realised that Rotface's head was bowed as he struggled with the packs. Stiffener's blow hit the rat, but only grazed his skull.

Rotface dropped the packs. He was a big, solid rat. Shaking his head, he went for his dagger. 'Hah! 'Tis only an old rabbit. Come on, Grandad, let's see the colour of yer insides!'

Stiffener Medick was not given to exchanging badinage with vermin. Coolly he sprang forward, feinting with a left at the rat's stomach. Immediately the rat stabbed downward with his blade. A swinging right hit him like a thunderbolt, breaking his jaw, and he collapsed with a sigh. Stiffener was off down the passage, the two packs in either paw, the torch clamped in his jaws.

Lord Stonepaw and the others fell on the food with gusto, though the badger shook his head disapprovingly. 'You could have got yourself slain. Why didn't you wake me?'

Stiffener turned his attention from a fruit scone. 'You need yore sleep, sah. So did those two vermin. Couldn't box for acorns, either of 'em!'

Blench winked at him. 'That's ole Stiffener for ye, lays 'em out stiff he does! Here, my dearie, try some o' my plum pudden.'

The boxing hare accepted it, chuckling. 'Only did it 'cos I couldn't stand the thought of vermin gettin' used to yore wunnerful cookin', marm. Now if'n those two grandsons o' mine was with us, young Southpaw an' his brother Bobweave, they'd 'ave put those two rats down an' gone lookin' for more. Pair o' rascals. Talk about fight? Those two'd swim the great sea just t'be in on a good scrap. Course, I taught 'em, y'know.'

Ungatt Trunn had now taken up residence in the mountain. He liked the view from Lord Stonepaw's chamber. Sprawling on the bed, he sampled the badger's best mountain ale, whilst chewing a savoury cheese and onion flan from Blench's kitchen. A knock sounded on the door. At a nod from Ungatt, the guard opened it. Grand Fragorl glided in, standing to one side as Groddil, Captain Swinch, Rotface and Grinak were ushered in by the stoat Captain Fraul. Putting aside food and drink, the wildcat rose from the bed. He circled the four culprits slowly, his banded tail swishing as he noted their trembling paws.

'I take it that the news is not good. Talk to me, Groddil.'

Fighting to keep his voice calm and level, the stunted fox made his report. 'Mightiness, we have searched through endless dark caves beneath your mountain, with no taste of food nor drink passing our lips. It is cold down there and totally dark. Alas, Great One, we found no trace of the stripedog or his creatures, though it was not from lack of trying.'

Ungatt leapt on to the window ledge and stood there, framed by the sky outside. 'Who are these two Horderats? Why are they here?'

Captain Swinch rapped orders at Rotface and Grinak. 'One pace forward, you two, stand to attention, eyes front, tell His Mightiness what happened to you!'

The rats' heads shook uncontrollably as they rattled forth their concocted story to their fearsome master. They did it piecemeal, alternating one to the other, Rotface nursing his broken jaw.

'We was sent back fer vittles by Cap'n Swinch, sire.'

'Aye, an' when we returned with 'em the main search

party wasn't there, Mighty One, so we was sort of lost.'

'But we never ate nor rested, sire, we searched for 'em. We searched an' searched an' searched, sire.'

'Enny'ow, Mightiness, there we was, a-searchin', when all of a sudden we was surrounded. It was the stripedog an' more'n a score o' those rabbits!'

'Er, but well armed they was, sire. We fought 'em like madbeasts – there was blood everywhere!'

'Mightiness, there was too many of 'em. They stole the vittles an' left us fer dead, sire!'

Ungatt Trunn was on the hapless pair like a hawk with two chickens. Rotface and Grinak screeched as the wildcat's claws sank into their shoulders. He shook both of them, snapping their necks, and then with a mighty heave he hurled the two carcasses out of the wide window on to the rocks below. He was not breathing heavily, nor was there a trace of anger or bad temper on his face as he turned from the window ledge. He stared impassively at Groddil and Swinch as though nothing had happened.

'Tomorrow at first light you will return to your task. The stripedog is alive and hiding down there with his hares. He will not escape me, because you will find him. Take as many to assist you as you wish, take supplies, extra torches, anything, but remember this. Return empty-pawed and you will wish you had died quickly, like those two fools who stood lying barefaced in front of me. Fail me and your deaths will take the best part of a season, as an example to all. Do you understand what I have just said to you both?'

Swinch and Groddil retreated, bowing.

'As you command, Mightiness!'

'We will find the stripedog and his hares, Great One!'

Ungatt waited until they had made it to the door. 'Wait! Captain Fraul, have these two staked out on the shore below, where I may see them from this window. They are not to have food or water. Choose two strong soldiers to beat them with the flats of their own sword blades, and tell them to lay on hard. It will serve as a warning to my forces that nobeast fails to carry out the orders of Ungatt Trunn, not even a captain or a magician. They may be released at dawn tomorrow to continue their search.'

Ripfang and Doomeye, the new recruits, were chosen to administer the punishment. They stood over their staked-out victims holding the swords high, looking up to the window. Ungatt signalled that the beatings should begin with a wave of his paw. Ripfang smiled apologetically at the two quivering figures pinioned on the sand. 'Orders is orders. No 'ard feelin's, eh?'

Swish thwack! Swish thwack!

The sound of the flogging was soon drowned out by Swinch and Groddil's screams.

Ungatt Trunn turned from the window and prowled down to the dining hall with his Grand Fragorl hurrying behind. Threescore captive hares were herded into a corner, ringed by armed Hordebeasts. Captain Roag, a tough female weasel, saluted the wildcat smartly. 'These sixty of the lesser orders await your judgement, sire!'

As usual, the Grand Fragorl addressed her master's words to the prisoners in her toneless cadence. 'You longears are of an inferior species, not fit to live in the shadow of the higher orders. It is only on the whim of my master that you still draw breath. Ungatt Trunn, he who makes the stars fall and the earth tremble! Ungatt Trunn the Fearsome Beast who drinks wine from the skulls of his enemies, Conqueror of the World! You live now only to serve him in slavery. If your work is not satisfactory, one of you will be hurled from the top of this mountain each day. You hold the lives of your own comrades forfeit!'

Sailears could not restrain herself from crying out, 'I hope I live to see the day you're chucked from the mountaintop, cat!'

A spear butt struck her in the face and she went down.

The rat who had delivered the blow raised his weapon again, point down, to slay the old hare.

Ungatt stopped him. 'Halt! Leave that creature be!'

Parting ranks, the guards allowed Ungatt passage to Sailears. He stood over her, shaking his head. 'I wish my creatures had spirit like yours, hare. What is it that creates such bravery and loyalty to some old fool of a stripedog?'

Ignoring her swollen jaw, Sailears levered herself upright. 'You wouldn't jolly well know, cat, an' you prob'ly wouldn't understand if I tried to tell you, wot!'

The wildcat stood, paws akimbo, smiling slightly. 'All I know about is conquest. I rule through fear, not affection. I'll wager you know where the stripedog is hiding at the moment, eh?'

Sailears maintained a defiant silence, exploring a loosened tooth with her tongue. The wildcat shook his head admiringly. 'Aye, I can see you do! More than likely you'd rather die than tell me, and so would all your comrades. No matter, I'll find him. Just remember now that you are my slaves – you are all prisoners until you die!'

Then Sailears did a strange thing. She placed one paw against her head, the other over her heart, and smiled. 'If that's what y'think then you've lost, cat. We all are free, here in our minds an' here in our hearts!'

Ungatt turned on his paw and strode off, calling back, 'Don't push your luck or I'll show you how easy it is to break a creature's spirit!'

He was answered by a concerted roar from the prisoners. 'Eulalia!'

Whispering something to Fragorl, the wildcat departed the dining hall without a backward glance. The Grand Fragorl held her paws up to gain the hares' attention.

'His Mightiness has decreed that you starve, every one of you, the next two days for your insolence. Take them away and lock them up!'

Before any of the Horde could lay paws on the captives,

Torleep, a fine upright old hare, rapped out some orders. 'Form twelve ranks five deep, you lot! Look lively now, dress off to y'right! 'Ten . . . shun! Straighten up at the back theyah, laddie buck, show these vermin how it's done! Chin in, head back, shoulders straight, eyes forward, ears stiff! That's the stuff! Now, by the right, quick march! One two, one two! Right markers, keep those lines straight!'

Off to their prison cave they marched, surrounded by Captain Roag's bewildered vermin, who could not comprehend how a defeated band of ancient hares could sing in captivity, although sing they did, loud, long and courageously.

'I'm a hare of Salamandastron,
An' foes don't bother me,
I'll fight all day an' sing all night,
This song of liberty!

Liberty! Liberty! That's for me,
The mountain hares are wild an' free!
One two three hooray!
You can't stop sunrise every day!

I'm a hare of Salamandastron,
I wander near an' far,
You'll know me when y'see me,
'Cos I'll shout Eulalia!

Liberty! Liberty! That's for me,
From good dry land to stormy sea!
One two three hooray!
You can't stop sunset every day!'

Ungatt Trunn could hear it from where he stood at the mountain's main shore entrance. He looked at the black charred doors, still solid upon their hinges, and out to the shoreline, crowded by his mighty hordes. To nobeast in particular he commented aloud, 'Fools, nought but old fools!'

Striding down to the unconscious forms of Groddil and Swinch, he picked up a pail of seawater and hurled it on their backs. They were revived, moaning with pain. Ungatt leaned down close, so he had their attention. 'I want that stripedog found!'

He was about to threaten further when a vision of the other badger flashed into his thoughts. Big, shadowy and as forbidding as the war blade he carried across his back. Straightening up, the wildcat gazed out to sea. He could not explain it, but his confidence felt shaken. Moreover, he did not know whence the warrior badger would come, or the day he would arrive. The wildcat was certain of only one thing: the badger would come!

14

Sunshaded, green and tranquil, the stream stretched, lazily meandering through the woodlands on this the questors' first full day together. Dotti and Gurth sat up for'ard, chattering away in molespeech; Ruff and Brocktree were aft, paddling. The otter nodded approvingly at their new crew member's velvety back. 'Looks like we found a treasure there, matey. That brekkist ole Gurth cooked up this mornin' would've made his dad proud o' him. Bet yore glad we brought him along.'

Brocktree could not help but agree with his companion. 'Aye, and he's not feared of boats or water, like most moles. He looks as strong as you or I, Ruff!'

'D'ye think so? Well, we'll find out soon enough. Ahoy there, you two in the prow, pick up yore paddles an' lend a paw here. Let's make a liddle speed, eh?'

Gurth was a bit inexperienced, but as soon as he got the knack of wielding a paddle, there was none better. Enjoying himself hugely, he commented, 'Hurr, Dott miz, this be better'n diggen at tunnel 'oles. Ee can keep ee paws noice'n'clean. Oi loiks boaten on ee stream gurtly. Et be foine furr ee choild such as oi!'

The haremaid found herself panting as she struggled to keep stroke with Gurth. His strength and endurance seemed boundless; he was not even breathing heavily. 'Whurr did ee getten t'be so strong, zurr Gurth?'

'Ho, oi 'spect et be all ee vittles oi scoffed. Gudd grub an' lots o' sleepen, that be's ee stuff. Least that's wot moi ole mum allus sez!'

In the early noon a watermeadow appeared to the south. Dotti's keen ears soon picked up sounds from its far side. She called sternwards to Brocktree.

'I say, sah, some kind o' jolly old hubbub goin' on over there. Shall we wander over an' take a look, wot?'

The Badger Lord scanned the sidestream, searching for an entrance, but it seemed to be blocked by dead wood cast there from the streamflow.

'There's no way into the watermeadow. Perhaps we should leave our log here and skirt the banks.'

'You'm set thurr, zurr, oi'll sort 'er owt!'

Gurth grabbed a hefty beech limb with his big digging claws. With a mighty tug he tore it free from the debris of driftwood, creating an entrance for them.

'Thurr y'be. Naow take 'er in noice'n'easy, miz Dott.'

Ruff chuckled. 'I never seen that done afore by a mole!'

The watermeadow was extremely hard to negotiate. They were constantly shaking thick bunched weed and long waterlily stems off the paddles. From the far side the sounds of urgent shouts and creatures thrashing about in the rushes echoed over the water.

'Get ahead o' the rascal. Cut 'im off, Riggo!'

'I got 'im. No I ain't – the liddle scallywag's away agin!'

'Kangle, Furrib, there 'e goes. Stop the scamp!'

This was followed by a sharp screech and a splash. 'Owow, the blighter spiked me. 'E's fallen in, chief!'

'Fur'n'snouts, look out, 'ere comes a pike, a big 'un!'

The pointed log prow broke through a reedbank, and the four travellers took in the scene at a glance.

Several shrews were dancing in agitation, pointing wildly at the water. A tiny hedgehog was going down for the second time, splashing and gurgling. He was in deadly danger. Gliding smoothly towards the hogbabe was a pike, its rows of needle-like teeth exposed as its jaws opened in anticipation, the dorsal fin near its tail sticking out of the water, dragging weeds along.

Dotti yelled out in dismay. 'By the left, look at the size o' that brute. He'll crunch the little tyke in one bite, spikes and all!'

The shrews threw up their paws hopelessly.

'He's a dead 'un all right!'

'Nought we kin do now, mates!'

Gurth tried to reach out with his paddle to the hogbabe, but he was too far away for it to do any good. 'Burrhurr, ee pore likkle h'aminal!'

Then Ruff dashed the length of the log to gain momentum and leapt high, soaring over Gurth and Dotti in a spectacular dive, roaring whilst he sailed through the air, 'Ye great slab-sided wormgargler, come t'me!'

Vegetation and spray flew everywhere as the big otter hit the water purposely to divert the pike from its prey. Instead of swimming for the babe, Ruff went like lightning at the fish. He shot by the pike like an arrow, swirled and brought his powerful tail crashing against its flat vicious head. Rearing up out of the water, he threw himself on the predator. They both went down. Brocktree, Dotti and Gurth paddled furiously, taking the log in between the pike and the hogbabe. Gurth hooked the tiny creature's little belt with a digging claw and fished him on board.

The shrews were jumping up and down with excitement, yelling encouragement to Ruff. 'Yiiiiihaaaaa! Hold him, big feller, you got the Riverwolf!'

Flashes of otter fur and green-gold scales revolved furiously in the clouded water, then the two broke the surface. Ruff had his paws clamped like a vice about the pike's mouth, holding it tight shut, while harsh wet slaps rang out as the mighty predator battered its tail, fins and body against its captor, struggling to break free and attack him. Ruff used his tail rudder like a club, striking the pike's head madly.

Whack! Smack! Splat! Thwock! Bang!

The pike fell back under Ruff's assault, eyes glazing over, speckled body going limp. Releasing it, the otter practically flew through the water and surged on to the log, blowing water.

'Whooh! That'll put paid to 'is gallop for a while, Dotti, though he'll wake up with a headache like nobeast's business. 'Tweren't easy, though. You ever tried stunnin' a full-growed pike with yore tail?'

Dotti peered behind at her small round scut. 'Er, 'fraid I haven't, old chap. A hare's tail's not exactly built for biffin' pike with, wot!'

The pike must have had a thick skull. Partially recovered, it displayed its savage nature by charging the log. Brocktree thumped it, none too gently, on its snout with his paddle. 'Gurcha! Away with you, or I'll really put something on your mind. Be off, sir!'

With an angry swish of its tail, the fish ripped off into the depths, its voracious appetite unsated.

Dropping her paddle for a moment, Dotti rummaged through one of the packs until she found a piece of material which she used as a towel. She handed it to the hogbabe and he draped it round his tiny body, muttering mutinously to himself.

'Gone an' gorall wet now. Kinfounded sh'oo, pushen me inna water. Skikkles didden wanna baff!'

Gurth nudged Dotti as they watched the infant hedgehog. 'Yurr, miz, be ee likkle bloke awroight?'

The haremaid could not resist smiling at the disgruntled babe. 'Yurr. Ee'm furr rowdled, but ee'll live, oi 'spect, Gurth!'

No sooner did they touch the shore than Ruff was surrounded by shrews clapping him on the back.

'Yore a rough ole beast, matey!'

'You beat the Riverwolf! You showed 'im!'

'Aye, 'e was champion o' these waters till you came along!'

'Lemme shake yore paw, warrior. I'm Log a Log Grenn!'

Ruff shook heartily with the shrew Chieftain. 'Pleased t'meet ye, Grenn. Couldn't let the liddle 'un get ate, so I had to tailwhop ole Riverwolf.'

'Hoho, an' a fine job ye did of it, mate. Come an' take lunch with us. Beach that log an' bring yore friends.'

The shrew camp was little more than blankets stretched over branches to form makeshift tents. Introductions were made all round and Grenn called for food. Brocktree watched in amusement as the shrews argued and fought over who was going to serve Ruff. They squared off at one another, scruffy fur standing up aggressively, pawing their small rapiers and adjusting their multicoloured headbands to jaunty angles.

'Oi, back off there, fiddlepaws, I'm servin' mister Ruff!'

'Talk t'me like that, twinjynose, an' I'll serve ye yore teeth on a plate. *I'm* waitin' on mister Ruff!'

Dotti helped herself to hot shrewbread and a bowl of steaming vegetable stew.

'Touchy lot you've got here, Grenn marm. Are they always like this?'

Log a Log Grenn calmly shrugged off an arguing shrew who had stumbled against her. 'Always, long as anybeast can remember. We shrews can't 'elp bein' wot we are, born to argue. I want to thank you an' yore pals for rescuin' Skikkles. We found the liddle tyke wanderin' round a while back. Wot a pawful that babe is. I never knew anybeast with such a mind of'n his own, ain't that right, Skikkles?'

The babe in question waved a severe paw under Grenn's nose. 'Me name's Skikkles, not Skikkles!'

Dotti attempted to help out by translating, using her

talent for accents and dialects. 'Oh, I see. Your name's Skiddles!'

The hogbabe scowled darkly, huddling deeper into the towel. 'Tchah! Shoopid rabbik. Me name not Skivvles, it Skikkles!'

Dotti tried another alternative. 'You say your name's Skittles?'

He smiled patronisingly at her, as if the message had finally got over. 'Tha's right. Skikkles!'

'His name's Skittles,' Dotti explained to Grenn, 'but he's a bit young to pronounce it properly, so he calls himself Skikkles.'

Grenn placed a bowl of stew in front of Skittles, who promptly buried his snout in it. 'There's one or two things I could call 'im, an' they wouldn't be Skittles. That'n's a right liddle terror!'

Skittles poked his stew-covered nose over the bowl at her. 'Me name not jus' Skikkles, y'know. I called Skikkle Bee Spikediggle, tha's me real long name.'

Dotti broke shrewbread and dipped it in her stew. 'What does the Bee stand for?'

Skittles eyed her ferociously. 'The Bee's for Burrtrump, but I pull you ears very 'ard if you tells anybeast!'

Dotti narrowed her eyes and gave Skittles a savage grimace. 'If you ever call me rabbit again, or even rabbik, I'll tan your tail bright red, then I'll announce to everybeast that your middle name's Burrtrump. So how d'you feel about that, master Skittles, wot?'

Skittles decided that the haremaid had him over a barrel, and stumped off without another word.

Ruff was the centre of attention. The shrew females wiggled their snouts at him in a very flattering manner, while the males served him the best of their food, which together with the shrewbeer they brewed was voted totally delicious by the friendly otter. Young shrews began showing off their prowess to impress him. They fenced and performed tricks with their rapiers, and wrestled, a favourite sport among Log a Log Grenn's tribe.

Dotti and Gurth sat watching them. The haremaid was quite impressed. 'I say, well done, chaps. By the left, Gurth, these shrews are jolly good wrestlers, wot?'

The strong mole nodded politely. 'They'm furr t'middlin', miz, but moi dad's moles be knowen more about wrasslin' than they 'uns, gurtly more, ho arr!'

Dotti was intrigued. 'I don't suppose you wrestle, do you?'

Gurth twiddled his claws, smiling modestly. 'Burr aye, miz Dotti, oi be champyun wrassler of ee moles. Oi winned ee gurt sil'er bucklebelt at et, lukk!'

He opened his tunic and showed her the belt he wore beneath. The buckle was of wrought silver, depicting two moles tussling. Gurth's name was etched on it in molescript: Gwrt.

'Course, oi doan't loik a-showen et off'n to everybeast.'

Dotti nudged her molefriend. 'You sly old tunneldog. How about givin' me a small demonstration? Go on, please – test your skill on those shrews.'

Fastening up his tunic, Gurth shrugged and flexed his muscles. 'Oi vows oi woan't 'urt 'em, miz.'

Standing in the midst of the wrestling shrews, Gurth called out his challenge in a deep bass voice. 'Oi be ee choild o' Longladle, borned daown ee darkest deep tunnel! Oi'm farster'n loightnen, 'arder'n ee rocks an' stronger'n moi mum's ale!'

Here he bent and scarred a furrow in the ground with his claw. 'Who be's bolden enuff to step o'er ee loine an' wrassle oi?'

Several of the shrews lined up, rubbing their paws in anticipation. Gurth signalled the first one. 'You'm lukk a moighty beast, zurr. Step ee oop!'

The shrew charged recklessly. Gurth sidestepped neatly, cuffing him as he hurtled by. The shrew somersaulted once and landed flat on his back, completely winded.

'Hurr, gudd h'effort, zurr. Oi'll take two of ee next.'

Two more impetuous shrews flung themselves at him. Gurth did no more than grab their tails, twist and send them crashing, head on into one another. He bowed. 'Thankee, gennelbeasts. Ennywunn else troi they'm luck?'

A much bigger, older shrew crossed the line and went into an expert wrestler's crouch, holding his paws ready to grip. Smiling broadly at him, Gurth accepted the grip.

'Yeeowowow! Leggo! Yer breakin' me paws!'

Gurth turned to Dotti, still holding his opponent. 'Oi tole ee, miz Dott, they'm gudd, but not gudder'n oi!'

He released the shrew and ambled back to his seat. However, another shrew, bolder than his compatriots, leapt on Gurth's back and locked all four paws round the mole's neck in a submission stranglehold. Gurth reached behind, tweaked the shrew's tail experimentally, then gave it a sharp tug to the right. His opponent fell to the floor, frozen in the same position as when he landed on Gurth's back. Smiling and shaking his head, the champion wrestling mole sat down beside Dotti.

'Hurr hurr hurr. Ee'm wurr a cunnen h'aminal, miz, but goin' agin ee rools. Oi'll let 'im lay thurr awhoile. May'ap 'twill teach 'im ee manner or two.'

Dotti gazed adoringly at her molefriend. 'I say, you were magnificent! Would you teach me to wrestle like that, Gurth? Please!'

'Burr aye, 'ow cudd oi afuse such an' 'andsome creetur as ee, marm? Us'll start a-trainin' this vurry h'evenin'.'

Dotti winked at Lord Brocktree. 'See, the old fatal beauty always does the trick, sah.'

They lingered at the shrew camp until late evening, and finally accepted Grenn's invitation to stay overnight. Even then, Ruff and Gurth had become such firm favourites that the shrews pleaded with them to extend their visit. Dotti liked being with the shrews. She enjoyed their company, and being garrulous and talkative herself she joined in all the arguments with gusto. Lord Brocktree took quite a bit of convincing that he should take a few days off from his quest, but under the combined persuasive powers of his three friends he yielded gruffly. The Badger Lord would not admit it, but he had become very fond of the hogbabe Skittles and was loath to part from the little fellow. He hid his feelings by pretending that Skittles was an unwanted pest. They wandered the camp together, the tiny hedgehog seated astride the badger's sword hilt, up on his friend's huge shoulders, carrying on lively conversations.

'Get down from there, you wretch. It's like having a big boulder perched on my back, you great lump!'

'You make Skikkles geddown, I choppa your 'ead off wiv dis sword, B'ock!'

'Oh, well, I suppose you'd better stay up there. Keep to the hilt, though – don't go near that blade, you nuisance!'

'C'mon, B'ock, gee up, we go lookin' for berries!'

'Great seasons o' famine, will somebeast rid me of this pestilence? What sort of berries d'you want, eh?'

'Nice sweety ones, dat's wot Skikkles like.'

Ruff sat with Log a Log Grenn, sampling shrewbeer and chuckling at the antics of Skittles and Brocktree. 'Will ye lookit him, marm. Big softie. That liddle 'og has Brock twirled about his paw! Ahoy there, Dotti, have ye wrestled that mole to a standstill yet?'

The haremaid neatly tripped her instructor, so that he fell sitting next to Ruff. Gurth smiled approvingly. 'No, zurr, miz Dott bain't winned oi yet, but 'er soon will. She'm a gurt clever wrassler – lurns quicker'n anybeast oi ever h'instructered, burr aye!'

Dotti sat with them, accepting a beaker of dandelion and burdock cordial from Grenn. 'Huh, don't listen t'that fat fibber. I'm sore as a peeled onion all over from bein' blinkin' well thrown by him. Still, I am learnin' one or two jolly good wrestlin' wheezes – breakfalls, holds, locks an' whatnot, wot.'

Grenn poured cordial for Gurth. 'Mayhap you'll need 'em if yore bound t'follow Lord Brock to the mountain by the seas. From what he tells me his dreams are worried. He sees visions of great trouble there.'

Dotti sipped her delicious drink, which had been cooling in the stream for a night and a day. 'Well, he could be right, marm. Badger Lords ain't like the rest of us, they're fated beasts who see strange things.'

The shrew Chieftain was gnawing her lip, staring off into space, when Ruff nudged her. 'Go on, Grenn, say it. You wants t'come with us, don't ye?'

She stood up and stretched before answering. 'Guosim shrews need somethin' t'do. Look at 'em, cookin', wrestlin', arguin'. Huh, we've been too long in one place now. Nothin' better for shrews than havin' somethin' t'do – keeps them up t'the line. Aye, Ruff, if'n ye'll have us, the Guosim are with you all the way!'

All four clasped paws. Grenn was highly pleased, now that she had made her decision. Gurth twiddled his digging claws politely, asking a question which was puzzling him. 'Whoi do ee be called Guosims, marm, furrgive moi h'iggerance?'

Grenn explained proudly about the shrew tradition. 'Guosim. Guerrilla Union Of Shrews In Mossflower, that's what the letters of our name stand for. I'm called Log a Log because all shrew Chieftains are. We're rovers, bold waterbeasts and fierce warriors, sworn to uphold good an' defeat evil. All Guosim shrews are bound under oath to help one another in battle.'

Gurth winked. 'Purty yoosful to 'ave along, oi'd say, marm!'

Lord Brocktree returned, both paws full of small hard pears which he spread on the ground before lifting Skittles down to earth. The badger sighed. 'Couldn't find any berries, but the pestilence here came across these wild pears, sweet, but hard as stones. He wouldn't rest until we'd picked some, dreadful rogue!'

Skittles seated himself on the badger's footpaw. 'Well, sh'oos be good cookers, they do sumfin wiv 'em.'

Grenn picked up a pear and tasted it. 'He's right. We've got lots of sweet chestnuts from last autumn. Once these 'ere pears are stewed down the cooks can make some lovely pear'n'chestnut flans.'

The hogbabe looked up and winked with both eyes. 'See, B'ock, I tol' you. Make nice flangs, Glenn, Skikkle be's 'ungry. I never 'ave a flang, mus' be nice!'

Dotti took the hogbabe's paw.

'Come on then, famine face, gather 'em up an' we'll go an' lend a paw with the shrewcooks.'

When Brocktree heard the news that the Guosim were joining them, he was overjoyed, though he changed his plans on the spot. 'Right, no more lying around here. I vote that we break camp in the morning and get under way!'

Ruff objected. 'Ahoy there, Brock, hold yer paddles, matey. There's me, Gurth, Dotti, Grenn an' about a hunnerd shrews. If'n we wants to lie round for a day or two then you'll find yore prob'ly outvoted!'

Lord Brocktree's eyes told the otter that he was not about to have his decision overruled. Swinging forth his battle blade, he stuck it quivering into the ground. 'Let's be reasonable about this, friend. Let me explain the rules. One Badger Lord carries two hundred votes and his sword carries another hundred. Agreed?'

Ruff looked from the sword to the badger. Sunlight gleamed from the blade, lighting Brocktree's eyes with a formidable gleam. He smiled nervously at his huge friend. 'Reason, that's wot I likes, mate. Vote carried. We go after brekkist tomorrer!'

BOOK TWO

At the Court of King Bucko

also entitled

The Tribulations of a Haremaid

15

Fleetscut's wild yells wakened the squirrels. Jukka rubbed irately at her eyes as she approached the dancing hare, Ruro hurrying to join her. Jukka loaded a stone into her sling.

'Methinks the time has come to silence that longeared windbag!'

Ruro placed a restraining paw on her leader's shoulder. 'Mayhap he is more to be pitied than punished, Jukka. I think his mind has snapped, crazed from the hunger. Fleetscut, wouldst thou not like to lie down an' rest, old friend? I'll pick some roots for thee to nibble upon, eh?'

But the old hare continued to prance about and shout. 'Nibble roots? D'you think I've gone off me bally rocker? Look, there 'tis! Plain as the washin' on me granny's line!'

Ruro stared out into the dawn light. Ahead, to the northeast, lay forestlands. 'Oh, I see, 'tis the trees. Well, that be a welcome sight.'

Fleetscut bounced up and down with impatience. 'Not the trees, you benighted bushtailed buffoon, the sign, as it says in the confounded poem. "March on through two moons and suns, my sign you'll see, I think!" Well there 'tis, the sign. Your young eyes are better'n mine – you should be able to distinguish it. Huh, I'm nearly blind from the starvation, blinkin' Unvittled Eyeshrink I think they call it. But I can see the sign!'

Jukka interrupted Fleetscut's wild tirade. 'Then cease actin' like a drunken toad and point it out!'

The old hare calmed somewhat at the sight of the loaded sling. 'Right, pay 'tention there, follow the line of me paw, wot. Now, d'ye see those two tall silver firs yonder, eh? Notice anythin' about 'em, wot? They've had most of the lower boughs chopped away and a thin dead trunk placed high on two notches atween 'em!'

Jukka nodded. 'Aye, 'tis true, I see them.'

Fleetscut smote his forehead with a paw. 'Thank me grandpa's whiskers for that! So, marm, does that cross-piece not look t'ye as if it's been purposely placed there? Use your noggin, squirrel – that's a letter H. It stands for Hare. H is for blinkinflippinbloomin' Hare. D'ye catch my drift at last, wot?'

Jukka commented drily, 'Well done, hare, thou canst spell the name of thine own species. Ruro, break camp. We'll make for yonder sign straight away.'

Fleetscut followed them, muttering, 'Good job the chap wasn't a squirrel. How in the name o' fur would he bend trees into an S shape, eh? Stiffen me, but I think the old tum's finally glued itself t'me backbone. Hope I make it there before I perish an' shrivel up, wot!'

Fortunately the old hare did not perish, nor shrivel up, and they marched into the tree shade by mid-morn. Grood stared up at the giant H sign. 'Gorrokah! How did anybeast get that splitten flitten gurgletwip up so high?'

Jukka cuffed his ears soundly. 'Language, Grood!'

Fleetscut found some young dandelions and devoured them. He came across some wild ramsons, tasting strongly of garlic. He devoured them too and continued his foraging, stumbling over the footpaws of squirrels resting in the treeshade.

'I say, you chaps, move your carcasses. Stoppin' a poor beast gettin' at nature's bounty. Bounders!'

They averted their faces from his breath, disgusted.

'Whooh! Get thee gone, longears. Thou smellest like a midsummer midden at high noon. Ugh!'

Fleetscut discovered some basil thyme and stuffed it down. 'Confounded cissies. Try sniffin' yourselves after a couple o' days' marchin' without a wash betwixt ye. What a pong! Hello, here's luck, a couple of lamb's lettuce, yummy!'

He ate them, flowers and all. Plus some harebells, sweet violets, chicory and butterwort. The greedy old hare then went on to strip a small apple tree. He returned to Jukka's tribe about early noon, and found them recuperating their strength by dozing in the pleasant green shade. Fleetscut stuffed down apples as if it were his last day on earth, sour juice foaming out over his whiskers.

'Grmmff, shlick, shloop! Caught you nappin', eh? Well, no hard feelin's, you miserable bunch o' cads, I could do with a spot of the old shuteye meself, wot wot!'

Spitting pips and stalks he lay down and instantly fell into a deep slumber.

Afternoon shadows were beginning to lengthen when Jukka stirred. She shook Ruro and Beddle. 'Best make a move before eventide. Which way now?'

Ruro retrieved the parchment of bark scroll, which was hanging from Fleetscut's tunic. 'It says here: "Discover then a streamwolf's ford, tug thrice upon the royal cord." Where wouldst thou suppose that to be?'

Jukka judged by the sunshadows. 'Nor'east has served us well thus far; we'll continue that way. Beddle, get them up on their paws. A ford means fresh water, that's good.' None too gently she turned and roused the old hare with a few kicks of her footpaw. 'Waken thyself, windbag, or we leave ye here!'

Fleetscut came awake, doubled up with agonising stomach cramps, which he let everybeast know about with long piteous wailing.

'Owowowowowowooooow! Ouf! Umh! I knew I'd die. We made these woodlands too late, you chaps! Owowowooch! Your old pal's a goner. Bury me here, please, quick as y'can. Ooooooh! Anti-Trampin' Plague, that's what 'tis. Oooooh!'

Obligingly several squirrels began kicking leaf loam over the suffering hare. He sprang up, spitting out leaves. 'Gerroff, you rotters. What d'ye think you're up to?'

'Thou asked us to bury thee. We would not deny thee that.'

'Aye, longears, th'art green in the gills. Methinks th'art close to Dark Forest gates!'

Fleetscut picked wet brown leaves from between his ears. 'Dark Forest gates indeed! Ouchouchooch! Oh, me poor belly!'

Ruro grinned and squeezed her friend's shoulders pityingly. 'Couldn't have been anything that thou ate, of course?'

Fleetscut straightened up indignantly, then immediately folded over again, hugging his stomach. 'Might have been a blighted worm in one of those apples!'

Beddle winked at Ruro. 'Oh, pray tell, sir, which one? Thou great fodderbag, thee ate a whole treeful, every one of them sour. 'Twould have slain any other beast!'

Jukka leaned on her broad-bladed spear impatiently. 'Ruro, do something for the bladder-headed oaf, or methinks he'll wail on until the crack o' doom.'

Fleetscut sat back against a sycamore, holding his distended stomach with both paws. He shut his eyes and mouth firmly, but not before remarking pointedly, 'Madam, I'm not eatin' that mishmash. Are you tryin' to hasten me flippin' demise, wot?'

Each of the squirrels had gleefully contributed a trickle

of their water. Ruro had a small fire going, over which she was boiling hound's-tongue leaves, milkwort, green alkanet blossoms and two sulphur tuft mushrooms in an old iron war helmet. The smell this concoction produced when she mashed it was horrendous. Jukka nodded to Beddle and Grood as Ruro removed the helmet from the flames.

'Take hold of the blockhead and grip him tight. Ruro, make him take it all!'

Beddle and Grood held Fleetscut's head, while other squirrels piled on and sat on his limbs. Beddle pinched the old hare's nostrils so that he could not breathe. The patient held out until he seemed fit to burst, then opened his mouth wide. 'Assassins! Hare-murderers! Wharooop!'

Ruro poured the offensive mixture down Fleetscut's throat like a ministering angel, whilst Jukka looked on in grim satisfaction. Fleetscut bucked and writhed to no avail. Ruro managed to get the last of it down his mouth, and sprang to one side as the hare began shuddering all over.

'Let him go. Stand back, everybeast!'

Fleetscut leapt up like a startled fawn, scut twitching, ears erect, eyes popping wide, jaws quivering. He shot off among the trees like a shaft from a bow.

'Foul toads! Pollywoggles! Great barrel-bummed poisoners! Wharrroooogggghhhh! Bluuuuuurgh!'

Moments later he lolloped back, rather unsteadily, with a wan smile pasted on his drooping features.

'Never killed me, did you, smartytails, wot!'

A stern voice boomed from the edge of the camp. 'Belaaay, put one paw near the rabbit an' we'll drop you all where y'stand!'

A single-bladed hatchet thudded into the ground between Fleetscut and Jukka. Instantly, the woodland was thick with hedgehogs. The squirrels were surrounded. The hog leader, a massive creature, made twice as big by the grass and leaves stuck to his quills as camouflage, strutted past Jukka and retrieved his hatchet. In the other paw he carried a shield of toughened beech bark, studded with shells. Staring fiercely at the squirrels, he puffed himself out, cheeks, stomach and chest.

'Bushytailed mice, eh! Well lissen, bullies, I wouldn't stand to see an 'og treated in that way, tortured an' poisinged, nor a rabbit, neither . . .'

Fleetscut tapped his quills politely. 'Er, 'scuse me, old lad, but I'm a hare an' they were—'

Rounding on him, the big hedgehog roared, 'Who asked you, eh? Don't dare interrupt when Baron Drucco Spikediggle has the floor, or you'll get yourself chopped up into frogmeat, you will!'

Fleetscut pawed away the hatchet hovering under his nose. 'Beg pardon, but don't waggle that thing at me, I'm still feelin' a bit frail, doncha know. I was merely explain—'

Baron Drucco went into a fury then, raising his hatchet and shouting in a voice which caused the leaves sticking round his mouth to blow away. 'Belaaay that gab, rabbit! I won't stand it from my 'ogs an' I won't take it from you. If I whack your 'ead off that'll cure you of talkin'. Wot d'you think, Rabble?'

The other hedgehogs began banging their hatchets against their shields, each vying to shout louder than the rest.

'Hohoh, that's the stuff, baron!'

'Chop that rabbit's 'ead off!'

'That'd stop 'is chatter, baron!'

'Does yer 'onour want us t'chop these bushmice up too?'

A small wiry female hogwife pushed her way through. Grabbing the baron's hatchet from his paw, she brandished it expertly, clipping the tip off one of his head-spikes. Her voice was almost a shriek, high and shrill.

'Yer blatherin' big pincushion, pin yer ears back an' lissen t'wot the rabbit's tryin' to tell yer.'

The baron deflated totally. Picking up the tip of his headspike, he chewed on it like a toothpick. 'Mirklewort, yer showin' me up in front of me own rabble.' He ducked as she swung the hatchet again.

'Show yer up? Every time you open that great trap o' yourn you show yerself up, breezebarrel!' Then, turning quickly aside, she whispered to Fleetscut, 'You 'ave yer say now. Shout out loud, mind. That's all this rabble pays 'eed to, beasts wot kin shout – even rabbits!'

Fleetscut yelled at the top of his voice, and to his surprise the hedgehog rabble went silent and listened.

'I'm a hare, d'ye hear, a bally hare! These squirrels are my friends! They weren't harmin' me, just helpin' me through a serious illness, that's all! No need to go choppin' anybeast up round here, chaps, wot! Wot wot!'

Determined to shout louder than Fleetscut, the baron hollered at a volume that hurt the hare's ears, 'Well why didn't yer say so at first, instead o' causin' all this trouble an' strife, eh?'

The baron's wife, Mirklewort, swung the hatchet once more, clipping off another of his headspikes. 'Because yer never gave 'im a wifflin' chance to, antbrain!'

Sulkily the baron picked up the headspike tip and stuck it in his mouth, next to the first one. Mirklewort pulled them out and stamped on them.

'Will yew stop that, Drucco? Y'll 'ave eaten yerself up one day, carryin' on like that! Ask these creatures if they'd like some blackcurrant an' plum crumble. Go on, snitnose!'

Baron Drucco's offer was readily accepted by Fleetscut and the squirrels. While the latter trooped after Drucco to the hogden the old hare, well aware of where the ruling power in the tribe lay, made a wobbly though elegant leg to Mirklewort, offering his paw.

'Allow me to escort you, marm. A pretty hogwife should never jolly well walk alone, wot!'

She accepted. 'Well well, ain't this grand? That 'usband

o' mine wouldn't give yer a push off a rock!'

Baron Drucco's tribe were known as the Rabble. They lived in rabble conditions, even though their camp was nought but a temporary one. However, neither Jukka nor Fleetscut could pretend that Rabble blackcurrant and plum crumble was anything other than first class. The guests seated themselves on a rotten elm trunk and dug into sizeable bowls of the stuff, steaming hot and covered in sweet maple sauce.

'Yew'll 'ave ter forgive us,' Mirklewort remarked casually. 'The camp's a bit untidy. Of course, it ain't wot we're used to, is it, Drucco?'

The baron licked white sauce from his snout and sniffed. 'I should wifflin' well 'ope not. Still, wot's a liddle untidiness atwixt friends, eh, that's wot I allus say.'

Jukka shifted to accommodate a beetle grubbing its way out of the rotten log they were seated on. 'A little untidiness indeed,' she murmured low to Fleetscut. 'Methinks the place looks like a battlefield in the midst of a midden!'

The area was littered with chopped off headspikes, broken bowls, fruit and vegetable skins and other debris, far too dreadful to mention. Fleetscut coughed politely and made conversation, lest anybeast had heard Jukka's remarks.

'Ahem, I take it that you don't live hereabouts then, marm?'

Mirklewort wiped spilled crumble from her lap with a withered dock leaf, which she then devoured. 'Ho graciousness no, we're only up 'ere lookin' for our babe, liddle Skittles. The wifflin' wanderin' wogglespike – er, haha, I mean the darlin' h'infant 'og – went an' got 'isself losted. We've seen neither nose nor spike of 'im for a frog's age. Oh, I do 'ope 'e ain't been consoled by vermins.'

Baron Drucco looked up in the midst of stealing a

dozing compatriot's bowl of crumble. 'Don't yew mean consorted?'

Fleetscut chipped in, making sure his tone was loud enough. 'I think the word you're lookin' for is consumed, chaps. Actually, we met up with two hedgehog types, Grassum and Reedum they called themselves, couple o' days back. They found your babe an' adopted him, but the little tyke escaped from them and wandered off again, wot. We're keepin' a weather eye out for your Skittles, though. Some goodbeast should find him sooner or later. Don't you jolly well fret, folks.'

Baron Drucco succeeded in filching the bowl of crumble from his rabblemate, placing his empty bowl in the hedgehog's paws and digging into the fresh one. 'Aye, long as 'e don't get consecuted by vermins, wifflin' liddle nuisance. Oh, did I tell ye, one o' the reasons I wanted to come up this way was to enter the contest. Hah, I 'spect that's why yore wanderin' this neck o' country too, eh?'

The old hare put aside his bowl. It was grabbed by a rabblehog who began licking the inside of it thoroughly.

'Contest, what contest, baron? First I've heard of it.'

Baron Drucco cuffed the sleeping hedgehog alongside him into wakefulness. 'Wot, eh, wossamarrer?' the rabblehog spluttered. 'Oi, somebeast's etted me pudden!'

The baron cuffed him another few buffets. 'It's etten, not etted, swillbrain! Never mind that. Gimme that contest thing you found.'

The hedgehog searched his spikes, ruminating aloud, 'Where'd I putten it? Sorry – putted it. Aha, 'ere 'tis!'

An extremely grimy birchbark strip was thrust into the hare's paw. He opened it gingerly. Wiping off remnants of bygone meals and a few unidentified smears, Fleetscut read aloud:

'Come mother, father, daughter, son,
My challenge stands to anybeast!

I'll take on all, or just the one,
Whether at the fight or feast!
Aye, try to beat me an' defeat me,
Set 'em up, I'll knock 'em down!
Just try to outbrag me, you'll see,
King Bucko Bigbones wears the crown!'

Jukka the Sling raised her eyebrows at the old hare. 'Methinks Bigbones has a fine opinion of himself, an' that's the hare thou art going up against. Well, good luck to thee. Yon fellow must have the might to back up his challenge.'

Mirklewort poked a grimy paw at Fleetscut. 'Hah, so y'are goin' to take up the challenge, eh! Don't yer think yore a bit long in tooth an' seasons?'

Fleetscut patted the top of his grey head and then his chest. 'Marm, there may be winter on the mountain, but there's spring at its heart. I must accept the challenge if I'm to raise an army to take Salamandastron, for we need this Buckowotsit and his followers on our side. So I'll search old Bigchops out an' throw down the bally gauntlet, wot!'

Drucco raised his dripping spikes from the pudding bowl. 'Aye, me too. I'll take a wiffle at it!'

'But you can't, sah,' Fleetscut objected. 'You're a blinkin' baron of hogs. How can y'be a king of hares, wot?'

Drucco shrugged and collared another bowlful from a smaller rabblehog. 'Huh, 'ares or 'ogs, all the same t'me. I knows 'ow t'be boss an' put me paw down firm. 'Ard but fair, that's me!' He emphasised the point by draining the tankard belonging to the hedgehog on his left, rubbing his stomach and belching aloud. 'Ah, that's betterer! Wot d'yer say we join forces an' seek this King Bucko out together, eh? We ain't got a clue where t'find 'im. Wot about you, cully?'

Without consulting Jukka, Fleetscut drew out the poem

he was carrying. 'Right y'are, baron, we'll go together. Safety in numbers, wot. Listen t'these directions. "Discover then a streamwolf's ford, tug thrice upon the royal cord, then my honour guard will bring, loyal subjects to their king!" Does that make any sense to you, old chap?'

Drucco scratched his stubby headspikes reflectively. 'Aye, it's poetry, ain't it, all those funny words put t'gether like a song, but y'speak 'em, 'stead o' singin'. That's the answer, it's poetry!'

He sat back, looking quite pleased with himself, until his wiry little wife gave him a shove, which sent him sprawling on his backspikes.

'Pay no 'eed t'that nincompoke,' Mirklewort snorted. 'A stone's got more brains than 'im. I think I might know where 'tis. Round 'ere they calls all the pikefishes streamwolf. Two of our scouts found a place coupla days back. A shallow crossin' just afore the stream breaks inter the river. That's a ford, ain't it?'

Jukka picked up her short spear. 'Canst thou take us there, hogwife?'

Ignoring her husband's struggles to get up off his back, Mirklewort bawled at the rabblehogs, 'Belaaaay! Break camp, 'ogs. Barleyburr, Shunko, take us t'that place you scouted out, if'n yer can unmember where it was. Stir yer spikes or we'll leave yer behind, Drucco!'

The combined forces cut into a winding path, which took them into what seemed a dim maze of thick ancient trees. Apart from the odd sunshaft breaking through the foliage, it was silent, still, and clothed in a soft green radiance. Jukka and Fleetscut marched together at the rear. The squirrel was highly displeased with the old hare's tactics and told him so in no uncertain manner.

''Twould have been fitting had thou asked me about joining my tribe up with these spiked, ill-mannered vagabonds. Rabble they be named and rabble they are – I like them not. An' who gave thee authority to decide whither we go, eh? Thou art no better than them, long-ears, treating us in such fashion, after we came all this way with thee!'

Fleetscut's dislike of Jukka still persisted. Moreover, he was feeling better now, full of crumble and ready for an argument.

'Well pish tush, me old bushtail, y'know what we always say at Salamandastron? If you don't like it then y'can jolly well lump it. So there! Come all this way with me, indeed! I never asked you to, marm. You an' your squirrels can go sling your hooks, wot! Aye, go on, back t'your safe little pine grove. Though it'll probably be swarmin' with all kinds o' bottle-nosed blue-bottomed vermin by now. Huh, I could say I wish you good luck, but I blinkin' well don't!'

The squirrel leader bared her teeth viciously. 'I don't need thy good luck wishes, old 'un. Ye branded me coward – I'll show ye I'm not, nor my warriors. We're with thee to the last step o' this journey, end where it may!'

Fleetscut curled his lip in contempt. 'Oh aye, you're with me all the way. For vengeance, no! For honour, hah, what would you know about honour? Jukka the famous Sling. Tchah! To see what weapons an' plunder y'can get your paws on, that's why you're with me, lady. An' you call these hedgehogs ill-mannered vagabonds? Let me tell you, treewalloper, you're no better'n them. Matter o' fact they're more honest about it than you, wot!'

Glaring and snorting at one another, the two continued without further words.

16

Lord Stonepaw had been watching the passage outside the cavern for sight or sound of foebeasts. Both he and Stiffener were taking turns on sentry, but there had been little to report in the last several hours. The Badger Lord arrived back in the cavern to find his hares grouped round old Bramwil, urging him to recall something.

'C'mon, old chap, you say it's called Littlebob hare, eh?'

'Now think carefully, how did it go?'

Bramwil was very old and confused. He looked pleadingly at the faces around him. 'Eh, wot, surely y'can recall it yourselves?'

This announcement was followed by snorts of impatience.

''Twas before our time. Nurse Willoway was long gone then!'

Stonepaw joined them. Placing a paw around Bramwil's skinny old shoulders, he silenced the rest. 'Calm down now, friends. What's going on here?'

'Bramwil thinks he knows a way out, sah!'

'But the old buffer's gone an' forgotten the bally thing!'

Stonepaw raised his eyebrows reprovingly at the speaker. 'A hare can forget lots of things when he reaches the winter seasons, you should know that. Look at us – we're no bunch of spring chicks any more. I'm older than you all. Don't pick on Bramwil. He can't help it, can you, old lad?'

Bramwil pounded a feeble paw against his grey head. ''Tis in there, sire, the old skiprope rhyme that Nurse Willoway used to teach young leverets. But alas, it was so long ago I can't remember it. Though I'm sure it was called Littlebob hare, or somethin' like that . . . hmmm!'

Stonepaw scratched his stripes pensively. 'I was here in Nurse Willoway's time. She was a stern creature. I'll never forget those herbal tonics and physics Willoway brewed up for the young 'uns. What a smell! Glad I never had to take 'em. Wait! Littlebob hare? I recall that – 'twas the one little haremaids used to chant when I swung the rope for them to skip. I'll tell you what, old friend. You and I will sit down someplace quiet together with a bite of cheese and some ale. We'll work it out together, and Blench can write it down as we remember it. Right, Stiffener, your turn for sentry go. Blench, get some charcoal from the fire and a flat piece of stone; the rest of you, take a nap and stay clear of Bramwil and me!'

Torleep put his ear to the barred oak door of the cell where the captives had been locked. He listened carefully, trying to distinguish the voices he could hear coming from somewhere beyond, but he was distracted by a fat, hungry old hare called Woebee, bewailing the fact that she was short of food, as some – or most – hares will. Torleep tried ignoring her, an impossible feat.

'Bit of a frost that was, Sailears old gel. If you an' Torleep hadn't cheeked the Trunn beast we might've had a morsel between us to keep fur'n'ears together. My word, I can't ever recall starvin' like this. I'm gettin' pains in me tummy. What time is it? Just past noon, wot. I'd normally be sittin' down to me post-luncheon snack now. Rosepetal an' maple wafers, scones with strawberry preserve an' meadowcream, with a nice pot o' mint an' comfrey tea. Now we haven't got a crust or a confounded swig o' water 'twixt the lot of us. How long'll we have t'put up with this state of affairs? Starvin's no fun!'

Torleep let the crystal monocle drop from his eye. His temper was fraying dangerously listening to Woebee's endless monologue – she seemed to go on and on and on. Normally polite, he rounded on her brusquely. 'I say, marm, d'you mind givin' the old jaws a blinkin' rest, wot? Confound it all, we could be a lot worse off!'

Woebee sniffed indignantly. 'Indeed, sah? A lot worse off, y'say? Pray how?'

Torleep pointed stiffly down with his paw. 'Well for a start, we could have been locked up in the cellars, in the flippin' dark! Granted we've got no food, but at least we can see daylight!' He gestured to the round hole which formed a window.

Sailears nodded her agreement. 'Lovely view of the sea from up here, wot. S'pose Trunn thought that if they'd locked us up in the cellars Lord Stonepaw an' the others may've broken us out.'

Woebee poked her head out of the window hole. The cell was really high up on the mountain. Down below the beach looked like a mere yellow ribbon, beyond which the great sea stretched until it was lost in a blue haze. 'Maybe we'd have been better off down below. There's absolutely no escape from this high-up place. I say, Torleep, I can hear those voices you mentioned clearer from here.'

Hurrying to the window, Torleep confirmed her observation. 'Stap me, you're right, marm. Now I beg you, please be silent whilst I eavesdrop. May hear somethin' jolly important!'

Two of Ungatt Trunn's horde captains were holding a conversation in the chamber below the cell. Well out of Ungatt Trunn's hearing, Roag the weasel and Mirefleck the rat were discussing the Hordes' position.

'Our soldiers'll take a lot o' feedin', Roag, mark my words.'

'The Great One ain't no fool, he knows that. Tomorrow the fleet's puttin' out to sea for fishin'. There's a couple o' patrols goin' to forage the cliffs an' dunes for birds' eggs!'

'Wastin' their time. No birds or eggs out there – we killed off the seabirds out at sea, afore we got here, an' the rest flew off. I still don't see where all the vittles will come from.'

'Oh, they'll find somethin' sooner or later, I s'pose. Bet we get sent with our troops on an inland forage. Meanwhile it ain't too bad for the likes of us – we get to live off'n the stripedog's larders for a while. Good vittles, eh?'

'Aye, that they are. Come on, we'd better get downstairs. The Mighty One's still carryin' on about the stripedog an' his followers hidin' in the cellar caves. I'd hate t'be them when they're captured. You know what Trunn's like -they'll die long'n'slow.'

'I 'eard the Mighty One's starvin' this lot up above so that sooner or later one of 'em'll break an' tell where the stripedog's hid 'imself.'

'I've 'eard that too, but suppose they don't tell an' he finds the stripedog an' those others? What d'you think he'll do with this lot in the cell above?'

'Oh, they won't be no use any more. Long'n'slow, that'll be their fate, long'n'slow . . .'

In the cell above, every hare had heard the conversation. When the captains had gone, there was a deadly silence among the prisoners. Woebee could not prevent a sob escaping her lips.

Torleep patted her ears. 'Don't fret, marm, they won't catch Lord Stonepaw. He's a lot cleverer than those rotten vermin give him credit for.'

Sailears stared out of the high window longingly. 'I just wish there was somethin' we could jolly well do to escape this place. Nothin' worse than sittin' round just waitin', wot!'

Captains Mirefleck and Roag were passing the wildcat's chamber when the door opened and Ungatt Trunn emerged with Fragorl at his heels. Both captains halted and saluted smartly.

Their leader nodded. 'Ah, I was just about to send for you. Listen now, I want you to take your troops – *all* your troops – down to the bottom caves. Flood those caves and passages with Hordebeasts. Show those other idiots down there how to snare an old stripedog and a few hares. I want them taken at any cost. Don't fail me!'

Mirefleck and Roag saluted stiffly and marched off, shouting orders to their column leaders. Ungatt Trunn addressed the silent Fragorl.

'I've got a small task for you, too. Take whom you like and find me some new spiders. There must be lots in this cave-riddled mountain and the rocks outside. Bring them to me in the stripedog's chamber – they can build webs there and redecorate it for me. Treat them carefully when you find them.'

'I live only to serve your word, Mightiness!' The Grand Fragorl glided soundlessly off.

Old Bramwil was blinking drowsily by the time they had pieced together the skipping rhyme. Stonepaw was tired too. He stifled a yawn. 'Well, I hope we haven't forgotten anything. Read it out, Blench.'

The cook read aloud from her neat lines of script, soon picking up the skiprope chant, which little hares had called out long ago as they held their smocks and skipped.

'Down in the cellars where nobeast goes,
Littlebob hare went runnin',
He ran an' ran an' followed his nose,
Where rocks never let the sun in.
He got very tired an' sat by a pool,
Then found out to his cost sir,

That he was nought but a silly fool,
Who'd got himself lost down there.
"Oh woe is me," cried Littlebob,
"'Tis dark an' so unsightly,
I must find some way out o' here,
To where the sun shines brightly."
So he climbed up to the coiling snake,
All damp an' slippy-feeling,
An' found beyond the big plum cake,
A hole right through the ceiling.
He went up through an' chased the blue,
An' made it home for tea sir,
He beat the tide an' spinies too,
But his mamma tanned his tailfur!'

In the silence which followed, Stonepaw turned to his hares. 'Well, let's see if we can make it home for tea, friends – or out of here at least!'

Trobee scratched between his ears. 'Beg pardon, sah, but are you sure you got it right?'

'As far as I can recall we did, right, Bramwil?'

The ancient hare did not reply to the Badger Lord; he had drifted off to sleep. Blench gave her opinion. 'H'it looks fine t'me, sire. Most of it's just a leverets' story, 'bout a liddle feller gettin' hisself lost down 'ere. 'Tis the last eight lines is wot we want, from that bit about the coilin' snake. Right?'

Trobee was still a bit bewildered by it all. 'Where in the name o' salad do we find a climbin' snake, wot?'

A hare called Willip corrected him. 'Not a climbin' snake, 'twas a coilin' snake. It says Littlebob climbed up to it. Up there!' She pointed up at the cave ceiling.

Like stargazers, the badger and his hares wandered about the cavern, heads thrown back, staring at the stalactite formations.

'Oops, got a drop o' water in me eye!'

'Watch where y'going, old chap. Go an' bump into

some otherbeast – you've near knocked me over twice now, wot!'

'Stop right where y'are, Trobee, or you'll walk straight into that pool!'

'Oh, I say, haha, one of those thingies hangin' down looks just like old Purlow with a great long nose. Hahaha!'

'Huh! Well at least I've got a decent nose, not like that apple pip stuck on the end of your muzzle. Tchah!'

'Ahaaah! There 'tis, I see it! There 'tis! . . .' Splash!

The Badger Lord's huge paws scooped a dripping Trobee up from the pool. 'Where? Point it out, quickly!'

Dancing to and fro, shaking freezing water from his fur, Trobee tried to resight the coiling snake.

'Er . . . er . . . where was I? Oh, confound it, I've lost the bloomin' thing now. Dearie me, there's only one thing for it. Get ready to fish me out again, sah. Here goes . . .'

Trobee flung himself in the air, and an instant before he hit the pool his paw shot out. 'There!'

Stonepaw marked the spot in a flash. Unable to stop himself laughing, he hauled Trobee out of the water again. 'Hohoho! Good old Trobee. Not only impressions of a bird an' a fish, but you did find it, over there in the far corner! Don't check it again, though. That pool looks to me as if it might go down for ever, and I might not manage to catch you next time!'

Bramwil doddered forward, rubbing sleep from his eyes. 'Not like you t'be takin' a bath before summer, Trobee. What's goin' on here, sah?'

Above the rock ledges in the cavern's dark-shadowed corner the stalactite hung, formed by water dripping for countless ages and leaving minuscule limestone deposits which added gradually to its length. At some point in time the water took a different course, threading its way around the main column and forming into a type of embossed spiral winding about the stalactite: an unmistakable representation of a coiling snake.

Stiffener, being the most agile, was brought in from sentry duty and replaced by Purlow. The boxing hare weighed up the route, shaking his head doubtfully.

'Those ledges look much too slippery for our hares t'climb, sah. Did we bring any rope with us?'

Stonepaw looked crestfallen. 'We haven't any rope at all.'

'Then use bowstrings'n'belts, you puddens!' Old Bramwil waved an apologetic paw. 'Didn't mean t'call you a pudden, sah. Beg y'pardon.'

The Badger Lord chuckled. 'You can call me what you like as long as you come up with ideas like that, my old friend. Belts'n'bowstrings, eh? Right!'

Cord girdles, woven belts and tough bowstrings were soon lashed together into an awkward but serviceable rope. Stiffener coiled it about his shoulders, spat on his paws and clambered on to the first ledge. It was worn smooth, wet and slick with trickling water.

Willip scraped up a bit of damp sand from the stones at the pool edge, moulded it into a ball and tossed it up to Stiffener. 'Here, catch! Rub this on your paws – 'twill help.'

The grit did the trick. Up Stiffener went, clinging like a fly to the slippery rock ledges, with his friends below calling out advice to him.

'Pin y'self flat against the wall an' reach up for that bit stickin' out above.'

'Move y'paws left a touch, Stiff . . . bit more . . . that's it!'

'Now lie flat on y'tummy an' wriggle along!'

'See that crevice? Wedge into it an' climb up there!'

Gradually, bit by painstaking bit the boxing hare made his way upward until he reached the stalactite they were certain was the coiling snake. Leaning out from the ledge he took hold of it, inspecting the dark ceiling above. Bramwil called up to him. 'D'you see the big plum cake? That's what the rhyme says you want t'look for. Any sign?'

Stiffener arched his neck back, searching. 'Sire, can you move one o' those big lanterns this way?'

Stonepaw shifted a lantern directly beneath the hare.

'So there y'are, me beauty! I found it, mates,' Stiffener called. 'Be back down in a tick. Stan' clear, now!'

The makeshift rope unravelled, its end hitting the floor. Stiffener came down it paw over paw in a manner that would have done credit to any squirrel. He landed lightly.

'Up there, just right o' that coilin' snake thing, there's the fat wide end of a stalactite which must've snapped off. Looks jus' like a big ole plum cake, though not as good as the ones you bake, Blench marm. T'other side of it is a hole, goes straight through the ceilin', sah. Any'ow, I swung across there an' tied the rope round a liddle nub o' rock, inside the hole, so we can all climb up there. I reckon the holespace might be wide enough to take a beast yore size, sah.'

Lord Stonepaw hugged Stiffener fondly. 'Splendid work, Stiffener. You're a real corker!'

Bramwil was the first to go, with Stiffener right behind him, lest the old fellow got into difficulties. Surprisingly he did quite well, though at one or two points Stiffener had to get his head and shoulders beneath Bramwil and push. Heaving the ancient hare through the hole, Stiffener started back down again.

Stonepaw noticed the boxing hare was beginning to breathe heavily. 'You won't last out, clambering up and down that rope all the time. We'll have to think of an easier way.'

Stiffener squatted until his breathing eased. 'Yore right, sah, I ain't gittin' any younger. I got an idea though. Let's get two of our strongest up there with me, say, Purlow an' Trobee. The three of us can stop up in the hole, run a fixed noose into the rope an' hoist the rest up one by one. Wot d'ye think, sah?'

Stonepaw agreed readily. 'An excellent idea! Trobee,

up y'go, friend. Purlow . . . Purlow?'

A worried frown flashed across the badger's face and he hurried to the concealed entrance, picking up a torch as he went. There was no sign of Purlow standing sentry in the narrow rift. Stonepaw heard yelling and clattering from outside. Forcing his great bulk through the crack, the Badger Lord pushed out into the passage and followed the sounds.

Around the first bend, Purlow was being set upon by six or more vermin. He fell with two on top of him, the rest scrabbling to get at him. Stonepaw came hurtling into the fray, laying about him with the blazing torch.

'Eulaliaaaa!'

Ripping the two Hordebeasts off Purlow, the Badger Lord dispatched both by smashing them head on against the rock walls of the passage. Taking to their heels, the others fled, running wildly for their lives. Stonepaw pulled Purlow upright and retrieved his torch. 'Are you badly hurt, my friend?'

Though blood ran from Purlow's jaw and back, he shook his head. 'I'll be all right, sah, but they've found our cave! 'Twas my mistake to step out into the passage holding a torch. I heard sounds, y'see, and walked right into the vermin like a fool!'

The badger threw a paw about Purlow to steady him. 'Come on, we'll soon have you up through the hole and out!'

But even as he found the cavern entrance, Stonepaw could hear the din of many vermin charging along the underground tunnels towards the secret cave that was no longer a secret.

17

Surrounded by a virtual flotilla of shrew logboats, which were a bit more sophisticated than Ruff's simple treetrunk, having been hollowed out and crossbenched, Dotti and Gurth sat for'ard on their elm log, digging their paddles deep and calling out the pace in true Guosim fashion along with Log a Log Grenn's shrews. Dotti liked the shrews, aware of a real sense of comradeship in their company. The vessels sped downstream together with a big shrew called Kubba calling the stroke in his fine bass voice.

Taking his orders from Grenn, he bellowed out, 'Ahoy, Guosim, we ain't stoppin' 'til we join the river, so let's git our guests there good'n'fast. The stream's a-runnin' well an' we'll camp near the river fork. So bend yore backs, an' let's show our friends how Guosim shrews do it. Right, take y'stroke from me. One . . . two . . . waylaheykoom!'

Everybeast bent to the paddles, roaring back at Kubba, 'Shrumm! Shrumm!'

Kubba called the stroke on every third beat: 'Waylaheykoom!'

Dotti and her friends joined the Guosim's answer: 'Shrumm! Shrumm!'

'Oh the river is deep an' swift an' wide.'

'Waylaheykoom!'

'An' there's my matey at my side!'

'Shrumm! Shrumm!'

'With the sunlight beamin' through the trees.'

'Waylaheykoom!'

'We'll all remember days like these.'

'Shrumm! Shrumm!'

'Oh oh waylaheykoom shrumm shrumm shrew, I won't forget a friend like you!'

Brocktree and Ruff cheered when the Guosim quickened the pace. Showing off their prowess, experienced shrews twirled their paddles high on alternate strokes, clacking the blades against those of their neighbours and dipping back without breaking pace. Ruff was full of admiration for their skill. 'Haharr, wot a fine ole bunch o' waterbeasts this gang are!'

Before long Gurth and Dotti had learned the trick.

'Hurr hurr, miz Dott, us'n's be gurt pagglewallopers, burr aye!'

Then the entire thing developed into a race. The logboats fairly flew downstream, spray shooting up from their bows. The four friends were caught up in the exhilaration of it all, keeping up with the breakneck stroke, yelling out friendly jibes and exchanging banter with the Guosim.

'Hah, there's woodworm in that log paddlin' faster'n you lot!'

'Ho, is there now, cheekychops? You'll soon be eatin' our spray from behind, matey!'

'Gurr, doan't ee strain you'mselfs, zurrs. Jus' ee stop in us'n's wake, naow!'

'Wake, is it? We thought ye were asleep, hohoho!'

'Scallywag, I'll bend my paddle o'er yore 'ead fer that!'

'Tut tut, me ole messmate, you'll 'ave to catch us first! Give 'em vinegar, Kubba – show 'em the ole double-stroke!'

'Come on, sah, wield that paddle as if it were your sword, wot!'

Kubba's booming shout rang out over the sunflecked waters.

'Ship yore paddles, stop that fuss,
Let the stream work carryin' us!'

Everybeast stowed paddles, allowing the boats to skim elegantly along on the silent current.

Brocktree leaned back, breathing heavily. 'Whew! We must have covered a day's distance in half a morn there. What d'you say, Ruff?'

'Aye, we made the fishes look as if'n they was stannin' still.'

Dotti flopped down upon the prow, wiping spray from her ears. 'By the left an' by jingo, I'm kerfoozled! What about you?'

Gurth's smile split his dark-furred features almost in half. 'Uz floo loik burds, miz. Et wurr wunnerful!'

The remainder of that memorable day on the stream passed in similar fashion, sometimes racing, other times cruising, with banter, shanties and good comradeship prevailing over all. In the late afternoon Grenn passed on orders to make landfall at a recognised Guosim camping spot, a shallow sunlit cove. They waded in the clear water, stretching and getting the feel of paws on solid ground again. A few of the younger shrews went deeper for a swim. Gurth watched the cooks setting up their fire and digging out supplies and cauldrons. The kindly mole gave their rations a quick look over before having a word with Dotti.

'Gurth says you lot can have the evenin' off,' the haremaid announced to the delighted shrewcooks. 'He'll be chef today. You chaps are in for a treat – my molepal's going to make gurt tunnel stew, followed by preserved apple'n'plum pudden with sweet chestnut sauce. How does that sound, wot?'

The cooks patted Gurth's back and hugged him

thankfully. Then in the true manner of shrews they hung about, observing him at work, offering advice and criticism and arguing among themselves.

'You needs to peel those turnips thinner. Don't waste any.'

'Pay no 'eed to that'n, Gurth. You peel 'em 'ow you like, but I'd roll me pastry wider if I was you.'

'Rubbish. The mole's rolled it too wide as it is, can't y'see!'

'That cauldron'll boil over if'n you don't watch it!'

'Shows 'ow much you know, sniggletail. A watched cauldron never boils, that's wot my mum allus said!'

'Yore doin' that dried fruit all wrong, Gurth. 'Ere, let me show yer 'ow 'tis done!'

Dotti had a quick word with Lord Brocktree, who soon settled the argument. Drawing his great battle blade he sliced a dead limb from an old willow with one mighty stroke.

'Some wood for your fire, Gurth. Oh, whilst I've got my sword out, d'you want me to stop any shrews from interfering with your cooking? I could whack off a few tails, eh?'

By the time Gurth turned to answer the shrews had fled. 'Thankee, zurr Brock. They'm surpintly muddlin' argifyin' likkle h'aminals. Oi never see'd ought like um!'

Log a Log Grenn approached Dotti, Ruff and Brocktree and pointed downstream. 'I was going to take a stroll along the bank. We have to cross a ford before we reach the river tomorrow – just thought I'd best check t'see if the ford level is high enough to sail over. If not we'll have to carry the boats along the bankside. Would ye like to take a walk with me, friends?'

Brocktree sheathed the sword upon his broad back. 'Be with you in a moment, marm. I want to check on Skittles. D'you know I've not seen hide nor hair of that rascal since morn?'

Ruff pointed out a group of young shrews frolicking in

the stream, Skittles splashing and giggling with them. 'There's the rogue. He's been with that gang all day, travellin' up front in the lead boat with Grenn.'

The shrew Chieftain turned her eyes to the sky. 'I always make the young 'uns sit in my boat so I can keep an eye on 'em. But seasons o' vinegar, I've never had to cope with one like that Skittles – he's more trouble than a barrel o' beetles!'

The Badger Lord smiled and shook his head. 'Aye, he is that. As soon as I mentioned getting a wash this morning he vanished like smoke. Look at him now, playing in the stream like a little fish. I couldn't get him near water for the life of me. Come on, let's get going before he notices us.'

They padded silently off down the bank. Before they had got round the bend, however, the hogbabe sprang out of the water in front of them, a wicked grin on his face. He scrambled up on to the badger's back, seating himself on the sword hilt before anybeast could stop him.

'Heeheehee, finked you was goin' off wivout Skikkles, eh?'

Brocktree turned his head, growling in the hogbabe's face. 'Be off with you, pestilence!'

Skittles tweaked the badger's nose impudently. 'See, I nice'n'cleaned now, B'ock. I come wiv ya, mate!'

Lord Brocktree turned his face to the front, smiling hugely, though his voice was gruff and stern. 'Huh, I suppose you'll have to, seeing as you're up there, but sit still and no nonsense out of you, sir!'

Skittles saluted. 'An' no nonsinks outta you, sir, or I chop you tail off wivva yore sword. Chop!'

It was a pleasant walk in the warm evening. Dragonflies hovered over the stream, hunting for midges and mayflies, pepper saxifrage and yellow-cupped silverweed grew in profusion close to the stiller edges, noon had turned to early evening gold, with pink and cream cloudbanks massed prettily to the south. Log a Log

Grenn halted them in sight of the ford.

'You can glimpse the river not far from here, friends. Stay well on the banks, now. If the water's deep enough on the ford our boats should pass over it with no trouble. I'll have to test it with a stick, so keep well on land. The waters hereabouts have streamwolves aplenty huntin' in 'em, an' they hide themselves well, so 'tis best to take care.'

On reaching the ford, Grenn demonstrated what she meant by tossing a few crusts she had brought along into the water. Four long pike shot out of the reed cover and fought each other viciously for the food.

'Wowow! Where a they comed from, B'ock?'

Brocktree glanced back at the startled hogbabe on his shoulder. 'Streamwolves lie in wait for food, then they pounce! Just like the one Ruff saved you from in the watermeadows.'

Whilst the pike were busy, Grenn poked a stick into the ford. ''Tis deep enough – our craft should pass over safely. Though I wouldn't trail my paws in there if I was you, Skittles. Look, further down the bank, you can see the river where it meets the stream.'

Dotti skipped down the bank apiece. 'I say, chaps, cranberries – scads of 'em growin' down here!'

Dainty pink flowers with curling petals stood swaying on wispy thin-leafed stalks; beneath them the small orange-hued berries grew in profusion. They were sweet but sharp to the taste. The friends gathered in the welcome addition to their supplies, sampling the fruit as they picked.

'Mmm, nice'n'tasty, marm. I wager Gurth an' yore cooks could make a batch or two o' cranberry tarts with these!'

Dotti chided the juice-stained hogbabe. 'Steady on, Skittles, you'll make y'self ill if you scoff too many. Don't be greedy now!'

Lord Brocktree raised an eyebrow at Ruff. 'That's the

best one I've heard for a while – a hare telling another creature not to eat too much. Wonders never cease!'

Dotti overheard the remark, and turned primly on the badger. 'Manners don't cost anythin', y'know. My mater always said enough was as good as a feast, sah. Merely advisin' the little tyke . . . Skittles, come back here, you rip!'

But the hogbabe was off on an adventure of his own. He dashed away into the surrounding bushes, chortling. 'Yah yah, can't catch Skikkles!'

They raced after him, fearing that he would turn and run into the ford. For a hogbabe, Skittles was surprisingly nippy. He put on a good turn of speed, dodging through shrubbery and around treetrunks. Grenn and Ruff went one way, Dotti and Brocktree the other, hoping to head him off. Then they heard Skittles's shrill screams cut the evening air.

'Yeeeeek! Leggo a me, leggo a Skikkles!'

Dotti was brushed to one side as Brocktree grabbed the battle blade from his back and crashed off through the foliage like a juggernaut.

Panggg!

A slingstone ricocheted from the sword blade. Jukka the Sling stood barring Brocktree's path, whirling her loaded weapon, teeth bared, ready to do battle.

'Hold hard, stripedog, or the next one puts thine eye out!'

'Oh corks! You benighted bushtailed buffoon, pack in slingin'. Can't y'see that's a Badger Lord?' Fleetscut stuck out his paw just in time. Jukka's sling wrapped around it, the stone load clacking sharply as it whacked the old hare's paw. He hopped and leaped about in pain, yanking Jukka crazily round with him.

'Owowouch! Y'blitherin' blisternosed bangtail, you've gone an' busted me poor old paw. Owoooh!'

Everybeast seemed to arrive on the scene together then: Baron Drucco, Mirklewort, a rabble of hogs and the squirrel tribe. Grenn came dashing up with Dotti and Ruff hard on her heels. Brocktree leaned on his sword hilt, perplexed. 'What in the name of all seasons is this?'

Skittles appeared from beneath a bush and sat down nonchalantly on Brocktree's big footpaw, shaking his head. 'Name a seasons, worrall diss, eh?'

More pandemonium ensued.

'My liddle babe, me treasure! Where in the name o' carnation 'ave yew been, yer foul-needled maggot?'

'Ahoy there, marm, curb yore tongue. The liddle bloke's been with us!' Ruff tried vainly to placate the angry hogmother, but only succeeded in offending her mate.

'Shut yer trap, babe robber. If'n my wife axes where in the coronation 'e's been then let 'im tell 'er!'

'Excuse me a tick, folks, but what's all this about carnations an' coronations? Shouldn't the word be tarnation, wot?' Dotti interjected.

'Beg pardon, marm, but shouldn't you keep your long ears out of other beasts' business? Bad form, marm!' Fleetscut said severely.

'Who are you jolly well callin' longears? You're a hare y'self, y'dodderin' old paw-wobbler – a fig for you, sah!'

'Thou art a bit young in seasons to be cheeking thy elders in such manner, miss. Mind, or I'll teach thee a lesson!'

'I say, you broomtailed paw-breaker, d'you mind beltin' up? This is my quarrel, wot!'

Claaaanggggg! 'Silence! Silence I say!'

The ring of Brocktree's sword blade upon a rock, coupled with his stentorian roar, created instant quiet. The Badger Lord sheathed his weapon. 'Next beast I hear arguing will have me to deal with! Now, back to the bank and gather cranberries, all of you! Don't stand there gawping at me – we have the best cooks in all Mossflower back at our camp. If you want hot cranberry tarts for supper tonight you lot would be better off picking berries than arguing. We'll sort all our differences out over a decent meal. Now get moving!'

Muttered introductions were made as the party bent to pick cranberries. Brocktree and Dotti filled Mirklewort and Drucco in on Skittles's encounter with the Riverwolf, and the trial it had been trying to keep him in order. Titles, histories and names of friends and relatives were exchanged. Bags, aprons, helmets and pouches were filled until the area was stripped relatively clean of the good fruit. They trudged back along the bank in the failing light, Baron Drucco shaking his head in despair of his offspring, as he explained to a smiling Brocktree.

'Four times – *four*, mind – that liddle tailsnip 'as gone missin' four times since 'e was borned, an' 'im not more'n two seasons old. No wonder me spikes is goin' grey – those the missus ain't chopped off wid me hatchet.'

Dotti and Fleetscut had apologised to one another, and were getting on quite amicably.

'Well stap me, so you're old Blench the cook's niece, wot? Bet you can't cook as well as your jolly old aunt, eh, m'gel?'

'Beg pardon? Me, cook? I'd burn a salad, sah. Us of the fatal beauty type are pretty awful cooks if y'ask me.'

Gurth's apple'n'plum pudden with sweet chestnut sauce was set to one side as the Guosim cooks set about making cranberry tarts, which involved arguing.

'These'll go nice with the sweet chestnut sauce, mate!'

'Who taught you to cook, bottlesnout? Rosehip an' honey syrup, that's the proper thing to 'ave with 'em!'

'Rubbish. Y'don't need any sauce or syrup with cranberry tarts. A few crystallised cuckoo flower petals, that's all anybeast in their right mind would sprinkle 'em with!'

'Huh, too late now. They're scoffin' 'em anyway!'

Stories were told around the stone oven campfire as it reflected in the night stream, and new-made friends relaxed on the bank. Brocktree and Fleetscut sat together.

The Badger Lord was extremely disturbed about the bad news from Salamandastron.

'My father Stonepaw did right in sending you to gather an army, Fleetscut. For one of your long seasons you have done well, despite the difficulties you were under. Relax now, old fellow, I take charge as from hereonin.'

The old hare bowed respectfully to the son, as he had always done to the father. 'Do you have a plan, lord?'

Brocktree's dark eyes glowed in the firelight. 'Oh yes, Fleetscut, I have a plan. Trust your Badger Lord!'

'I always have, sire, without question. D'ye mind me sayin', you remind me of your dad when I was nought but a leveret, though a bit bigger an' fiercer if that's at all possible.'

Brocktree's great striped muzzle nodded. 'It's possible, my friend. 'Tis said to wield a battle blade the size of mine, a badger must suffer from the Bloodwrath.'

Fleetscut fell silent then. He had heard tales of badgers, the most reckless and savage of warriors, all affected by the violent scourge known as the Bloodwrath. Nothing could stop such a beast in combat; not weapons, nor force of fangs and claws. This new lord was a truly perilous beast.

That night Lord Brocktree and the tribe leaders Jukka the Sling, Baron Drucco, Log a Log Grenn, Gurth son of Longladle and Ruffgar Brookback the otter made a pact. Between them they would gather a great army and take Salamandastron; free it from the claws of Ungatt Trunn.

Lord Brocktree's stern voice caused neck hairs to bristle. 'The lands our creatures live on must not be tainted by vermin hordes. Babes should be safe to wander alone. This will not be accomplished by one tribe alone. I need you all – anybeast that loves freedom, hedgehogs, shrews, squirrels, moles, otters, mice, voles and especially hares. We will go with you to the realm of this self-proclaimed hare king. He must be challenged and defeated. Then he and his followers must be persuaded to join us. They will all be fine fighting hares.'

Gurth stared up at the badger's massive form. 'Hurr well, if'n anybeast be's gurt 'nuff to beat hurr king, that 'un'll be ee, zurr!'

Brocktree was looking straight at Dotti as he replied. 'No, Gurth, 'tis only fair that a hare challenges a hare. Tell me, Fleetscut, what is the next clue to this king's whereabouts? Is there anything special we must search for?'

The old hare repeated the lines he had committed to memory.

'Discover then a streamwolf's ford,
Tug thrice upon the royal cord,
Then my honour guard will bring,
Loyal subjects to their king!'

Brocktree tossed a few logs into the oven fire. 'We've already found the streamwolf's ford. Let's get some sleep now. Tomorrow we've got a royal appointment, what d'you say, Ruff?'

'Haharr, royal me rudder. If'n that 'un's a king I'm a h'emperor of h'otters, mates!'

Dotti lay awake for a while, wondering why the badger had stared at her so pointedly when he referred to a hare's only being challenged by another hare. But she did not dwell on it overlong. Just before sleep claimed Jukka, she heard the young haremaid mutter aloud to herself: 'Ahem, all those of my subjects still awake, take note of this proclamation. Queen Dorothea Duckfontein Dillworthy is about to take her fatal beauty sleep, so put a clap on your jolly old traps, wot wot?'

The shrew Kubba wandered back into camp as the cooking fires were being rekindled next morning. He saluted Log a Log Grenn with a flourish of his rapier.

'Got up an hour afore dawn, marm, scoured the bank by the ford an' found wot yore lookin' for!'

'Jolly decent of you, old beast,' Fleetscut called back from his place on the breakfast line. 'You mean y'found the royal wotsamacallit? Where was it?'

Kubba sheathed his rapier. ''Tain't much, mate, just a big thick red cord, 'angin' from a whoppin' great 'ornbeam. I'll take ye there after brekkist. Float me log, I'm starvin'!'

Brocktree stepped out and shook Kubba's paw. 'Take my place at the front of the line. Well done, sir!'

An hour later, their hunger sated by cheese and oatmeal cakes, the remaining cranberry tarts and some good Guosim cider, everybeast adjourned to the ford bank. Kubba pointed out the hornbeam tree, around the leeside of which hung a red tasselled rope, its length going off, up amid the foliage.

'That's the one, though I ain't tugged on the rope yet.'

Brocktree performed an exaggerated bow to Dotti. 'Would ye pray do the honours, milady?'

The haremaid curtsied prettily and fluttered her eyelids. 'Why, thankee, m'lud. Methinks I'll give it a jolly old tug once or thrice, providin' the blinkin' tree don't fall on me bonce, wot wot!'

Dotti took firm hold of the cord and gave it three hefty tugs. The thin boughs in the hornbeam crown shook, dislodging a colony of jackdaws. Flapping angrily into the air they set a din of harsh cries ringing into the quiet woodlands.

Baron Drucco watched the birds settle back on to the tree. 'Haw haw haw! You'd think 'e could afford proper bells if'n 'e's supposed t'be a king like 'e sez 'e is. Wot do we do now? Shall I give the rope a few more tugs?'

Once again, he was not fast enough to escape Mirklewort's hatchet. She clipped one of his headspikes and pushed him down on his bottom, so that he was sitting against the hornbeam base. 'Yew leave that rope alone, nincomscoop. We sit an' wait. Ain't that right, yer badgership?'

Brocktree unwound Skittles from his sword hilt and sat down alongside Drucco. 'Right, marm, we wait!'

Jukka and Grenn deployed both their tribes to the shrubbery, where they concealed themselves. The rest sat and waited. Morning was well on before anything happened. It was Gurth who leaned close to Brocktree and announced in a bass whisper, 'Oi, yurr's sumbeasts a-coomin' this way, zurr!'

The Badger Lord sat casually, eyes half closed. 'I see them too, friend. Everybeast sit still now, stay calm.'

The air hissed, and a light javelin buried its tip in the ground, not far from Ruff's footpaw. Twoscore rough-looking mountain hares, some still showing white fur patches from last winter, marched up armed to the teeth.

Their leader's voice, like his companions', had a strong burr of the far northern mountains about it. 'Arrah weel now, laddies, whit've we here?'

'Why don't you ask me that, instead of the laddies?' Brocktree replied, his eyes still half closed. 'They've only just arrived with you.'

The leader pulled his javelin point from the soil. His voice had an insolent tone to it. 'Hearken t'me, stripe-dawg, ye're en noo position t'be saucy wi' me. Mah hares are upright'n'armed ready, ye an' these beauties o' yourn are settin' doon unprepared, d'ye ken?'

The Badger Lord uttered a short bark. Guosim and squirrels emerged from hiding, rapiers and slings in evidence. The mountain hare saw his troop were surrounded.

Brocktree rose to his full height, sword in paw. 'Oh, I ken all right, hare. I ken if you give impudence to Lord Brocktree of Brockhall you'll find your ears dangling from yonder alarm rope. So keep a civil tongue in your head!'

The hare was visibly cowed, and his tone became more reasonable. 'Mah apologies, lord, 'cept have t'be careful o' strangers aboot these parts. Whit was it ye were wantin'?'

Jukka the Sling dropped from a hornbeam bough. 'Thou wilt take us to this one who calleth himself king. Move!'

'Look fit enough, don't they, wot?' Fleetscut remarked to Ruff as they followed the hares on a tortuous path through the woodland. 'Touch o' trainin' an' discipline should bring those laddies up t'the mark!'

At the centre of the party, Brocktree had called Dotti to his side. He gave her murmured instructions. 'Don't speak until I tell you when we get to where we're going, miss. Don't get flustered or indignant, just act calm and look as if you're capable of taking care of yourself.'

The haremaid felt slightly nervous, and started babbling. 'Yessah, take care o' meself, act calm, you can bet your bally stripes I will, most carefullest calmest blinkin' hare ever twiddled an ear, sah, that's me, wot! An' as for gettin' flustered or indignant, by the left, sah, there's not a beast alive can muster flea, er, fluster me, an' I can be rather undignant when called upon. Why, I recall when Grandpa got stuck in the chimney—'

Brocktree's paw cuffed her ear lightly. 'Stop babbling, miss. Listen!'

A profusion of noises from afar could be heard on the still woodland air. Loud cheering, drumbeats, singing, shouting and many other unidentified discordant sounds. The hare leader, taking care to keep clear of Brocktree, remarked with jaunty cynicism: 'Och, brace yerselves, mah babes, yer aboot tae enter the court o' King Bucko Bigbones, the roarin' beast hisself!'

Dotti took a deep breath and swallowed hard.

18

Trobee had already climbed the rope of belts and bowstrings and was sitting in the entrance of the ceiling hole when Lord Stonepaw hurried into the cavern, supporting Purlow. Stiffener Medick ran to help them. Calm as ever, the boxing hare ignored the increasing sounds of Trunn's Blue Hordebeasts as they charged towards the hiding place.

'I see ole Purlow's taken a few knocks, sah. Sounds like we got trouble comin' to visit, eh! C'mon, Purlow, let's get you up the rope.'

Stonepaw lifted the wounded hare on to the rope, then turned to the others waiting their turn to climb.

'I want you all up and through that hole as quick and safe as possible. Stiffener, you'll be last hare up. Stay here until the last one's gone. Understood?'

The boxing hare threw a stiff salute. 'Sah! But what about you, sah?'

The Badger Lord's voice was like thunder. 'Never mind about me. I've given you an order and I expect it to be obeyed! Blench, you go next, help Trobee and Purlow to haul the others up into the hole. I don't need to tell you that speed is of the essence. Go!'

The din outside was very close now. Stonepaw

grabbed a javelin and a chunk of rock and lumbered towards the entrance. Stiffener was at his side, paws clenched. 'I'm comin' with you, sah!'

The Badger Lord stiff-pawed him in the chest, knocking him back a pace. Stonepaw's voice had sunk to a growl, and there was danger in his eyes. 'I gave you an order, Stiffener Medick. Are you disobeying me?'

Tears sprang to the boxing hare's eyes. 'You know I've never disobeyed yore orders, sah, but there'll be too many vermin for you out there. You need help, sah!'

Stonepaw ruffled Stiffener's ears fondly, as he had done many times when the old hare was young. 'Not this time, old friend. You must get away to lead our warriors; I must hold the entrance to buy you the time to get them out. It is my duty as their lord. Promise me one thing, though. You will try to free Sailears and the others if they are still alive. Promise?'

Stiffener wiped a paw across his eyes and saluted Lord Stonepaw one last time. 'Promise? I swear it on me life, sah! You give 'em blood'n'vinegar, sah. Slay some for me, eh, wot!'

The first blue rat's head poked around the rift which formed the cavern entrance. Stonepaw turned his back on Stiffener and charged, bellowing the war cry of Salamandastron.

'Eulaliiiiaaaaaa!'

It was as if the long seasons had fallen away from the old badger; strength coursed through his veins like wildfire. Vermin hurtled about him like dandelion clocks in the wind. Wedging himself in the rift, Stonepaw went at them as they crashed on him in waves, Mirefleck and Roag screeching in the background, urging their Hordebeasts on.

'Take him alive! Throw ropes around him!'

'Wound him! Don't kill the stripedog! Mighty Ungatt Trunn wants him alive!'

'Ten seasons' rations to the ones who capture the stripedog!'

Stonepaw flung the rock and slew Captain Roag. He hammered, stabbed and battered at the seething mass with his javelin. Ropes parted like dead grass between the badger's jaws and big blunt claws, and his voice echoed thunderously through the underground passages and caves as he wreaked destruction on his hated foes, regardless of wounds. The Bloodwrath was upon him.

'Eulaliiiaaaa! Come to the Lord of Salamandastron! Eulaliiiiaaaa! Blood an' vinegaaaaar!'

Stiffener followed the final hare through the hole. They were gathered in a huddle, bloodless paws gripping weapons tightly, peering down, unable to see anything, their ears filled with battlesounds from below. Seizing a torch, the boxing hare gestured forward into the tunnel which lay before them. 'No hangin' about, now. Come on, let's go!'

Blench threw her ladle forcefully through the hole, stifling a sob as she jammed a paw in her mouth. 'Oh, sire, me pore lord!'

Trobee tried to force his way past Stiffener. 'Blaggards! Fiends! Let me at 'em!'

The boxing hare winded him with a sharp rap to the stomach. 'Lissen t'me. You lot ain't goin' anyplace but out of 'ere. I made a promise to Lord Stonepaw an' I means t'keep it. We'll get out all right, but we'll be back to free any of our pals who are alive an' imprisoned. Nothin' we can do now but go. I ain't lettin' my friend ole Stonepaw sacrifice 'imself so we can climb back down an' get killed. Is that clear? I'm in charge now, so march!'

Pulling up the rope, Stiffener coiled it about his waist and snapped out orders. 'Trobee, you an' Purlow lead off, column o' twos, I'll bring up the rear. Here, take this torch, Blench!'

Stooped almost double they took off along the tunnel.

It was wide enough to take two hares, but low-ceilinged, dark and damp.

Groddil came scuttling to the edge of the mêlée. All he could see was blue vermin pushing forward into the rift. The stunted fox nodded at Mirefleck. 'So, this was where they were hiding. Have they taken the stripedog yet? Remember, the Mighty One wants him alive.'

Mirefleck watched vermin trampling their slain companions whilst Captains Fraul and Swinch urged them on with whips.

'Get through there, you slackers, into the cave an' 'elp yer mates to capture that beast. Come on, move yerselves!'

Mirefleck curled her lip scornfully at the magician. 'Ye want to find out how 'tis goin', Groddil? Then why not join our brave soldiers an' see for yerself, eh?'

Groddil shot her a hate-filled glare, but did not move.

Force of numbers had finally driven Stonepaw back into the cavern, and now they were coming at him from all sides. A quick glance told him that his hares had escaped safely. He battled on doggedly, wounded in a score of places. Snapping off an arrow which had pierced his shoulder he roared and charged, wreaking havoc with his shattered javelin. But there was no end to the vermin. Lord Stonepaw began to feel weary and old. Fraul sneaked through, with a bunch of soldiers bearing between them a large stone-weighted net. He signalled them to climb upon a low ledge. Some others followed through, and swiftly he whispered orders to them. 'See, the stripedog won't last much longer. Get behind and drive him over, close to this ledge as y'can.'

The plan worked. Stonepaw was beaten back. Facing his attackers, he could not see the trap that awaited him. Back, back he went, stumbling upon the carcasses of those whom he had slain on either side. Fraul shouted as the badger's shoulders brushed the ledge.

'Now!'

Instantly the badger was borne to the ground by the cumbersome coils of the net and the lumps of stone tied to its edges as weights. Letting his javelin fall he lay flat, gasping for breath. A roar of triumph arose from the vermin. Groddil hobbled through the rift to watch. Nudging Captain Swinch, the fox sniggered.

'We've got him now. The stripedog's finished!'

Swinch swaggered forward boldly and kicked at the prostrate badger trapped beneath the net. 'How d'ye feel now, stripedog? Aaaaagh!'

Wreathed in ropes Stonepaw surged forward, crashing the horde captain into the ledge and finishing him. Groddil howled: 'Stop him, he's away again, stop him, stop him!'

Rearing up, Stonepaw pulled the net along with him – it was far too snarled up and heavy to be rid of. He looked for all the world like some primeval colossus from the dawn of time. Bellowing and roaring, he swept one of the big lanterns from the ledge and smashed it into the barrel of lamp oil near the entrance. Then, giving the barrel a powerful kick, Stonepaw crashed it into the rift. Flames crackled and leapt.

Fearing he would be trapped in the cavern and slain, Groddil pranced about screaming hysterically. 'Kill him! Finish him off! Hurry, you fools, kill him!'

Stonepaw began to laugh aloud, the sound booming eerily until it filled the cavern. Dragging rocks and net he threw himself on to the closest group of vermin, wrapping his fearsome paws about as many as he could grab. Four he held, with another three trapped in the net, to be swept along with him to the edge of the bottomless pool. They bit and scratched and stabbed, to no avail. With one last war cry, Lord Stonepaw of Salamandastron summoned up his final strength and jumped.

'Eulaliiiiiaaaaaa!'

Groddil and the Blue Hordebeasts packed around the

pool rim. Pale green luminescence deep down in the icy water shrouded itself around the dark wriggling mass which sank down, down, down, until it was lost to sight. Wordlessly they stared at the waters, the silence broken only by water dripping, flames crackling and the agonised moans of their wounded.

Thus died Lord Stonepaw, he who had ruled the mountain longer than any other Badger Lord.

Hares halting in front of him caused Stiffener to stop sharply. 'Trobee, Purlow, what's goin' on up there?' he called to the leaders.

'A blue light! There's a blue light up ahead, Stiff!'

The boxing hare made his way up to the front of the column. The tunnel was beginning to tilt slightly uphill, and the stones beneath his paws contained small shallow pools. From round a bend up ahead there shone a soft blue light.

Stiffener took the torch from Blench. 'Trobee, Willip, come with me. Purlow, you stop here with the others an' rest yoreself.'

Willip sniffed the air as they drew nigh to the blue light. 'Well, great seasons o' salt, there's only one thing smells like that, chaps – seawater! Haha, I was right! Listen!'

Stiffener's ears picked up the faraway sound. 'Aye, marm, that's the sea right enough!'

'He went up through an' chased the blue,
An' made it home for tea sir,
He beat the tide an' spinies too,
But his mamma tanned his tailfur!'

Trobee smiled proudly. Stiffener cast a curious eye on him. 'You feelin' all right, mate? Is that blue light affectin' ye?'

Trobee chuckled happily. 'I'm feeling fine, Stiff old

chap. I was just repeating the last lines of Bramwil's skippin' poem, the one about Littlebob hare, wot! My old memory must be improvin'.'

When they rounded the bend, the blue light was clearer, with water patterns shimmering off the rough rock walls. The ground began a downslope. Trobee went back to fetch the others, while Willip, who was a sensible creature, summed up their position.

'Seems like we'll come out very close to the great sea. It must run up here rather strong at high tide, but this slope stops most of it. Can't be high tide now, though – this tunnel's too jolly dry. So I suppose we're all right to proceed, wot. The poem says that Littlebob beat the spinies too. Anybeast know what a blinkin' spiny is?'

Stiffener shrugged. 'Just have t'find out as we go, marm. Look, we don't know when 'igh tide is due, so we'd better shake a paw.'

Despite the tragedy they had left behind, the hares felt their spirits rising after being down in the gloomy caves for so long. The blue light promised a good clear day and fresh air, wind, breeze, the sight of green growing things, and most of all freedom. They started singing to set up a good pace, sloshing through pools and stumbling over rocks, but returning to their irrepressible nature.

'There's hares on the mountain much older than I,
An' still they can manage to scoff the odd pie,
I remember ole Grandma had no teeth to boot,
She used to eat rock cakes an' lots o' hard fruit.
Older'n I, scoff the odd pie,
No teeth t'boot, rock cake an' fruit,
A hare is a marvellous creature!

My uncle Alf with long seasons was grey,
"Stale pudden an' pasties'll do me," he'd say,
"Oh fetch me good cider an' no fancy cuts,
An' a big rusty hammer to crack hazelnuts."

Older'n I, scoff the odd pie,
No teeth t'boot, rock cake an' fruit,
Seasons was grey, pasties he'd say,
No fancy cuts, crack hazelnuts,
A hare is a marvellous creature!

My auntie Dewdrop was old as the hills,
She wondered why ducks always ate with their bills,
"Their tummies must flutter," the old gel would cry,
"I once knew a duck ate a dragonfly pie."
Older'n I, scoff the odd pie,
No teeth t'boot, rock cake an' fruit,
Seasons was grey, pasties he'd say,
No fancy cuts, crack hazelnuts,
Old as the hills, ate with their bills,
Auntie would cry, dragonfly pie,
A hare is a marvellous creature!'

19

Ungatt Trunn was furious, though he did not let it show. Groddil, Fraul and Mirefleck lay flat on their faces in front of the wildcat, each waiting to be interrogated by him. Lord Stonepaw's former bedchamber was festooned with fresh spiderwebs, flies caught by horde vermin buzzed about, and the fire was stoked up high. Trunn let his eyes wander to the spiders waiting in their webs. Flies never changed their ways; sooner or later they would blunder into the sticky gossamer snares. The Grand Fragorl drifted silently about in the background, sprinkling powder on the braziers to make them give off blue incense.

The wildcat flicked his tail in Captain Fraul's direction. 'Suppose for a moment that I have you executed. Then the flies would feed off your miserable remains, and my spiders would catch the flies and devour them. So, in a roundabout way, they would have eaten you. Do you agree, Fraul?'

The stoat captain, too terrified to speak, merely nodded his head in frightened agreement of the horrific idea. Ungatt Trunn's tail curled beneath Fraul's chin, lifting his head so they were eye to eye. The wildcat leaned forward, a wickedly curious look upon his features.

'Hmm, and do you imagine that that would make my spiders become as thick and empty-headed as you?'

Fraul's throat bobbed visibly as he nodded once more.

Ungatt Trunn poured himself a goblet of dark damson wine, then sighed and sat back, watching the spiders. Ignoring Fraul's bobbing head, he turned his attention to Mirefleck. 'I'm disappointed in you. I was under the impression that you had the makings of a good captain. Mayhap there's time yet for you to reflect on your stupidity. What do you think, Mirefleck? Shall I let you live, give you the opportunity to improve your ways? Or would you like to feed my spiders?'

The rat did not stir or nod, sensing that the wildcat was merely ruminating. She was right. Trunn smiled, as if humouring Groddil.

'Ah, my faithful fox magician, you disobeyed me again. I wanted the stripedog alive, yet I've been told that many who were down there heard you shouting for him to be slain. I know you three are telling the truth about the stripedog's death. There were too many witnesses for it to have been a lie. But think, Groddil. There's something you forgot. Can you recall what it is, my friend?'

Groddil was far too petrified to answer, though he knew his master was about to tell him. Still smiling, Trunn spoke.

'What became of nearly a score of hares? Did you magic them away? Perhaps they vanished into thin air, or faded into the rocks down there. Tell me?'

Groddil had no choice but to reply. 'Mightiness, I am told there was only one of the longears seen, who escaped, helped by the stripedog. What became of him and his companions nobeast can say, sire. We could find no trace of them, though we searched hard and long.'

Ungatt Trunn disregarded the fox. He was staring at two rats, who were providing the prisoners' escort for Groddil, Fraul and Mirefleck. 'Aren't you two the new recruits to my Blue Hordes? Refresh my memory – what are your names?'

The rat with a disfigured tooth curving on to his chin replied for them both. 'Yer 'Ighness, we're brother searats, I'm Ripfang an' this is Doomeye, my kinrat.'

Trunn nodded as he assessed the pair. 'Former pirates, eh? I like that. Well, this is a lucky day for you. I'm promoting you both to the rank of captain. Exchange uniforms with Mirefleck and Fraul. From now on they are to be the lowest of Hordebeasts. They will be your servants, bring you food, carry out your wishes and keep both your accommodations and your kit clean. You have my permission to treat them as harshly as you please.'

Stripping the uniforms from the former captains, Ripfang and Doomeye grinned in wicked anticipation. The wildcat observed the mixture of shame and relief on the faces of his demoted officers before continuing.

'Not so fast. You aren't off the hook yet, my friends. Before you take up your duties with my new captains you will return to the cave where the stripedog perished. Take our friend Groddil with you; he'll enjoy it, I'm sure. Now, here's what you must do. The three of you will stay down there, until you capture the hares, or find out how they escaped. These two captains will take an escort to guard you. Each day that you are not successful in your task you will be flogged with willow canes and given no food. Oh, cheer up. There's water aplenty down there, a great pool of it – you won't get thirsty. Ripfang, Doomeye, get these idiots out of my sight!'

The unhappy trio were marched unceremoniously off. Ungatt Trunn curled his tail about the Grand Fragorl's neck and drew her close to him, purring pleasurably.

'Did you see their faces? I spared them, humiliated them, they looked relieved. Then I sentenced them to a living death and they just looked blank. I tell you, Fragorl, pleasure comes through power, and power is everything!'

*

The hares sat down to rest a moment in the long, downsloping tunnel. Bramwil rubbed the back of his neck and complained, 'Ooh! 'Tain't much fun marchin' with the old neck bent all day. Ceiling should be a bit higher, wot?'

Stiffener smiled at the ancient hare. 'Marchin' all day, ye say? How d'you know whether 'tis day or night? Looks all the same to me down 'ere.'

Bramwil tugged at Blench's smock. 'Er, how're things on the vittle front, marm? Give young Stiffener a carrot – he can't tell night from bally day, wot. I can though, an' I'll tell ye how. That blue light ahead is goin' dimmer, so it must be evenin' out there!'

Blench turned her bag inside out and shook it. 'H'ain't a crumb o' vittles left, ole Bram. Yore right, though – it must be gettin' dark outside, the light has faded.'

'I could do a spot o' damage to a rhubarb tart right now. Wouldn't mind if it was hot or jolly well cold . . .'

Stiffener glared at Willip in the torchlight. 'A word in yore ear, marm. Don't start talkin' about scoff, 'tis the fastest way for a hare t'go mad. You'll have everybeast goin' on about feasts they were at seasons ago. All that ripe fruit an' crumbly cheese an' summer salad, aye, an' bilberry cordial. Look, you've got me at it now!'

Trobee's stomach rumbled, and he sighed unhappily. 'Yes, let's. Well, what else is there to bloomin' well talk about? My tummy's in a blinkin' turmoil!'

Stiffener peered down the tunnel. 'Then think about 'ow lucky we are. Light fadin' means we got a good chance of not bein' spotted under cover o' darkness. There's somethin' in our favour, mates.'

Purlow started up, batting at his scut. 'Yowch, confound it, somebeast just bit me!'

Stiffener swung the torch in his direction. 'Where?'

'Right on the end o' me bobtail, old lad, where d'y'think?'

Stiffener shoved him roughly aside. 'I never asked where y'were bit, I meant where was the beast that bit ye?'

Blench held out her no longer empty bag with both paws. 'Ah, look, bless 'im, 'tis only a liddle crabthing. Got a spiky back too. Big claws for such a young 'un, though.'

Purlow wagged his paw in the crab's face. 'You small cad, how dare y'bite my tail? Wait'll I tell your mama!'

Trobee grabbed the torch from Stiffener and stared wide-eyed. 'Zounds! You won't have long t'wait, old lad. Here comes his mama right now, an' the whole confounded crab clan!'

They were spiny spider crabs, with spiked backs covered in sharp spines, long red legs and fearsome-looking claws. Very aggressive crustaceans indeed. Blench tipped the baby crab on to the floor in a hurry.

'Oh corks, there must be 'undreds an' 'undreds o' the villains. Wot d'ye suppose they want?'

Stiffener weighed up the dangerous situation. 'So that's wot the rhyme meant, the spinies! Listen to that waternoise buildin' up down there – the tide must be comin' in. We're in those crabs' way. They're tryin' t'get further up the tunnel to stop theirselves bein' washed away by the waves. I don't like the way they're clackin' those big nipper things an' openin' their jaws. Maybe they think we're vittles, somethin' good to eat!'

Scuttling sideways, the teeming masses of crabs advanced, claws held high and snapping open and shut, blowing froth and bubbles from their gaping mouths. The noise of them could be heard over the advancing tide outside. It sounded like a shower of hailstones as their hard-shelled legs rattled against the rocks. The hares looked to Stiffener.

'What d'you think we should do?'

The boxing hare decided instantly there was only one answer to Bramwil's query. 'We've got to run for it, straight through the middle o' those blighters, an' not stop for anythin'. They're tryin' to get away from the sea, we're tryin' to get to it, might be a bit of an 'elp. Trobee, me'n'you will take the lead an' see if'n we can batter through. The rest of ye, stay close together. Willip, Blench, stick in the middle, keep tight 'old of Bramwil. Well, 'ere goes, mates. Eulaliaaaa!'

The charge carried them helter-skelter down the tunnel, straight into the crabs. Trobee and Stiffener bulled aside as many as they could, striking about with a couple of javelins. It was an almost impossible task; hares and crabs were so tightly packed in the narrow tunnel confines that it was difficult to make way. Powerful claws tore the javelins from their paws, spiny shells bumped them painfully, pointed legs scratched at them in the wild scramble. Some crabs were toppled over backwards and the hares ran over their hard-shelled undersides, avoiding kicking legs and snapping pincers. However, it could not last. The tunnel was far too narrow, and soon became completely jammed with a jumbled mêlée of hares and crabs.

Stiffener looked up. A gigantic specimen was bearing down upon him with both claws ready for action.

'Trobee, throw me the torch, quick!'

The boxing hare scorched his paws as he caught the torch and thrust it savagely into the big crab's mouth. It gurgled and hissed, latching both claws on to the torch. It was a scene of complete chaos, with trapped hares shouting amid the forest of clacking pincers.

'Aagh, get this thing off me!'

'Owouch, me ear!'

'Leggo, you rotter, gerroff!'

'Hold Bramwil up, don't let him fall!'

'Eeek, there'th one god me nothe!'

Then the wave came.

Peak of high tide sent a monstrous roller crashing up the tunnel entrance with all the awesome power of the stormy sea. Boiling white, blue and green, it shot up the bore of the rocky passage and hit the mass of hares and crabs like a mighty sledgehammer, shooting them hard uphill. Then it sucked them back in a whirling vacuum of seawater. Stiffener spun like a top, jolting against rocks and crabshells, his nose, mouth, eyes and ears choked by the salt water. The entire world became white and filled with roaring noise as he went ears over scut. Stomach down he was hurled flat, his mouth gaping wide as he skidded along until it was full of sand.

A moment later he was upright in the night air, waist deep, with waves bashing him. Coughing up grit and brine, he wiped the stinging seawater from his eyes. A familiar figure waded towards him. Blench.

'Watch out, Stiff, 'ere comes Willip!'

A wave sent Willip crashing into the boxing hare's back. He staggered up and joined paws with her and the cook. 'Keep tight 'old, marms. Let's find the others. Where's ole Bramwil got to, anybeast seen 'im?'

'Hi there, young feller, over here, wot!'

Only then did Stiffener realise that it was raining hard. Bramwil was sitting on the shore in the downpour, waving a piece of driftwood, several others with him.

Trobee came swimming along, his head popping up alongside Stiffener. He saluted, sank, and resurfaced spitting a jet of seawater into the air. 'Phwah! All present an' correct, I think – there's Purlow floppin' about upcoast. Ahoy there, Purlow, how d'ye do!'

'Fine, old chap. How're you? Lots of weather we're havin' for the time o' season, wot wot?'

'Keep yore voices down, mates,' Stiffener called out in the loudest whisper he could muster, 'there might be vermin patrols around. Bramwil, we'll meet ye in the lee o' those rocks.'

It was a cold, windy, wet and moonless night as they huddled together on the north side of a ragged rockspur. Bramwil could just make out the shape of Salamandastron's dark bulk to the south of where they sat.

'This chunk o' rock is part of our mountain, a great spur, buried beneath the sand an' stickin' up again here by the sea.'

Willip crouched down and scuttled towards the end of the rock protruding into the sea. 'Bramwil's right,' she reported when she came back. 'I saw the mouth of the tunnel we came out of, though 'tis so thickly overgrown with seaweed a body would never know 'twas there, wot.'

Bramwil shivered, shaking his saturated fur. 'Well, we made it, chaps, we're alive an' free. But with no weapons or food. What next, young Stiff, eh?'

Stiffener blinked rain from his eyes. 'Can't stay 'ere, that's fer sure, mates. We'd best move while the goin's good. There's some rock ledges an' dunes east of 'ere – I picked blackberries there last autumn. Let's take a look over that way, eh?'

In the hour before dawn they topped a rise in the sandhills. Some white limestone cliff ridges loomed up on their left. The rain was becoming heavier, whipped sideways by the wind. With both ears plastered flat to his head and his fur thoroughly sandgritted and wet, Stiffener looked back in the direction of Salamandastron.

'See, lord, I kept me vow so far, an' don't you fret now. I'll be goin' back to our mountain, an' if there be a single hare alive there I'll rescue 'em. I promise!'

20

Dotti had never in her life seen anything like the court of King Bucko, nor had any of her travelling companions. It was situated in a broad, beautiful woodland glade, backed by a steep rocky hill, with a stream bordering one side, fringed with crack willow, guelder rose and osier. But there any resemblance to a peaceful sylvan setting ended. It was packed to bursting with teeming life. Lord Brocktree's party wandered about, relatively unnoticed. There were moles, otters, voles, hedgehogs, mice, squirrels and shrews everywhere, but hares formed the main presence. Hares, big, strong, young and bold. Fleetscut nodded at them. He had to raise his voice so that Dotti could hear him above the din as they pushed and jostled their way through.

'Well stap me ears, we've got a right bunch o' corkers here, miss. There's a lot o' mountain hares – one can tell by the remains of their white winter patches, wot. As for the rest, there's a few gypsies, but a chap can recognise the offspring of Salamandastron hares. D'y'know, I can pick out the ears an' faces of most – look just like their mothers an' fathers they do. Dearie me, it makes me feel jolly old, I can tell ye. Some o' these great lumps o' fur'n'bone, huh, I bounced 'em on me knee when they were tiny leverets!'

Dotti giggled at the thought it conjured up. 'Heehee, you'd get a blinkin' broken knee if you tried bouncin' any o' those big hulkin' boyos now, wot?'

A carnival atmosphere reigned over the court. Groups of hedgehogs competed with oak clubs on hollow logs, trying to outdrum one another; squirrels were performing acrobatic feats, flying over the heads of the crowd. A mob of young otters lounged against a stack of barrels, with foaming tankards in their paws, roaring out bawdy songs with no pretence whatsoever to harmony or tune, volume seeming to take precedence over all else. Shrews and voles wrestled in packs, one team against another. Mice and moles were cooking over a huge open fire, laughing as they exchanged friendly insults about the results of each other's culinary efforts. A motley orchestra had set itself up on the lower hill slopes. All manner of creatures scraped on fiddles, rattled tambourines, shrilled on flutes and whistles, battered away at bohrans – flat single-headed drums with double-ended striking sticks – and twanged a variety of odd stringed instruments. Some mountain hares even droned away on sets of bagpipes.

Lord Brocktree was the only badger present at the massive gathering, standing out head and shoulders above other beasts. His backslung battle sword received many admiring glances, and not many creatures tried to bump or jostle him – in fact, not any.

The Badger Lord winced, clapping paws over both his ears. 'By my stripes, how any creature could put up with this infernal din is beyond me! Let's find somewhere less noisy!'

They took refuge on the streambank beneath a couple of crack willows, which afforded generous shade. Log a Log Grenn signalled two of her Guosim. 'Kubba, Rukoo, find your way back t'the ford an' see if you can find a sidestream to bring our boats up here.'

Jukka sprang moodily to a low willow branch, where

she jabbed her short spear viciously into the trunk. 'I like it not, this place of loud fools. 'Tis an affront to the ears an' eyes, a gathering of madbeasts!'

Fleetscut noticed she was staring accusingly at him. 'Well pish tush an' a pity about you, milady. What d'you want me t'do about it, eh? Do I run around shushin' them all up, or would y'prefer me to carry you back to your pine grove, wot?'

Whirling her loaded sling, Jukka sprang down. 'Thou hast insulted me enough, longears. Let's settle this thing betwixt us, here an' now!'

Brocktree was between them suddenly, knocking the sling awry. 'Cast one stone, Jukka Sling, and I'll snap off the paw that does it and feed it to you!'

A hare, with six others attending him, marched up to Brocktree. 'By the cringe'n'the left, sah, you'll be the Badger Lord who's come a-visitin', wot! His Majesty King Bucko wants a word with you. Don't know who you other bods are, but y'd best wait here, wot!'

Fleetscut placed himself in front of the officious young hare. 'Aye, but one of these other bods knows who you jolly well are, earwag. Son of Bramwil, if I'm not mistaken. Hmm, y'won't remember me, but I knew you. Little fat feller with a runny nose, always sniffin' an' weepin'. What was it they called you? Dribbler, that was it!'

The hare, a fine fit-looking beast, sniffed and turned on his heel, stating huffily, 'That, sah, was a nickname. I'm properly called Windcoat Bramwil Lepus the second. You may bring your retinue with you if you wish, Lord Badger!'

Stifling a smile, Brocktree addressed his creatures. 'Fall in and follow me, retinue. Let's go and see this Bucko!'

Steps made from logs led up to the fork of an old cherry laurel, padded and draped with hanging velvet to form the royal throne. King Bucko Bigbones was bigger than most hares and obviously strong-framed. He lounged casually in the tree fork, one footpaw dangling, the other up against the outward-leaning left limb. A broad belt girdled his ample waist, decorated with coloured stones, polished arrowheads and lots of medallions. Around his head, though cocked jauntily over one eye, he wore a gold circlet interwoven with laurel leaves. In one paw he held a sceptre of sculpted oak with a crystal chip set in its top. He cast an eye over his visitors as if they were of no great interest.

'D'ye no bow yer heids or bend a knee tae a king?'

Brocktree's answer was equally dismissive. 'We bow to no creature, even self-appointed kings. Do you not find it common courtesy to rise in the presence of a Badger Lord, instead of sitting draped up there like a drunken beast?'

The Royal Guard surrounding the tree throne put paws to their weapons, but the king shook his head at them. 'Nae call fer that, yon beastie'd prob'ly floor the lot o' ye. Jings, but yer a big 'un, an' saucy too, as I heard. By the rocks! That's a braw battle blade ye bear. Ah'll trade ye for et, anythin' ye like!'

Brocktree raised a paw to touch the double-hilted weapon. 'My sword wouldn't do you any good, and it's not for sale or trade. You and another like you couldn't lift it.'

King Bucko laughed and bounded down the steps, paw outstretched. He gripped the badger's paw and applied pressure. 'Och, I like ye well, mah friend. D'ye mean tae challenge me?'

Brocktree stood smiling easily, allowing Bucko to squeeze his paw to the maximum. Then the Badger Lord squeezed back. White-faced and trembling, the hare was forced to his knees. He managed a pained smile. 'Jings, ah hope ye *don't* challenge me. Would ye not let mah paw free afore ye flatten et completely?'

The badger released his paw. Bucko stood up, massaging it and smiling ruefully.

'Don't worry, I won't be challenging you,' Brocktree assured him, 'but one of my party will. I'll let you know who when the time's right.'

Bucko glanced over Brocktree's followers, then dashed up to Skittles and knelt in front of the hogbabe. 'Hah, so you're the wee terror who wants tae fight King Bucko, eh? Let's see whit ye can do then, mah laddie!'

Skittles needed no second bidding. He jumped upon the hare and began pummelling with his tiny paws. 'I fight ya, Skikkles be's a good fighterer!'

Bucko held him off, shouting in mock horror, 'Ach, get the wild wee beastie off me or ah'll be kill't!' Still rubbing his paw he winked at Brocktree. 'Just as weel ye never breakit mah paw. Ah've got a challenge tae answer shortly. Gang ye along an' watch – 'twill be a bit o' sport tae entertain ye. Guards, bring mah battlegown!'

The guards draped King Bucko in a magnificently embroidered cloak and he set off, with Brocktree and the others following.

A log-circled ring had been cleared further down the streambank. Dotti stood between Ruff and Gurth to view the combat. Creatures packed the circle's edge, fifty deep, while others climbed trees or took to the rocks. An enormous hedgehog stood to one side of the ring, a gang of his followers stroking his spikes and massaging his hefty gnarled paws. He kept shrugging his shoulders and sniffing a lot. King Bucko entered the ring to deafening applause. Throwing off his cloak, he joined both paws over his head and shook them at his followers in salute.

There was a line scratched at the ring's centre. Bucko stepped up to it, flexing both knees and rolling his head about to limber up. The big hedgehog stepped up, threw a few punches in mid-air and snuffled. A fat bankvole came next, who stood between the contestants and roared out the rules in a voice that would have put a choir of crows to shame.

'Good creatures h'all, h'attend my words!' The crowd

fell silent as the bankvole swelled his chest out. 'Thiiiis daaaaay! H'a challenge 'as been given to yore king, Bucko Bigbones, the Wild March Hare of the North Mountains! By none h'other than Picklepaw Ironspikes, Champeeyun h'of the Southern Coasts! Roooools are as follows! No weapons or h'arms t'be used by either beast. Apaaaaart from that . . . h'anythin' goes! Theeeee fightah left standin' picks up the crown as victoooooor!'

Silence continued as Bucko gave his crown to the bankvole, who marched ten paces over the ground and held it high. He dropped the crown, and as it hit the ground the fight started. Dotti could not hear herself think for the noise.

'Och, gev hem the auld one two, Yer Majesty!'

'Show 'im the Picklepaw Punch, go on, Ironspikes!'

'I'll give ten candied chestnuts to one on 'Is Majesty!'

'A silver dagger to a copper spoon ole Ironspikes drops 'im!'

'Watch out for his jolly old left, sire!'

'Don't wait around, Ironspikes, gerrin there!'

With a footpaw each on the line the fighters faced each other. Both ducked and weaved, though it was only the hedgehog throwing massive barnstorming swipes with left and right. As yet the hare had not offered a single blow. He stood firm, merely bobbing and bending backwards, avoiding each haymaker as it whooshed by overhead or either side of him. Bucko was smiling, Ironspikes almost purple with anger and exertion. Dotti could not help whispering to Gurth, 'What's King Bucko doing? Why doesn't he try to hit the hog?'

Gurth kept both eyes on the fighters, assessing them. 'Ee king be a gurt scrapper, miz, ee'm wurrin' ee 'edgepig daown. Lukkee naow, miz Dott, ee king gotten ole Ironspoikes!'

The haremaid could not see how Bucko had the hedgehog beaten. Suddenly Ironspikes dropped one of his paws and straightened up, just for a split second, but that was enough. Bucko crouched and swung a massive sideways left as he came up. Bumpff! It connected with Ironspikes's jaw, his eyes rolled and he fell like a stone, spark out!

Dotti had to shout to make herself heard over the cheering. 'Oh corks, what a fighter, what a punch! I'll bet nobeast could beat King Bucko, eh, Gurth?'

The good mole smiled at his young friend. 'Hurr, miz, nobeast cudd beat ee king at boxen, but oi bet moi tunnel a clever wrassler wudd, burr aye!'

King Bucko picked up the crown and replaced it on his head, and the hares draped his cloak about him. He leapt over the logs, right where Dotti was standing, and winked roguishly at the haremaid.

'Och, 'twas a piece o' cake, lassie. Yon hog was nought but a great fat brawler. Ahey, you're a pretty wee thing, ain't ye!'

Dotti did not want to appear over-impressed by Bucko, so she stiffened both ears and looked distant. 'Actually pretty's the wrong word, sah. I'm a fatal beauty really. Runs in the family, y'know.'

Bucko smiled as he chucked her under the chin. 'Och, away with ye, missie, ah've seen fatal beauties an' yer no one o' those. Still, like ah say, yer a pretty wee thing.'

He swept by her and was carried off on the shoulders of his jubilant supporters. Ruff noticed Dotti's quivering lip and angry features, and put a paw about her shoulders. 'Ahoy there, me ole mate, wot's wrong with yore face?'

The haremaid shrugged Ruff's paw off. 'Nothing. There's absolutely nothing wrong with my face. But I'll jolly well tell you something, Ruff. I don't like that cad Bucko King, or whatever he calls himself. I'd like to take the blighter down a peg or three, wot!'

Ruff stared at her in surprise. 'An 'aremaiden like you, Dotti, d'you think you could beat 'im?'

The noise was audible as her teeth ground together. 'I

don't think . . . I *know* I can beat the blusterin' bounder!'

Campfires burned all over the glade area as night fell warm and soft. Lanterns hung in the trees reflected their colours into the stream. King Bucko's court was celebrating yet another victory by their ruler; the noise and merriment continued unabated. Dotti sat with Fleetscut beneath the willow. The rest of their party had gone off to join in the fun and games.

The old hare had a worried look as he spoke to his young friend. 'I say, dash it all, miss Dotti, I was the one who should've challenged Bucko Bigbones, not you, a young haremaid, wot!'

Dotti poured cider for Fleetscut. 'Sorry, old chum, y'far too old, he'd eat you. Besides, you ain't the one he bloomin' well insulted. The honour of the Duckfontein Dillworthys was at stake – I had to challenge the rotter. Not a fatal beauty, eh? I'll show him!'

The dark bulk of Lord Brocktree loomed up out of the night. He joined the two hares beneath the willow, shaking his head at Dotti. 'I delivered your challenge to Bucko Bigbones. Sorry, miss, he wouldn't accept it.'

The haremaid sprang up, eyes flashing angrily. 'Wouldn't accept it? What d'you mean, sah?'

The Badger Lord shrugged. 'He just flatly refused to accept any challenge from a young maid. I delivered the message formally, with due gravity and ceremony – it was all done with proper dignity.'

Dotti was quivering all over, apart from her ears, which stood up ramrod straight. 'And what did the blaggard say? Tell me, sah, word for word!'

Brocktree's huge paws fiddled about with a thin branch. 'He said you should be at home,' he explained, almost apologetically, 'helping your mama to do the washing, and that the whole thing was a silly little joke. Then he laughed with his cronies for a while and told me to tell you there was no way he was going to fight a haremaiden. Said one tap of his paw and your face wouldn't be so pretty, not with a broken jaw. His final words were: "Learn to cook and stay clear of real warriors, before you become fatally injured, with no chance of ever becoming a fatal beauty." That's it, as best as I can remember, miss.'

Dotti grabbed Fleetscut roughly and hauled him upright. 'Give me that barkscroll you were telling me about, the one found by that Rabblehog. Give it t'me this bloomin' instant!'

The old hare rummaged in his tunic and produced the battered and stained scroll. Dotti snatched it from him.

'Listen t'this, sah – the blighter's own challenge!' Her voice shaking with temper, she read the lines aloud.

'Come mother, father, daughter, son,
My challenge stands to anybeast!
I'll take on all, or just the one,
Whether at the fight or feast!
Aye, try to beat me an' defeat me,
Set 'em up, I'll knock 'em down!
Just try to outbrag me, you'll see,
King Bucko Bigbones wears the crown!'

She waved the tattered barkscroll in Brocktree's face. 'Now, sah, you've heard it. Is that a challenge or not, wot?'

The Badger Lord nodded gravely. 'Couldn't be any clearer, 'tis a challenge right enough!'

Dotti quickly rolled the scroll and jammed it in her belt. 'Huh, that's flippin' well good enough for me. Come on!'

She stormed off, her footpaws almost punching holes in the ground. A wide grin spread across the badger's face. He took hold of Fleetscut's paw, tugging him along in her wake. 'Hurry along, old one, I wouldn't miss this for a feast prepared by Longladle himself. Things are going to plan, even better than I dared hope they would!'

King Bucko was in high good humour. He sat on his

treefork throne, swilling dandelion beer and laughing uproariously with his comrades as he relived the fight with Ironspikes that afternoon.

'Och, the fat auld fraud wiz swingin' both paws like a windmill an' puffin' like a northeast gale, d'ye ken. So ah just ducked an' came up wi' mah guid auld left cross. Whacko! Did ye see the big braw pincushion topple, hahaha!'

'Aye, y'pick the easy marks, don't you, Bucko?'

The laughter ceased. All eyes turned on Dotti, who was standing, paws akimbo, on the bottom log step. The king waved his sceptre dismissively at her. 'Ach, awa' wi' ye, lassie, go an' look fer some babbies t'nurse.' Sycophant hares around the throne guffawed loudly.

Dotti bounded up the steps and shook out the bark-scroll. She thrust it under the king's nose. 'It says here that you'll fight mother, father, daughter or son. That's what it says. Right?'

The big mountain hare flicked the scroll from her paws with his sceptre and tossed it over his shoulder. 'Mebbe et does, mebbe et don't. Whit are ye gettin' so stirred up aboot, mah pretty one?'

Dotti's paw prodded him hard in the chest. 'Don't you ever call me your pretty one, you great blowbag! I'm here to take up your challenge!'

One of the guards tried to lay paws on Dotti for prodding his king. He froze as a swordpoint from below tickled his tail. Lord Brocktree was staring up at him.

'Stay out of this, or I'll make it my fight with you!'

Dotti prodded Bucko again, harder this time. 'Well?'

The king's former good humour was fast deserting him. 'Ach! Ah'm nae goin' tae fight wi' no wee haremaid. Whit d'ye think I am, a bully?'

Dotti marched off down the steps, her nose in the air. 'Since you ask, sah, I'll tell you what I think you are. You're no king, just a liar an' a coward!'

In the horrified silence that followed, King Bucko came

bounding down the steps after her, paws clenched tight. 'Yerrah! Ye whey-faced whelp, we'll settle this right here an' noo. Ah'll no have a lassie cheekin' me!'

He scratched a line in the ground with his sceptre and tossed it aside. Placing his footpaw on the line, he snarled, 'Get yer fuitpaw on this mark here an' spit like this!' He put up his paws in fighting stance and spat over the other side of the line.

Dotti gave him a frozen glare. 'Didn't your mater ever tell you 'tis rank bad manners to spit? Disgusting habit, sah, but quite in keeping with your form, wot.'

Lord Brocktree stepped in, pointing his sword at Bucko. 'No quick paw-the-mark scraps here, Bigbones. Let's do it properly at the designated time. Now, do you accept this hare's challenge, answer yes or no?'

The mountain hare's expression was murderous as he grated out his reply. 'Aye, stripedawg, ah accept the challenge. Ye'll be hearin' from mah seconds afore midnight!'

Brocktree tipped a paw to his stripes courteously. 'Thank you, I'll look forward to it. I bid you good night.'

As they strode off, the badger took Fleetscut's paw. 'Hurry, go and get Gurth, Jukka, Ruff and Log a Log Grenn. Tell them to meet us by the willows on the streambank. Go!'

Dotti looked shaken. Brocktree patted her back gently. 'Calm down now, miss. Temper's the sign of a loser – it affects the reason too much. We've got to start your education and there's not a lot of time to do it in. That's always provided you want to win, eh?'

Dotti managed a smile. 'Oh, I want to win all right, sah!'

21

Stiffener Medick was leading his friends over the dunes towards the cliffs. Dawn's first slivers of light showed pale-washed grey over behind the limestone heights. Rain teemed down unabated, squalled by the wind that flattened the dunegrass. Wet and weary they stumbled onward, assisting one another through the soft sand. Stiffener nearly jumped out of his skin when an otter popped up right in front of him.

'Aye aye, wot's this then, the old hares' outin'? Ain't picked out very good weather for it, mate, 'ave ye?'

Immediately recognising the creature as a friend, Stiffener blew a dewdrop of rain from his nose and grinned. 'No we ain't! Tell you somethin' else too, we've lost our picnic baskets – linen, cutl'ry, vittles, the lot!'

The otter threw a paw round the boxing hare's shoulders. 'Worse things 'appen at sea, eh? Not t'worry, me ole lad, we'll find ye a dry berth an' a mouthful round the fire. My name's Brogalaw, Skipper o' Sea Otters, but let's get you an' yore fogeys in out the rain, then we'll natter.'

Brogalaw led them to the cliffs. He clapped paws to his mouth and shouted at the blank stoneface, fighting to make himself heard above the storm: 'Ahoy the holt, 'tis only Brog wid some ole hares wot've escaped from the wildcat's bluebottoms on the mountain!'

Trobee coughed politely to gain the otter's attention. 'Beg pardon, old boy, but how'd you know that?'

Brogalaw winked. 'Tell ye later, matey.'

A sea buckthorn bush growing against the cliff face was pushed aside at one corner. The homely face of an otterwife appeared, her nose twitching disapprovingly. 'Lan' sakes, Brog, get those pore beasts in out the weather.'

They filed inside, staring about. It was a big, rough and ready cave, full of otters and a fully grown grey heron which stood immobile on one leg, watching as Brog grouped them about the fire. Bread was brought to them, with cheese baked on top of it. From a cauldron by the fire, the hares were served with steaming bowls of stew. The otterwife watched appreciatively as they ate hungrily.

'Good, ain't it? That's my special tater'n'whelk'n'leek chowder. I'm Brogalaw's mum, Frutch. Ahoy, Durvy, break out some seaweed grog an' give this crew a beaker apiece. Haharr, that'll put the life back in ye!'

Stiffener could hear the rain outside battering the cliff face as he sat on the warm sand round the fire with his friends, listening to Brogalaw's story.

''Tis like this, messmates. We're sea otters, see. Lived down the coast, south apiece. Quite 'appy we wos, 'til ole Ungatt arrived with 'is blue vermin. I tell ye, we just about got away with our lives that day. 'Ad to run fer it an' 'ide, we did. Those vermin commandeered our best two ships, stoled 'em y'might say. So there you 'ave it. We sneaked up the coast after 'em, tried to take our ships back. No luck, o' course – far too many of the swabs fer us. Enny'ow, 'ere we be, sittin' in this cave, waitin' our chances, an' 'opin' fer better times t'sail along!'

Old Bramwil told the hares' tale of woe to the sea otters. The goodwife Frutch, a soft-hearted creature, wept silently as she listened, dabbing her apron to the tears. 'Oh, woe is you, pore beasts, least they never slayed nor imprisoned none of ours. Can't we 'elp 'em, Brog?'

The sturdy sea otter Skipper raised sand with his rudder. 'There there now, me liddle mum, don't go floodin' us all out wid yore tears. Y'll 'ave me blubbin' soon. Wot sort o' creatures'd we be if'n we didn't give aid to others worse off'n ourselves, I ask yer? Course we'll 'elp!'

Stiffener thanked him on behalf of all the hares. Bramwil moved nervously away from the great heron. 'Er, don't mind me askin', Brog, but what's that big bird doin' living with you, wot?'

Brogalaw stroked the heron's snakelike neck fondly. 'Oh, this feller. Nice ole cove, ain't he? Name's Rulango. Been with us since he was a chick, never speaks, fends an' feeds for hisself an' washes twice a day in the sea, don't ye, mate?'

Brogalaw stopped stroking and the heron nudged his paw with its long pointed beak, wanting him to continue. He chuckled. 'I forgot to tell ye, don't ever start strokin' his neck feathers. You could stroke all season an' it still wouldn't be enough for 'im. This bird likes t'be stroked plenty! Now, let's get ye sorted. There's pals o' yours, you think, still on the mountain, but y'don't rightly know where, eh?'

Blench toyed with the chowder ladle. It was a nice one. 'Aye, that's true, sir. I can't stand the thought that those vermin villains might be doin' nasty things to 'em!' She began sobbing. Frutch sat down beside her and gave her a clean kerchief, and they sobbed together.

Brogalaw twiddled his ruddertip awkwardly. 'Ho, I can't be a-doin' wid this. Lookit them, waterin' the chowder down. Action, that's wot we need. Durvy, me'n'you'll take a scout round the mountain. Rulango, me ole fishgrubber, would you take a flight round the mountain an' see wot y'can see? Sail careful, though –

watch out fer those blue vermin. Still, if'n the bad weather 'olds out, most of Ungatt's rascals should stay inside the mountain. Well, no time like the present. Let's get under way, mates!'

Stiffener rose, dusting warm sand from himself. 'I'll come with ye, Brog.'

The sea otter would not hear of it. 'Yore much too wearied. Y'need sleep, Stiff mate. Come on now, y'ole cod-fish, a nice nap by the fire'll do yer a power o' good. We'll be back by the time you wake. If we ain't then tell Blench an' me mum a few funny stories, cheer 'em up, you'll be doin' me a big favour. G'bye now!' Brogalaw, Durvy and Rulango were gone before anybeast could argue.

Ripfang and Doomeye, like most searats, were hard and cruel, and they were enjoying their new positions as horde captains. They sat by a small fire they had made from the remains of the oil barrel staves. Ripfang poked at it with a long willow cane while he watched the three creatures searching the cavern, calling out to them at frequent intervals.

'Hey there, Fraul, stay where I kin see yew. Don't go hidin' in dark corners where y'can catch a quick nap!'

'How are we supposed to find anythin' if we can't search?' the former stoat captain complained.

Ripfang strutted over to him, swishing the cane. 'Git that paw out. I'll teach yer t'cheek an officer!'

Fraul hesitated. Doomeye fitted an arrow to his bow. Aiming at the stoat, he drew string. 'Do like 'e sez, stupidface. I'm warnin' yer, I never miss.'

Completely humiliated, Fraul was forced to hold out his paw. Swish! Ripfang delivered a stinging cut of the lithe willow. Fraul's face went tight with pain and he dropped his paw.

Ripfang smiled at him, lifting Fraul's paw with the cane. 'Like some more, or 'ave yew learned yer lesson, winklebrain?'

Fraul kept his eyes fixed on the ground. 'Captain Ripfang sir, I've learned my lesson, Captain Ripfang.'

The searat smirked at his brother. 'See, my one's learned now. Every time 'e speaks t'me it's gotta be either sir, or captain, or Captain Ripfang. 'Ow's yore one doin'?'

Doomeye kept the arrow notched as he called to Mirefleck, who was trying to appear unobtrusive behind a fat stalagmite: 'Stand out where I can see yore worthless 'ide, yew scum!'

Mirefleck hastened to obey, her shouts echoing in the cavern. 'Yessir, Captain Doomeye sir, right away, sir!'

Doomeye looked slightly exasperated. 'This one does everythin' y'tell 'er. She ain't much fun. Prob'ly 'cos she knows she can't run faster'n an arrow.'

Ripfang sat back down by the fire. 'How d'ye know she can't? Go on, try 'er!'

A wicked smile hovered on Doomeye's face. He sighted along the arrow and shouted sharply at Mirefleck, 'Run!'

Mirefleck was fast, but not as quick as an arrow.

Doomeye looked stunned, and dropped the bow. 'Yew made me do that. I didn't mean to slay 'er. Wot'll the wildcat say? 'E might 'ave *me* killed with an arrer.'

Ripfang gave his brother a playful shove. 'Don't be daft. 'Ere, watch this an' lissen. Fraul, Groddil, get yerselves over 'ere, on the double!'

The hapless pair scurried across, saluting.

'Yessir, Captain Ripfang sir!'

Ripfang adopted a serious face and a grave tone. 'Did yew 'ear that Mirefleck? Shoutin' an' sayin' nasty 'orrible things about 'Is Mightiness, terrible things, things yer couldn't repeat. Did you two 'ear 'er?'

The willow cane pointed from one to the other as they answered.

'Yessir, Captain Ripfang sir!'

'We both heard her, Captain Ripfang sir!'

Ripfang shrugged and winked at his brother. 'See?'

Doomeye grinned as recognition dawned upon him, then he was struck by another idea. 'Aye, an' did you both see that 'un attack me'n'this other captain an' try to escape?'

The answers came back as expected.

'Yessir, Captain Doomeye sir!'

'We both saw it all, Captain Doomeye sir!'

The two captains tittered like naughty beastbabes who had wriggled out of being punished. Ripfang nodded towards the body of Mirefleck. 'Tie that thing with rocks an' sling it in the pool, then git on wid yore searchin'.'

Groddil bowed respectfully. 'We need rope to do that, Captain Ripfang sir.'

Doomeye looked at the stunted fox as though he were stupid. 'Then go an' get some rope, lots of it. We needs to tie youse two up tight tonight. You'll be stayin' down 'ere. Us captains got to get some decent rest an' 'ot vittles. Well, don't stan' there lookin' gormless, move yerself!'

Groddil did get lots of rope, a great coil of line from one of the ships. That night, he and Fraul were bound together from tails to necks. Ripfang tested the knots, then pushed the two bound captives down.

'Make sure yer get a good sleep now, you'll be busy tomorrer. Hahahaha! G'night!'

When the two captains had gone, Fraul growled at Groddil angrily. 'Why did ye bring so much rope? I can 'ardly move a whisker. We'll be no good fer anythin' in the mornin'!'

Groddil's reply was even angrier. 'Then be still and shut your useless mouth. I didn't bring all this rope down here just to be tied with it. Those two mudbrains don't know it, but I've found where the longears made their escape from. There's a way out of here!'

'A way out? Where?'

'I'll tell you when you've chewed through this rope. Now get your teeth working, stoat. We'll need this rope to reach the place – that's why I brought so much!'

Groddil lay still. They were back to back, but he could hear Fraul gnawing at the rope. 'And don't be all night about it. We'll be lucky to last another two days with no food and those cruel fools guarding us. Chew harder, Fraul. It's either get away tonight or we're both dead-beasts!'

Ungatt Trunn did not sleep that night either. His dreams were haunted by the shadowy form of a Badger Lord with a sword, a big double-hilted war blade, getting closer each night.

Earlier evening of that same day saw Brogalaw and Durvy returning to their cave. Stiffener and the hares were awake, eagerly awaiting any news the sea otters could disclose to them. But there was none.

Brogalaw stood before the fire, steam rising from his fur. 'Rain ain't let up by a drop. I tell ye, the wind fair chases it round every rock on that mountain!'

Durvy joined his Skipper, and they both sipped bowls of broth. Not wishing to appear ill mannered or impatient, Stiffener let a short time elapse before asking the question.

'Did you catch sight of any hares, Brog?'

'Sorry, matey, but we didn't. Searched high'n'low though, didn't we, Durvy?'

'Aye, we did that, but all we saw was foul weather, wet rock an' the odd glimpse of blue vermin. Nary a hare. Is Rulango returned yet?'

Frutch fed the fire with driftwood. 'Oh, that ole bird'll turn up when it suits him. I'd wager he's out fishin'. Rulango likes to fish in the rain.'

Thoroughly dejected, the hares lounged about, constantly looking towards the entrance to see if the heron would show up. Night fell and there was still no sign of him. Two younger otters took out a whistle and a small drum and began playing a pretty tune. The one beating the drum began to sing.

'Oh I am a sea otter I lives by the sea,
I knows every tide ebb'n'flood,
An' I'll never break free from the sea, no not me,
'Cos the sea's in a sea otter's blood.
Haul yore nets in mates an' let everybeast wish,
That tonight we'll be dinin' on saltwater fish!

Well I've seen 'er stormy, sunny an' calm,
An' I've tasted the good briny spray,
Just show 'er respect an' she'll do ye no harm,
She'll send you 'ome safe every day.
Throw those pots in mates, down deep t'the sea,
Tonight you an' me'll 'ave lobster for tea!

Them waves come a-crashin' on out o' the blue,
Aye big rollers all topped white with foam,
I sees my ole boat prow a-cut 'em clean through,
An' I sings then a-sailin' back 'ome.
We're ashore now mates, let yore mains'l go limp,
I've brought my ole mum a great netful o' shrimp!'

Scarce had the otters finished singing when Rulango stalked into the cave. Brogalaw stroked the great heron's neck. 'Well now, about time you showed up, mate. Did you 'ave a good feed o' fish out there?'

Rulango nodded several times. Brogalaw tickled his crest. 'Yore an' ole scallywag, fishin' while these good-beasts are waitin', gnawin' their whiskers for news o' their mateys. So, what've ye got t'say for yoreself?'

Rulango tapped the sandy floor with his widespread talons. The sea otter smoothed out an expanse of the sand, winking happily at Stiffener. 'Our friend's got news for us. Watch this. Right ho, me ole bird, tell these creatures what ye saw.'

The heron began drawing in the smooth sand with his beak. Stiffener moved close, interpreting what he saw. 'There's the coastline an' the sea . . . now he's sketchin' out our mountain. Look at this, Bramwil!'

The ancient hare joined Stiffener and watched admiringly. 'I say, this bird is a good artist. That's Salamandastron sure enough, viewed from the seaward side if I'm not mistaken. What's that? Oh, I see, it's him, circling round the rocks, about three-quarters of the way up. Hmm, he's drawing a circle in the mountain. Wait, 'tis a window hole, near the top level. But I don't understand – what are all those funny leaf-shaped things he's sketching inside the window hole?'

Stiffener stared hard at the leaf shapes. 'Strange-lookin' things. I can't tell what they are.'

However, Brogalaw identified them without hesitation. 'Why, bless yore 'eart, matey, they're long ears, just like yours. Good bird, you've found where Trunn's keepin' the hares locked up. Is that right?'

The heron nodded his head emphatically, then retired to a corner, where he perched on one leg.

Blench viewed the sketch with dismay. 'Oh lawks, we've no chance of climbin' up that 'igh. Wot's t'be done, Stiffener?'

The boxing hare bit his lip and scratched his whiskers. 'Aye, what's t'be done? A difficult question, marm!'

Trobee slumped moodily by the fire. 'Of all the rotten luck, chaps. The blinkin' bounder has locked 'em up in a place far too high for us to do anythin'. I mean, how in the name o' sufferin' salad are we supposed t'get up there, eh, eh, wot, wot?'

Brogalaw's mother, Frutch, looked appealingly at him. 'Oh, say you can 'elp the pore beasts, Brog!'

The Skipper of Sea Otters closed his eyes patiently. 'I'll give it a try, Mum, but don't go gettin' yore 'ankychief out an' weepin', or I won't be able to think of anythin'. Quiet now an' let me ponder this.'

Frutch blinked back grateful tears. She avoided reaching for her kerchief as she smiled at Blench. 'Don't ye fret, m'dear. My Brog'll find a way to 'elp ye!'

Silence reigned in the cave. Outside the wind whipped up the rain into a fresh assault on the cliff face, and waves could be heard breaking on the shore. Brogalaw nodded to himself a few times, as if confirming his thoughts. Then he opened his eyes.

'Right, mates, 'ere's the top'n'bottom of it all. 'Tis too 'igh for us t'climb up to 'em. But they could climb down with the right 'elp. This is my plan. We needs ropes, good long 'uns. Once we've got 'em, Rulango can fly the ropes up to yore mates an' they can lower themselves down!'

It was a splendid idea, but Willip found an obstacle. 'I don't see any great long ropes hereabouts. You'll forgive my sayin', Brog, but the plan won't jolly well work without ropes.'

Brogalaw was forced to agree with Willip. 'Yore right, marm. Ahoy, Rulango's drawin' again!'

The Skipper of Sea Otters took one look at the sketch.

'Yer a crafty ole wingflapper, mate. Durvy, Kolam, Spraydog, come with me'n'Rulango. There's work t'be done!'

22

Cloaked in lengths of old sailcloth, two Blue Horderats stood deck watch on the bows of one of Ungatt Trunn's vast flotilla of vessels, which were anchored in the bay facing Salamandastron. Both rats blinked rain from their eyes, staring miserably at the mountain.

'Bet they're all sittin' snug an' dry in there tonight, mate.'

'Aye, quaffin' grog an' fillin' their bellies wid vittles.'

'Nah, I wouldn't go s'far as to say that. Vittles is short an' grog's only fer Ungatt Trunn an' 'is cronies. I'll bet we gets stuck on 'alf rations in a day or so.'

'Mebbe yore right, cully, but I wager they're all warm'n'dry an' sleepin' their fat 'eads off, snorin' like 'ogs.'

'Huh, an' look at us beauties, stannin' out 'ere on deck watch in the storm, soakin', cold, 'ungry an' sleepy!'

'Whoa! Wot was that?'

'Wot? I didn't see nothin'. Wot was it?'

'Like some kinda big bird, swooped down aft there!'

'Never! I thinks you needs some shuteye. Y'see funny things when yore tired, or at least you thinks you sees 'em.'

'But I did see it, I'm certain I did, down at the stern end!'

'Well, let's go down an' take a look. If 'tis there a quick chop of me cutlass'll settle it. I'll take it down t'the galley an' we'll share it wid the cook.'

Both rats staggered down the slippy deck, clinging to the rails, and climbed the stairs to the stern peak.

'Well, where is this big bird o' yours?'

'Er, it musta flew off, but I saw it!'

'Arr, yer talkin' through yore tail, mate. There wasn't no big bird 'ere. All the birds is long gone.'

'Oh, they 'ave, 'ave they? Then tell me, where's that big thin heavin' line that was coiled up, right where yore stannin'?'

'I don't know, cleversnout, you tell me?'

'The big bird took it!'

'Why, 'cos it thought it was a giant worm? Don't talk rubbish, mate. The 'unger's gone to yore 'ead. That fox Groddil musta took it. He was 'ere t'day, lookin' fer ropes.'

'No, I'd take me affidavit the rope was 'ere when we came on watch. I saw it!'

'Aye, just like y'saw the big bird. Lissen, mate, you keep on seein' big birds an' vanishin' ropes an' I'm not comin' on deck watch with you any more!'

Rulango dropped the last rope to Brog and his otters, who were waiting in the sea. Silently they coiled nine strong thin heaving lines about them and swam off shorewards, swift and sleek.

Durvy caused great merriment back at the cave as he related what he had heard, imitating the vermin voices expertly, whilst Brog knotted the heaving lines into one massively long rope. Purlow watched the long coils building up into a great thick cylinder.

'Great seasons, nobeast'd be able to lift that whackin' huge thing. How do we move it to the mountain?'

Brogalaw had thought it all out carefully. 'Nine of us forms a line, each one carryin' only a single rope's length.

When we reaches yore mountain, Rulango takes the end an' flies up t'the window an' passes it to 'em. No fancy twiddles, mate, a plain'n'simple plan. But not to worry. Me an' my crew will do it – you rest 'ere.'

Stiffener had a word to say about that. 'Sorry, Brog, but I'm comin' with you, mate. 'Tis my sworn duty. I wouldn't feel right, lyin' warm an' dry here whilst your otters were out facin' all the danger. I'm going!'

The otter Skipper shook his paw warmly. ''Twill be a pleasure to 'ave ye along, Stiff mate. Now there's no time to lose whilst 'tis night an' bad weather. If we puts a move on, there's a chance we could get yore messmates down from the mountain afore daylight. Hearken, crew, we got a hard'n'fast night's work. Let's be about it!'

Though he was an old hare, Stiffener's seasons of exercise routines had kept him fit, and he bore his section of the rope as well as any sea otter. Brogalaw dog-trotted along in the lead, staying to the clifftops, which were easier to travel than the deep sands of the dunes. All nine creatures wore hooded cloaks of soft green-dyed barkcloth. Spume was whipped from the high-crested waves by the rain-sheeting wind, while dried-out seaweed flotsam from the tideline tumbled crazily about on the wet sand. The skies were moonless, strewn with banks of dark scudding cloud. Ahead of the column, Rulango winged low over the stunted grass, striving to keep a straight course to the distant mountain. Brogalaw had spoken truly: it was a task which was proving to be both hard and fast.

They halted not far from Salamandastron's base. Brogalaw and Stiffener, accompanied by the heron, went ahead to scout out the lie of the land. The other seven sea otters sat down on the lee side of a hillock, still carrying the rope. They rested, but stayed alert, ready to go again at a moment's notice.

On reaching the sheer rock face, Brogalaw and his friends crouched in the shelter of a bushy spur.

'Ahoy, Stiff, yore familiar with this place,' the sea otter

whispered. 'Be there any exits or entrances round 'ere, mate?'

The boxing hare blinked out into the rainwashed night. 'Not round 'ere, Brog. Ssshh! Somebeast's comin'!'

On leaden limbs, a weasel sentry plodded by, keeping his head down against the weather, glancing neither left nor right. Brogalaw breathed a sigh of relief as the weasel was swallowed up by the night. 'Ship me rudder, mates, that was close!'

However, he spoke too soon. The sentry coming in the opposite direction heard the otter as he marched by. Thrusting into the shadows with his spear, he called for assistance to the weasel who had just passed that way.

'Hoi, Skel, back 'ere, quick!'

Stiffener heard a note of uncertainty in the guard's voice as he shouted round the spur at them: 'I knows yer in there. Come out now an' show yerselves. Skel, will you 'urry up? I got prisoners cornered 'ere!'

Stiffener came out at top speed, bounding and leaping. He caught the nervous guard unawares and floored him with a massive uppercut. Flinging aside his cloak, the hare grabbed the fallen guard's helmet, shield and spear. Clapping the helmet on, he held the shield high, masking his face, beckoning Brogalaw and Rulango to step out, as if he had captured them.

Rather slow and cautious, the weasel sentry appeared out of the darkness, and approached Stiffener warily. 'Where'd ye find these two, Reggo?'

Stiffener pointed round the darkened spur with his spear. 'In there!' he muttered gruffly.

The weasel edged forward and peered round. He saw his companion lying sprawled on the ground and turned quickly. 'You ain't Regg— unh!'

Stiffener's oaken spear butt rapped him sharply between the eyes and he dropped without a sound. Brogalaw and Rulango dragged the two unconscious guards into the bushes.

The otter Skipper began looping the rope end round the heron's long bony leg. 'We'll stay down 'ere an' pay the line out, mate. You fly up there an' give 'em your end, they'll know what t'do.'

Stiffener glanced up at the sky. 'Too late, Brog. 'Twill be dawn in an hour or so. The journey here took longer than we thought. My friends are old – they wouldn't stan' a chance in broad daylight, out on the mountain face.'

Brogalaw was reluctantly forced to agree. 'You got a good point there, Stiff. So, what's the drill now?'

Stiffener made a quick decision. 'Only one thing for it, friend. Let Rulango take the line up. When they makes it secure I'll shin up there an' tell 'em what's goin' on. I'll take me cloak an' stop with 'em. You an' the bird go back an' hide out with yore otters for the day. All of you come back 'ere at nightfall an' we'll do it then. 'Tis the only safe way.'

Most of the prisoners were sleeping in the high mountain cell. Torleep and Sailears were on duty rota, standing by the window, listening to see if they could hear any news from the chamber below them. Torleep leaned on the sill and rubbed his red-rimmed eyes.

'These two new brutes, Ripfang an' Doomthingy, not much at gossipin' are they? Snore snore all night, that's all they've blinkin' well done. I say, marm, what's the matter?'

Sailears was facing the window. She tried to keep her voice calm as she explained the situation. 'Don't move, Tor, stay completely still, eyes front, don't turn round whatever y'do. There's a whackin' great bird of some sort perched on the window ledge. Bloomin' creature could take your head off with a single swipe of his beak from where he is. Don't move! Let me deal with this, wot.'

She put on her most winning smile and spoke softly out of the window. 'Dearie me, you are a fine big feller, ain't you? What brings you up here on a night like this, friend?'

For answer, Rulango lifted his leg. Sailears was taken aback. 'Well biff me sideways, he's brought us a rope!'

Torleep turned slowly and found himself staring into the heron's fierce eyes. He moved closer and waited a moment. 'Well, he ain't taken m'head off, so he must be a friend come to help us. Am I right, sah?'

Rulango nodded twice, shaking the rope-draped leg. Under the bird's watchful eye, Sailears unfastened the line and began knotting it to an iron ring set in the wall.

'Take it from me, my fine feathered friend, if I were twenty seasons younger I still wouldn't live long enough to thank ye for the favour you've done us, wot!'

Torleep was wakening the sleepers. 'C'mon, chaps, up on y'paws, we're bein' rescued. Woebee marm, I'd be obliged if you keep the old voice down, wot!'

Rulango flapped off into the greying dawn. Sailears had half of her body out of the windowspace when she looked down. 'Well, I'm blowed! Guess what? There's somebeast, a hare I think, tryin' to climb up the bally rope. Look at this, Torleep?'

Torleep squinted down through his monocle. 'By the left, you're right, marm, looks like a hare. Hey there, you chaps, lend a paw to haul the feller up here!'

When Stiffener was eventually hoisted into the cell and they recognised their old companion, there was profuse hugging, kissing and paw shaking. The boxing hare put a paw to his lips, urging them not to make too much noise. 'Coil the rest o' that rope in afore anybeast sees it, mates.'

Doomeye lay back on a straw pallet, facing the long rectangular window of the chamber below the hares' cell. Half asleep, he rubbed his eyes.

'Ripfang, you awake, brother? Was that a rope I saw goin' up in the air just then?'

Ripfang sat up and yawned.

'Aye, 'twas prob'ly Groddil an' Fraul escaped. Tryin' to catch a passin' cloud, the fools was. Hawhawhaw!'

Doomeye probed at one eye, blinking furiously. 'Musta been an eyelid dropped down over me eye. That blue dye plays 'avoc with my eyesight. Thought it was a rope!'

Ripfang was now up and about. 'Y'never know, it mighta been. Let's go an' check on them longears they got locked upstairs.'

But the two rats never got that far. On emerging from the chamber they were faced with the sinister form of Ungatt Trunn's Grand Fragorl.

'His Mightiness would have words with you. Follow me.'

The wildcat looked as if he had passed a sleepless night. He sat in front of a blue-smoking brazier, draped in a silken blanket. Ripfang and Doomeye stood stiffly at attention, both thinking that he knew about the wanton slaying of Mirefleck. Trunn surveyed his two new captains from the corner of a red-rimmed eye.

'You two were searats – you must have sailed many places and seen lots of strange things, eh?'

Ripfang, being the more eloquent, spoke for them both. ''Tis so, Mighty One. Why d'yer ask?' He quailed as the frightening eyes turned to meet his.

'Never answer a question with a question when speaking to Ungatt Trunn; that way you may see the next sunset. In all your travels, have you ever met a badger, a big beast who carries a double-hilted sword on his back? Think now, did you ever encounter such a creature?'

'No, Yer Mightiness, we never met such a beast, sire.'

The wildcat dismissed them with a wave of his tail. 'Leave me now. Go about your duties.'

On their way down to the dining hall, Doomeye chuckled with relief. 'Heehee, I thought 'e'd found out about Mirefleck.'

'Shuttup, oaf. 'E will if'n yew keep shoutin' it round. Funny, though, 'im askin' about a badger like that?'

'Aye. I've never even seen a badger, 'ave yew?'

'Not real like, but sometimes I gets 'orrible dreams about one, a big 'un, like Trunn said, but not carryin' a sword like the badger 'e wants t'know about.'

'Is that right? I never knew you dreamed about a badger, Ripfang. Er, 'ow d'you know wot a badger looks like if'n you ain't ever seen one?'

'I never said I ain't heard of one! Look, will you shuttup about badgers? I don't like badgers, an' I can't 'elp it if I dream about one, can I? Let's go an' get some brekkist. I'm starvin'.'

But breakfast was disappointing. Doomeye prodded with his dagger at the tiny portion of mackerel on a dock leaf and wrinkled his nose, sniffing at it suspiciously.

'One stingy liddle cob o' fish – goin' bad, too, I think. Is this all the vittles we gets? I thought we signed on fer better grub than rotten fish. 'Ey yew, c'mere!'

The Blue Horderat cook saluted. 'Anythink I kin do fer ye, cap'n?'

'Cap'n? Oh, aye. Wot's wrong wid the vittles round 'ere?'

'That's all there is, cap'n. Wish 'Is Mightiness'd get that fox of his to magic up some more provisions.'

Ripfang puffed out his narrow chest. He felt it was beneath him to bandy words with a mere low-ranking skivvy. 'Right, well. Anythin' else to report?'

'Aye, two outside guards deserted, cap'n,' the cook informed him with an insolent grin. 'There'll no doubt be a few more if'n the grubstakes don't improve.'

Ripfang had taken a dislike to the cook, so he prodded him several times on the end of his bulbous nose. 'Bad fortune to 'em if'n they do – we'll fetch 'em back an' use 'em t'bait up the fish 'ooks. Now stop yer gossipin' an' git back t'work. Oh, those two who've gone missin'. Bring us their pieces o' fish – that's an order!' He nudged his brother and winked broadly at him. 'One o' the joys of bein' a cap'n, eh!'

Outside the weather was beginning to clear. Mist rose from the damp rocks and a warm breeze started to sweep the clouds away. Summer had begun. It was to be a most memorable season for all.

Most memorable!

23

The storm had not penetrated inland; it was driven upcoast and out to sea. Dotti sat on the streambank, breakfasting on fresh fruit salad with her friends. The haremaid was now under instruction as a contender for King Bucko Bigbones's crown.

Grenn read out the rules which had been delivered by the king's seconds. 'Two days from now the three events will commence: the Bragging, the Feasting and the Fighting. The Bragging will take place on the eve of day one. Whichever beast wins the Brag will be the creature voted by common consent of the crowd to have outbragged the other. Dawn of day two the Feasting will commence; the victor will be the one left sitting, still eating, at sunset, or until one creature yields to the other. Noon of day three is the Fighting. No weapons or any arms whatsoever are allowed to be taken into the ring. All supporters and seconds must have vacated the ring by the time the crown is dropped. The king has the right to decide whether the contest be from scratch, or moving freely. The moment one beast cannot rise and continue fighting, the other will be declared the winner. Note: in the event of Bragging or Feasting being won, lost, or declared a tie, the winner of the Fighting will be declared outright king. These are the approved rules!'

Fleetscut laughed scathingly. 'Bucko's rules made by himself, eh? He's only got to win the jolly old Fighting an' he's home'n'dry, wot?'

'That's right, ole feller. King Bucko makes the rules in his own court – you've got t'be better'n him to change 'em!'

'Aye, an' you've got to blinkin' well prove it, too!'

They turned to see two extremely fit-looking young hares lounging nearby, taking everything in.

'I'll give you young whelps something to think about if you don't move yourselves!' Brocktree growled.

The hares did move, not away, but closer. They were obviously twin brothers, alike as peas in a pod. They spoke alternately, beginning or finishing off sentences, as if each knew what the other was thinking. Fleetscut was watching them closely as they addressed the badger.

'Don't get touchy, sah, we're on your an' the pretty one's side.'

'Rather, on the pretty one's side especially, wot wot!'

'I'm Southpaw an' this fat ugly one's Bobweave!'

'Fat ugly one? Go 'way, you bounder, let miss Dotti say. C'mon, miss, ain't I the best-lookin' one who cuts the finest figure? Tell the truth now!'

Fleetscut approached them, his paw extended. 'I'll tell you the truth, you young rips. Bobweave an' Southpaw, eh? You're the orphaned twins, grandsons of Stiffener Medick. I can see it in you both, fightin' hares born an' bred, wot!'

'Rather! How d'ye do, sah!'

'Pleased t'meet you, old chap!'

They exchanged greetings with all the party. Dotti took an immediate liking to the twins. Though they had the biggest, toughest-looking paws she had ever seen on a hare, both were extra gentle when they shook her paw.

Brocktree had changed his attitude, and was quite cordial with them. 'So, friends, you have the looks of two very perilous beasts. How can you help us?'

Fleetscut threw a sudden barrage of punches at them. Still smiling and hardly taking notice, they repelled every blow in a casually expert manner. The old hare nodded. 'Your grandpa talked about you night'n'day. Said you were the finest boxers on earth.'

They shuffled modestly.

'Oh, we keep ourselves busy, sah.'

'Always up t'the jolly old mark, y'know.'

Dotti was bursting to ask the athletic pair a question. 'Er, beg pardon, chaps, but if you two are so good, then why haven't you challenged King Bucko?'

'Quite simple really, miss Dotti.'

'Right. If I challenged Bucko an' floored him, then I'd be King Southpaw. But I couldn't give old Bobweave orders.'

'True, miss, an' if I challenged Bucko an' won, I'd be King Bobweave. Hah – imagine me tryin' to give Southpaw orders?'

'Besides, Bucko Bigbones, between you'n'me'n'the gatepost, he's a great big windbag, but he can be sly an' dangerous as well. Makes all his own rules – an' breaks 'em too, wot!'

Jukka Sling was beginning to wave her tail impatiently. 'Then canst thou tell us how the maid will defeat him?'

'Well, we can't tell you exactly, marm, but we can help her by pointin' out Bucko's weaknesses.'

Gurth chuckled appreciatively. 'Hur hur hurr, you'm be a-doin' us'n's a gurt favour if'n ee can, young zurrs. Tell away naow – we'm all ears!'

Dotti learned a great deal by listening to Bobweave and Southpaw. King Bucko liked to play jokes, but he hated the joke being on him; he was vain, quick-tempered and resorted to cheating at the blink of an eye. But he was surrounded by loyal mountain hares and, moreover, he was no fool at fighting and always won at any cost.

Ruff wagged a serious paw at the haremaid. 'So you

see, miss, Bucko ain't no pushover. We got to figger how y'can use his faults agin him, upset his apple cart.'

'Smacka 'im tail wivva big stick. Dat's wot Skikkles do!'

Mirklewort shooed her babe off with a dire warning. 'H'I'll smack yore tail wid a big stick! Go an' play, yer liddle plague. Can't yer see this is a serious conservation?'

Skittles climbed up on to Brocktree's sword hilt and sulked. The Badger Lord reached up and patted the hogbabe's paw. 'Maybe Skittles has provided us with the answer!'

'Burr, you'm mean smacken ee king's tail wi' sticks, zurr?'

Brocktree scratched his stripes thoughtfully. 'In a manner of speaking, yes. We smack his pride. Can you see what I'm getting at?'

Log a Log Grenn caught on to the idea immediately. 'Aye, that's 'ow Dotti'll win, by keepin' cool an' calm. Turn the jokes on Bucko, get the supporters on 'er side.'

Jukka began warming to the plan. 'Play the good-mannered well brought up haremaid. Use thy wit against the braggart. Make him fall into his own traps!'

Dotti's friends all began making suggestions to help her.

'Use his own weight against him. Duck an' weave!'

'Aye, show him up to his supporters as a fraud an' a cad, wot!'

'Keep y'nose in the air an' dismiss Bucko as a ruffian!'

'Hurr, make ee king wrassle ee, miz Dott. Doan't ee box 'im!'

'Don't fret, miss, we'll show you one or two boxin' tricks!'

'Rather, an' when he's least expectin' it, you can use 'em!'

'Right! We'll outthink him at every turn!'

All that first summer's day they sat on the streambank, working out a master plan. Dotti practised her new role of the cool calm and distant haremaid, though she had trouble avoiding the admiring glances of Southpaw and Bobweave, who were obviously smitten with her. Every now and then the twins would be so overcome that they would move further up the bank and box the ears off one another.

Kubba and Rukoo paddled up at mid-noon, with the logboats strung out behind them. Kubba shipped paddles and looked questioningly at Grenn. 'Wot's goin' on 'ere, marm? Are ye wagerin' on which of those two hares'll knock the other's block off first?'

The Guosim Chieftain helped to moor the vessels. 'Somethin' like that. I'll tell ye about it later.'

Over the next two days Dotti wrestled with Gurth, was instructed in the art of boxing by two very enthusiastic young hares, and listened to the wisdom of her elders. It was all very helpful and instructive, except for one thing. Part of her training included a strict diet: no food and precious little water. For a creature of her young appetite it was nothing less than sheer, brutal torture. When meals were served she was forced to sit in one of the logboats, guarded by Ruff, out of the sight of food. Nursing a beaker filled with water with a light sprinkle of crushed oats added to it, she glared at her otter friend.

'Rotten an' stingy, that's what you lot are, miserable grubswipers. When I'm a kingess – or d'you think queen sounds better? – I'll banish the whole bally gang. Everybeast who refused a fatal young royal beauty a morsel, away with 'em!'

Ruff swiped her ears playfully. ''Tis only for yore own good, young 'un. You'll thank us for this one day.'

'Oh, an' pardon me, what day'll that be, sah, wot?'

Glancing over her shoulder, Ruff whispered, 'Hush ye now, miss, 'ere comes Bucko hisself.'

A light skiff with two mountain hares plying it drew alongside. Bucko was seated beneath a canopy with a jug of pale cider and a trayful of pasties and tarts. He grinned roguishly at his challenger.

'Weel now, 'tis a bonny summer noontide, lassie. Would ye no care for a tart or a pastie . . . mebbe a beaker o' this guid pale cider? Join me, pretty one?'

Dotti blinked serenely. 'Thank you kindly, but I'd rather not. I've just finished quite a large luncheon.'

Bucko bit into a tart, and blackcurrant juice ran down his chin. 'Mmm, nought like a fresh blackcurrant tartie, mah pretty!'

Dotti took a dainty sip of her clouded oatmeal water. 'Nought like a fresh mountain hare, I always say. Kindly remove yourself downstream, sah, your table manners offend me. There may be a few mad toads down there who'd be glad of your company. Toads aren't too choosy, y'know.'

Bucko bolted the rest of the tart and licked his paws. 'Och, an' ye'd know aboot toads' manners, I ken?'

Dotti gave him her sweetest smile. 'Indeed I do. Mother always held them up to me as a bad example. Pity your mother hadn't the sense to show you.'

Bucko scowled. He tried to stand up but the skiff swayed. 'Ah'll thank ye tae leave mah mither oot o' this. Another word aboot her an' I'll teach ye a braw sharp lesson!'

The haremaid stared down her nose at the irate king. 'Pray save your threats until the appointed time, sah.'

Bucko signalled his hares to row on. 'Ye'd do weel to mind that there's many a beastie got themselves slain by their ain sharp tongue!' he called back to Dotti.

Dotti waved delicately to him with a clean kerchief. 'Just so, sah, an' you'd do well to know that there's many a creature with a sloppy tongue slipped an' broke their neck upon it. Toodleoo an' all that!'

Ruff squeezed Dotti's paw as the hare's boat pulled upstream, his face wreathed in a big smile. 'Full marks, miss. You was magnificent!'

Dotti kept up the pose, simpering and fluttering her

lids. 'Why thank you, my good fellow. Did it earn one perhaps a smidgeon of that woodland trifle which Gurth made, wot?'

The otter shook his head firmly. ''Fraid not, miss.'

'Yah, go an' boil your beastly head, y'great slabsided boatnosed planktailed excuse for a worthless water-walloper!'

Brocktree poked his striped head through the willow fronds. 'Did our young lady say something then, Ruff?'

'Bless 'er grateful liddle 'eart, she did, sir. She was just thankin' us fer all the trouble we're takin' over 'er eddication. She's fair overcome with gratitood!'

The Badger Lord waggled his paw at Dotti. 'Mustn't get over-excited now, must we, missie? Time for your afternoon nap – remember 'tis the Bragging challenge tomorrow evening. Can't have you overtiring yourself, can we?'

Sitting with the luncheon party, Jukka Sling put aside her bowl of cold mint tea. She listened wide-eyed to Dotti telling Ruff and Brocktree what she thought of them.

'Zounds! Methinks yon haremaid could give young Grood a lesson in choice language. Grood, cover thy ears!'

It was the evening of the first day. Crowds gathered at the log-bounded arena amid a festive air. There was music, singing, the sound of picnic hampers being shared and banter from supporters on both sides. Candied fruit and treasured possessions – knives, belts, tail and paw rings of precious materials, some studded with glinting stones – were changing paws as betting opened. As usual, Bucko was the firm favourite. Nobeast had ever seen him lose, so they weren't about to wager on an outsider.

Amid a roll of drums and a blast from a battered bugle, King Bucko Bigbones entered the ring, with an honour guard of his cronies. He wore his broad belt, his cloak, two silver paw rings and the laurel-twined crown perched on his brow at a jaunty angle. Whirling the cloak dramatically, he shed it and threw the garment to his minions. Then he paraded round the perimeter, acknowledging the cheers by leaping high, with one clenched paw held up.

Dotti wore a demure cloak of light blue, with the slightest hint of a frill at its neck. She carried her bag and stood patiently whilst Mirklewort and Jukka made final adjustments to her flowered straw bonnet, specially loaned to her by Mirklewort for the occasion. Southpaw and Bobweave gallantly helped her over the log barrier, and she entered the arena alone. The bankvole referee puffed himself up officiously and roared in his stentorian voice, 'Gentlebeasts aaaaall! Praaay silence for the Braggin'. Kiiiing Bucko will not remove 'is crown for this h'event. The winnaaaah will be judged by the popular h'opinion h'of your very good selves. The challengeaaaaah this h'evenin' is Miss Dorothea Duckworthy Dillfontein h'of Mossflowaaaaah!'

There was a smattering of applause. Dotti tapped the bankvole. 'Correction, my good sah, the name's Duckfontein Dillworthy. Would you kindly reannounce me, please?'

The pompous bankvole was forced to comply with her request. This brought a few encouraging laughs and some shouts.

'That's the stuff, miss. You tell the ole windbag!'

'A gel that jolly well stands up for herself, wot. Good show!'

The bankvole cut them short with a glare, then he shouted, 'Let the Braggin' staaaaaaaart!'

Silence fell on the crowd. Dotti stood quite still in the centre of the ring and said nothing. Bucko paced about the edges, as if stalking her. Suddenly he did a splendid cartwheel and a breathtaking leap. He landed very close to Dotti, who did not flinch, and began his brag.

'Yerrahooo! Ah'm the mighty monarch frae the

mountains! Mah name's King Bucko Bigbones. Whit d'ye think o' that, mah bonnie wee lassie?'

Dotti ignored him and waved cheerily to her friends. 'Isn't he clever? He knows his own name. It must have taken him simply ages to learn it, wot?'

There was a ripple of laughter from the crowd.

Bucko stamped until dust rose, and leapt clear over Dotti's head. Still she did not move from her place. Bucko thrust out his barrel chest and thumped it.

'Ah'm nae feart o' anybeast. Ah wiz born on a moonless night 'midst thunder'n'lightnin'!'

Amid the hush that followed, Dotti carefully wiped a speck of dust from her paw with a lace-edged kerchief. 'Tut tut, what dreadful weather you had. Did you get wet?'

This time the laughter increased. Raucous guffaws could be heard, some with a distinct mountain hare tone to them. Bucko had to wait for the merriment to subside, his jaw and his paws clenched tight.

He thrust his face forward until he was eye to eye with Dotti, and his big voice boomed forth. 'Yerrahoo, wee beastie, have ye ever looked death straight in the eye, eh? Then look at him whit stands afore ye!'

The crowd waited with bated breath. Dotti peered even closer at her opponent, until her nose touched his. 'Hmm, you do look a little peaky, sah. All that shouting can't be doing you much good – all that jumping about, too. Have you got a pain in your tummy, is that it?'

Roars and hoots of laughter greeted this remark. Creatures at the ringside were wiping tears from their eyes.

'Yahahaha! Pain in the tummy, that's a good 'un!'

King Bucko was shaking all over. Glaring murderously at Dotti he gripped both paws, raising them over her head as if he were going to bring them down and crush her. She nodded in prim approval of his action. 'Bit of exercise, sah, good! My mother always says exercise is the best cure for tummy ache. Come on now, hup! Down! Hup! Breathe through your nose, head well back, sah!'

She moved just as Bucko's paws came crashing down, one of them catching her shoulder, knocking her slightly off balance. The crowd booed.

'Foul! Foul play, sir!'

'He struck the little haremaid!'

Several hares, Baron Drucco, Ruff and the bankvole referee leapt the logs and rushed forward. The hares and Drucco restrained Bucko, and Ruff placed a paw about Dotti, while the bankvole placed himself between the contestants, bellowing, 'Disqualification! Yore Majesty 'as broke the roooools! No creature, h'I said nooooo creature, h'is allowed to strike h'another at a Braggin' challenge. H'out o' this h'arena, sire, h'out this very h'instant!'

Bucko grabbed his cloak and pushed through the crowd, knocking creatures this way and that in his haste to flee the scene of his disgrace.

Jubilation reigned. Dotti was swept shoulder high and carried round the ring several times. Stamping, whistling and shouting, the crowd cheered her to the echo. Gurth and Fleetscut waved to her as she was borne past them; the old hare was overjoyed.

'I say, good show, absolutely top hole performance from the young 'un, eh, Gurth, wot wot!'

'Hoo urr, our miz Dott winned fur'n'square, zurr, but she'm 'ave t'do wotten she'm be told, an' not go a-getten swell-'eaded. Ee king be still gurtly dangerous. Hurr!'

When the shouting had died down, Lord Brocktree refused numerous offers for Dotti to attend feasts and parties in her honour. He whisked the haremaid back to their camp beneath the willows. Deaf to her protestations and appeals for food, Brocktree and Grenn ordered her to bed down in a shrew logboat. Moreover, they posted sentries on the streambank, to ensure that she did as she was told. Log a Log Grenn was as stern a taskmistress as any badger.

'You get some sleep now, young 'un. Fergit food. As of dawn tomorrer, yore goin' t'wish you'd never seen drink or vittles. The contest goes from sunrise to sunset – 'twill be a long day for ye, so close yore eyes. You Guosim, keep yore eyes open, or ye'll answer to me!'

Southpaw and Bobweave had been missing since the end of the Bragging contest. Grenn joined the others on the streambank as supper was served. 'Are those hare twins back yet?'

Baron Drucco peered out into the darkness. 'No sign of 'em yet, marm. You know 'ares, they've prob'ly gone off to some celerybrayshun or other.'

Grenn looked to Mirklewort. 'Celerybrayshun?'

The hogwife touched her snout knowingly. 'Don't let our big words fool ye, marm – Drucco means they've gone off to a party. Oh no they 'aven't, 'ere they come now.'

Southpaw and Bobweave slipped into camp and helped themselves to supper.

'Sooper dooper, scones with strawberry preserve, wot!'

'An' hot mulled pennycloud'n'bulrush cordial. I say, you chaps certainly know your vittles from your vitals, eh!'

Gurth tapped his digging claws impatiently. 'Did ee get yon jobs, zurrs, tell us'n's?'

The hare twins laughed, as if sharing a secret joke.

'Oh, the jobs of waitin' on table, you mean?'

'I'll jolly well say we did, eh, South?'

'Rather. That old head cook'll do absolutely anythin' for three flagons o' pale cider, wot!'

Drucco waddled angrily over to them. 'So that's wot's 'appened to me fine pale cider. All three flagons! I was savin' that for me Season Spikeday!'

Mirklewort clipped one of his headspikes neatly with her axe. 'Stop moanin', Drucco, yew'll wake Skiddles. Lissen, if'n we wants the 'aremaid to win we've got to make sacriphones!'

Fleetscut chuckled. 'Aye, an' some sacrifices too, marm.'

Mirklewort nodded sagely. 'Them too!'

Brocktree took off his sword and lay down by the fire. 'Good. I hope this plan of yours and Ruff's works out, Grenn.'

Unsheathing her rapier, the Guosim Chieftain stuck it in the ground and lay down next to it. 'Aye, I hope so too. 'Tis costing the Guosim their last keg of old plum'n'beetroot wine!'

Ruff chided her. 'Oh, come on, Grenn, stop whinin' about yore wine. Hoho, that's a good 'un, whinin' about wine!'

But Grenn did not see the joke. 'We've carried that keg with us more seasons than I care to remember. There ain't a wine like it in all Mossflower – ask any Guosim. One drop of it can cure any ailment of 'ead or stomach. It can clear up coughs, sniffles an' colds in the wink of an eye, take my word for it!'

The hare twins shared the last of the scones.

'Should do the trick then, wot!'

'Aye, provided miss Dotti knows her blinkin' lines!'

24

Dawn arrived bright and sunny. Ruro shielded her eyes as she glanced skyward. 'More like midsummer's day than the second day o' the season, what thinkest thou, Fleetscut?'

'Goin' t'be what we hares call a bloomin' scorcher, marm!' The old hare turned to Dotti as she walked with her friends to the Feasting challenge. 'How d'ye feel today, young miss? Chipper, wot?'

The haremaid's reply was summed up in two fervent words. 'Flippin' famished!'

Fleetscut stared at her sympathetically. 'I know exactly what y'mean, miss. But remember, pace yourself, don't go wallowin' in there an' scoffin' like a gannet in a ten-season famine. Cool an' jolly well calm, that's the ticket for you, m'gel, cool an' calm.'

The crowd had already gathered around the arena, but they parted to allow Dotti's party to enter the ring. Bucko was already there, surrounded by supporters. His minions had spent most of the night planting tales of provocation, enlarging the insults to their king until it appeared to the gullible ones that he was the injured party.

A table with two chairs was laid in the centre of the

ring, bare save for two plates, two goblets and cutlery. Bucko was already seated, and Dotti took her place at the table's far side. Bucko tilted his chair back on to two legs and smiled sarcastically.

'Och weel, here the lassie is. Better late than never, eh? Don't weep, now – ah willnae raise a paw to ye, pretty one. But mind, ah'm wise tae all yer wee tricks noo, ye ken?'

Dotti shook out a clean kerchief, of which she had brought a goodly supply to use at table. She greeted him civilly. 'Good morrow to you, sah. I hope you're in good appetite.'

'Dinnae fret yersel', lassie, ah could eat every morsel yon servers put up for both of us. Aye, an' still go hame an' enjoy mah dinner!'

Dotti carefully wiped the rim of her goblet, not looking up. 'You can? Oh, that is nice to know, sah!'

Further conversation was curtailed as the bankvole referee entered the ring, followed by a line of servers pulling trolleys laden with food and drink. His considerable voice had lost none of its volume.

'Hearken to me! H'attend all creeeeeeatures! Toooooday is the Feastin' challenge! Choice of vittles is left to the contestants, h'as is choice of drinks! No wastin' of fooood h'or drink by spittin' out or throwin' h'away. Theeeeee contest will take place until sunset, h'or until one or t'other contestant is unable to finiiiiiish! Let the Feastin' begiiiiiin!'

The servers began loading food on to the table. Southpaw set lots of salad, both fruit and vegetable, on Dotti's side, and winked furtively at her.

'Good luck, miss!'

Bobweave tapped the keg of plum'n'beetroot wine, filled Bucko's goblet and came round to serve Dotti. The haremaid covered her goblet with a paw.

'I'll take water or cold mint tea, if y'please. That wine looks far too jolly strong for me.'

Bucko swigged from his goblet and smacked his lips. 'By the mountain rocks, that's a guid drop o' stuff! Ach, a shame et's too jolly strong for the wee lassie, but ah'm a King o' Hares, an' naething's tae strong for Bucko!'

He piled salad, a wedge of cheese and an onion and leek turnover on his plate and dug in eagerly. Dotti could tell that he too had been fasting. She piled salad on her plate and forced herself to eat at a normal rate, though the ten chews per mouthful routine that her mother had enforced at home was too much for her.

Bucko quaffed his wine and signalled for a refill. With lettuce leaves, watercress and scallions hanging from his mouth corners, he gulped the lot, waving his fork at Dotti. 'Nibble away there, pretty missie, ah'll show ye the way a king eats. Mmmmff! This is braw wine, suits me fine! D'ye not fancy a dram of et, mah pretty?'

Dotti dabbed her lips with a kerchief. 'No thank you, sah, I prefer mint tea.'

Bucko held his goblet daintily and mimicked her. 'I prefer mint tea, sah! Ach, away wi' ye, ye wee fuss-budget. Here noo, watch how a wild March hare warrior eats!'

He bolted down the wedge of cheese, tore apart a warm rye farl, stuffed it in his mouth and washed the lot down with another goblet of wine before attacking his turnover. Dotti was so hungry, after nearly three days, that she almost did likewise. However, she checked herself at the last moment, allowing Southpaw to serve her some sliced apples.

By mid-morning Dotti was still maintaining her sedate pace, though she had eaten a latticed pear tart, some gooseberry crumble with meadowcream topping, two plates of vegetable salad and a plate of fruit salad. Which was only about a quarter of what King Bucko Bigbones had downed. His supporters were yelling encouragement, egging him on.

'Ye show her how 'tis done, sire!'

'Aye, scoff her under the table, Yer Majesty!'

Bucko dug his spoon into a steaming apple sponge pudding. 'Ah'm verra partial tae apple sponge. Here, server, brang me yon pitcher o' custard so ah can pour et over this!'

In the crowd, Jukka murmured to Drucco, 'Keep silent now. Don't encourage her to eat fast – leave that to yonder bigboned fool.'

Drucco could not help shaking his head in admiration. 'By the spike, that longear king can scoff, though, no doubt about that. The beast's a glutlet!'

'Yew mean 'e's a blutton, ain't I right, Ruff?'

Ruff nodded, knowing it was useless to argue. 'Correct, marm. Look, Bucko's callin' the referee over!'

The officious bankvole listened as the king registered his complaint. 'Ah'm fair sweatin', ye ken – yonder sun's beatin' doon on mah heid like a furnace. Can ye no brang me a sunshade?' The referee went to the ringside and consulted with several other pompous-looking bankvoles. After much paw-waving and arguing, the huddle broke up and he returned to the table.

'H'I'm h'afraid there's nothin' in the rules that says you can 'ave a sunshade, sire!'

Bucko was forced to eat on as he questioned the decision. He swigged wine and set about a heavy fruitcake. 'Weel now, mah guid feller, is there anythin' in yon rules whit states that ah cannot have a sunshade?' Bucko stole one of Dotti's used kerchiefs and mopped at his brow whilst the bankvole considered the quandary.

'Hmmm, er, yes, well. Tell you wot h'I'll do, sire. H'if the young miss requires a sunshade then you shall both be h'entitled to 'ave one. But if'n she don't, sire, then h'I'm h'afraid you'll 'ave to do widout the sunshade, sire. Miss Dorothea, do you want h'a sunshade, miss?'

Dotti nibbled a woodland trifle thoughtfully. 'Not really, thank you, 'tis far too nice a day. Actually I quite enjoy the early summer sun, don't you, sah?'

The bankvole shrugged apologetically to Bucko. 'There you 'ave it, sire – no contestant shall 'ave unequal advantage of the other. You'll 'ave to feast on. Sunshades are out, h'I'm h'afraid!'

Bucko sprayed cakecrumbs as he glowered at his opponent. 'Ah'll still beat ye, wee miss prissypaws!' He downed another two goblets of wine, cold from the keg, thinking it would cool him down.

It was midday. The sun was beating down on both contestants. Dotti was full. She did not want to look at, smell, or taste any more food that day, but she carried on, keeping up a good front, as she had been instructed by her friends. She marvelled that Bucko, hot and perspiring as he was, carried on bolting down huge quantities of food. He ate indiscriminately now, not choosing one thing over another. Pies, puddings, breads, salads, flans and pasties were devoured without favouritism. He was slopping the wine about quite a bit, but still going at it. Bucko, like all March hares, was unpredictable. He was wolfing his way through a strawberry shortcake when he paused and winked at Dotti.

'Ye can'nae defeat me by consumin' yer vittles slow. Hohoho, ah'm watchin' ye, pretty one. Weel now, two can play at that wee game, missie – ah can eat as slow as ye. Aye, an' still be settin' here taenight at sunset!'

Dotti put aside her mint tea and chose a small almond tart. For the first time, Bucko noticed that she appeared slightly disturbed. She fussed about wiping her spoon. 'Then do so, sah – 'tis no concern of mine at what rate you fill your flippin' face!'

Bucko grinned triumphantly and began chewing his food slowly. He drained his goblet leisurely and picked up a honeyed scone. Slowly he chewed it, ever so slowly, washing it down with lingering draughts of wine.

Shortly before mid-afternoon, most of the onlookers moved into the willow shades on the streambank. Dotti plodded on with a single slice of dry bread, hating the very thought of food, her appetite completely sated. Southpaw and Bobweave ignored her, focusing all their attention on Bucko, refilling his goblet, heaping up his plate, leaning over him as they did and yawning. Bees buzzed somewhere nearby, not a breeze disturbed the hot noon air, the remainder of the crowd at the ringside had fallen silent.

Then the eyelids of King Bucko Bigbones began to droop. His head started to nod forward on to his chest, and a morsel of wild cherry turnover slipped from his half-open mouth. Bobweave winked at Dotti; the haremaid held her breath. Bucko's half-filled goblet toppled gently over on to the tabletop. He did not seem to notice. The king's eyelids drooped lower . . . lower . . . then closed softly, his ears flopped forward and he started to snore.

Dotti continued eating as silently as she could, nibbling on the same slice of bread. After what seemed like an age, she saw Lord Brocktree stamp heavily across to the referee. Blinking, as if he himself had not been caught napping, the bankvole struggled upright.

'Ahem, you shouldn't really be 'ere in the ring, sire.'

Brocktree nodded in solemn agreement. 'I know, sir, and I apologise, but from this angle you can hardly see that one of your contestants has stopped eating.'

'Where, er, what, er, stopped h'eatin' ye say, sire?' The bankvole waddled anxiously across to the table. Dotti stopped eating her bread to point at Bucko.

'I'm terribly sorry, but this chap's been like that for quite a while now. Would you wake him, please?'

But Bucko could not be wakened. His head fell forward on to an apple pie and he lay there snoring lustily. The bankvole was extremely upset. He climbed on to the table, taking care not to tread on any food, and shouted, 'Miss Dorothea, erm, erm, Miss Dorothea the winnaaaaah!'

He went on to roar about how the king had forfeited the day by not being able to continue, quoting chapter and verse of the rules (set down by Bucko himself) and calling on the other bankvoles to bear him out as witnesses.

King Bucko slept on, oblivious of what was going on around him. A crowd of mountain hares lifted him on to a food trolley and bore him off. Still snoring, with his cheek resting in an apple pie. Defeated!

Fleetscut and the hare twins set about demolishing the remainder of the feast. Dotti tried not to watch them, her eyes glazing over in disgust. 'Yuurgh! How can you dreadful savages even think of food! I never want t'see another flippin' pie, bloomin' pudden, or blinkin' salad again in my young an' fatally beautiful life, d'ye hear? Get all vittles out o' my sight!'

The trio obeyed her instructions with alacrity.

'Gettin' these painful reminders out o' your sight, miss. I say, don't hog all that trifle, old lad!'

'Rather! We'll try not to prolong the agony, miss. Pass the scones an' honey, will you, Fleet!'

'Pass 'em yourself – you young rips are too fast for me. A bit of respect for age, please. That damson pudden's mine! Desist, wretch, or I'll report you to your grandpa, wot!'

Lord Brocktree's eyes twinkled as he shook Dotti's paw. 'Two down, one to go, miss. That was a decisive victory, I'd say. I wonder if they've managed to wake Bucko yet?'

Dotti twitched her ears disapprovingly. 'D'you know, sah, I've got a feeling we cheated.'

Log a Log Grenn replaced the bung in her wine keg. She held it up and shook it, listening to the swish it made.

'Nearly 'alf a keg the blaggard supped. Cheated, you say, young 'un? We never cheated at all. Bucko defeated himself by showin' off an' bein' so greedy – ain't that so, Jukka?'

'Aye, 'tis true, miss. 'Twas no small thing to vanquish him at his own game, in his own court, an' under his own rules. Bucko had defeated all comers, I'll warrant, by fair means or foul, until he met thee. Thou art a worthy champion!'

Dotti attempted to rise and fell back, holding her waist. 'Y'mean I'm an overstuffed wreck. D'y'know, I think my ears have gone fatter!'

Jukka heaved Dotti upright, a smile hovering on her normally serious features. 'Up ye come! Grenn, take her other paw. Methinks a good long walk until nightfall will cure thee, miss. If that proves useless there is always an old squirrel remedy for one who has overeaten, eh, Fleetscut?'

The old hare glared at Jukka. He had not forgotten. 'Take the walk, young 'un, tramp about 'til your bally paws feel ready t'drop off. If y'don't I know what'll happen. That bushtailed poisoner'll boil up half the woodlands in a pot an' sit on you 'til y'drink it. Take my word, just the smell of that squirrel's foul concoction'd make a worm gag, and rot the feathers off a blinkin' buzzard!'

Brocktree and Ruff watched the haremaid totter off between the squirrel and the shrew. Ruff sat back on his rudder. 'Our liddle Dotti, eh, a future Queen o' Hares. Who'd 'ave thought it?'

The Badger Lord replied confidently, 'I would, friend, that's why I chose her. That young 'un has courage, nerve and wit. She'll make a truly perilous queen.'

'Tchah, she still gorra biff Bucko tomorrer. I fink she be's too likkle for dat!'

Brocktree looked over his shoulder at Skittles, seated on the great sword hilt. 'Aye, you've got a point there, wretch. Under Bucko's rules Dotti's two wins count for nothing if he beats her tomorrow. Our plans and her work will have been all for nothing.'

'Hah, B'ock plan 'arder an' work more. Skikkles 'elp!'

Brocktree tickled the hogbabe's footpaw affectionately. 'Well said, mate. I wish I'd been as clever as you when I was a badgerbabe.'

Skittles scoffed at the idea. 'Chahah, no likkle one's cleverer'n Skikkles, not no big 'uns neiver, me cleverer in all d'world, ho aye!'

'I wouldn't argue with 'im, mate,' Ruff murmured solemnly to his badger friend. 'He's got hold o' the sword!'

They walked back to the camp under the willows together. Brocktree's mind was seething with a host of thoughts: his father old Stonepaw, Salamandastron, the mountain that was his spiritual inheritance. The army he needed to raise so he could regain it. And Dotti. All of his plans, hopes and dreams rested in the paws of a young haremaid. Granted, she did not lack courage or determination. But Bucko was an experienced warrior, a wild March mountain hare, with countless victories under his belt. Nor was he particular about the way he accomplished them. Was Skittles right? Would Dotti prove too young, small and inexperienced to overcome King Bucko Bigbones in this the most difficult of her three challenges?

25

Ungatt Trunn acquired a new enemy on the night that Groddil made his escape from the underground cavern. Battered, bleeding and totally exhausted, the fox was swept out into the sea. He floated awhile, letting the tide sweep him along, half dead, but half alive. He had craftily hung back in the blue tunnel, letting Fraul run eagerly in front of him. Straight into the spider crabs.

The stunted fox clung to a piece of driftwood, salt water stinging his eyes as he was swept south on the current. He watched Salamandastron recede and swore to himself that he would return one day. Outwardly Groddil shivered with the cold, but inside he was burning with the unquenchable fires of vengeance.

The following evening Ungatt Trunn presided over the trial of four Blue Horderats. These had been brought before him by Karangool, the only other fox serving in the Hordes beside Groddil. Karangool held the title of Captain in Chief in all the wildcat's vast armada. Karangool was a disciplinarian; he lived by his master's rules and laws. Very little aboard the ships escaped his keen notice.

He gave his evidence in a strange clipped voice. 'Wharra these beast charge with, Might'ness? I tell you.

They fish, keep fish themselfs, eat 'em!'

The four Horderats knelt before Ungatt Trunn, roped together by a thick line about their necks. He watched his spiders awhile, then turned to the rats as if noticing them for the first time.

'You know what you must do with any fish you catch?'

Karangool kicked the rat closest to him. 'You, ansa!'

'Give 'em t'the cap'n o' the fishin' party,' the rat mumbled.

The wildcat's voice carried no anger, nor any emotion whatsoever. 'So you know my law. Why did you disobey it and eat the fish?'

Without any urging, one of the four stood up, his face a mask of sullen defiance. ''Cos we 'adn't 'ad no vittles fer two days. We was 'ungry!'

Ungatt Trunn smiled, and the rat shuddered. He knew what was coming; he had witnessed that smile turned upon otherbeasts.

'Do I look fat and well fed, does the Fragorl, or your captain? We are all hungry until proper foraging grounds have been found. But we do not steal food from the mouths of our comrades – that is why we are the Chosen Ones.' He beckoned the Grand Fragorl with his sceptre. 'Give orders to all my captains to assemble their creatures on the beach at high tide tomorrow. These four will be made an example of; my Hordes will witness their execution. Guards, take them away and watch them well. Karangool, stay. I would talk with you.'

When the guards, prisoners and Fragorl had departed, Ungatt Trunn questioned his Captain in Chief.

'What are they saying aboard my ships? Is it mutiny?'

'Might'ness, not yet. I whip 'em, work 'em 'ard, but no food? They talk, whispa, steal! Need food t'live!'

With all the sinewy litheness of a great cat, the Conqueror bounded from his throne and swept out of the room. 'Follow me. I think I have the answer!'

Karangool was fairly quick on his paws. However, he

had a job keeping up with his master as they bounded upstairs.

A guard captain was waiting at the stairhead. At Trunn's nod, he fell in behind them.

Sailears pulled Stiffener out of the shaft of evening light which framed him in the window. 'Hide yourself! Somebeast's comin'!'

Stiffener stowed himself behind some of the older ones huddled in a corner. He heard the key grate in the lock. Torleep joined Sailears, and they stood together in front of the others as the door swung open. Threatening with his spear point, the guard captain jabbed at them.

'Back, you lot! Get back an' stand still!'

Ungatt Trunn and the hard-faced fox walked in. Torleep took a pace forward, his voice shaking with indignation.

'I demand food for these hares. We've had nothin' but one pail of water since we were locked in here. Disgraceful, sah!'

The guard captain struck him down with the spear butt. 'Silence, longears. Lower orders do not speak in the presence of mighty Ungatt Trunn. I'll slay the next beast that speaks without permission!'

Sailears and several others knelt down and began ministering to the fallen Torleep. Ungatt Trunn nodded towards the hares and smiled, raising his eyes at Karangool.

'Yes?'

The fox nodded, satisfied. 'Yes, Might'ness!'

They swept out, the door slammed shut and the key turned.

Torleep sat up, rubbing at his swollen face. Stiffener hurried to his side as he murmured in a half-dazed voice, 'Huh, what d'you suppose that was all about, eh?'

Woebee sobbed. 'Oh, did you see how that villain an' the fox looked at us? My blood fair ran cold, I can tell you!'

Stiffener helped Torleep up on to his footpaws. 'Don't blub, marm, it ain't 'elpin' anybeast. I've got a pretty good idea what they was sizin' us up for, but we won't be hangin' around to find out the truth of it.' Unstowing the rope from where he had hidden it throughout the day, the old boxing hare began giving orders.

'It'll be dark soon an' Brog will be waitin' down below with 'is otters. Sailears, is there any way we can jam that lock so they can't come bargin' in 'ere?'

'Give me a tick an' I'll think of somethin', Stiff.'

'Right y'are, marm. I'll make the line fast an' watch at the window fer Brog an' the crew. Torleep, if yore feelin' better, line 'em up in order t'go. Oldest an' shakiest first, fittest last. We can lower the first lot, second lot can shin down without 'elp.'

Sailears had a brainwave about the lock. 'Woebee, give me that necklet you're wearin', please.'

The fat old hare clapped a paw to her neck. 'You can't have this. It was left to me by my mum, an' Grandma had it before her. 'Twas always in our family, an' I won't give it up. Not my necklet, 'tis far too precious t'me!'

Sailears slapped Woebee's paw aside and wrenched the necklet off, losing one or two beads in the process. 'Don't be so silly, marm, this is a matter of life an' death, d'ye hear? An' it could mean *your* life or death. Anybeast got a bit o' fluffy cloth about them?'

'Here, take the corner of my shawl. Itchy fluffy old thing, I never liked it really.'

'Oh, thank you. I'll need to borrow the pin you fasten it with – looks good and pointy.'

Using the pin, Sailears poked the homely knitted shawl end into the keyhole, popping in a bead here and there. She went at it until the lock was packed tight with fluffy shawl and slippy beads.

'There now, try turnin' a blinkin' key in that lot, wot!'

Day's final sunrays melted scarlet and gold into the western horizon; a pale sliver of silver crescent moon was visible in the deep dark blue sky. Suddenly the great heron Rulango filled the window space.

Stiffener breathed a sigh of relief. 'Good to see you, mate. Is Brog an' the crew down there?'

One emphatic nod, and the heron flew off.

The boxing hare spat on his paws and rubbed them. 'Right, miz Woebee marm, step up 'ere. Yore the first!'

As soon as the rope end encircled her oversized waist, Woebee went into a wailing panic attack. 'Oh oh, I'll never make it, I'm not goin', I'll slip an' fall, I know I will! No no no, I'm not goin', I'll stay here! Oh me, oh my, ooooooounh!'

Torleep bristled at Stiffener. 'I say, old chap, did I see you strike that lady? Bad form, sah, jolly bad form!'

Stiffener patted Torleep's chin, none too gently. 'Now now, don't go off the deep end, ole feller, I didn't 'urt 'er, 'twas just a tap in the right place. 'Twas either that or leave 'er be'ind. You wouldn't like one too, just to 'elp y'down an' save yore nerves, sah?'

Torleep assisted Stiffener and Sailears to lower Woebee's limp bulk down on the line, woffling away. 'See what y'mean, sah, very good, slides down easy, don't she, wot! No bally need for that sort o' thing with me, y'know, don't mind heights at all, not one little bit. Paw over paw, wot, that's me, old chap, turn a bally squirrel green with envy, rappellin', abseilin', call it what y'will!'

A tug on the line told them Brog was ready for the next escaper. Things went smoothly for the next hour or so. Stiffener had got all the oldest ones down and half of the fitter ones when Torleep held up a paw of warning.

'Hist, it's those two beasts from down below, Ripthing an' his confounded brother!'

Stiffener froze. He could hear the voices. 'That's torn it. They'll see them goin' by their window!'

Torleep listened more carefully. 'Hang on, they ain't below, they're at the blinkin' door!'

Ripfang's voice could be heard clearly from beyond the door. 'Oh, very good, Doomeye, wot a clever brother I got, eh? Steals the key off the guard cap'n an' now 'e can't even open the flamin' door wid it! Cummere, let me try!'

There followed a deal of poking, scratching, and some very colourful language. Doomeye could be heard giggling.

'Heeheehee, yore good at this, ain'tcher? Now you've got three beads an' some damp fluffy ole blanket. Any more in there, Rip?'

'Look, shut yer stoopid gob an' gerron lookout, willya? The guard cap'n might come back at any time now. Yore the one who started this, you woggle-'eaded wipesnout!'

'Who, me? I never said a scringin' word!'

'Oh, didn't yew? Let's go an' 'ave a look at those longears, 'e says. Me'n'you'll pick out a nice fat 'un, 'e says. One of Karangool's cap'ns told me they're goin' to the cookin' pots tomorrer, that's wot you said, blither'ead!'

'Let me 'ave anudder go. I'll turn the key!'

Stiffener signalled the next candidate for the line. 'Come on, mate, move. Next one right be'ind – we can't afford to 'ang about any more. Shift yore paws there!'

Bang! Thud!

'Ahoy in there, git this rubbish out the lock'ole, or it'll be worse for youse when we open this door!'

The banging of a spear butt against the heavy door timbers continued. Stiffener watched another hare disappear over the sill into the night, clinging tight to the rope. When he judged the hare was far enough down he quietly called for the next one. A loud groan of frustration sounded from outside.

'Now lookit wot yer done, idiot, you've gone an' broke the key off in the lock, yew senseless rat!'

'Well 'ow was I t'know it'd snap, rusty ole key? Never mind, Rip, we kin batter the door down, eh?'

There were only three hares left in the cell now.

Stiffener guided the next one on to the rope. An argument between the two searats was in full flow.

'Batter the door down? 'Ave yew got mud fer brains? Wot 'appens when the door falls off its 'inges, eh? I'll tell yer wot, there'll be two of us wid a spear apiece facin' three score o' beasts, ye slimebrained toad!'

There followed a scuffling sound and the clacking of spear staves as the pair turned on one another. Stiffener winked at Torleep. 'We did it, mate. Come on, out ye go!'

'Wot, oh, er, after you, old chap.'

'Get a grip o' that rope, Torleep, no time now for bowin' an' scrapin'. Out!'

The boxing hare watched the taut rope anxiously, waiting for Torleep to get far enough down it to let him take his leave of the hated prison cell. In the passage outside the altercation between the two searats continued.

'Owow! Yew bit me tail. Savage!'

'Well, you shouldn'ta called me a slimebrained toad. Fancy callin' yore own brother a name like that. Look wot you've done to me skull! Split it, see, that's blood that is!'

Stiffener vaulted on to the sill, took a firm grip of the taut line and began his descent, with the quarrel still going on.

'Split yer skull? That's only a scratch – there ain't no blood at all, just a liddle bump! Doomeye, come back, where are yer off to?'

Doomeye scuttled off down the passage. He turned at the stairhead and stuck his tongue out. 'Snagglefang!'

Stung by the reference to his single tooth, Ripfang brandished his spear and chased after his brother. 'Right, that's done it. There was no call fer that. I'll crack yore skull good'n'proper when I get yer!'

Willing paws guided Stiffener to the ground, then Brogalaw was hugging him fiercely. 'Good to see your ole face again, mate!'

The boxing hare looked about at his friends. 'Thanks for yore help, Brog. I kept my promise to Lord Stonepaw.

There ain't a hare left on Salamandastron.'

'Oh, 'tis so sad. Our home is nought but a vermin den now!' Woebee wept into her apron.

Stiffener put a paw about her shaking shoulders. 'There there, don't take on so, marm, we'll be back, I promise you. Sorry I 'ad to knock you out like that. 'Ope it didn't 'urt too much, marm?'

The old harewife dried her eyes and sniffed. 'You did the right thing, sah. I was bein' very silly, carryin' on like that. If I'd had enough sense I'd have hit me for such shockin' behaviour! Oh, isn't it good that nice mister Brogalaw an' his otters helped us like this!'

The sea otter Skipper bowed gallantly. 'Thankee, marm, but may'ap we could carry on this discussion elsewheres. It don't do to linger round 'ere. Durvy, take our friends t'the cave. Rulango, go with 'em t'see none get lost. Me an' the rest o' the crew will follow, wipin' out our trail. See ye back at the holt, Stiff.'

With Durvy leading, Stiffener in the rear and the heron hovering overhead, the escaped prisoners scurried off towards the clifftops. Brogalaw and his crew began cutting bushy branches from the shrubbery growing out the rocks to erase the trail.

'Don't leave a pawprint showin' anywheres, mates, or those bluebottoms o' Trunn's will be payin' our holt a visit!'

One of the crew stirred the captured sentries with his paw. Bound and gagged tightly, they rolled their eyes fearfully.

'Wot do we do with these two beauties, Brog?'

Brogalaw gnawed his lip thoughtfully. 'I know they're only vermin, but I ain't never slayed an 'elpless beast afore an' I'm not startin' now. Leave 'em tied up 'ere. The moment we're gone they'll start breakin' themselves loose. They can be Trunn's problem – leastways that scum'll know he's not havin' things all 'is own way when they makes their report. Right, let's make a move, mates.'

The Hordebeasts wriggled furiously with their bonds, once Brog's party had departed. But a sea otter knows his ropes. It would be some time before the prisoners could hope to be even slightly loose.

26

Brog and his crew arrived back at the cave in broad daylight. It was a fine summer morn, with light breezes coming in from the sea. Stiffener and the hares had only just got there ahead of Brog's party. The trek along the cliffs, after climbing down from a mountain top, had worn the older ones out, and Durvy had been forced to make a few rest stops along the way. Greetings and introductions were still being made as Brog entered the cave. He joined Stiffener and put a paw to his brow in mock despair.

'Seasons o'saltsea, Stiff mate, couldn't you 'ave left that ole Woebee creature be'ind? We got three of 'em blubbin' now!'

Brogalaw's mother Frutch and Blench the cook were being helped by Woebee to stir the chowder pot. All three were sobbing and sniffling gratefully for the hares' deliverance.

Brog nodded to the two musical young otters, who broke out their small drum and whistle and struck up a song.

'Now have ye been away far,
To tarry an' to roam?

Well sit ye by the fireside,
Welcome to yore home!
The kettle's on to boil,
Flames a-burnin' bright,
No more you'll sleep alone,
'Neath those stars at night,
Take off yore trav'llin' cloak,
Come put yore paws up 'ere,
Put a smile in my ole eye,
Take away this weary tear,
You've come home mate!
An' in time for supper too,
So it feels just great,
To say welcome home to you!'

Frutch brightened up immediately. She kissed her son's cheek. 'Oh, Brog, you got 'em t'sing our song. Remember I used to bounce you on me tail an' sing it t'you when you was just a liddle fat otterkit? Such a chubby smilin' babe you were!'

The sea otter Skipper's tail curled with embarrassment. 'Mum, d'you 'ave to go on like that in front o' everybeast!'

Stiffener patted his friend's well-muscled back. 'I wouldn't complain if'n my mum was around to say things like that, mate. Let's see if we can learn about wot's goin' on among the vermin inside Salamandastron from Sailears an' Torleep. Might 'elp us to make a few plans, what d'ye say – me liddle fat otterkit?'

The boxing hare dodged a swipe of Brog's rudderlike tail and led him over to where the two hares sat.

Later that night the fires burned low. Nearly fourscore hares had been found places to sleep and Blench was helping Frutch and Woebee to bake bread for breakfast. Stiffener and Brogalaw listened long and carefully to the two hares' account of all they had heard and seen whilst in captivity. Then, allowing the pair to get some rest, they sat together making plans.

'So, that's the lie o' the land, Brog. What d'you think?'

The sea otter added some old pine cones to the fire. 'One thing's clear, Stiff – the bluebottoms are low on vittles. Feedin' an army that size takes some doin', mate. Trunn will have t'send foragin' parties into the land 'ereabouts. D'ye catch my drift?'

Stiffener smiled grimly. A good scheme was forming. 'Aye, I'm with ye, Brog. We don't 'ave the numbers to go up against Trunn an' invade the mountain. But we can certainly try to cut off the villain's food supplies, eh!'

'Right y'are, messmate, an' this's 'ow we'll do it. I'll post Rulango to keep a lookout from the air – he can fly well out o' arrow range. Whenever he sees a foragin' party set out, he'll report to us which direction they're a-goin'.'

Stiffener warmed to the idea eagerly. 'Our crews can harass them, cut 'em off, steal their supplies, duck an' weave, hit 'em when they're least expectin' it!'

Brog chuckled as he poked a stray pine cone back into the fire. 'They say an army marches an' fights on its stomach. Hah, let's see wot those vermin can do on empty stomachs! Even if they tries to go seaward an' fish we can hammer 'em. My crew was born in salt water – they knows more about the sea than any vermin from the land!'

Stiffener Medick and Skipper Brogalaw clasped paws.

'We'll teach 'em the art o' war, mate!'

'Aye, an' 'twill be the 'ardest lesson they ever learned!'

Mid-morning sunlight shafted into the passage from the cell window when the door was smashed down. Ungatt Trunn stared blankly at the empty prison. After a moment, he strode inside and leaned on the sill. Fragorl, the guard captain and a patrol of Hordebeasts stood apprehensively in the passage, waiting for the wildcat's wrath to descend on them.

Trunn removed his helmet, closed both eyes and

massaged his temples slowly. When he finally spoke, his voice was a barely controlled growl with a high-pitched hiss behind it.

'I don't want to know who stole the key, nor who snapped it off in the lock. I don't want to hear excuses or explanations from any of you. I don't want to know how the hares escaped, or where they've gone. But before the sun sets today, I want to see threescore longears back here. Take your patrols, scour the countryside, send vessels to search the waters and coast north and south of here. But before you go, come down to the shore and watch what happens to four creatures who ate a few fish without asking. Then, all of you, ask yourselves this question. If the mighty Ungatt Trunn could have four beasts executed for a couple of mouthfuls of fish, what fate would he devise for the entire guard patrol of this level, who managed to let sixty valuable prisoners escape? Think!'

Captain in Chief Karangool came marching up as the wildcat emerged from the mountain.

'Might'ness!'

Ungatt Trunn eyed him warily. 'What is it, captain?'

'Two soldiers, they find sentries who desert, at dawn!'

A sigh of relief almost escaped the wildcat, but he checked it. 'Ah, the pair who deserted the night before last. Where were they found? Who were the soldiers who found them?'

'They walk here, into main gate. Two soldiers on sentry round mountain were there.'

The wildcat spoke his mind aloud. 'So, the two sentries who were supposed to be patrolling round the mountain all night spent their time idling in the shelter of the main gate, by the guard fire no doubt. They were wakened by the two other fools walking in, so they arrested them. Is that it?'

'Ya, Might'ness!'

'Where are the two deserters now?'

'Sentries know Might'ness rules 'bout runaway beasts. They slay 'em for break of your law.'

The wildcat made a pawmark in the sand and stared at it. 'Why am I surrounded by halfwits and dunderheads?' he hissed.

'Might'ness?'

'Nothing, captain. Have the two sentries tied up with the four to be executed. Make certain Fragorl tells everybeast why they must pay the penalty. Sleeping on guard and shirking their patrol duties, and so on and so on. I've got other things to think about. Captain, before you sailed for me, what did you do?'

Karangool indicated a faded tattoo on his paw and the hole in his ear, where a big brass ring once hung. 'Might'ness, I was corsair, long 'go.'

The assembled Hordes on the beach stood watching their leader conversing earnestly with his Captain in Chief.

'Tell me, did you ever come across a badger?'

'One time.'

'A male badger, in his prime, carrying a double-hilted war blade over his shoulder?'

'Nah, Might'ness, old female badger I see, dead.'

Trunn suddenly lost interest in the conversation and stalked down to the execution site. Hordebeasts heard him muttering to himself as he passed them.

'I cannot see your face, but I see you every night. Yet nobeast has even heard of you. But we will meet, ah yes, badger, we will meet. And then you'll see what a wildcat looks like before you die.'

Noon sun had passed its zenith when Rulango alighted on a dune close to the cave. Brogalaw was waiting for him. He cleared a patch in the sand, to let the heron sketch out his report of what he had seen. Brogalaw stared tight-lipped as the drawing unfolded before him.

Stiffener came out of the cave with Frutch, munching

on a slice of flat pastry with obvious enjoyment. Frutch carried two more pieces on a platter. Stiffener popped in the final bit, licking crumbs off his paw. 'Beech'n'hazelnut slice, eh, marm? Yore own recipe, too. No wonder Brog looks well, feedin' off vittles like yores.'

Frutch twitched her rudder at the compliment. 'Our bird likes it too, y'know. 'Tis a mix of sliced nuts an' plum preserve baked atop a shortbread biscuit.' Nearing her son and the heron, Frutch called, 'I brought yore favourite slice, fresh from the oven!'

Rulango stood on one leg and looked distant, while Brog hastily obliterated the picture from the sand with his footpaw.

'Good ole Mum. Brought the raspberry cordial too, did ye?'

'Land sakes, I'll fetch the oven out an' the table'n'chairs if'n you like, Brogalaw. Talk about chasin' after an ungrateful son. Here, y'great lump, get this down ye!'

Brogalaw and Rulango set about their slices eagerly. Frutch stroked the big bird's neck affectionately. 'Bless 'is feathers, there's a bird who never complains an' knows wot's good for him. What's he been drawin', Brog?'

The sea otter appeared suddenly absent-minded. 'Oh, 'twas nothin' for you t'worry yore pretty ole 'ead about. Ahoy, Mum, we're thirsty. Where's that cordial, eh?'

She trundled off down the dune. 'I'll go an' fetch it.'

Stiffener tapped a paw in the sand. 'So then, matey, just wot was yore bird sketchin'?'

Brog dropped his voice a tone. 'D'you know wot that wickedbeast did to six of 'is own? Had 'em bound together with rocks an' drowned in the sea. Aye, 'tis true. All the bluebottoms, whole hordes of 'em, was made to stand an' watch the pore wretches, screamin' an' pleadin' for their lives. Stiff, wot makes anybeast foller a master like that?'

Stiffener doodled sand patterns with his paw. 'Who knows, Brog? Fear, wantin' to be on the side of a conqueror who always wins. Maybe the vermin join 'is ranks 'cos deep down they're as bad'n'evil as Trunn hisself.'

The sea otter Skipper shuddered and shook himself. 'Time we started strikin' back now, Stiff. Let's take a look at this otter'n'hare crew of ours, see wot weapons they're best suited to besides knives'n'forks.'

27

It was noon of the third day at the court of King Bucko Bigbones, time for the Fighting challenge. Spectators were packed tight around the arena; others sat on the hillside or climbed trees. However, there was no air of festive gaiety. This was serious business; the outcome would decide which hare picked up the crown. The high bright sun presided over a silent and solemn crowd. A furtive whisper rustled about Bucko and his seconds as they made their way to the ring through the path which fell open before them.

The mountain hare had discarded his broad belt for the event, and a paunch which had not been visible before was now clearly evident. Creatures commented on it in hushed tones.

'I say, whatever happened to the trim waist he had, wot?'

'Too much scoff an' not enough exercise if y'ask me!'

'Maybe so, but ole Bucko still looks dangerous enough to do the job. I wouldn't fancy facin' him, no sir!'

'Och aye, yon king's a big braw beastie, near twice the size o' the wee lassie. Ah'm thinkin' 'twill all be o'er if he lands the bairn one guid blow!'

Bucko took the log barrier at a bound, his cloak

swirling as he tossed it to his seconds. He jammed his sceptre between two of the logs, balancing the laurel-wreathed gold coronet on it. Then, grim-faced, he sat down to wait, acknowledging the presence of the bankvole referee with a curt nod. Glancing up at the sun, Bucko judged which would be the best position to take up without being dazzled. After a while some of the onlookers began whispering among themselves. Dotti had not yet put in an appearance. Bucko sat calm and motionless.

Lord Brocktree and his party led Dotti through the aisle of creatures which opened from the stream side. He and Ruff stepped into the arena, followed by Dotti and Gurth. The haremaid was simply clad in a short green tunic. She sat down on the logs on the opposite side to Bucko, giving him scarce a glance.

Waddling to the centre of the ring, the bankvole began his preamble. 'Good creatures, h'attend meeeeee! Toooooday h'is the day o' the Fightin' challenge, an' the rooooools h'are h'as folloooows. No weapons h'or arms can be heeeee—'

Bucko stood up and cut him short. 'Och, awa' an' stop wearin' yer auld gob oot. We ken the rules as guid as anybeast here. Let's get on wi' it!'

A roar of approval arose as the pompous bankvole fled the ring. Ruff winked at the haremaid as he and the others stepped outside the logs bordering the arena. 'Go to it, missie. Remember wot you've got t'do!'

Dotti leapt up and dashed to the line scored in the earth. She scraped her footpaw along it, calling to her opponent, 'Come on, Bucko, let's have you up to scratch, come an' face me across this line. I'm waitin'!'

The mountain hare swaggered slowly across, but he did not put his footpaw on the mark. It was obvious he expected some sort of trick. He winked knowingly at Dotti.

'Yer a canny wee beastie, but ah'm no fooled by ye. You

an' yer friends've cooked somethin' up, ah can tell. So yer no' gettin' mah footpaw on yon mark. D'ye ken whit the rules say, pretty one? Ah'll tell ye. Them rules say, the king, that's mahself, has the right tae decide whether this contest be frae scratch or movin' freely!'

He smiled at the disappointment which clouded her face. 'So, mah bonny wee thing, 'tis goin' tae be movin' freely, that's mah decision. Och, dinnae look sae sad aboot it!'

Dotti twitched both ears impertinently. 'Oh, I don't know, sah, you may be the one who ends up lookin' sad, wot?'

Bucko did actually look sad for a moment as he pondered his big clenched left paw. 'Ye've brought this on yersel', missie. Ah'll be fair grieved tae lay ye oot flat – ah've no raised mah paw tae a lassie afore. Ah promise not tae hit ye too hard.'

Dotti moved a little closer to him. 'Thankee, sah, an' I promise not t'let you hit me at all. Now, do we stand here jaw-waggin' all afternoon, or shall we get on with it? What d'you say, eh?'

Dotti was ready. She saw the hard knobbly paw move in a quick arc. Falling flat, she kicked Bucko's footpaws from under him, leapt upright and fled. The crowd roared aloud at her clever move.

'Haha, did y'see that? She sat him down good'n'hard!'

'Aye, an' without even landin' a proper blow. Hohoho!'

Bucko scrambled upright, flicking dust from his scut, and went after the haremaid like a charging bull. Dotti skidded to a halt as he rushed by her. This time she stood her ground when he turned and charged once more, waiting until he was almost on top of her. Again she went down, falling flat on her back, both hind legs shooting up like pistons. Bucko's own weight and momentum carried him straight on to her. Air whooshed from his stomach as it came in contact with Dotti's footpaws, and he went ears over scut, landing hard on his back in a cloud of dust. Dotti was up and running again.

Bucko arose, but not so speedily this time, one paw clutching his stomach. He did not give chase, but circled swiftly and cut off Dotti's escape as he backed her against the logs. This time it was his turn to throw himself down, his long powerful footpaws lashing out at her.

Thunk! King Bucko gasped aloud with pain. Dotti had jumped backwards on to the log boundary, and the noise was audible as her opponent's footpaws hit the wood. She cleared his head at a bound and trotted to the centre of the ring. Bucko took a moment to pull a splinter from his footpaw, then he got upright purposefully and limped out to meet her.

They faced each other, Dotti breathing hard, but Bucko breathing harder. His eyes were red with wrath.

'Stan' an' fight me, ye wee whelp!' He lashed out with a surprisingly quick left paw.

Dotti dropped into a crouch, hearing it whistle overhead. She stayed stooped, putting into practice what the twins had taught her. One two three! Dotti whacked at the stomach protruding in front of her. Bucko's flailing right thudded against the side of her head. Stars exploded in her eyes, and the crowd noise suddenly seemed very distant. Bucko's left looped round her head and tightened on her neck.

'Och, ye've got her noo, Majesty!'

Roaring darkness filled Dotti's brain as the breath was cut off in her throat by Bucko's grip. Dimly she could hear the hare twins bellowing in unison: 'The old bread basket, miss! Give it him in the basket!'

She knew what they meant. Swinging her right furiously she pummelled the king's stomach, and as he gasped she slid out of his stranglehold. She found herself facing his back, and shoved hard, knocking Bucko face down.

He struggled up, spitting earth and wiping dust from

both eyes. Lowering his head for a vicious butt, he hurtled forward. Dazed as she was, Dotti knew she had to act quickly. Holding position, the haremaid sucked in her stomach and arched her back. The mountain hare's bowed head struck her fractionally, jarring her hip. Clenching both paws, she brought them down in a sharp double blow on the back of Bucko's neck.

Once! Twice!

Still bent double, Bucko carried on another three paces, staggering crazily. Then he crumpled and fell.

A deathly hush fell upon the crowd. Dotti walked across and stood over the fallen king. A voice from the crowd split the silence.

'Finish him off!'

Dotti turned and glared in the direction of the shout. 'Why don't you try it yourself? Come on! This hare is a brave fighter. He could still finish you off from where he lies, whoever you are!'

Bending wearily, she tried to lift Bucko, but she collapsed with fatigue alongside him. The mountain hare opened one eye and gave her a battered smile.

'Mah thanks to ye for that, lassie. 'Twas weel said!'

Lord Brocktree and Ruff supported Bucko back to the log surround. Dotti followed, limping as she leaned heavily on Grenn and Jukka. They sat sharing a pail of water from a ladle, the victor and the vanquished. Brocktree and Ruff positioned themselves behind the pair, stopping the numerous paws trying to pat their backs.

'Well done! What a sooper dooper scrap, wot!'

'Och, 'twas wan tae tell yer bairns aboot in seasons tae come!'

'Bravely fought! Never seen anythin' like it in me bally life. What courage!'

'Staaaand baaaack there, h'everybeast, give these two h'animals room t'breathe. Staaaaaand baaaack, h'I say!' The bankvole referee pushed his way through, bearing the crown and sceptre.

Bucko placed a paw about Dotti's shoulder. 'Ah'd take et if I were ye, Dorothea. Ye beat me fair'n'square, lassie. Ah couldnae think o' anybeast more deservin' of mah title than ye. Och, yer a fatal beauty so y'are!'

'And you, sah, are a valiant an' brave warrior!' She passed the crown and sceptre to Lord Brocktree. 'Here y'are, sah, crown an' thingummy. Don't rightly know what I'm supposed to do with the confounded things.'

Bucko was taken aback. 'Ach, ye mean ye don't want mah croon an' sceptre?'

Dotti shook her head. 'No, not really. The plan wasn't for me to become queen or kingess or anythin' like that. No, we had a bigger idea, and one which we think will appeal to a great perilous warrior like y'self, sah! Don't you realise you've practically got a blinkin' great army here at your court, Buck?'

The former king shrugged ruefully. 'Aye, 'twas mah intention that one day ah'd knock 'em intae shape as an army. Then ah could've found mah enemy an' marched against him with these braw beasts at mah back.'

Brocktree patted Bucko's shoulder. 'Well, your time has come, sir. You can help us rally this crew into a great fighting force to follow us to Salamandastron and face Ungatt Trunn.'

'Ungatt Trunn the wildcat? Haud on there, Brock, yon's the very foe ah'm bound tae find an' slay!'

Dotti gaped in surprise at the mountain hare. 'You're jokin', of course, sah?'

'Ach, 'tis nae joke, lassie. Feel mah back!'

The haremaid ran her paw across the welted ridges of flesh beneath the fur of Bucko's back. 'He did this?'

For the first time since she had known the tough hare, Dotti saw a single tear course down his cheek.

'Flogged me with the flat o' mah own sword 'til it breakit o'er mah back, an' drove mah hares from oor hame in the North Mountains. That's the beastie they call Ungatt Trunn for ye. Aye, the whippin' was carried oot by a fox called Karangool, on Trunn's orders. Karangool, och, there's a vermin wouldnae sleep easy if he knew Bucko Bigbones was still alive an' drawin' breath. The rogue thought he'd left me fer dead, ye ken!'

Dotti felt a wave of pity sweep over her. She squeezed the mountain hare's big scarred paw. 'Let's go somewhere more private an' discuss this. Would you care to take a bite o' supper with us, 'neath the jolly old willows, cheer you up, sah, wot?'

Bucko swiftly regained his composure and jauntiness. 'Och, ah'm fair famished frae all that fightin'. Lead on, Brock mah friend, auld Bucko can vittle wi' the best o' 'em!'

'Haharr, I'll wager 'e can, too,' Ruff murmured to the badger as they set off for the bank. 'Never knew a hare who couldn't. We'll let ole Fleetscut defend Dotti's Feasting title for 'er!'

'I say, top hole, wot. That's jolly decent of you, sah!'

Ruff tweaked the old hare's ear. 'You wasn't supposed to 'ear that, faminechops.'

It turned out to be anything but a private supper on the streambank. Coloured lanterns and torches decked the trees in the soft summer night. A celebration feast for Dotti's victory had been secretly prepared by the Guosim, Gurth and some moles he had met, and Bucko's cooks, who were determined to give their old master a good send-off and welcome the new mistress. Dotti was so pleased that she rummaged through her worn bag and whipped out the harecordion.

'I couldn't sleep last night, so I composed a ditty, in the hope that I'd win the challenge today. Good job I did, wot. Right, my good subjects, gather round an' I'll sing it to you. I know you'll jolly well like it!'

Brocktree clapped a paw to his brow. 'I'm sure we will.'

The terrible twins Southpaw and Bobweave rubbed their paws in anticipation.

'I say, we didn't know y'could warble, miss?'

'Spiffin', wot. I'll bet you're rather good at it.'

Brocktree viewed the eager pair with a jaundiced eye. 'I guarantee 'tis something you won't forget lightly!'

Dotti forestalled any further chatter by launching into her ditty with a wobbly falsetto.

'Ho whack folly doodle oh Duckfontein,
Dillworthy is my family name!

A fatal beauty have I, goodbeasts,
I'm completely unrehearsed,
Havin' never been, kingess or queen,
Woe to me I'm doubly curs'd,
Oh the crown lies heavy on the ears,
Of a simple maid like me,
Now everybeast must scrape an' bow,
An' bend a jolly ole knee . . . heeheeheeheeheeeeee!

Ho whack folly doodle oh Duckfontein,
Dillworthy is my family name!

What a royally difficult life I've got,
But I regally say to m'self wot wot,
A Duckfontein must show no pain,
'Tis fame an' fortune's lot,
My super subjects will adore,
My spiffin' sweet young voice,
An' loyally cry out, more more more!
Each night they'll all rejoice . . . joy hoi hoi hoi hoice!

Ho whack folly doodle oh Duckfontein,
Dillworthy is my family name!

Affairs of state that just can't wait,
An' decisions of high degree,
The balance of a pudden's fate,

Rests hard 'twixt lunch an' tea,
Let anybeast yell "Come let's feast!"
Whilst the royal beauty doth sleep,
They'll rue the day that they met me,
Dorothea . . . Du . . . huck . . . fontein . . . Dill . . . worth
. . . eeeeeeeee!'

As Dotti's ears quivered on the last off-key note, the harecordion groaned as it discharged a deafened gnat. A mole hurled himself into the stream to escape the discord. The streambank was empty, everybeast having fled during the second painstaking verse. Only Southpaw and Bobweave sat adoringly in front of her, applauding wildly.

'Bravo, miss, put a blinkin' nightingale to shame, wot?'

'Rather! Are you goin' to give another rendition, Dotti? Sing us another of your charmin' ditties, wot!'

Dotti looked slightly baffled. It was the first time anybeast had actually sat through her singing and requested more.

'Jolly decent of you, chaps, but the old vocal chords need feedin' – I'm rather peckish right now. You could do me a favour, though, an' see if y'can clean out my harecordion. Confounded thing's full of gnats an' such. Must still be some old pale cider in there attractin' the blighters.'

She tossed the harecordion to the twins and wandered off to see if she could find some food. Southpaw and Bobweave set about boxing each other for the privilege of cleaning out their idol's instrument.

'Give it here, Southie. She was lookin' at me when she chucked the thing over!'

'Rats t'you, old chap, but I'll give you a swift right!'

'Oof! Here, have some o' this, chum! Now will y'let me clean it? Yowch, that does it. Get those paws up!'

Away from the main merriment, three shrewboats, lashed together, floated gently on the stream. Sipping shrewbeer and dining on pasties, salad and cheese, Brocktree, Fleetscut and Bucko sat with the tribal chiefs Ruff, Grenn, Drucco and Jukka to confer on important matters. The former king had formed an alliance with the others.

'Ah dinnae know where this Salamawotjimacallit place is, but ah'm gan with ye, an' mah wild mountain hares'll be a-comin' tae, the noo. We widnae miss a braw battle for nought!'

Gurth sat with Dotti, the willow leaves lightly brushing their heads. Between them lay a flagon of gooseberry crush and a thick vegetable flan. The sturdy mole waved his tankard towards the logboats.

'They'm avven gurtly apportant talks, miz. Oi wuddent be approised if'n we be on ee march boi mornen, hurr aye!'

The haremaid broke off a piece of flan. Forgetting her table manners, she spoke through a mouthful in moletalk. 'Oi wuggent noider, zurr!'

Joyous sounds of happy creatures rang through the warm velvety night. Music, singing and feasting were everywhere. Those who were weary slept curled on the grass, full and contented, not worrying about the perilous days which lay ahead of them.

Dawn's first birds trilled to the rising sun, waking the dew-scattered sleepers in the wide forest glade. Dotti was already up, abandoning her fatal beauty sleep in favour of the momentous events she knew were about to take place. The haremaid joined Brocktree and the company of chieftains, standing on a rock protruding from the hillside. In groups, last night's revellers drifted into the clearing below. Brocktree leaned on his battle blade, Skittles perched on his footpaw. He waited patiently until everybeast was standing grouped before him. Then, at his nod, Bucko took the fore.

'Hearken tae me, mah beasties. There's an auld hare

here, who comes frae a mountain an' bears a message for all warriors. Ah've nae doubt ye'll listen to whit he has tae say. Judge for yerselves, ah'm nae langer yer king!'

Bucko stood back, allowing Fleetscut to come forward. The old hare held the crown in his paw. 'Mount Salamandastron is where I come from, as most of you know, wot. Now there's those here t'day who were born there, whose parents an' grandkin are comrades o' mine. I've been gone from there a while now, but I know for certain that any hares left alive on the mountain will be slaves and prisoners of the wildcat Ungatt Trunn and his Blue Hordes!' He waited until the angry shouts died down. 'Hah, I see that y'know the vermin, wot. When Bucko was king he intended to form you into an army to hunt Trunn down an' face him. Well, that still goes. Only difference is you won't be marchin' under a king; our leader is the rightful heir of Salamandastron, Brocktree!'

There followed a mixture of cheering and surprised cries. Fleetscut held up the crown. 'You hares, let me tell you the law. Some among you will remember the rhyme you learned from your elders.

'"We follow our comrades in peace and war,
The hare is a perilous beast, we know,
But who commands, who makes our law?
The Badger Lords, 'twas always so!"

'Do you hear that? This is Lord Brocktree of Brockhall, a Badger Lord of Salamandastron by birth and by right, and this crown, won for his cause by his brave champion Dorothea Duckfontein Dillworthy, is the symbol of his leadership!' Fleetscut passed the crown to Brocktree. Every eye was upon the great badger as he took his place in the vanguard of the tribal chieftains. Unwinding the laurel leaves from the thin gold coronet, he cast them aside. His powerful paws crushed the circlet into a narrow double strip. This he wound about his sword hilt, with no more effort than he would have used on a green willow withe. Then the Badger Lord's voice boomed like thunder about the glade, setting every creature's neck hairs on end.

'Friends! Warriors! Goodbeasts all! I am going to defeat the evil one, Ungatt Trunn. I am going to take back from him and his Hordes the mountain that is mine. Today, now! I march for Salamandastron! Those who would follow me, call out this war cry. Eulaliiiaaaaaaaa!'

The entire glade exploded in an earsplitting roar.

'Eulaliiiiaaaaaaa!'

Dotti knew then the force and power of a Badger Lord. She was swept along beside him, howling like a mad-beast, surrounded by blades, slings, spears, bows, shields, javelins and bared teeth, all surging irresistibly forward like a gigantic wave. Brocktree's paws pounded the dust high as he ran, whirring his battle blade like a sunlit lightning flash, his huge form standing out like a beacon.

'Eulaliiiiaaaaa! Eulaliiiaaaaa! Eulaliiiaaaaaaa!'

For all his seasons, Fleetscut kept pace alongside the haremaid. She saw him, tears flowing down his weathered face, brandishing a short-hafted squirrel spear, yelling hoarsely between the battle cries.

'I never let ye down, Lord Stonepaw. I'm comin' back home now, sire . . . Eulaliiiiiaaaaaaaaa!'

BOOK THREE

Comes a Badger Lord

also entitled

A Shawl for Aunt Blench

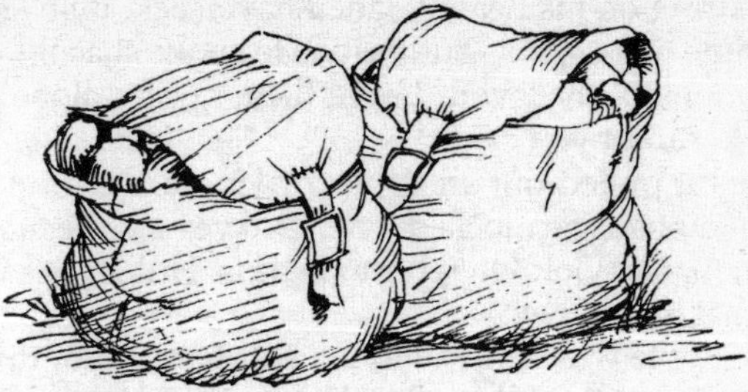

28

South of Salamandastron in a sparsely wooded copse, a group of about thirty Blue Hordebeasts and their stoat captain, Byle, sat in a clearing. They had been foraging for food, quite successfully, if anybeast were to judge by the bulging haversacks scattered about. Byle was a newly promoted officer, determined to do well. He was very happy with the results of the forage, but also quite hungry. So were the vermin under his command. Byle strode about, checking the haversacks were all fastened tight, aware of the surly glances of his minions. They wanted to eat some of the food, instead of having to tramp back to the mountain and deposit it, untouched, with Ungatt Trunn's supply officers. It was a tricky situation for Byle, but he put on a jovial air and attempted to flatter the mutinous-looking vermin by praising their efforts.

'Hoho, we did well today, cullies. I wouldn't be at all surprised if you wasn't all promoted f'yer good work!'

A rat spat, narrowly missing Byle's footpaw. 'Promotion! Wot good's that, eh? Ye can't eat promotion!'

The new captain laughed nervously and winked at another rat. 'Haha, you was up that tree like a squirrel after those apples. Where did ye learn t'climb like that, mate?'

Instead of answering, the rat began undoing the drawstring on his heavily laden haversack. Byle knew it was time to assert his authority. He spoke sharply. 'Now now, none o' that, you. Leave them apples alone or I'll have to report yer!'

The rat pulled out an apple, making a wry face at his companions as he mocked Byle. 'Did ye hear the nice new cap'n, mates? Goin' to report me he is. Huh, that's if'n he makes it back alive!'

The apple was halfway to the Horderat's mouth when a slingstone struck his paw. He screamed and dropped the apple.

'First beast t'move is a dead 'un!'

A figure clad in a hooded brown barkcloth cloak appeared from behind a juneberry bush, its face hidden behind a woven reed mask, a long whip held in its paw. Byle gasped. 'The Bark Crew!'

The creature behind the mask chuckled harshly. He cracked the whip in Byle's face. 'Haharr, right first time, vermin. Yore surrounded by threescore of us. Duck yore 'eads. Quick!'

Instinctively the forage patrol ducked their heads. Broken twigs and leaves showered down on them as a volley of slingstones rattled through the trees overhead. Four arrows quivered in the ground close to Byle. The whip snaked out, wrapping itself round his paw.

'See wot I mean, stoat? D'you an' this worthless pack want to live? Answer me!'

Since the start of summer the dreaded Bark Crew had become the terror of Ungatt Trunn's foraging patrols. They seemed to be everywhere at once. Byle knew of Hordebeasts and captains who had been slain when they offered resistance to the brown-cloaked raiders. His voice quavered helplessly as he replied to the sinister figure.

'Don't s-s-s-slay us, s-s-sire. We wants t'live. W-w-wot d'ye want us to do?'

Other members of the Bark Crew entered the vermin

camp, bows, swords and javelins much in evidence. The Crew leader pulled Byle forward on the whip around his paw.

'Get rid of yore weapons, all of 'em! Those uniforms, too – strip 'em off an' shed 'em. Move yoreselves!'

Menaced by the Bark Crew, the vermin piled their arms in a heap and pulled off their uniforms. They huddled together awaiting the next command.

'Sling those 'aversacks o' vittles on spear poles!'

They threaded the laden haversacks three to a spear haft. When this was done, they were ordered to lie face down on the ground. Walking between the prostrate figures, the Bark Crew leader consulted his companions aloud.

'Wot d'ye say we do with this scum, eh, mates?'

The Crew were in no doubt as to the fate of their captives.

'Rope 'em up to some rocks an' drown 'em!'

'Nah, sounds too Trunnish t'me. Toss 'em off the cliffs!'

'I vote we tie these vermin to trees an' use 'em for target practice. I likes shootin' at blue targets!'

The Crew leader had to crack his whip several times, to stop the forage patrol weeping, sobbing and begging to be spared. He turned Byle over roughly with his footpaw.

'Stow yore scringin' an' bellerin', stoat. You ain't worth wastin' arrows on, so I'm goin' to let ye live.'

Lined up in threes, within minutes the foraging patrol stood facing a rift in the clifftops, in view of the sea. Taking Byle none too gently by his neck scruff, the Bark Crew leader made him repeat his orders.

'We marches straight t'the sea, sire. If'n we looks left right or back we're deadbeasts. We wades into the sea up to our necks an' goes that way back to the mountain. I'm to make my report to Ungatt Trunn that this was the work of the Bark Crew, an' to say that he's a worthless piece o' crab bait, an' that he's goin' to starve t'death with 'is vermin army!'

The whip cracked viciously over the forage patrol's heads.

'Next time we see yore faces we'll roast ye alive! Quick march, one two, one two!'

The vermin needed little urging to march quicker than they had ever done before. Down the rift, across the shore and straight into the sea, without a backward glance.

Brogalaw removed the woven reed mask from his face and clasped paws with Stiffener.

'Another win for the Bark Crew, matey. Did ye notice 'ow thin some o' the vermin are startin' to look?'

Stiffener watched the dark dots far off in the sea, each one representing a Hordebeast wading neck deep back to Salamandastron. 'They'll look a lot thinner afore we're done with 'em, Brog. Did you say we 'ad threescore of us surroundin' 'em?'

Brogalaw looked around. Their party numbered twenty-two, counting himself and Stiffener.

'I thought sixty was enough t'do the job, mate. I was goin' t'say we 'ad fivescore, but that would've really been fibbin'.'

'We could jolly well do with fivescore to carry all the loot we liberated from those rascals today,' Willip complained as they turned back to the copse. 'Ah well, at least we've got plenty of grub and weapons. What d'you think, Stiff? Should we blindfold the next lot an' make them tote the spoils back to our hideout? Save a lot of bloomin' wear'n'tear on our old carcasses, wot?'

Brog picked up one end of a spear haft, slung with haversacks. 'C'mon, Willip me ole mate, git the other end o' this thing on yore pore ole shoulder, or we'll miss supper.'

'Hah, d'you know, I suddenly feel young again, Brog?'

'Aye, I've noticed, every time I mention food, you ole lollop-eared grubwalloper. I thought sea otters could scoff until I watched hares sit down to vittles!'

*

A bright summer evening was drawing to its close. Ungatt Trunn stood on the beach with his Grand Fragorl and Captain Karangool, watching as Byle and his foraging patrol stumbled through the shallows on to the sands. They presented a very odd picture. Seawater had washed out the blue dye from their fur from tail to neck; only their faces and heads remained blue. Byle staggered up and saluted the wildcat, his body drooping with exhaustion.

'Mighty One, we were ambushed . . .'

Ungatt's upraised paw silenced him. 'Let me guess, Captain Byle. It was the Bark Crew again. How many of them were there this time? Fivescore . . . ten?'

'Fivescore at least, Mightiness. The Bark Crew chieftain gave me a message to deliver, sire.'

The wildcat's tail whipped from side to side angrily. 'Don't tell me if it's merely insults. Get your patrol out of sight before others see what a pack of clowns you look!'

Byle bowed and saluted dutifully, then signalled his patrol to get inside the mountain.

Later, Ungatt Trunn sat closeted in his chamber with Fragorl and Karangool. He watched his spiders, his two aides watched him, holding their silence and blinking in the thick smoke that swathed the room.

The wildcat pointed upwards. 'Young spiders never seem to get the flies, it's always the older ones. I suppose because they're more experienced, better hunters, wickeder, more ruthless, would you say?'

Karangool nodded. 'Ya, is so, Might'ness.'

Trunn turned his gaze upon the fox. 'You're a ruthless creature, but I need you here. My mistake was in sending out well-behaved new captains. What we need is wicked ones – cruel, evil creatures who bend the rules to suit themselves. Searats and corsairs were always like that, eh, Karangool?'

The fox's normally stern face broke into a fiendish grin. 'Ya, Might'ness. I sailed with bad ones in good old days!'

The wildcat stroked his whiskers reflectively. 'I'll wager you did, my friend. Fragorl, those searat brothers I had stripped of their rank, tell the guards to bring them up from the dungeons. Fetch food from the kitchens, too. Good food, not fish heads and stewed grass.'

Ripfang and Doomeye thought they were being brought in front of Ungatt Trunn because he had decided on a slow agonising death for them. They kicked, bit and struggled with the guards as they were hustled into the wildcat's chamber. Nobeast was more surprised than they when Ungatt ordered their chains removed and the guards dismissed. Panting and rubbing their limbs where the manacles had been, they sat on the floor, their sly eyes flicking from the food to their ruler. Ungatt Trunn nodded towards the tray, which contained a flagon of damson wine and the last of Blench's fruit scones.

'You must be hungry. Eat.'

They stared at him, openly suspicious. Karangool sipped from the flagon and bit off a piece of scone. 'Eat, food not poison!'

Like a pair of ravening wolves the two rats fell upon the food, stuffing it down and slopping wine. Ungatt Trunn lectured them as they crammed the vittles into their mouths.

'By rights you should be dead now, both of you. Did you think I was fooled by your lies about Groddil and the other two? Maybe you did slay them and throw their bodies into the pool, but not because they insulted me, as you said. No, you killed them for some reason best known only to yourselves. I could have had you executed, but I chose instead to have you locked up and starved, until I decided what I should do with you both.'

Ripfang looked up, a mess of chewed scone falling from his lips. 'So yew ain't 'avin' us done away wid. Thankee, cap'n, er, I mean Yer Mightiness.'

'Oh, don't thank me. Thank them.'

Ungatt's paw was pointing up to the spiders. Doomeye

grabbed the flagon from his brother and swigged at it. 'Wot, does 'e want us ter say thanks to them things?'

Ripfang elbowed his slow-thinking brother hard. 'Shut yer gob, wifflebrain! Ye'll 'ave to excuse 'im, sire, Doomeye ain't very bright. So, me lordship, wot is it yer wants us t'do for yer, eh?'

The wildcat assessed Ripfang. He was young still, but experienced and hardened to cruelty and death. Evil was stamped on his features, from the treacherous flickering eyes and scarred nose, to the unsightly single fang protruding downward from the centre of his lipless mouth.

'I suppose you slew quite a few in your seasons as a searat?'

Ripfang snatched the flagon back from Doomeye and guffawed. 'Me'n'me brother 'ere, we killed just about anythin' that moved, all types o' beasts, young, old, males or shemales. Harr, an' we slew 'em any way we could, an' a few ways wot don't bear thinkin' about, ain't that right, Doom?'

Doomeye dug foodscraps from between his blackened teeth with a dirty claw. 'Aye, yer right there, Rip, any way we could, we murdered 'em!'

The wildcat sat back and purred. 'Excellent. Now listen to me if you want to keep eating food like that and regain your rank as captains in my Hordes.'

Brogalaw stroked the heron's neck. 'Good job you found this other cave, Rulango. My ole mum was beginnin' to create an' kick up somethin' awful about all the loot we was bringin' back.'

The cave was upcoast, slightly north of the sea otters' dwelling, a fortunate find indeed. Stiffener took a torch from its wall mount to light their way out. From floor to roof, the place resembled a well-stocked larder cum armoury. Weaponry and uniforms lined its walls, while at the centre there was an enormous heap of fruit, vegetables and edible roots. Plunder, taken from the foraging patrols by the Bark Crew. Outside they doused the torch in the sand and camouflaged the cave entrance with a dead sea buckthorn bush.

Trobee kept a branch to cover their tracks. 'I say, let's get back an' see what luck old Durvy had today. Maybe his crew brought back some shrimp, wot!'

Brog's mother Frutch was in the process of giving Durvy and his crew a good dressing down.

'Seasons o' seaweed'n'salt, what are we supposed t'do with all this shrimp, that's what I'd like t'know, master Durvy. There can't be a single shrimp left in the sea!'

Durvy dodged a swipe of the ottermum's ladle. 'Belay wid that weapon, marm, I'm only doin' wot yore son told me to. You ain't supposed to biff members o' the Bark Crew wid ladles, that's takin' the side o' the enemy!'

Brog rescued the ladle from his mum and hugged her. 'Wot's for supper, ye liddle plump battler?'

Frutch tugged at his whiskers. 'Put me down, ye great ribcrusher, or I won't be fit t'cook anythin' for anybeast. Sufferin' sandhills, did any pore ottermum have t'put up with such a son!'

Brog's nose twitched at the two cauldrons which his mum, Blench and Woebee had perched on the fire. 'Mmmmm, skilly'n'duff, me fav'rite!'

The three cooks denied it stoutly.

'We never did no skilly'n'duff, did we, Blench?'

'No marm, we got shrimp soup, followed by shrimp stew, ain't that right, Woebee?'

''Tis for sure, an' a nice shrimp salad for afters!'

Brog's face was the picture of misery. 'But I could've sworn I smelled skilly'n'duff?'

Frutch plucked her ladle from his paw and whacked his tail. 'Of course 'tis skilly'n'duff, ye big omadorm, with lots o' plums in the duff, the way you like it. Now make y'self useful, an' you too, mister Stiffener. Lend a paw to get those cauldrons off'n the fire.'

Over supper, Durvy told of his crew's exploits at sea that day.

'Ho, we kept the bluebottom fishin' fleet busy, mates. We swam under their vessels an' shredded the nets, stole all their shrimp, an' – hahaha, tell Brog wot you did, Konul.'

''Twas like this, see,' a sleek ottermaid, with a face born to mischief, explained. 'I waited 'til they dropped anchors to fish. Soon as they cast their nets I attached each boat's net to the next boat's anchor flukes, snarled 'em up good an' proper. Heehee, you should've seen the vermin haulin' away at those nets. All the vessels came bumpin' together – there was bluebottoms floppin' an' fallin' this way'n'that. Harder they hauled, the worse it got. Them boats was knocked together so 'ard that three of 'em sprang leaks. Last I saw they was tryin' to paddle back to shore an' balin' out at the same time, draggin' most o' the fishin' fleet along with 'em. I tell ye, Brog, 'twas a sight to see!'

Another of Durvy's crew piped up. 'Aye, then they started fightin' among themselves. So I slices through the anchor ropes an' off they went like big flappin' birds with the wind behind 'em. That ole fleet hit the shore so 'ard that they was all run aground!'

Sailears chuckled with delight at the sea otters' story. 'Wish I could swim like you chaps, then I could jolly well go along with you.'

Durvy gallantly refilled her bowl from the cauldron. 'Yore doin' just fine as the onshore Bark Crew, marm. I reckon those rascals must really be feelin' the pinch now, wot d'you think, Stiff?'

'I think yore right. They're learnin' a hard lesson the hard way. Even if Trunn an' the officers kept the best for themselves, I'll wager they've more or less gone through wot stores was left in Blench's larders.'

Stiffener little knew how truly he spoke. At that exact

moment, Ungatt Trunn was prowling into Salamandastron's dining hall, followed by Fragorl, carrying her master's plate. Taking it from her, the wildcat shoved the platter under the cook's nose.

'What do you call this mess of rubbish?'

Wiping his paws on his greasy apron, the cook avoided eye contact with his master, stammering nervously, 'Mightiness, 'tis all we've got left. Yew 'ad the Fragorl take the last o' the good stuff up to yore chamber. I drained the wine kegs to fill a pitcher, an' those scones was well stale, but they was all I 'ad left.'

Trunn stared round the deserted tables as the cook continued, ''Tain't worth anybeast turnin' up 'ere fer vittles, Mighty One. There ain't nothin' to serve 'em. Them Bark Crew are t'blame, I say, stealin' the food out'n our mouths like that. I been mixin' some mouldy flour wid chopped seaweed an' dannelion roots. Don't know wot I'll do when that's gone, sire.'

Ungatt Trunn pushed the plate into his trembling paws. 'Stop babbling and whining, cook, and keep your voice down. After tomorrow there'll be food aplenty for all. Put the word about that this is my promise to you.'

Marching hurriedly from the dining hall, the wildcat was rounding a torchlit passage leading out to the shore when a shadow fell over him. He fell back with a horrified gasp, shielding his face with a paw. The shadow was that of a great double-hafted sword hilt. Trunn stood petrified at the sight. It grew larger and came closer. A strangled cry was torn from his throat, and he shrank back against the rough rock walls.

Two gaunt rats rounded the corner, carrying between them three driftwood spars lashed together, the shadow of which looked for all the world like a giant double-hilted sword haft. They chatted to each other as they toted their burden.

'I thought yew said this'd get all seaweed tangled round it?'

'Well, we jammed it atwixt those rocks on the tideline. It should've got some seaweed stuck to it at 'igh tide.'

'But it never, did it? Huh, talk about bright ideas!'

Noticing Ungatt Trunn they dropped the contraption and saluted.

'Mightiness!'

The wildcat wiped a trembling paw across his ashen face. 'Take that thing and burn it,' he shouted hysterically. 'Burn it! D'you hear me! Burn it!'

Blank-faced, the two rats were knocked to one side as the wildcat swept by them on his way to the shore. They looked at one another and shrugged.

'Wot was all that about, mate?'

'Search me. Get that torch off'n the wall an' put a light to this thing, afore 'Is Mightiness comes back!'

'Was I seein' things, or did 'e look frightened?'

'Looked like 'e'd seen a ghost. This won't burn, 'tis damp.'

'Well git yore sword an' chop it up 'til yew find the dry bits.'

Ungatt Trunn sat on the sand, which was still warm from the day's sun. Much as he had hated and despised Groddil, he missed the fox magician's soothing words. Every day the spectre of the badger looming in his mind was growing larger. He was surrounded by his Blue Hordes, yet trapped alone by the visions of his own imagination, with nobeast to explain them or chant encouraging prophecies.

He stared disdainfully at the silent Grand Fragorl, in attendance as ever. 'Well, what have you got to say for yourself?'

'Nothing, sire,' the ferret replied warily.

His footpaw shot out, sending her sprawling in the sand. 'Nothing. That's all you ever say. Get out of my sight!'

Fragorl made an undignified retreat on all fours. It was wisest to do what Ungatt Trunn said immediately and without question, when he was in one of his dark moods. Which were growing more and more frequent as the days went by. Some Hordebeasts grubbing for seaweed nearby heard their leader laugh bitterly and talk aloud to himself.

'The mountain of my dreams. Hah! More like the mountain of my nightmares. So, these are the days of Ungatt Trunn, eh?'

29

After breakfast next morning, Durvy was leaving with his crew to harass the fishing fleet. Frutch shook her ladle at him, and he held up both paws placatingly. 'Don't say it, marm, we've got the message. No more shrimp!'

Brogalaw entered the cave, with Rulango stalking in his wake. 'Ahoy, 'ere's a bird who's very partial to shrimp. Feed our friend well, Mum, he just sketched me out an important message. Stiffener, get the Bark Crew together, mate. There's a small party, about twenty-five bluebottoms, left the mountain at dawn. Rulango reckons they're 'eaded thisaways, armed with bags an' 'avvysacks.'

Stiffener donned his barkcloth cloak and mask, arming himself with sword, bow and arrows. He beckoned to the rest of the hares and otters who were gearing themselves up.

'Another foragin' party. Let's send those vermin back sore-tailed an' empty-pawed, eh, mates!'

Woebee threw her apron up over her face. 'Begone the lot of ye. I don't 'old with masks'n'cloaks, fair scare a body they do. Away with ye!'

Torleep bowed courteously. 'No need t'fuss yourself, marm. 'Tis only us under this lot.'

Ripfang and Doomeye had taken a hundred and fifty Hordebeasts out of the mountain long before dawn. They concealed themselves in the crags and crannies behind Salamandastron. Each of them was personally picked by the rat brothers; there were a lot of former searats and corsairs among their ranks. All in all they were a mean and savage-looking bunch, armed to the teeth.

Ripfang climbed down from his lookout spot. 'The forage party decoys are well on their way, 'eadin' nor'east to the clifftops an' dunes to scout for berries an' roots. Doomeye, take yore gang an' sweep southeast. Git well back from the cliffs afore ye start closin' in.'

Doomeye fiddled with his spear, as if reluctant to go. 'Which way are yore lot goin'? The short way, I'll bet.'

Ripfang tossed a long dagger and caught it neatly. 'We'll be follerin' the same route as the foragin' party, I been drummin' that inter yer 'alf the night. That way we'll catch this Bark Crew in a pincer movement, from back an' front. Simple plans allus works best, I told yer!'

Doomeye stuck out his bottom lip sullenly. 'I still don't like it. From wot I've 'eard this Bark Crew just appear out o' nowhere. They say they're like spirits!'

Ripfang brandished his dagger impatiently. 'That's 'ogwash an' yew know 'tis. I'll tell yer who I think they are – those threescore escaped longears, that's who. Are you lot as 'ungry as I am, eh?'

There was a rumble of agreement, from both mouths and stomachs. Ripfang made a slashing movement with his blade. 'Then wot are we waitin' for? There's meat on the paw fer the takin'. Y'want to eat, then move yerselves!'

Doomeye kicked at the dirt, staying where he was. 'You still 'aven't said why me an' my gang got t'go the long way round. 'Tain't fair.'

Ripfang flung the dagger, burying it in the earth right between his brother's footpaws. 'Lissen, lump'ead, yew get goin', right now. Otherwise I'm goin' back inside to report to Ungatt Trunn, an' you can see 'ow well y'do takin' charge o' this lot!'

Doomeye got up huffily and signalled his party to move off. 'All right all right, keep yer fur on, we're goin'! Huh, never thought I'd see a brother o' mine snitchin' to the chief on 'is own fur'n'blood. Enny'ow, wot's the signal for the ambush? I've forgotten it.'

Ripfang turned his eyes skyward, as if seeking help from above. 'Wot's to forget, shrimpbrain? I've told yer ten times already. Firrig 'ere will give two curlew cries – that's the signal for youse to attack. Y'do know wot a curlew sounds like, don'tcher?'

Doomeye led his party out of the rocks, shouting back at his ill-tempered brother, 'Course I do. It sounds just like you tryin' to snore through that single pickle-stabber of yores, twiddletooth!'

Ripfang flung a rock at Doomeye, but it fell short. 'I'll get yew fer that, jus' see if'n I don't!'

Lying in concealment, the Bark Crew watched the foragers climb the cliffs at a place where a small streamlet trickled down. Brogalaw noted their every movement, murmuring low to Stiffener, 'They're stoppin' to take a drink now, some of 'em pickin' crowberries an' eatin' them. Nasty bitter-tastin' things. I've never liked crowberries, 'ave you, Stiff?'

The boxing hare shrugged. 'Not really. Still, you'll eat anythin' once the 'unger grips yore stomach. Dumb stupid vermin, I pity 'em in a way.'

Willip snorted. 'Save your pity for decent creatures, sah. These are the same rotten bounders who were plannin' on eatin' us when they had us locked up. Pity 'em, indeed!'

Brog saw two vermin detach themselves and climb to the top. A moment later they were calling back to the other foragers.

'There's nettles up 'ere, an' some bilberries!'

The rest of the party climbed up. Once on top they could not be seen by the Bark Crew, but their voices came back clear.

'More nettles than bilberries, I'd say. Ouch, they sting!'

'Well, that's wot nettles are supposed t'do, mate. Pick 'em, you can brew good beer with nettles.'

'Huh, will yew lissen to 'im? Wot beast could wait a season fer nettles to brew? We'd all be starved dead by then.'

'Oh, stop moanin'. Use yore blade an' cut the nettles – they'll do to make soup with.'

Brog picked up his javelin. 'Ain't goin' t'be so easy, while they're out in the open. Still, if we jump those bluebottoms quick it should do the trick. When I show meself, see if you can get a few round the back of 'em, Stiff. Sailears, you an' the others stay just below the clifftop, but show yore weapons, to let the vermin think they're surrounded. Well, here goes. Good huntin'!'

The forage party leader was a weasel. He did not know that his band had been sent out as a decoy. While the others were busy at their work, he stuffed a pawful of bilberries into his mouth.

'Tut tut, matey, stealin' food,' a voice nearby chided him. Without looking up, the weasel glimpsed the barkcloth robe and groaned inwardly. 'Yore a leader, y'should be settin' an example to those under ye!'

The sinister cloaked and masked figure stood framed by the weapons that poked up over the cliff. Raising his voice, Brog called harshly to the vermin: 'Move a muscle an' ye die. A Bark Crew javelin's a lot sharper than some ole nettles, you'll find!'

A rat knocked over his haversack, and berries spilled out. 'Ow no, 'tis the Bark Crew!'

Stiffener walked up from behind him and rested a loaded sling upon the rat's bowed head. 'Ow yes, 'tis the Bark Crew, y'mean. Toss yore weapons over by me, all of ye. Yore surrounded!'

Shielding his eyes against the sun, the weasel looked up at Brog. 'Y'ain't gonna kill us, are yer, sir?' he gulped aloud.

There was a touch of humour in the masked figure's voice. 'Not just yet. Pick those berries first, but leave the nettles. I don't want ye t'get yore paws pricked. Go on, pick!'

Nervously the forage party picked the bilberries. 'Why d'yer want to slay us?' a rat whined at Torleep. 'We ain't done no 'arm to nobeast.'

The hare gave him a resounding kick on his blue-dyed rear. 'Fibber, cad, bounder, don't look for mercy from me, sah!'

When the berries were all picked and bagged up, Brog made the vermin shed their uniforms. The weasel leader suddenly broke down and clung weeping to Stiffener's cloak. 'Aaaaahaaaaggh! Spare us, sire, spare our lives, please, I beg yer, don't kill us. Waaahahaaa!'

Stiffener's loaded sling rapped the weasel's paws until he was forced to release the cloak hem. The boxing hare's voice was laden with contempt. 'Spare your lives, eh, like you spared the old Badger Lord? But he went out like a true warrior, fightin' for his life. Look at yoreself, coward, blubbin' like a stuck toad!'

Torleep was slinging the bags on to a spear shaft when a strange noise cut the still noon air. Stiffener whirled round to face Brog. 'What was that?'

The otter yanked his friend to one side just in time. A slingstone buzzed by like an angry hornet. Doomeye's Hordebeasts came charging out of the eastern moorland, howling and yelling, firing slingstones and discharging arrows at the Bark Crew.

Torleep dashed to the cliff edge and glanced over. 'I say, there's more coming up this way!' He never had time to say more. An arrow thudded into his throat. Torleep tottered for an instant, then fell over the cliff.

Brogalaw gathered the Bark Crew swiftly. 'Take a

stand facin' for'ard an' aft, mates. Grab yore bows!'

Stiffener stood back to back with the sea otter, battling the vermin who were scrambling over the clifftop, whilst Brogalaw faced the crowd charging them from the moorland.

''Tis a trap, Stiff. They got us surrounded!'

The boxing hare whirled his sling, knocking a rat back over the cliff. 'There's a lot of 'em, but we ain't surrounded yet, Brog. They've got us in a pincer move from back'n'front. Keep pickin' off the outsiders – stop 'em circlin' us!'

The otter alongside Brog went down with a spear through him.

Doomeye's contingent had slowed their headlong rush and were advancing cautiously now. They tried to stay in a tight bunch, nobeast wanting to be strung out on the edges, where they would be picked off. Ripfang had his group halfway over the clifftop before he saw how furiously the Bark Crew were retaliating. Dropping back below the rim he called out orders.

'Keep yore 'eads down. We'll snipe 'em t'bits. Pick yore targets – there's only a score an' a half of 'em!'

Stiffener took out a weasel, with a spear that had just missed him a moment ago. Still back to back with Brog, he outlined a plan that was forming in his mind. 'I'd say we're outnumbered five to one, mate. We'll have t'make a break for it, sideways!'

An arrow hit Brog in the shoulder. He bit his lip and snapped off the shaft. 'I'm with you, mate. Best go north, away from the location of our cave. Do it soon, afore we lose any more beasts!'

Stiffener could feel the arrowhead that had pierced Brog scratching his back. Willip was down on all fours, blood flowing from a gash on her head. The weasel and his forage party were lying flat on the ground, paws covering their heads, unarmed and out of the action.

Brog grabbed the weasel and hauled him roughly up.

'Up on yore scringin' paws, you bluebottoms, an' form two lines, a spear length apart. Move or I'll kill ye!'

Whimpering and trying to evade missiles, the vermin were forced to obey. Brog ordered his Bark Crew into the space between the two lines. 'Keep goin' north then strike east the moment y'see some trees, mates. We got a livin' shield to take us out o' here. If'n these bluebottoms try to slow up or break away, you got my permission to slay 'em. Quick march!'

Confused by the sight of two lines of hostages from their own side, the vermin ceased fire, and the Bark Crew moved smartly off whilst they had the advantage. Ripfang hauled himself over the clifftops, yelling, 'Don't lerrem get away, fools, kill that Bark Crew!'

Doomeye came running up at the head of his vermin group. 'Oh, 'ard luck, Rip. They fooled us that time, eh?'

Ripfang punched his brother in the eye. 'That was you, puddlebrain, y'never waited for the signal!'

One of Doomeye's patrol, a ferret, stepped forward. 'Yew shouldn't 'ave punched 'im. Yore brother stepped on a thistle an' yelped out loud. We all thought it was the signal, so we charged. 'Twasn't 'is fault!'

Ripfang punched the ferret square on the nose. 'Who asked yew, slugface? I'm givin' orders round 'ere! Now get after 'em, the lot of yer, an' slay the Bark Crew!'

The ferret wiped blood from his nose and glared at it. Then he lashed out, cracking Ripfang between the ears with his spear haft.

'Yew ain't a cap'n any more. Trunn broke youse two back down t'the ranks, an' besides, we'd 'ave to kill our own mates to get at the Bark Crew. I ain't doin' that!'

Ripfang rubbed his head, grinning ruefully. 'Yore right, mate, yew ain't doin' that. Yore stayin' 'ere.' Quick as light he drew his cutlass and ran the ferret through, then waved the dripping blade in an arc. 'Anybeast else want to stay 'ere? Come on, who wants t'join 'im? Step up an' face me!'

They backed off, staring dumbly at the slain ferret. Suddenly, Ripfang was among them, laying about savagely with the flat of his blade. 'After 'em, all of yer! I don't care who y'bring down as long as yer finish the Bark Crew off!'

With Ripfang in the rear, cutlass drawn, they took off after the enemy, who had a good head start.

Stiffener cast a glance over his shoulder. 'Didn't take 'em long, Brog. 'Ere they come!'

The sea otter Skipper peered anxiously ahead. 'No sign of any trees yet, Stiff. Sailears, how's Willip doin'?'

'Still groggy, I'm afraid. An' there's a young otter here, Fergun, who's taken a javelin through the footpaw. Slowin' us down a bit, but that can't be helped, wot?'

Stiffener called Trobee and two otters, Urvo and Radd. 'Fetch double quivers an' bows. We'll hold the rear, mates!'

'Don't let them catch up,' one of the forage party sobbed. 'They'll kill us just t'get at youse!'

Brog clouted his head soundly. 'Shut yore mouth or I'll boot ye over the cliff!'

Stiffener and his three archers let the others go on ahead. Stringing shafts to their bows they brought down two Hordebeasts who were running ahead of the rest. After another volley they joined their friends. Trobee kept another shaft ready on his bowstring and walked facing back. 'I think we took out seven vermin back at the clifftops. Countin' the two we just dropped, that makes nine. Not bad considerin' we lost only three, two otters an' old Torleep.'

Stiffener turned to join him. 'Nine don't make a lot o' difference to the crowd they've got, Trobee. We're in big trouble unless we get some 'elp.' He raised his voice, calling to the front of the column. 'Any sign o' shelter ahead, trees, rocks, or whatever?'

'Not a thing, matey,' an otter's voice replied. 'All I can see is a big dead ole tree near the cliff edge up yonder, sorry!'

Brog's voice joined in the shouted conversation. 'Ahoy, did ye say a big dead tree? I know that 'un – used to fish up this way. If'n I ain't mistaken there's a whole circle o' rocks on the shore down there, above the tideline. Cut off an' take a peek, Sailears.'

Sailears left the group and bounded to the cliff edge. She was back shortly with good news. 'Brog old chap, you were right. A ring of rocks, not unlike a blinkin' small fort. Oh, well done, sah!'

Stiffener and his archers dropped back and fired off another two volleys of arrows. This time the vermin saw them coming and avoided them. Brog waved the archers to join the column. 'Never mind that now, mateys. Let's get down to those rocks!'

Doomeye was holding a pawful of wet sand to the eye which his brother had punched. Ripfang watched him and shook his head in despair. 'All's that'll get yer is an eyeful o' wet sand, yer ninny.'

Doomeye spat contemptuously at him. 'Think yew know everythin', don'tcher, yew rotten slime, punchin' me in the eye like that. Well, I ain't yer brother no more, see. I 'ope one of those arrers out of the air gets yew, right in yore eye, then y'll see 'ow it feels!'

'Look, they're climbin' down the cliffs t'the shore!' somebeast shouted.

Ripfang ran to the cliff edge and peered along. 'Tryin' t'make it to those rocks, eh? Well, we've got 'em now – we can easily surround those rocks. Slow down an' catch yore breath, mates, they ain't goin' nowhere!'

It was hot on the rocks. The sand at the centre of the stone circle was dry and hot too. The Bark Crew threw themselves down gratefully, shedding cloaks and masks. Sailears tended to the injured, while Brogalaw and Skipper watched the clifftops.

'Ain't got much time to rest, Stiff. 'Ere they come, climbin' down the cliff. How many would ye say they've got?'

'Oh, about a hunnerd an' two score more. Too many for us.'

Brogalaw stroked his whiskers thoughtfully. 'Yore right, but we still got enough to make a fight of it. One thing, though, mate – what d'we do with these beasts we captured? They might prove troublesome.'

Stiffener saw the last vermin stumble down to the shore. 'Well, we got no more use for 'em, an' we certainly can't feed the scum. I say we let 'em go, what d'ye think, Brog?'

'Aye, let's rid ourselves of the pests. Ahoy there, weasel, git yoreself over 'ere!'

The forage patrol leader practically crawled across. 'Yore goin' t'kill us, I know ye are, I kin feel it!'

Brog hauled him up sharply by the ears. 'Good news, blubberchops, we're lettin' you go, all of you!'

'Wha . . . er . . . y'mean yore lettin' us go, sir?'

'Aye, that's wot I said, though if you 'ang around 'ere weepin' an' moanin' all day we'll slay ye just for the peace'n'quiet 'twould give us. So you'd better run fer it!'

As Ripfang was giving the orders to form a circle round the rocks, Doomeye, who was still a fair shot despite his swollen eye, unshouldered his bow and shot off an arrow.

'Haharr, got one of 'em! 'E was tryin' to escape. Look, there's more of the Bark Crew!' Ripfang's cutlass chopped through his bowstring. 'Wot did yer do that for? Leave me alone, will yer!'

Ripfang pointed angrily at the fallen weasel. 'See wot you've done now, pan'ead, shot one of our own!'

Doomeye looked sheepish. 'Well, wot if'n I did?' he muttered sulkily. 'You said 'twas all right, long as we got the Bark Crew.'

Ripfang ignored him. He called to the forage party, who were half in and half out of the rocks, not knowing which way to go. 'Over 'ere, you lot. C'mon, we won't shoot no more of yer!'

They hurried across, keeping nervous eyes on Doomeye, who was restringing his bow. Ripfang sneered at them. 'Well well, wot've we got 'ere? A shower o' cowards with no uniforms or weapons. You lot better make yerselves slings an' gather some stones. Might look better on yer if you 'elp to capture the Bark Crew.'

Back at the rocks, Stiffener was assessing the situation. 'Well, we've given the vermin some reinforcements now. Still, we'd never 'ave killed 'em in cold blood. They can't wait us out, 'cos they ain't got the supplies to do it, though neither've we. The bluebottoms still outnumber us by far too many, but we're still dangerous an' well armed. They'll try to pick us off one by one, now that they've got us surrounded. Mebbe when dark falls they'll try a charge. What d'you think, Brog?'

The sea otter was sharpening a javelin against the rock. He nodded grimly. 'Aye, that's when they'll come. It'll be the Bark Crew's last stand. Haharr, but we'll make it a good 'un, eh, mates?'

Hares and otters gripped their weapons tighter.

'Aye, no surrender an' no quarter given or asked!'

'Take as many as we can with us!'

'Remember Lord Stonepaw and the others, chaps!'

This time Ripfang kept Doomeye close by, where he could keep an eye on him. Both rats lay behind a mound of sand they had set up. Ripfang watched the noon shadows beginning to lengthen. A cry rang out from the rocks.

'Eulaaaliiiiaaaa!'

The ferocity of the war cry caused the searat a momentary shudder. But he soon recovered himself. 'Hah, we've got ye outnumbered by far. Shout all ye want, it won't do youse any good when night comes an' we charge. I'll paint those rocks red with yore blood!'

No news had come back to the mountain of the trap that had been laid for the Bark Crew, but Ungatt Trunn felt in better humour than he had for some while. One of his captains had come across a hidden cupboard in the larders, containing three casks of aged rose and greengage wine. He donated two of the casks to be shared among his horde captains, and the remaining one he had broached himself. All afternoon he drank deeply from it. The wine induced a pleasant and languorous feeling, and he drifted off into a peaceful sleep as noon sunlight poured through the chamber windows.

Stretched on Lord Stonepaw's bed, the wildcat dreamed of nothing in particular. The North Mountains, where his old father reigned, his younger brother Verdauga Greeneye, waiting to inherit the throne. Or maybe he was not – he might be considering the life of a conqueror, like his elder brother Ungatt. The sleeper smiled. Nobeast living could claim to have won anything as spectacular as this mighty mountain. Salamandastron, the legendary home of Badger Lords. Ungatt Trunn sighed and turned in his sleep. Then the vision altered. A huge dark paw wrapped itself about his face, blinding and smothering him. The Badger Lord, he had come, he had come!

'Mmmmffff! Uuuurgh! Help me! Gmphhhh!'

'Sire, lie still whilst I get this blanket from your head.'

Writhing wildly, Ungatt Trunn lashed out, and caught his Grand Fragorl a blow which sent her spinning across the room. Ripping and shredding with lethal claws, the wildcat tore the homely blanket from about his head and sat up panting, his head aching abominably. All semblance of good humour had deserted him. 'Who gave you permission to enter my chamber?' he growled at Fragorl.

The ferret rose groggily. 'Sire, you called for help. I came to assist you.'

The wildcat tossed the tattered blanket aside and made to rise. 'Assist me? You whey-faced poltroon, you dared to think that you have the right to assist me? Begone before I throw your worthless hide from the window!'

The Grand Fragorl fled the chamber, followed by a wine goblet, which smashed on the door as it slammed.

'I could have taken this mountain unaided! Ungatt Trunn the Earth Shaker needs help from nobeast. Go on, whine, starve, moan, blunder about, all of you! This is my mountain, I rule it alone, I can hold it alone! Every creature here depends on me, I don't need any of you!'

Outside, the two guards moved further down the passage, away from the door.

'Shift along there, mate. Don't get too close when the chief's in one of 'is dark moods.'

'Aye, the cap'ns are all like that too. Wot d'you suppose started it all?'

'Guzzlin' wine on a midsummer noon, on empty stomachs too. I done it meself once. Doesn't improve the temper, I can tell ye. Wish it'd get dark, so the night watch could come an' relieve us. 'Tis dangerous stannin' round 'ere.'

Ignoring the glories of a setting sun on the sea's far horizon, the Bark Crew perched in the rocks, anxiously scanning the humps of sand surrounding them. Behind each one, several vermin lay, armed and ready, waiting for the shades of night to descend. Brogalaw spoke without turning to Stiffener, his eyes roving back and forth.

'Wot grieves me about all this is no matter 'ow many we takes t'the Dark Forest with us, 'twon't make much difference to the numbers Trunn 'as to serve 'im.'

The boxing hare checked the shaft on his bowstring. 'Shame, ain't it, but that's the way o' things, Brog. Willip, are you all right, mate?'

The old hare adjusted the makeshift bandage on her brow. 'Fit enough t'fight, sah! But I'm jolly hungry, doncha know. Funny how a bod can think of food at a blinkin' time like this, wot? Can't help it, though – the old tum's rumblin' twenty t'the dozen!'

The sea otter chuckled and shook his head. ''Tis no wonder they call hares perilous beasts. Death facin' us, an' that 'un has dinner on 'er mind!'

Stiffener shrugged. 'Wot's on yore mind, Brog?'

Brogalaw glanced at the darkening sky. 'My ole mum, the rest o' my crew, Durvy, young Konul an' the mateys I grew up with. I'd just like to clap eyes on 'em one last time. Any beast you'd like t'see, Stiff?'

'Hmm, those twin grandsons o' mine, Southpaw an' Bobweave. You should've seen 'em, Brog. Two braver fighters you'd never come across in a season's march. I reared 'em, y'know, until they grew restless an' left the mountain. Mebbe 'twas just as well they did, the way things turned out.'

As the night drew on, voices began chanting from behind the sand humps which the vermin had put up for protection.

'Ungatt! Trunn Trunn Trunn!'

Brogalaw's grip tightened round the javelin. 'Haharr, 'twon't be much longer now, mates. 'Ear 'em gettin' their nerve up to charge.'

The speed and volume of the chant increased.

'Ungatt! Trunn Trunn Trunn! Ungatt! Trunn Trunn Trunn!'

From the rock circle the otters and hares answered with their own defiant war cry.

'Blood'n'vinegar! Eulaliiiiiaaaaaaaa!'

Stiffener centred his arrow on the dark forms breaking cover. 'Stand fast, mates, 'ere they come!'

The vermin charged.

30

In a wide valley formed by four grass-topped sand dunes, Lord Brocktree put aside his empty plate and beaker. He lay back upon the sand next to Fleetscut and sighed contentedly, gazing up at dizzying myriads of stars strewn about the soft night sky.

'Tomorrow you say, around late noon?'

Fleetscut left off munching wild raspberries from the prone position and nodded. 'Indeed, sah, we should reach Salamandastron about then, providin' we're up an' about by dawn, wot.'

Ruff joined them, Bucko too, both highly pleased.

'Well, we did it, Brock, a half-season march!'

'Och, an' ye said et were nae mair than a wee patrol!'

Fleetscut wrinkled his nose mischievously. 'Had t'say somethin' t'keep you chaps goin', wot? Bit of a fib, but we made it. Heehee, sorry 'bout that, my wee patrol turned out t'be somethin' of a long patrol, wot wot!'

The Badger Lord closed his eyes and mused. 'Long patrol, hmmmm. I'd say that was a— Whooooofh!'

Skittles had jumped from somewhere high up one of the dunes. He landed like a stone on Brocktree's stomach, driving the wind from him completely. The hogbabe seized his friend's whiskers and hauled on them.

'Cummon, B'ock, we go an' fish f'fishes inna big water!'

The badger gasped breathlessly as he tried to sit up. 'Dotti, get this fiend off me! Throw him in the sea!'

Dotti had been trying to patch up the battered shawl she was taking as a gift for her aunt Blench. She stuffed it carelessly back into her bag and grabbed Skittles's paw. 'Come on, wretch, we'll go down t'the water for a paddle.'

Skittles held out his other paw to Bucko, whom he was quite friendly with. 'Buck go for paggles too?'

The mountain hare rose, dusting off sand. 'Aye, ah like wettin' mah paws in the sea. C'mon, laddie.'

'Goin' paddlin', miss Dotti? Splendid! We'll join you, wot?'

'Rather! Nothin' like a jolly old paddle 'neath the stars!'

Southpaw and Bobweave joined the ever-growing paddling party.

'Burr, oi bain't feared of ee gurt sea, oi'll cumm too!'

Mirklewort chased after them, waving a towel. 'Wait fer me. I'll need to give my liddle babe a good dryin' when he's paddled. Seawater can cause cornfluggenza, y'know. That's wot my ole grandma used ter say, an' she knew!'

Southpaw winked at Bobweave. 'Cornfluggenza, eh? Sounds pretty serious, wot?'

'Oh, I don't know. With a blinkin' name like that you wouldn't know whether to eat it or suffer from it, old lad.'

When they reached the tideline the sea looked enchanting. A half-moon cast a path of golden ripples out from the horizon, and small foam-crested waves ran ashore, spangled with starlight, hissing softly on the cool wet sand as they broke. Those who wore smocks tucked them up into their belts. Holding paws in a line they jumped over each wave as it arrived, splashing and laughing joyously.

'Oh one two three, come to me,
From far o'er the briny sea,
Four five six, each wave flicks,
Past my paws, the sand it licks,
Sev'n eight nine, all in line,
This one rolling in is mine,
One to ten, rise and wane,
Swelling as they come again!'

Bucko Bigbones splashed water at Gurth. 'Yeehoo! Ah've no done this since ah was a bairn!'

The smiling mole splashed back. 'Hoo urr, oi bain't never dunn ee pagglen afore, zurr. Gurt fun 'tis furr a choild loik oi!'

Skittles wriggled free of Dotti and Bucko. Throwing himself flat, he lay on his back in the sea, spouting water like a tiny whale. 'Yeeuk! Dis water tasters salty t'me!'

Mirklewort, who had stayed dry on the shore, dashed into the shallows brandishing her towel frantically. 'Spit it out, yew naughty 'og, or ye'll get seahytiss an' yore teeth'll drop out! Owww! Why diddent I 'ave a liddle nice-mannered 'ogmaid, 'stead o' this umthreekerr-fumchin!'

The instant Skittles saw his mother bearing down on him he took off. In a spray of giggles and splashes he romped away along the edge of the tideline. Dotti and the rest gave chase. Skittles, as they had noticed before, could move surprisingly fast for an infant hedgehog.

'I say, come back, you little rip!'

'Och, the wee pincushion's awa' like a fish!'

'Get ee back yurr, maister Skikk!'

They pursued him until he could run no more. The hogbabe sat down in the shallows, twitching his head-spikes resignedly. 'Skikkles 'ad 'nuff now. Muvver can dry me!'

The paddling party sat down on the beach, whilst Mirklewort scrubbed at her son with the towel. 'Wot've yew been told about runnin' off, yew drefful liddle 'og? Wait'll yer father 'ears about this, yew brigand!'

Gurth silenced her with a wave of his digging claws. 'Yurr, 'ush ee, marm. Miz Dott, can ee 'ear ought?'

Dotti's finely tuned ears quivered this way and that. 'Matter o' fact I can, Gurth. South of here, it seems t'be comin' from. Sounds like some sort of a ding-dong goin' on!'

Southpaw and Bobweave were up and running south along the shoreline, calling back to the others.

'Sit tight, chaps, we'll be back in a tick, wot!'

'Aye, you stay an' rest y'self, miss Dotti. We'll investigate!'

Bucko sat the well-dried Skittles on his lap. 'Hoots, laddie, bide here they say. Look at yon pair go!'

Dotti borrowed the damp towel to wipe her footpaws. 'Indeed, sah, I think the bloomin' wind would have trouble tryin' to keep up with those twins!'

Gurth found some flat pebbles, and they passed the time by skimming them across the shallows.

Neck and neck, sand spurting from their paws, the hare twins raced back, looking as fresh as when they left. Both were excited and disturbed at the same time.

'Vermin, those blue vermin old Fleetscut mentioned!'

'About a hundred an' fifty o' the blighters!'

'Got a small bunch o' hares'n'otters surrounded, the cads!'

'That's right, an' they're attackin' the poor creatures!'

'Jolly unfair, I'd say. Those otters'n'hares are takin' a terrible hammerin'!'

Bucko Bigbones grabbed a chunk of driftwood. 'Dorothea, awa' wi' ye, bring Brocktree an' the tribes! Mirklewort, bide here wi' Gurth an' the bairn, point the way for 'em! Ye twins, find yersel' a weapon apiece an' take me tae the battle. We'll lend a paw 'til oor clans arrive!'

*

Willip lay dead on the rocks. Stiffener stood over her body, a whirling sling in one paw, a sword in the other, slashing and whacking at the vermin as they hurled themselves at him. A spear had chopped a chunk out of one of Trobee's ears, and he and Sailears had been driven from their position. They stood out on the sand, backs against the rocks, thrusting hard with their spears. Brogalaw shouldered an otter who had been struck twice by arrows. The sea otter Skipper was using his broken javelin as a club. He roared out to Stiffener, his voice ringing over the mêlée.

'Stiff, there's two outside the circle. Get 'em back, mate!'

Stiffener bounded down on to the sand. Cracking the skull of one rat and slashing ferociously at two others, he drove them away from Sailears and Trobee, giving them space. 'Git back up on those rocks, you two, quick!' Turning, he ran a weasel through and flattened a stoat with a swift hefty punch.

Ripfang had done what all careful vermin officers usually do; he had stayed out of the battle, directing it from the rear and laying about the half-hearted ones who tried to hang back. He had kept Doomeye with him, but his brother had bloodlust in his eyes now that he could see victory in sight. The searat licked his cutlass blade and danced on the spot with frustration.

'Lemme at 'em, Rip. I wanna kill a few!'

Ripfang nudged him sharply. 'Nah, yew don't wanna do that, Doom. Look, they've retreated fer their last stand. There ain't many left, but they got nothin' t'lose now, so they'll be real dangerous. Stay out!'

But Doomeye dashed forward, waving his blade. 'I ain't scared! C'mon, Rip, let's see the colour o' their guts! Yahaaarrrr, char—'

Doomeye got no further. Bucko laid him senseless with the chunk of driftwood he was swinging. Ripfang turned and dodged just in time to avoid his second blow. 'Wha

. . . you ain't one o' them, are yer? I ain't seen you before.'

Southpaw and Bobweave needed no weapons. Both their long hind legs crashed into Ripfang's head, knocking him out cold.

Only ten hares and otters were left, forming a tight circle in the sand at the centre of the rock circle. The vermin stormed over the rocks and leapt at them, but were repulsed by the ferocity of the reception they received from the gallant defenders. However, the vermin knew they had won the battle and they pressed home their assault once more. Stiffener had lost his weapon, and was using only his knotted paws now. Brog pounded away at the wave of foebeasts with all he had left, a shattered javelin and a lump of rock.

Over the clash of battle the Skipper of Sea Otters called out to his remaining friends: 'Give it one last go, mateys. We'll meet by the banks o' the sunny streams, along with those who've already gone!'

Suddenly a cry arose from outside the circle.

'Eulaliiiiiaaaaa!'

Bucko and the twins came roaring in. They crashed into the enemy's flank and broke through to join the beleaguered party. Momentarily the vermin fell back.

'Ah'm Bucko Bigbones, the mad March hare frae the North Mountains. Och, 'tis a grand auld evenin' tae be battlin'!'

Stiffener wiped blood from his eye and gaped in amazement. 'By the fur'n'fang, what are you two doin' 'ere?'

Southpaw and Bobweave crouched in fighters' stances, grinning at the hesitant vermin surrounding them.

'What ho, Gramps? Nice time t'pay a visit, wot!'

'Thought we'd drop in an' lend a paw. Left or right, no difference to us, old chap!'

A venturesome ferret, who had aspirations to captaincy, charged forward, urging the rest on. 'There's only three of 'em. Charge!'

He collapsed under a frightening barrage of hefty blows from Bobweave, who shouted as he delivered the punches, 'Sorry t'make a liar out of you, old lad, but listen. Eulaliiiiaaaaaa!'

His war cry echoed back at him like rolling thunder.

'Eulaliiiiaaaaaa!'

Blue Hordebeasts were battered in all directions as Lord Brocktree mounted the rocks, swinging his mighty sword. The vermin fled screaming, though none of them got more than twenty paces. Squirrels, shrews, hares, otters, moles and hedgehogs fell upon them. They took no prisoners. Stiffener sat down upon the sand, staring at the Badger Lord, completely bewildered.

'It's like seeing Lord Stonepaw when he was young, but bigger, much bigger. Who is this badger?'

Fleetscut ambled up and sat down beside his old friend. 'That's the great Lord Brocktree. Big, ain't he? A regular one-beast army an' no mistake, wot!'

'Fleetscut! My dear ole chap – where did you spring from? Is this your doing – did you find Southpaw and Bobweave, and bring Lord Brocktree to our aid? Tell me everything!'

'Later, ole friend. There's business to do first.'

Introductions were made all round, then the Badger Lord took command. 'Log a Log Grenn, see if any vermin survived. I want no more killing – bring them to me. Jukka, tell your squirrels to take these dead Hordebeasts and leave them below the tideline. The sea will take care of them.'

Immediately, Jukka's tribe set about stripping the dead vermin of armour and weapons. Fleetscut could not help making a loud observation, within Jukka's hearing.

'Scavengers! Nought but a pack o' carrion crows!'

Jukka hurled herself at him, but the sturdy Ruff leapt between the beasts as they strained to get at each other.

'Thou longeared glutton, who gave thee the right to talk of my tribe in such a manner?'

'I did, that's who, you bunch of bushtailed carcass-thieves!'

Brog came across to help Ruff hold them apart. 'Whoa now, less o' that talk. Stow it, you two. At this rate you'll end up no better than the vermin we're against!'

'Aye, lissen t'the sea otter an' get some sense in yore skulls. We're supposed t'be friends, not foes!'

They backed off from each other, glowering.

Ripfang, Doomeye and a round dozen vermin, who had been knocked unconscious and still looked distinctly groggy, were paraded in front of the stern-faced Brocktree. He silenced their excuses and pleas by picking up his sword. 'Stop whining. There's nought worse than cowards crying. Now, are your leaders slain, or are they here? Speak!'

'Those two, sire, Ripfang an' Doomeye!'

Both searats glared daggers of hatred at the one who spoke.

Brocktree looked the brothers over. 'Heed me if you wish to live. You and your creatures will bury our dead. Here, in this sand at the centre of this rock circle. Carry them carefully, treat them respectfully. My creatures will be watching you, to see that you do.'

On all fours, the vermin were forced to dig a hole with their paws. Brog, Stiffener and the remainder of the Bark Crew placed their slain friends gently in the grave. When it was filled in, the Badger Lord turned his attention back to the huddle of trembling vermin.

'This shall be the epitaph of these brave warriors, that they died fighting against superior odds, with no hope. Yet they never deserted their comrades, in whose memories they will live on. If fortune had been reversed, do you think they would have trembled and wept for their lives? Do you?' His voice rose so sharply that the vermin sat bolt upright. Brocktree did not wait for their answer, but continued, 'No, they would not act as you do now, they had courage! And I will not act now as you would have, had you been the victors of this fray. I will not kill you – your miserable lives are spared. But I want you to take a message back to your master, from me, Lord Brocktree of Brockhall!'

31

It was late morn of the following day. Ungatt Trunn exited by a window space, high up on the mountain, and strode up a winding path to a lookout post. Karangool was there with two sentries. He saluted the wildcat. 'Might'ness!'

Both sentries slid past Trunn and backed off down the path, saluting and bowing furiously. He watched them, puzzled. 'Where are those two going?'

The saturnine fox pointed north and slightly west. 'Ambush party be comin' back, Might'ness.'

The wildcat's first reaction was to smile, but his face stiffened as he glimpsed the fourteen figures, neck deep in the sea, ploughing their way homeward. Wordlessly he swept past Karangool, back down the path. The fox followed him. As they came out on to the shore, Karangool looked back. Fragorl was watching from a chamber window, but now she ducked down out of sight, not wanting to be involved with what would follow. Wisely, Karangool dropped behind a pace or two.

Ungatt Trunn stared in disbelief as the pitiful party stumbled out of the sea. As before, the blue dye had gone from their coats; only their heads were still blue. Each had their paws bound tightly in front. Moreover, they could not avoid walking in a straight line. They had been linked together, at neck height, by four long pikes, lashed two by two, the poles pressing close against their necks. At either end of the pikes were long metal spearheads, which had been twisted together, two at each end, sealing the fourteen like peas in a pod. They collapsed on the sand, fighting for breath, for seawater had swelled the wooden pikeshafts, tightening their grip about the captives' necks.

Karangool signalled some vermin. They prised the pikes apart, slicing at the ropes that held them together. When they were freed, Ripfang and the rest lay exhausted, rubbing their throats as they gasped in fresh air. The fox inspected the metal pikeheads, wondering what creature possessed the strength to twist them into two spirals like that.

Trunn snatched the cutlass from a nearby Hordebeast. Karangool averted his eyes as the wildcat honed the blade on a rock, putting a sharp jagged edge on it. This he placed against Ripfang's throat.

'Where are the bodies of the Bark Crew? Where are the hundred and a half soldiers I sent out to deal with them? Answer me truthfully and I will spare you a slow death!' The wildcat stepped back a pace and swung the sword high to one side. He brought it slashing down, expertly stopping the blade a fraction from Ripfang's exposed neck, and roared, 'Tell me, you worthless lump of offal!'

Ripfang spoke four words as if they were a magic spell. 'I saw the badger.'

The sword clattered against a rock as it fell from Trunn's paw. He sat down in the sand next to Ripfang, as if pushed there by a giant paw.

'Leave us. Everybeast go!'

Karangool, the guards nearby, Doomeye and the others scattered, leaving Trunn and Ripfang together, alone on the shore. The tail flicked out and pulled the searat close.

'I will not slay you. I have a half-cask of wine; it is yours if you tell me all. What did he look like, what did he say, who was with him, what manner of beasts? Tell me.'

Ripfang relaxed and squinted up at the sun. 'Er, an' I'm still a cap'n, an' me brother Doomeye too?'

'Yes, of course. Now tell me . . . please.'

The searat pulled Trunn's tail from round his neck. 'Where's this 'alf-cask o' wine first? I'm thirsty.'

As night fell, campfires blazed openly in the dunes facing the cave in the cliffs. Frutch sat out on a tussock at the cavemouth, her son by her side. Several others sat around close, enjoying some of the ottermum's plum and nut slices, hot from the oven. She looked about at the teeming scene and clapped a paw to her cheek. 'Well dearie me, well I never, fates a mercy! I never did see so many creatures in all me born days!'

Brogalaw hugged his mother and planted a big kiss on her brow. 'Ahoy there, Mum, are you goin' t'keep on sayin' that all night? You missed out "well nail my rudder"!'

Frutch wiped her eyes on an apron corner, passed Dotti another slice and patted her son's paw thankfully. 'Well seasons o' saltwater an' nail my rudder, where did ye find all these nice beasts, Brog?'

The sea otter grinned at his new friend Ruff. 'Well, at least she's changed 'er tune, mate. Oh, look out, 'ere comes tears by the blinkin' pailful!'

Blench and Woebee joined Frutch. In a trice they were all passing kerchiefs, weeping and snuffling. Dotti licked crumbs from her paw and looked quizzically at Brog. 'Beg pardon, sah, but do they always do that?'

'Only when they're 'appy, miss. P'raps you'd like to give 'em a song? That always calms 'em down a mite.' He winced as Brocktree's paw dug him in the side. 'Oof! Wot did I say?'

The Badger Lord shook his head mournfully. 'You'll find out, my friend, you'll soon find out!'

Stiffener remonstrated sternly with the hare twins. 'Stop fightin', you two. Wot are you doin' with the young 'un's bag?'

'Just gettin' miss Dotti's harecordion out, Gramps.'

'No you ain't, chum, *I'm* gettin' it for miss Dotti. I say, Gramps, wait'll you hear her sing. She's a pip!'

Dotti rescued her instrument, smiling sweetly at her admirers as she explained to the weeping trio, 'My fatal beauty, y'know, does it every time. Did I tell you I was nearly a queeness, or somethin' like that? Never mind, ladies, I'll sing you a cheery old ditty, wot!' Without further ado, Dotti launched into her song.

'Did ever I tell you when I was born,
Pa cried we were clear out of luck,
He sent me out searchin' for honey,
An' my head in a beehive got stuck!
Poor mother was so forgetful,
She put a plum pudden in bed,
An' covered my brother with custard,
"That'll do us for supper," she said!

Oh woe is me, what a family,
There used t'be just six of us,
But now there's thirty-three . . . heeheeheeheeeeee!

The day Grandma took up knitting,
She couldn't tell yarn from fur,
But she clacked her needles all evening,
An' knitted herself to the chair!
My sisters left home for ever,
Then returned wet an' soakin' with tears,
The fire had died, so 'twas I got 'em dried,
I pegged 'em all out by their ears!

Oh woe is me, not another more,
There used t'be thirty-three of us,

But now there's thirty-four . . . hawhawhawhaaaaaw!

Old uncle was hard of hearing,
He'd a trumpet to hold by his ear,
Poor auntie was so short-sighted,
That she often filled it with beer!
When a squirrel dropped by for a visit,
She tidied the place in a rush,
Auntie swept the floor an' varnished the door,
By using his tail as a brush!

Oh woe is me an' hares alive,
There used t'be thirty-four of us,
But now there's thirty-five . . . iiiiiiiiiiiiive!'

Blench had been staring hard at Dotti, gnawing the hem of her kerchief, whilst the haremaid was singing. They had not been introduced. The old cook's ears suddenly stiffened as she recognised the family likeness, and her paw shot out accusingly.

'Dillworthy! I knew it as soon as I clapped eyes on you, miss. Those young hares called you Dotti. You must be Daphne's daughter, Dorothea!'

Dotti's harecordion gave out an unearthly squeak, as both she and it were squeezed in a vicelike hug.

'Aunt Blench?'

'Of course it is, ye young snip. I should've reckernised that voice right away. Last time I saw ye was when you were a liddle fluffy babe, yellin' for lettuce broth. What a racket!'

Overcome by the emotion of the moment, Dotti burst into tears, as did her aunt. Brog led them back to his mum and Woebee, who joined them in a good loud weep. Ruff groaned and covered both ears. 'Rap me rudder, mate, 'tis 'ard to tell wot's worse, lissenin' to Dotti's caterwaulin' or yore mum's cryin' choir!'

Baron Drucco hurried them both into the cave. 'Let's

see if there's somewheres quieter in 'ere. I tell yer, we could use those four agin the enemy. Bet they'd drive 'em offa that Sammalandrocrum mountain!'

Log a Log Grenn went with them. As she patted Brog's shoulder she noticed him wincing. 'Yore shoulder's wounded, Brog!'

The sea otter managed a rueful grin. 'So 'tis, marm, but don't tell my mum, or there won't be a dry eye this side o' winter. I'll take care of it.'

The shrew beckoned one of the squirrels over. 'Let Ruro see it. She's the best ever for healin' wounds.'

An immense feeling of joy and relief reigned over the cliffs and cave, which the small party of hares and otters had used as their hiding place. The centre of it all was Lord Brocktree. The big badger radiated quiet strength and confidence. Creatures passed close to him, so that they could reach out and touch his huge form, or admire the massive sword, with Skittles perched half asleep between its double hilts. Now they could sit out in the open, feeling safe and reassured by his presence. Sailears summed it all up in a single phrase.

'At last we've got a leader, a real Badger Lord!'

Cooking fires were stoked up to full pitch that night. Frutch left off weeping to show her multitude of guests what sea otter hospitality was all about. The ottermum and her helpers were happy to accept the offer of assistance from Guosim cooks, squirrels, hedgehogs, and the ever-smiling Gurth, son of Rogg Longladle.

'Yurr, missus, whurr did ee foind all ee shrimpers?'

Woebee hauled out another netful, which Durvy and his crew had brought back that afternoon. 'From our very own fisherbeasts, sir, good old Durvy an' the seafarin' Bark Crew!'

Konul the cheeky ottermaid raised her rudder in surprise. 'You was singin' a different tune this mornin', marm. Ye threatened to boil me whiskers if we brought back more shrimp. Good job we did, though.'

Blench appeared in their midst, swirling proudly. 'My niece Dotti brought me this shawl from my sister Daphne. It's been in our family a long time. Isn't it pretty?'

The shawl had been shredded, patched, torn, tattered and inexpertly repaired. But Blench was enchanted with the family heirloom and nobeast was about to hurt her feelings.

'Oh, it's, er, very unusual, but beautiful!'

'Rather! I like that light brown weave on the hem!'

The light brown weave crumbled off under Woebee's paw. It was mud which had turned to dust. Blench carried on swirling and showing it off, blissfully unaware.

'Lovely, ain't it? An' can ye smell that perfume from it? Reminds me of somethin', though I can't just think wot it is.'

'Hmm, a bit like pale ole cider, eh?'

Dotti trod meaningly on Ruff's footpaw and glared at him. 'Never! 'Twas a special perfume belongin' to Grandma. I had a lovely letter from my mother too, y'know, but it got lost.'

Southpaw and Bobweave took Dotti's paws and hauled her away.

'I say, miss Dotti, come an' lend a paw with the supplies!'

'These chaps have got a great caveful o' vittles up yonder!'

She made a hasty exit accompanied by the twins.

The feast was an epic triumph, with the centrepiece a great cauldron of shrimp'n'hotroot soup, cooked to Frutch's own family recipe. The Guosim cooks produced pear flans, apple pies, blackberry tarts and rhubarb crumble. Mirklewort and her hograbble contributed loaves and biscuits, hot from the ovens. Gurth placed himself in charge of drinks. He made mint and rosehip tea, a cordial of dandelion and burdock and a great deal of fruit punch. Brogalaw had the sentries relieved often, so that all could join in. Skittles tried to keep his eyes open, but he was so tired that he fell asleep with a ladle of crumble still in one paw. It was inevitable that singing and dancing would break out; there were many good dancers among the tribes gathered there. A sea otter shanty was started by Brog's two young singing otters, accompanied by drums, flutes and stone clappers. Amid much fancy pawstepping by hares, otters, hedgehogs and squirrels, the music rattled along at a breakneck pace.

'Oh rowtledy dowtledy doodle hi ay,
We're full of plum duff an' salt water!
Now the *Rowtledy Dow* was a leaky ole craft,
With aprons an' kerchiefs for sails fore an' aft,
An' all of her crew thought the cap'n was daft,
An' he was sure they was all barmy!
Her anchor was made from a big rusty pot,
That they hauled up each mornin' to serve dinner hot,
But the crew was too slow so the cook scoffed the lot,
An' a seagull flew off with the pudden!
So 'tis heave away mateys the wind's blowin' west,
An' the cabin mole's wearin' his grandma's blue vest,
While the mate's got a blanket tattooed on his chest,
To keep his fat stummick from freezin'!
Well there's fish in the sea better mannered than we,
For they washes their flippers an' don't slop their tea,
An' we'd be better off on the land don't yer see,
'Cos I think that the ould ship is sinkin'!
Oh rowtledy dowtledy doodle hi ay,
Nail a pie to the door for me mother!'

They sang it again, this time at double speed. Hares leapt high, seeing if they could wiggle their ears six times before hitting the ground again (Bucko could do eight earwiggles – he was the envy of all). Dancers had often to jig out of the way of hedgehogs revolving in mad spins.

Otters twined their tails and somersaulted over the fire. Squirrels high-kicked wildly, gritting their teeth as sand flew about. Around them all, the Guosim shrews joined paws and spun in a wide eye-blurring wheel. Right at the centre, Gurth danced sedately with Brog's mum, bowing and hopping gracefully, whilst Frutch curtsied and performed dainty little steps, holding her apron wide.

Old Bramwil sat chuckling with Brocktree. 'Will y'look at them, sire! I never saw such jiggin' in all me seasons, wot! I say, that pretty young 'un, Dotti, those hare twins won't leave her alone. They want every blinkin' dance with her!'

Brocktree chuckled. 'She'd be disappointed if they did leave her alone, a fatal beauty like our Dotti. Tell me, Bramwil, what was my father Stonepaw like? You served under him, didn't you?'

Bramwil wiped both eyes on a large spotty kerchief and blew his nose. 'Lord Stonepaw was the wisest, gentlest beast a hare ever knew. He was my Badger Lord and my good friend, sire.'

Brocktree knew he was upsetting the old hare, but he had to put the question which he had been too moved to ask when Stiffener had sat between himself and Fleetscut and told them that Lord Stonepaw was dead.

'I never knew him very well, you see. Badgers leave home whilst their sons are still young. 'Twould be a tense household with two grown male badgers in it. Now, I don't want every little detail, but please tell me, how did he die?'

Bramwil stared into the fire, answering without hesitation. 'He went bravely, lord, more courageously than anybeast could imagine, surrounded by those blue murderers! He laid down his life to give us time to escape.'

Brocktree put a paw about Bramwil's shaking shoulders. 'You've no need to distress yourself further, old one. I know now. My father died like a true Badger

Lord, full of the Bloodwrath, taking many vermin with him.'

Bramwil's tears sizzled in the embers at the fire's edge as he nodded and dabbed at his eyes. ''Twas so, lord, 'twas so!'

Brocktree rose, flickering flame shadows playing over his immobile face. Bramwil looked up at him. The Badger Lord looked like something carved from rock, which had stood there since the dawn of time.

At last, Brocktree shouldered his sword. 'Waste no more tears, you good old beast. Stonepaw would not want grief, he would want retribution. I am here now. It is the turn of Ungatt Trunn and his vermin to suffer. I will make them weep full sore before they die!' He strode off towards the clifftops, alone.

Bucko Bigbones threw himself down beside Bramwil, panting from the dance. He seized a flagon of cordial and drained it. 'Hey, auld 'un, I seen ye talkin' wi' the big boyo. Och, 'twill be a thing tae see when that'n takes hamself aff tae battle!'

Ungatt Trunn could not sleep. He wandered the upper passages of Salamandastron until he came to a small chamber on its north side, where he had chosen to store his own armour and weapons. His restless eyes sought out a long trident leaning against the wall. He took the weapon and hefted it. This trident had served him well many times in battle. Three barb-headed copper prongs gleamed dully in the torchlight; he ran his paw over the oaken shaft until it met the cord-bound grip at its middle. Grasping it firmly, he went to the window and stood staring out towards the cliffs in the distance.

'Brocktree of Brockhall, eh? So that's what they call you. I know you are out there somewhere, Badger Lord. I am Ungatt Trunn the Earth Shaker, who makes the stars fall from the sky. This mountain is mine by right of conquest. Here I stay – come to me!'

He pointed out of the window at the cliffs with his trident.

Brocktree stood on the clifftops, the night breeze ruffling his fur, though his eyes never once blinked against the wind. He gazed at the dark shape to the south, the mountain looming high on the western shore edge. Drawing his sword, he pointed it at Salamandastron, starlight shimmering along the burnished blade's length.

'I know your face, wildcat; soon you will see mine. I am coming. Eulaliiiiiaaaaaaa!'

32

Morning sun shone down on a strange scene. Durvy and his crew also witnessed it, and they turned from the water's edge and hastened back to camp. Leaders of all the tribes and crews were taking breakfast inside the cave with Brocktree, about to begin a council of war, when Durvy and Konul dashed in, breathless and excited.

'Come an' see! All the bluebottoms are paradin' out along the shore!'

The Badger Lord put aside his food. 'Where?'

'I'd say 'bout a third the distance 'twixt 'ere an' the mountain. 'Tis a sight t'see, eh, Konul?'

The cheeky-faced ottermaid was grim and shaken. 'Aye. You can't see the sands o' the beach for 'em!'

Rulango the heron stalked into the cave. Log a Log Grenn took a backward pace at the sight of the fearsome bird. 'Where did that monster come from?'

Brog went to Rulango and stroked his neck. 'I forgot to tell ye about this 'un. He's Rulango, the eyes'n'ears of the Bark Crew. Where'd you get to yesterday, mate?'

He cleared a patch in the sand, and Rulango sketched out several fishes. Brog nodded. 'Fishin', eh? Well, you've got to eat, just like anybeast. No need to tell us wot's down on the shore, we know.'

But the heron kept dabbing his talons down on the sand, until it was covered in tiny dots.

'See all these dots? Each one's a bluebottom,' Brog explained.

Rulango scraped out a row of scratches.

'He says that for every scratch there's that many again. Too many for 'im t'sketch!'

Brocktree shouldered his sword. 'Come on, I've got to see this. Bring your weapons!'

Brocktree took with him a selected small band, Dotti and the twins among them. Using the dunes as cover and keeping low, they threaded their way south, between the sandhills at the base of the cliffs. When Durvy judged they had gone far enough he led them west towards the shore. Dotti wriggled her way forward, joining Brocktree and Ruff in the long grass on top of a high dune.

'Oh my giddy aunt, look at that lot!'

Rank upon rank of Blue Hordebeasts lined the beach, twenty wide and ten deep, almost as far as the eye could see. Each section comprised vermin carrying different weapons. One group had pikes, another javelins, yet another was made up of archers; there were slingers, swordbeasts and club wielders, each headed by a captain. Ruff started a hasty calculation in the sand, but he soon gave up.

''Tis no use, matey. They'd eat our little army alive.'

Bucko and Fleetscut crawled up beside them and lay gaping.

'By the left, sah, I didn't imagine there were that many blinkin' vermin on earth!'

'Och, 'twould be plain suicide goin' up against yon vermin!'

However, the Badger Lord took no notice of their comments. His eyes roved slowly over the scene below. 'I don't see their leader. Ungatt Trunn isn't there!'

Dotti pointed out a figure standing at the head of a group of officers below the tideline. 'I say, sah, what about that chap? He looks like a sort of commandin' type, wot?'

The Badger Lord studied the one Dotti had singled out. 'He's no wildcat. Looks like a fox to me. Anybeast know who he is?'

Durvy shaded his eyes against the sun. 'That's Karangool, Cap'n in Chief of Trunn's fleet.'

Bucko was halfway up, his eyes blazing madly. 'Aye, so 'tis. Bide ye here. Ah'm bound tae kill the scum that slaughtered my family!'

Brocktree and Ruff bore the mountain hare down forcibly, though he struggled like a wild beast. 'Take yer paws offa me. Ah hae business wi' yon fox!'

Brocktree leaned heavily on Bucko, pinning him firmly. 'Your business is our business too, friend. I'm not getting this party slain or captured because of you. Now, do you want me to sit on you? I'm quite heavy, you know.'

Bucko spat out sand, but did not attempt to move. 'Ach, ye can let me go, Brock, ah'll deal wi' yon scum another time. Ah wiz behavin' like a fool!'

They released him and continued watching the vermin.

'What are you thinkin', sah?' Dotti murmured to Brock.

The Badger Lord never took his eyes off the Hordebeasts. 'Right at this moment I'm thinking lots of things, miss. My first thought is that Brog and the Bark Crew have been doing an excellent job. Hah! That's what I was waiting for. Did you see that rat? Front rank third column, there!'

'I see him. He's just fallen over. Tripped on his spear, d'you think, sah?'

'No, Dotti, he's fainted with hunger. The captains seem well enough, but take a good look at the rank and file vermin. Ruff, what do you see?'

'Look like they're 'avin' a pretty thin time o' things. I'd say they was starvin', the whole gang of 'em!'

Brocktree glanced back at the clifftops. 'Right, but more

of that later. I think we'd best make ourselves scarce. I can see your bird hovering up yonder, Brog – he'll be flying over here to tell you that there's more vermin leaving the mountain to come along the clifftops. The wildcat is a clever general. He wouldn't miss the chance of hitting us from behind, whilst we're busy watching his troops. Let's get out of here quickly and quietly.'

As they slid down the rear of the dune, Brog gave orders. 'Everybeast keep low. Back to the caves now, quickly. Durvy, take Urvo, Radd an' Konul an' cover our trail!'

Ungatt Trunn sat in council with Karangool and Fragorl. Ripfang was present, too. They waited respectfully until the wildcat spoke. 'Do you think they saw the parade?'

Karangool shrugged. 'Might'ness, who can tell? I did not see them.'

Trunn nodded at Fragorl to make her report. 'They could not have been there, O Great One. I led the ambush party along the clifftops. We searched the dunes, and there was no sign of them, not even pawprints, sire.'

Ripfang put in his opinion. 'I did like you said, Mightiness, took a ship along the coast. There was no sign of 'em watchin' from the sea.'

The wildcat paced the chamber, shaking his head. 'But I know they were there, spying on my Hordes. The badger is no fool. He would have taken the opportunity to assess our strength, I know it!'

Ripfang gave voice to what the others were thinking. 'That 'orde on the beach t'day, they coulda swept up both sides o' the cliffs an' scoured yore enemies out.'

Ungatt Trunn sat down, looking thoughtful. 'Yes, I could have done that, but it would leave the mountain undefended. Any good commander knows that this mountain is the prize; the beast who holds it fights from a position of strength. I want them to come to me.'

'Might'ness, what if they don't?'

Trunn's claws drummed a tattoo on the tabletop. 'Then I will have to do as Ripfang says, send the Hordes to root them out, eh, Ripfang?'

The other two were surprised that Trunn should ask the former searat's opinion. So was Ripfang, but he answered readily enough.

'Aye, yer right there, sir, but I wouldn't leave it too long if'n I was you. Every day yore beasts are gittin' more 'ungry. Yew can't afford a long drawn out wait.'

Ungatt Trunn turned his eyes to his source of inspiration. 'Spiders are like that too. They will wait, but not for long. The moment the time is ripe they pounce!'

Back at the store cave, Jukka gave out the last bundle of weapons, to be distributed around.

'There, 'tis empty now. This will be thy home for a while.'

Frutch held her lantern up to get a better view. 'I like the other cave better. This 'un's a bit poky!'

Blench tightened her apron strings resolutely. 'Don't fret, dearie, we'll soon make this comfortable. I'll get some moles to scoop out the back there, where the rocks are loose. We'll put the ovens agin that wall. Woebee, what d'you think about that ledge yonder?'

'Spread with moss an' sailcloth 'twill make fine seats'n'beds. I'm glad we used up the last o' the shrimp – mayhap we can get some decent meals cooked. Shall I ask the shrewcooks to lend a paw with the dinner, Frutch?'

'I'd be beholden t'them if'n they did. Such good cooks!'

Lord Brocktree was addressing a meeting in the big valley between the dunes outside the old cave. Everybeast fit to march or fight was in attendance. They sat on the dunesides and hilltops, listening to what their leader had to say.

'We saw many vermin on the shore this morning, more than a beast could shake ten sticks at. It was meant to be Ungatt Trunn's show of force, though the vermin looked so thin and starved that it was more a show of weakness! But still, they are far too numerous for us to meet in open warfare. Now I have some ideas of my own, but I am open to good and sensible suggestions as to how they can be defeated.'

Brog immediately held up his paw. 'I says we carry on cuttin' off their supplies. The Bark Crew was doin' a first class job, you said it yoreself.'

Ruff answered for the Badger Lord. 'Aye, mate, but if we carries on cuttin' off their vittles Trunn'll git desperate sooner or later, an' they'll come out in force after us. With the numbers they got, we'll lose!'

There was a murmur of agreement. Brocktree held up his paws. 'Good. That's what I was hoping you'd say – 'tis what I was thinking myself. But I have a plan!'

'Burr, then do ee tell uz ee plan, zurr. Us'n's gettin' orful 'ungered settin' owt yurr!'

General laughter greeted Gurth's good mole logic. Grenn had food brought out by the Guosim, Drucco's rabblehogs lending a paw.

It was late afternoon by the time Brocktree finished outlining his plan, which was wholeheartedly approved. Bucko winked admiringly at the badger. 'Ah ken noo why Badger Lairds are braw canny beasts!'

Brocktree's fierce dark eyes looked appraisingly round. 'Everybeast here has their own special part to play. I know 'tis a perilous and risky scheme, but I think it'll work. So, are you with me? Hold up your paws all in favour.'

Not one creature held back. Every paw went up. Skittles held up all four paws, lying flat on his back.

'Us wiv ya, B'ock mate!'

The difficult part was explaining to Frutch and the very old ones, who would be remaining behind, hidden in the supply cave. Brogalaw tried to placate his weeping mother.

'Hush now, Mum, we'll take that ole mountain

quicker'n you can say nail me rudder. You can 'ave a nice liddle room there, all of yore own, an' a rock garden too. You allus wanted a rock garden, didn't you, me ole darlin'?'

But Frutch was not to be consoled. 'Go an' do wot you gotta do, Brogalaw, but come back alive t'me, ye great tailwhackin' lump. Never mind tryin' to get round me wid mountain caves an' rock gardens. When this is all over I don't want none of it. Tell ye wot I would like, though – to go back down southcoast, to our ole 'ome. Oh, I do miss it!'

Blench loaned Frutch a corner of her apron to weep into. The old cook patted Brog's paw. 'We'll take good care of yore mum, Brog. You get goin' now. Get our mountain back for us. Fates'n'seasons o' fortune go with ye. Oh, an' keep an eye out for that niece o' mine. Dorothea's a brave hare, but young an' 'eadstrong.'

Brog gave the old cook a hug. 'Bless yore 'eart, marm, I'll do me best for us all, you got my word. Stay safe now an' don't weep too much, it makes the bread soggy.'

On the way out of the cave, Brog stopped to stroke the heron's long neck and speak softly to the bird. 'You stay 'ere now, my ole matey. Take good care of these old 'uns an' don't stay out fishin' too long. I'll see you when 'tis all done, I 'ope!'

Rulango laid his beak on Brog's shoulder and blinked, and the sea otter Skipper patted him roughly. 'Come on now, ye ole rogue, don't start gettin' soft on me.' Brogalaw did quite a bit of blinking himself, then he straightened up, sniffed loudly, and left the cave.

A great pile of wood, sea coal and grass had been heaped not far from the front of the old cave. Everybeast was gathered there when Brog arrived.

'All ready, Brock. I've just been makin' me farewells to Mum an' the old 'uns.'

Dotti clapped a paw to her mouth. 'Aunt Blench! I forgot to say goodbye to her!'

Brog shouldered his javelin. 'I already did that, missie. She said that you got to take good care o' me. Liddle Skittles was sleepin' an' Mirklewort is stayin' back to keep an eye on things. There ain't a thing to keep us now, so let's be about our work!'

Lord Brocktree turned to Jukka the Sling. Nobeast would have recognised her from the disguise she wore. The squirrel Chieftain had been dyed blue, her tail was shaven and she wore a Hordebeast's uniform. Brocktree nodded approvingly. 'You look like a true vermin, friend. Now you know what you have to do?'

'Aye, lord. As soon as the bluebottoms leave the mountain I will shoot a burning shaft from one of the high windows.'

Brocktree clasped Jukka's paw. 'Good luck!'

'Huh, an' try not to plunder anythin' until we get there!'

Jukka eyed Fleetscut coldly. 'When 'tis all over, thou an' I will have a reckoning!' Then she turned and hurried off towards Salamandastron.

Ruff shook his head in disapproval at Fleetscut. 'It's not good to go into battle with bad blood 'twixt you two. Right, who's next to go, mates?'

Durvy and Konul stepped forward with their crew. Strapped to each one's back was a torch, wrapped tightly to protect it from the seawater. Brog issued final instructions. 'Don't start anythin' until you see this fire in front o' the cave lit an' blazin' well. Fortune go with ye, mates!' The sea otters slipped silently off seaward.

Brocktree looked round at those left, and took Ruff's paw. 'Your turn now, friend. You and Brog look after yourselves!'

'An' you do likewise, Lord Brocktree of Brock'all!'

Dotti and Log a Log Grenn stood watching as Brog and Ruff led the squirrels and rabblehogs off into the gathering evening. They climbed the cliffs and began a long sweep south.

'Ah well, chaps, that leaves only us now, wot?' Dotti observed.

Bucko Bigbones exposed his teeth in a wide grin. 'Aye, lassie, so whit'n the name o' seasons are we hangin' aboot for? Let's be awa, mah bairns!'

Brocktree's hefty paw descended on Bucko's shoulder. 'You stay close to me, sir, and none of your mad March mountain hare antics out of you, understand?'

Bucko checked the six long daggers he had thrust in his belt. 'Ach, ah'll be as quiet as a wee molebabe, eh, Gurth?'

'Oi'm 'opin' ee will, zurr. Oi wurr a gudd h'infant moiself.'

Stiffener led the little army off through the dunes. 'We'll get up as close t'the tunnel afore dark as we can.'

Dotti fell in between Southpaw and Bobweave, who were simultaneously loading their slings.

'Splendid evenin' for a jolly old war, eh, miss Dotti?'

'Rather! I say, d'you want me to load your sling, miss Dotti?'

'Tut tut, old chap, *I'm* the sling-loader round here, y'know!'

The haremaid rescued her sling from the irrepressible twins. 'Oh, give it a rest, you two, I'm perfectly capable of loadin' me own bloomin' sling. Besides, Mother always told me to beware of sling-loadin' types.'

'Wise old mater, wot?'

'Pretty too, if she looks anythin' like her daughter!'

At a gruff cough from the Badger Lord, they fell silent.

Darkening clouds merged with dusky sky overhead, and the last crimson sunrays shimmered over the horizon, flaring briefly across the waves. A warm vagrant breeze stirred grass on the dunetops. Night fell, with moonshadows transforming the landscape into a patchwork of silver sand and velvet shadow. Dotti could scarce suppress a shudder of excitement and apprehension. The battle to win back Salamandastron had finally begun!

33

Ungatt Trunn paced the mountain passages like a caged beast, agitated and impatient. Everywhere he went, guards stood stiffly to attention in the torchlit corridors, holding their breath as he prowled by, his long cloak swishing. From the top level of the inner mountain he went, through every floor to the bottom. Only the sound of restless waves greeted the wildcat as he emerged, past the sentries, out on to the shore. Two searats rowed a small gig into the shallows. Leaping out, they dragged it ashore.

Captain in Chief Karangool stepped on to the beach. 'Might'ness, is quiet this night.'

Ungatt Trunn stroked his whiskers slowly. 'Too quiet altogether. I don't like it, captain. 'Tis as if something is waiting to happen. Can you feel it too?'

'Yah, Might'ness.'

Together they strolled back to the main mountain entrance. Patrols had been doubled around the perimeter, and six guards, with Ripfang at their head, marched around from the north side. They halted, saluting Trunn with their spears. He nodded to Ripfang.

'Anything to report, captain?'

'Nary a thing, sir. 'Tis like walkin' round a buryin'

ground out there, but we're keepin' a sharp lookout!'

Fragorl interrupted further conversation. She hurried out of the main entrance, her dark cloak flapping like a bird of ill omen. She pointed. 'Mighty One, over there, by the cliffside, northward, I saw it from my window, a fire!'

With Fragorl, Ripfang and Karangool scurrying in his wake, Trunn raced inside, taking stairflights in leaps and bounds.

He was breathing heavily by the time he reached the highest level. Vaulting through a frameless window space, the wildcat made his way to the high guard post. A ferret stood pointing his spear to the fire. 'There, sire!'

Even from that distance the blaze was visible, lighting up the cliffside with an orange glow. The others arrived behind Trunn. He heard Ripfang chuckle and whirled on him.

'Something appears to be amusing you, searat?'

Ripfang indicated the distant bonfire. 'You got to admit it, they ain't short o' nerve. Hah! S'posed to be 'idin' out from yer, sir, an' there they be, burnin' a whopper campfire. Aye, an' I'll wager they're cookin' too, stuffin' their gobs wid food they stole off us. Ho ho, if'n that ain't a sight ter see!'

Karangool watched the wildcat's paws shaking with anger. 'Might'ness, it could be trap!'

Ungatt Trunn grabbed him so hard that his claws sank into the fox's paw. The Captain in Chief winced as the wildcat sneered scathingly, 'Do you think I don't know that, imbecile? The insolence of those creatures, taunting Ungatt Trunn like that!'

Ripfang cleaned his single tooth with a grimy paw. 'Aye, that's wot 'tis, a taunt. Plain open defiance, like my ole cap'n used ter say. But wot are ye goin' t'do about it, that's the question, sir?'

'Karangool, take half of the entire Hordes, split them in three columns. One either side, clifftops and dunes, the third to go flat out along the shore and circle round behind them. I want the leaders alive; the rest must be slaughtered. Bring their bodies back with you!'

Shouting broke out from a sentry post facing the sea.

'Fire! Fire aboard the ships!'

Out at the western edge of the vast armada, flames could be seen licking around sails and rigging. Ungatt Trunn looked from one conflagration to the other.

'It wasn't a trap, it was a decoy to divert our attention. Well, I'm going to turn it into a trap. Karangool, take some crews out there, cut the burning vessels away from the others. Save the fleet! Fragorl, Ripfang, you will take command of those attacking the decoy fire by the cliffs. You heard my orders to Karangool. Go and carry them out!'

Ungatt Trunn went inside and beckoned the first creature he came across, a guard in the upper passages. 'You, gather together my captains, bring them to my chamber!'

In an instant the quiet of the summer night was shattered. Horde captains dashed about bellowing orders, the entire mountain bursting into a hive of activity.

Ungatt Trunn met the group of captains in the doorway of his chamber. He marched them out into the corridor and issued hasty instructions.

'I am taking over the defence of my mountain against any outside attack. Listen to me. Bar all entrances – that includes the window spaces and any paths going up the mountain. You six, take your patrols, bring in all outside sentries, repel any assaults from ground level. You four, spread your creatures about in the passages, watch out for enemy beasts trying to break in. I'll take the top levels. Send me up a hundred or more troops!'

Rulango returned to the new cave, minus the lighted torch he had been carrying in his beak. Frutch made sure the entrance was well camouflaged before she accompanied the big heron back inside. 'Did the fire light well when you dropped the torch on it?'

Rulango ruffled his feathers, spread both wings and did an odd hopping dance, nodding his beak. The ottermum smiled. 'Yore a good bird. See, I baked some slices for you!'

'Slicer for Skikkles too, eh, F'utch?'

'Bless yore liddle 'eart, o' course there is, my lovey.'

Stiffener winked at Brocktree. 'Nicely timed, sire. We won't even wet our paws, the tide's slipped out nice'n'quiet. Git the lanterns ready an' foller me. Best be quiet, though – it echoes loud in there.'

Dotti and the twins rounded the rock point, to see Stiffener holding back a jumble of kelp and seaweed with his javelin.

'C'mon, you young rips, in y'go, we ain't got all night.'

They entered the tunnel by which Stiffener and the prisoners had escaped. Southpaw lit their lantern from Gurth's torch.

'I'll be official lantern-bearer for you, miss Dotti, wot?'

To forestall further argument the haremaid agreed. 'Right, you do that, Southpaw. Bobweave, here, you can be the official sling-holder. I say, it's jolly damp an' gloomy in here, spooky too. Yeeeek! What's that?'

Brocktree pushed in ahead of them, covering Dotti's mouth with a huge paw as he investigated the grisly object.

Still partially clad in tattered rags of a uniform, the skeleton of Captain Fraul gleamed white in the lantern light. The eye sockets of the skull remained fixed in a ghastly mask of death. Tiny spike-backed crabs scuttled hither and thither over the vermin's bare bones, seeking any semblance of a gruesome meal. The Badger Lord shifted the skeleton to one side with a sweep of his footpaw, and little crabs scuttled everywhere, holding their nippers aggressively high.

Brocktree took his paw from Dotti's mouth. 'Nothing

to be feared of, miss. Looks like the skeleton of a stoat, if I'm not mistaken. Wonder how he got down here?'

Stiffener viewed the remains dispassionately. 'Who knows? One vermin less to deal with, I say. 'Tis those crabs we got to worry about, lord, there's lots'n'lots of the confounded beasts down 'ere. Pretty big 'uns, too!'

Bucko saw the long-stalked eyes, watching them from every crack and crevice. He thrust a torch at them and made them scuttle from its flame. 'Ach, they'll no be a bother tae us. We got fire, lots o' it. Ah think frae whit ye were tellin' us, Stiff, 'tis only the high tide a-rushin' up here whit disturbs 'em!'

The mountain hare was right. In the absence of waves crashing into the tunnel, the crabs kept to the wallsides. There was room enough for everybeast to proceed in single file. It was a long hard trek, though; sometimes they had to bend almost double in the confined rock tunnel. Brocktree had to wriggle along, flat on his stomach. Though they had only been going a few hours, it felt like days.

Fleetscut patted his stomach. 'I say, you chaps, hows about stoppin' for a morsel o' jolly old supper? I'm fair famished, wot.'

'You stay famished an' let young Dotti stay fair,' Stiffener called back. 'We'll be in the cave soon enough, then y'can eat supper.'

After an interminable age of groping along through the damp rocky spaces, the boxing hare halted. 'Saileears, Trobee, bring those ropes here, will ye?'

Lord Brocktree peered through the hole at the eerie blue-lit cavern beneath, with its stalactites, stalagmites, bottomless pool and echoing water drips. Dotti pushed through. She measured the hole's diameter with both paws, then tried to gauge the Badger Lord's burly width.

'Hmm, 'fraid you won't fit through that hole, sah.'

Brocktree unshouldered his sword. 'Seems you're right, miss. Stand clear, please.'

He brought the swordpoint down hard a few times round the hole's edge, knocking out large cobs of the veined limestone. They crashed down into the cave, some into the pool. Blue wavery reflections of moving water gave the badger's face a spectral, fearsome appearance.

'Hope nobeast heard those stones falling. There, I'll fit through the hole smoothly enough, eh, Gurth?'

'You'm 'ave ee gurt way o' solvin' probberlums, zurr!'

They did not have to climb down the ropes. Lord Brocktree stayed on top and lowered them, four at a time, two to each rope. When they were all down he lowered himself gingerly, using both ropes. 'There now, that wasn't too bad. Let's rest awhile and eat.'

Grenn's Guosim cooks had brought along some supplies, which they ate sitting around the pool. Brocktree hardly touched his food, but sat staring intently into the green-blue translucent depths. Grenn swigged from a flask of dark damson wine, watching the badger.

'So, what're ye thinkin' of, sire?'

Brocktree continued scanning the water.

'My father Stonepaw died in this cave – a hero's death to enable his followers to escape.'

Grenn nodded sympathetically. She uncorked another flask of the wine and tossed it into the centre of the pool. Being filled to the top, it sank into the depths, sending up a tracery of dark purplish wine, like smoke from an oily fire on a windless day.

'There. That'll let yore ole dad know you've come to the mountain to take vengeance for him.'

They all watched the bottle until it was lost to sight in the fathomless depths, leaving only a long solitary spiral of dark damson wine. Brocktree stood up, dry-eyed.

'Thank ye for that, Log a Log Grenn. Stiffener, will you lead off? I'm completely lost down here.'

The boxing hare scratched his ears. 'I ain't too familiar with Salamandastron's cellars either, sire. We only stumbled on this place by accident when we were runnin' for our lives.'

The ever-optimistic Dotti volunteered a suggestion. 'I don't suppose it'll be that difficult to find our way out o' here, wot. An' I'll bet once Jukka has fired off her signal arrow she'll come lookin' for us. She should have a pretty fair idea of the place, havin' to find her way in an' whatnot.'

Bucko picked up his torch and joined Stiffener. 'Guid thinkin', lassie. Ah don't fancy hangin' aboot this place, et makes mah back preckle. Let's be awa'!'

Jukka's heart had been pounding as she approached the main gates. Standing almost barring the way was a group of vermin, who looked different from the usual Hordes, and the wildcat, who was obviously Ungatt Trunn. Keeping her eyes straight ahead, the squirrel, hoping fervently that her disguise would not be noticed, strode boldly forward. She passed them, as if she were carrying on with some chore or other which was keeping her busy, and breathed a sigh of relief as she made the main entrance. Next moment she was almost bowled over by a hooded and cloaked ferret, who dashed out and accosted Trunn and the others.

'Mighty One, over there, by the cliffside, northward, I saw it from my window, a fire!'

Jukka pulled to one side as the wildcat came bounding past, with the rest trying to keep up with him. Nobeast would dare challenge her in such company, thought Jukka. She tagged on and joined the rear of the party.

When Ungatt Trunn reached the high level guard post, Jukka followed. However, she stayed almost hidden against the mountainside, keeping in the background as much as possible. Jukka saw the flames from both fires, and watched Trunn giving out his commands to Ripfang, Fragorl and the tall saturnine fox called Karangool. When the vermin had departed hurriedly, Jukka ventured out.

There were three lookout guards still at the post, a ferret and two rats. The ferret was obviously the most senior of the three. He eyed Jukka suspiciously, pointing at her with his spear.

'Hoi! What're yew doin' round 'ere?'

The squirrel knew her disguise had him fooled. She decided to brazen it out and spat on the ground in true vermin fashion. 'Ain't doin' anythin'. What're yew doin'?'

The ferret was taken aback at her insolence. 'Wot am I doin'? I'm the night watch in charge o' this 'ere lookout post, appointed by Cap'n Drull!'

Jukka made as if to stroll away, but one of the rats barred her way with his spear haft. 'I ain't seen you afore?'

Jukka sneered back at him. 'An' I ain't seen you, or I'd remember yer ugly face. Now get that spear out o' me way!'

The rat's courage failed him when he saw the dangerous gleam in Jukka's eyes, and he allowed her to knock his spear aside. Accompanied by the other rat, the ferret stepped in. They menaced Jukka with their spear-points. Slightly unsure of himself, the ferret adopted an officious tone.

'You got no business bein' up 'ere. Who sent yer?'

'Ungatt Trunn did, an' stan' to attention when yer speaks to me. The Mighty One was right, things are gettin' far too sloppy round these 'igh lookout posts!'

Shooting the two rats a warning glance, the ferret came to attention, the rats speedily following his example. Jukka was beginning to enjoy herself. She circled the trio, inspecting them critically, whilst she pounded her brain in an effort to think how she could rid herself of them. Jukka needed to be at the high guard post, to fire off her signal arrow.

She saw the ferret's throat bob nervously. She nodded understandingly and flashed him a brief smile. 'I'm only doin' me job, same as you, mate. Let's take a look at yore spear a moment. Trunn's orders, y'know. At ease!'

The trio stood easy, the ferret passing over his spear for inspection. Jukka studied it closely. 'Hmmm, pole's a bit splintery, could do wid a polish too. When was the last time yer sharpened the blade?'

Some of the starch had gone out of the ferret. 'Three days back, I think, or mebbe four,' he muttered.

Jukka pursed her lips critically and shook her head at him. 'This spear'ead ain't been sharpened in a season. D'yer know it's come loose? Could do wid a new nail. Look!'

She waggled the spearhaft, holding tight to the head. A rusty nail was all that held them together, and it soon snapped, leaving Jukka holding the haft in one paw and the head in her other. She raised her eyebrows knowingly. 'See wot I mean, matey? Ah, but don't fret, I won't report yer. Y'know, sometimes a spearpole wid no blade can be a useful weapon. I'll show yer. Youse two rats, put down those spears an' stand either side of yer officer 'ere.'

The sentries decided that this strange-looking inspector was not such a bad type. They obeyed, letting Jukka shove them about until she had them in the required position: outside the guard post, with their backs to the edge of the mountainside. There was a dizzying drop behind them.

Jukka threw away the spearhead and held the pole sideways. 'When I did me spear trainin', my ole cap'n showed me this trick with a spearpole. Watch an' pay attention now, mates.'

The pole moved in a blur. Whack! Thwack! Whock! Three stunning blows, one to the side of each rat's head and the last to the ferret. The pole butt hit him between the eyes. Without a sound the three guards fell backward over the edge. It was a long way down.

Jukka checked that the little fire was lit in the guard

post and laid out bow and quiver, selecting the shaft with the oil-soaked rags bound to its point. Sounds drifted up from below; she peered down. Vermin came flooding out of the main gates and from the shores round about. They marched off at double speed in three groups, with Fragorl, Ripfang and Doomeye at the head of the columns. Karangool exited next, followed by every ship's crew that was on shore leave, dashing towards the fleet. Then Jukka saw the mountain perimeter guards hasten inside. She heard the main entrance doors slam shut and captains yelling for the windows to be barred. At last all became quiet, and the shores in front of the mountain lay deserted.

Touching the arrowhead to the fire, she waited a moment until it was blazing well. Then, fitting the shaft to her bowstring, Jukka turned south and fired off over the mountaintop.

Waiting on the tideline, not too far south of Salamandastron, Brog and Ruff stood at the head of their small army. The sea otter Skipper was first to see the signal arrow, arcing through the night sky, like a tiny comet. He pounded Ruff's back.

'There she goes, mate, right on time!'

Ruff's answer was to throw back his head and howl.

'Eulaliiiiaaaaa!'

They thundered along the shoreline, paws pounding the damp sand, weapons waving, a wild fearless band, giving out the challenge to anybeast daring to oppose them.

'Blood'n'vinegaaaaar! Eulaliiiiiaaaaa!'

It was only a short distance. Inside the mountain, a weasel Hordebeast heard the war cries. Moving aside a slat of driftwood from a ground level window space he peered out and was immediately cut down by a sling-stone. The rat Captain Drull leapt aside as a javelin clattered through. Grabbing the driftwood he closed the space, shoring it up with the slain weasel and shouting,

'Stand to! We're under attack! Get to the arrow slits!'

A bewildered stoat confronted Drull. 'But cap'n, we blocked up the arrer slits, you tole us to.'

Drull booted him to one side and drew his sword. 'No I never. Get t'the main gate an' stand fast, that's where they'll try t'break through. Shift yerself!'

Jukka climbed back inside the mountain and began making her way down to the cellars. She was still on the highest level, racing along a passageway, when she ran slapbang into Ungatt Trunn. They fell headlong, both tripped by the wildcat's trident haft, down a short flight of stairs. Jukka landed on top, extricating herself from Trunn's cloak folds and mumbling hasty apologies. Momentarily forgetting herself, Jukka fell into her natural speech.

'I beg thy pardon, sire. Art thou injured, pray?'

Ungatt Trunn scrambled to get upright, locking eyes with her. 'You're no Hordebeast, I can tell. Come here!'

Jukka did the only thing she could do in the circumstances. She leapt over the wildcat and ran for it. Trunn was speedily up and after her, calling for assistance.

'Guards, stop that creature, she's a spy, stop her!'

Jukka took a sharp left along a corridor which branched off two ways, and jammed herself into a darkened niche as Captain Drull and a mob of guards raced by.

Drull came to a forced halt as he turned the corner and the wildcat grabbed him.

'Where's the spy? Did you see which way that spy went?'

Ignoring the question, Drull babbled into Trunn's face. 'Attack, sire, we're bein' attacked! They're all over the shore outside! They're attackin' us!'

Ungatt Trunn shook the unfortunate rat mercilessly. 'I'll go and see to the attack. You take these with you and find that spy, there must be others inside my mountain. Don't stand there dithering. Catch the spy!'

Jukka saw the wildcat race down the opposite arm of the corridor, and waited until he was out of sight before she emerged. Drull came skidding round the corner at the head of a large mob of vermin, almost face to face with her.

'That's the spy! Hey you, halt! Stop, I say!'

But Jukka was not about to stop or halt. She went off down the passage with the vermin pack hard on her heels.

34

Dotti blinked. Lights shimmered in her vision each time she closed her eyes, and she stumbled against Southpaw. He gallantly held her upright. 'Steady on, miss Dotti. Here, take m'paw!'

The haremaid was glad of his assistance. 'Whew, we've been blunderin' round in the gloom down here for absoballylutely ages. Those lights are makin' my eyes go all funny. D'you suppose we're lost?'

'Good grief, I jolly well hope not, eh, Bob?'

'What, lost? I dunno, but it looks like we could be, old chap. I think this is the second blinkin' time I've passed this rock. It's shaped like a salad bowl. I've come t'know it rather well, wot!'

Brocktree held up his torch, illuminating the rock in question. 'Is he right, Stiffener? Are we lost?'

The boxing hare's ears drooped in shame. 'I 'ates to say it, lord, but I'm afeared we are.'

A groan rose from those who had been following him.

'Lost? D'ye mean we've been traipsin' round here for hours'n'hours only to get lost?'

'Hmm, bit of a blinkin' frost if y'ask me, old lad!'

'Yurr, zurr Stiff dunn a gudd job, oi reckern. Us'n's nearly thurr, hurr aye!'

The Badger Lord sounded hopeful. 'What makes you think so, Gurth?'

The good mole wet his digging claws by licking them, and held them up as high as he could. ''Coz oi be's feelen ee fresh hurr frumm above, zurr. 'Tis ee thing uz moles do be a-knowen abowt!'

Bucko, who hated the dark, congratulated Gurth. 'Och, guid for ye, mah braw laddie. Lead on!'

Fleetscut chortled aloud. 'Well twoggle m'paws, the old salad bowl, I remember that when I used to pinch puddens an' come down here to eat 'em, when I was only a young 'un!'

Sailears chuckled drily. 'An' that must've been only last season. I recall cook Blench complainin' about a lot of missin' vittles, you lanky-shanked pudden-purloiner!'

But Fleetscut was not listening. He was away, helter skelter down the rock tunnels, his cries echoing into the distance. 'Haha, salad bowl, o' course! Can't fool old Fleetie. I know me flippin' way out, course I jolly well do!'

Dotti started to run after him, but Gurth stopped her. 'Ee woan't catch zurr Fleet, missie. You'm foller Gurth, oi'll get us'n's safe out, trust oi!'

Brocktree smiled at the stolid reliable mole. 'Friend Gurth, I'd sooner trust you than a cartload of Fleetscuts. We'll follow faithfully wherever you lead!'

Fleetscut halted for an instant to regain his breath, not too sure if he was on the right path. 'I say, you lot . . . where've they gone? Oh, never mind. Now, was it this way, or that? Oh corks, I'm starvin'. Hope those blue-bottoms have left a morsel in the larder for supper. Or maybe tea. Huh, it could be blinkin' brekky time for all a chap'd know down this confounded hole. Hello, is that them comin' from the other way? I must've been travellin' in circles, wot?'

The sounds Fleetscut was hearing drew nearer, but they did not resemble any noises his friends would make.

'Come on, we've nearly got the spy!'

'Catch the spy! Stop that spy!'

It was one long passage, with no exits left or right. Fleetscut looked rather nonplussed as Jukka came panting up out of the gloom, and held up his torch. 'Oh, it's only you. Stolen any good weapons lately, wot?'

Jukka collapsed beside him, words pouring out of her. 'Right behind me – a load of vermin coming fast! Where are thy friends? Are they not with thee?'

'No, they're back there a ways. Should imagine they'll be along in a while . . .' He caught sight of the yelling mob of vermin racing up the tunnel. 'Great seasons, there'll be murder if they clash with our lot. We weren't expectin' anythin' like this.'

Jukka grabbed him savagely. 'No time for explanations now, longears. Hast thou weapons? We must hold them here, thee an' me!'

The enormity of it dawned upon Fleetscut. He snapped his javelin in half and brandished the torch. 'We'll have t'stop 'em. Here, take this. Eulaliiiiaaaa!'

Holding a half of the double-pointed javelin apiece, they charged forward. Both creatures threw themselves at the vermin mob in the narrowest part of the tunnel. The move took the Hordebeasts completely by surprise. Battering away with the lighted torch and thrusting with his piece of javelin, Fleetscut battled side by side with Jukka. They gave no quarter and stood their ground, fighting like a pair of madbeasts, yelling when their javelins found marks and gasping with pain when vermin blades found theirs.

Further down the tunnel, Sailears held up a paw for silence. 'What was that, sah? Did y'hear it?'

Brocktree was already rushing by her, his blade drawn. 'Battle ahead! Eulaliiiiaaaaa!'

They thundered along the tunnel and hit the vermin like a tidal wave. The awesome Brocktree went straight through the Hordebeasts, his sword scything a harvest of death. Dotti had hardly a chance to whirl her sling. Bucko shoved her to one side as he went in like a battering ram.

'Oot mah way, lassie. Yerrrahaaah! Ah'm the mad March hare frae the mountains! Tak yer last look at me, ye vermin!'

Skulls cracked against rock as Stiffener Medick and his two grandsons went in weaponless, punching and kicking. Dotti staggered upright, ducking again as a rat went sailing over her head. Gurth placed her politely out of his way.

'Stan' ee asoide, miz, lest ee get you'm dress mussed!'

Sailears hugged Dotti to her. 'Don't look. We should never have brought a maid to this place. Turn your face away, Dotti, 'twill soon be done.'

It was done in a frighteningly short time. No vermin was allowed to escape and raise the alarm. Treading carefully, Sailears led Dotti forward, clear of the carnage. On the other side of the battleground, Bucko was waiting for them. He stood up from the two forms he had been crouching over, Jukka and Fleetscut. The mountain hare wedged a torch into the rocks above them. As she knelt by their side, Dotti could see that Jukka was already dead. Fleetscut had tight hold of the squirrel's paw. His eyes flickered briefly. He was whispering something, and Dotti had to put her face close to his before she realised that the old hare was talking to Jukka.

'Held the tunnel . . . they never passed . . . lots o' weapons for you, my friend . . . odd though . . . don't feel a bit hungry. Jolly cold, wot!'

Fleetscut smiled at Dotti, his eyelids flickered one last time, and then they closed for ever. The haremaid looked at Sailears through a shimmering haze of tears.

'They died as friends. Who'd have thought it?'

The older hare helped her upright. 'Jukka an' Fleetscut were the bravest of the brave. Come now, young 'un, let them share the long sleep together.'

Ungatt Trunn felt the cold paw of fear traversing his

spine. With no more than a hundred vermin at his command he stood facing the barred main entrance. Rocks and boulders thudded noisily against the fortified oaken doors. Without his vast Hordes the wildcat was virtually a captive inside the mountain he had captured. There were roars of derision from outside.

'We're comin' to get ye, Trunn!'

'Is that the earth shakin', or is it yore paws tremblin'?'

'Bring up the batterin' ram. I'm tired o' knockin' on this door, mates. Let's knock it down!'

There was no aperture uncovered for the vermin to see what was going on, or to retaliate from. Hordebeasts stood grouped in the entrance hall, staring in horrified fascination at the reverberating doors. Stoat Captain Byle looked beseechingly to Ungatt Trunn.

'They're bringin' a batterin' ram – did you 'ear 'em, sire? Where's Drull an' the others got to? We'll be slain!'

A blow from the wildcat's trident shaft knocked Byle flat. Trunn aimed a kick at the cringing captain. 'Get up, you whimpering worm, find Captain Drull and his sentries, bring them here immediately!'

Byle scurried off to do his master's bidding.

Brog looked quizzically at Ruff as they both flung rocks at the doors.

'We never brought no batterin' ram with us, mate?'

Ruff hurled a lump of limestone. It made a satisfying thud. 'Haharr, but Trunn don't know that, do 'e? We'll need those doors in one piece once we're inside. Remember, Brog, our job's to provide a diversion. Make as much 'ullabaloo as possible 'til Brock an' our pals can find their way to the doors an' ambush Trunn from the rear, inside. Look out!'

Ruff pulled Brog to one side as a gang of rabblehogs loosed their slings. Pebbles rattled against oak like a spring hailstorm. Baron Drucco yelled encouragement.

'Now give 'em a few yells, my 'ogs, tell those vermints

wot we're goin' t'do to 'em!'

'Yaaah, yer bluebottomed wifflers, we'll spike yer!'

'Yew can't get away from the rabble'ogs. We've thrown an accordion round yore mountain, so there!'

Brog and Ruff joined in with gusto.

'Chop yore 'eads off an' chuck 'em in yore faces we will!'

'Set lights to yore tails an' use 'em for candles, too!'

'Aye, we'll make the stars fall on ye all right, the moon too!'

On the other side of the door, Ungatt Trunn paced nervously about, waiting for Byle to return with the reinforcements he had sent him to get. 'Stand your ground,' the wildcat rapped sternly at his quivering vermin, 'the doors will hold! This trident will take the eyes out of anybeast who moves without my permission!'

Trunn spied Byle. The stoat captain was dithering around at the hall entrance, as if unsure of which way to go next. Dashing down the hall, the wildcat cornered him.

'Where's Drull and the guard patrols? I ordered you to bring them to me! Well, where are they?'

Forgetting all titles and protocols, Byle blurted out, ''Ow should I know? There's a badger wid a sword twice the size o' me, there's an army wid 'im, an' they're comin' this way fast!'

Trunn's trident prongs prodded the stoat's neck. 'Keep your voice down. You and I are leaving here.' He shouted to the Hordebeasts guarding the doors, 'Hold your positions, stay there! Captain Byle has found Captain Drull and the guard patrols. We're going to fetch them. I order you to hold the doors. We'll be back soon!'

'But sire,' Byle protested, 'we don't know wh—'

He froze into silence as the trident pricked his throat. 'One more word and I'll leave you behind with them. Now follow me up to the second level!'

*

Brogalaw waved his paws furiously. 'Whoa, mates, stop yore rock-throwin' an' shoutin, and lissen!'

The decoy attackers left off their activities. They did not have to strain their ears to know what was going on on the other side of Salamandastron's main doors. Screams, roars, yells and the thunder of Eulalias told them that the plan had worked. Lord Brocktree and his force had made it, up from the cellars to the entrance. Slaughter was raging unchecked against the vermin that Ungatt Trunn had deserted.

Ruff flung away a rock and grabbed his spear. 'To the gates, me 'earties, to the gates!'

Durvy and his crew raced up from the shore, their coats dripping with seawater. Konul shook herself vigorously. 'Ain't you lot got inside yet, Brog?'

Chuckling, the sea otter Skipper dodged a spray of water. 'Ho, don't fret yoreself, missie, we soon will be!'

The ottermaid pointed seaward. 'Then ye'd best make it quick, mate. Karangool an' his crews cut out the burnin' ships an' sunk 'em. But they caught sight of us an' they're 'ard on our rudders. See!'

Ten galleys were being rowed to land, crammed with horde crew vermin, led by Karangool. Brog issued hasty orders.

'Drucco, bang on them doors as if yore life depended on it, 'cos it does! Form up in four lines, mates, backs t'the doors, slings, arrers an' javelins. Stir yore stumps!'

Sounds of battle, loud and wild, rang out from behind the doors. The ships ploughed into the shallows and armed vermin began leaping ashore in droves. Drucco battered the door, a rock in either paw, bellowing with all his might, 'Brock! Brock! Open up, mate! We're 'ard pressed out 'ere!'

Karangool stood on the prow of his vessel, urging the vermin on towards the mountain. 'Slay streamdogs, they fired our ships, kill allbeasts!'

*

Ungatt Trunn tore driftwood and sacking from a narrow window facing east on the second level. He peeped out and saw a small band of squirrels below. The wildcat nodded, smiling at Captain Byle.

'We're lucky, my friend, it's all clear. Out you go!'

Two arrows took the stoat before he cleared the window. Trunn spoke up in a voice loud enough to be heard from below.

''Tis no use, mates, the foebeast's waitin' below. Round to the south side, quick. I know a good place there!'

He stood perfectly still and waited a short time. When he looked out again the squirrels had run off to cover the south face. With all the litheness of a wildcat Ungatt Trunn descended to the ground. Treading contemptuously on Byle's carcass he set off north towards the cliffs.

Once the vermin were above the tideline, Brog gave the first rank of archers their order. 'Now!' Eight vermin fell, transfixed by flying arrows. The rest paused, but Karangool drove them onward from his ship's prow.

'Rush them, they be only few to us!'

They continued the charge. The archers dropped back to reload as Brog gave a command to the slingers who took their place.

'Shoot an' fall back, mates. Now!'

Drucco foamed at the mouth as he pounded the doors. 'Open up afore we're slaughterfied! Open up, Brock!'

Ruff took out a front runner with a well-aimed rock. 'Too late, mate, we'll just 'ave t'go down fightin'!'

Brog judged the distance between himself and the charging vermin. It looked as if Ruff was right. The sea otter Skipper brought forward his spears and javelins.

'Kneel 'ere in line, mateys, points to the fore! Archers, place yoreselves between the spears. Right, now!'

Another deadly hail of shafts buzzed through the night air. Vermin fell, but they kept coming, their own front ranks unshouldering bows and fitting shafts to strings.

With a creak and a groan the mighty doors swung inwards. Baron Drucco fell face down, still pounding with his two rocks at the earth in the open gateway. Gurth and Bucko Bigbones poked their heads round the doors.

'Welcumm to ee mounting, zurrs, do you'm cumm in naow!'

'Och, mah bairns, ye'll catch yer death of arrers stannin' roond oot there!'

They piled in regardless, ears over tails in a jumble, and the great doors slammed shut in the vermin horde's face.

Lord Brocktree put aside his battle blade. The badger's eyes were red as flame on winter's eve. His huge chest rose and fell as he approached the otters, stumbling over the carcasses of vermin who would fight no more. He stood silent awhile, striving to control the Bloodwrath which coursed like wildfire through his veins. Brog and Ruff took a step backward from the fearsome sight. Brocktree shuddered violently, as if trying to rid himself of a phantom foe. Then he held both paws wide, bowed his head and spoke in a normal tone.

'This is my mountain. Welcome to Salamandastron!'

35

Morning was well under way, warm and still under a powdery blue sky. Ungatt Trunn had traversed the clifftops for most of the night, searching for the mass of Hordebeasts he had sent to investigate the fire to the north. Only now had he found them. Telltale spirals of smoke marked their campfires in an area between the dunes and the cliffside. Still carrying his trident, the wildcat padded silently down to where Ripfang, his brother Doomeye and some other former searats were cooking things in their shields over the flames. Catching sight of Trunn, they started to stand to attention, but he waved them back down with a few flicks of his paw. Seating himself between Ripfang and Doomeye, he turned to the more intelligent of the two, showing neither anger or anxiety.

'So, Ripfang, I don't see captives or the slain bodies of Bark Crew creatures. Nor do I see as many Hordebeasts as left the mountain last night. What happened?'

Taking his time cleaning a morsel of food from his single tooth with a knifepoint, Ripfang coolly pushed across a shield containing a form of stew in its curved bowl. 'You musta been trampin' 'alf the night, boss. 'Ere, 'ave a bite o' brekkist.'

The food did not look very appetising, but it smelt good. Trunn picked up a clean seashell, scooped some up and tasted it, nodding agreeably. 'Not bad at all. What is it?'

'When we was chasin' after Fragorl, we found clumps o' charlock growin' everywhere, an' stonecrop too, sir,' Doomeye explained proudly. 'There was a liddle stream o' sweet water, wid tutsan sproutin' round it. Got some periwinkles an' mussels off'n the rocks below the tideline as well. So we cooked 'em all up together. Tasty, ain't it? Wish we 'ad some pepperwort, though. I likes pepperwort.'

Ungatt Trunn cut him short, his voice calm and reasonable. 'Very resourceful of you. But, Ripfang, why were you chasing after my Grand Fragorl?'

'Well, it was like this, see, cap'n. Fragorl was wid the band who was supposed to 'ead out along the shore an' circle back be'ind the enemy. But sink me if'n that treacherous ferret didn't just carry straight on goin'!'

The wildcat was hungry. He scooped up more of the mess. 'You mean she deserted?'

'The very word, cap'n, deserted! Aye, an' she took a third of our force wid 'er. Went like a flight o' swallows flyin' south, but o' course they 'eaded north. We did like yer said, closed in on that big bonfire, but there wasn't 'ide nor 'air of anybeast there, just a fire. Knowin' 'ow you'd feel about ole Fragorl takin' off wid yore soldiers like that, we tried to track 'er down. But they was long gone.'

Trunn tossed away the shell and wiped his mouth. 'I see. Thank you, my friends, you are both faithful and trustworthy servants. I'll reward you well when the time comes. But for now we'd best get back to the mountain.'

'The mountain, eh?' There was a hint of irony in Ripfang's tone. ''Ow are things goin' back there, cap'n?'

Ripfang gulped as the trident prongs went either side of his paw. Pressing down, the wildcat pinned the searat firmly to the sand. Ripfang was immediately regretting the dangerous game of disrespect he had started.

Ungatt Trunn's gold-ringed eyes blazed savagely. 'Let's go back and see, shall we? I trust you are still loyal to my cause, Ripfang, that you swear to follow and serve me? Or perhaps you'd like to stay here?'

Ripfang knew what the fearsome wildcat meant by the phrase stay here. He averted his eyes from the murderous gaze. 'Loyal? Me an' me brother are loyal to ye, sire, that's why we signed up with yer in the first place. You lead an' we'll foller yer, sire, true blue an' never fail. Er, soon as yew let me 'ave me paw back, sire.'

The trident lifted, releasing Ripfang's paw. Trunn smiled. 'Good! Get the columns ready to march, captain.'

They took to the clifftops where the going was faster, Ungatt Trunn at the rear, his captains at the front. The brother searats held a muttered conversation as they marched at double speed.

'Did yer see 'is eyes, Rip? That 'un's mad, stark starin' mad!'

'Oh no 'e ain't, Doom. Dangerous, aye, but not mad. Somethin' strange 'as 'appened back at the mountain. Wotever 'twas, it brought Trunn out searchin' for us all through the night. I don't like it, mate, not one liddle bit!'

'Mebbe we should've run fer it, like Fragorl did?'

'Yore right, Doom. Too late fer that now, though.'

'So wot d'yer think we should do, Rip?'

'I dunno, but I'll think of somethin'.'

'Well, 'urry up an' think, will yer!'

'Shuttup. 'Ow can I think wid yew blatherin' down me ear?'

'So that's all the thanks I gets for cookin' yer brekkist. Well, keep yer ideas. I can think of ideas too, y'know!'

'Hah, yew can think of ideas? Who told yer that? Yore brain's got a full-time job just figgerin' out 'ow to put one paw in front o' the other so yew kin march!'

Doomeye purposely stamped on Ripfang's paw.

'Yowch! Watch where yore treadin', y'great lolloper!'

Doomeye's smile was full of malicious innocence. 'Sorry, Rip. Me brain mustn't 'ave been figgerin' right.'

Lord Brocktree had ordered the mid-level windows and arrow slits to be opened. Now his creatures stood at every aperture, well armed and vigilant. Dotti and the twins took their lunchtime snack gratefully from the Guosim cooks and placed it on the windowsill. As they ate, the Badger Lord halted his inspection of the defences to chat with them whilst he took his meal.

'No sign of Ungatt Trunn yet, miss?'

'Sorry, sah, the blighter hasn't shown up yet. D'you think he will? P'raps the rascal's scarpered, wot?'

Brocktree shook his great striped head. 'No chance of that, I'm certain. He'll be back; this isn't finished yet. Look at those vermin below. They've completely surrounded the mountain, yet there's not been a single slingstone or arrow from them. That fox, Karangool, he's sitting on the sand just waiting. Waiting for orders, if I'm not mistaken. Doesn't want to make a wrong move.'

Southpaw and Bobweave guffawed.

'Haw haw, the wrongest move old Trunn ever made was stealin' your mountain, eh, lord?'

'I'll say. The blighter must be a right puddenhead, wot? Should've stuck t'stealin' his grandma's pies!'

Brocktree waved a plum slice under their noses sternly. 'Never underestimate your enemy. I shouldn't have to tell you that – you're supposed to be fighters.'

The Badger Lord pulled his paw back with half the slice gone. Bobweave grinned as he chewed. 'An' never wave scoff near a hare's jolly old mouth. You should know that, sire, wot?'

Brocktree winked at Dotti, then tripped the hare twin slyly. Bobweave found himself flat on his back, with the great sword point prodding his stomach lightly. It was the badger's turn to grin. 'Never steal food from the Lord of Salamandastron – he has a dreadful way of getting it back. You should know that!'

Dotti and Southpaw fell about laughing as Bobweave wailed, 'I say, sir, steady on, you wouldn't chap a chop, er, I mean chop a chap open t'get a measly mouthful back, would you? Rotters, why don't you plead for my bally life instead of rollin' round grinnin' like daft ducks!'

Bucko Bigbones fitted an arrow to his bowstring and took careful aim, not wanting to hit the fox sitting on the sands below. It was a skilful shot. The shaft whizzed down, burying itself between the creature's footpaws. The mountain hare's voice rang out.

'Guid afternoon to ye, Cap'n Karangool, is it? Ah'm lookin' down anither arrer at ye, so dinna move! Mebbe ye cannae bring me tae mind – ah'm Bucko Bigbones, an' ah remember you weel. Aye, an' there's scars on mah back, so ah'll nae ferget ye. Ach, quit tremblin', fox, ah wouldnae slay ye wi' an arrer, 'tis far too quick an' clean, ye ken. But don't ye fret noo, we'll be meetin' soon, tooth tae tooth an' paw tae paw, ye've got mah sworn promise on that! Off with ye now!'

Karangool leapt up and ran, four arrows zipping close by before he made the shelter of some rocks and shouted to his archers, 'Get him, middle window, secon' level, big harebeast. Get him!'

Shafts rained through the window space. Bucko stood to one side smiling grimly. Brog looked up from collecting the fallen arrows. 'Ahoy, mate, a spot o' trouble?'

'Och no, ah was jist givin' yon fox somethin' tae think aboot, sort o' joggin' his bad auld memory a wee bit!'

Karangool did have a bad old memory. He could not recall, from numerous evil deeds in the past, why the hare was seeking revenge upon him. While he crouched behind the rocks reviewing his wicked career, Ungatt Trunn's claws tugged the back of his cloak.

'Why are you hiding here, captain?'

'Might'ness, not hidin', waiting for you.'

'Well I'm here, as you see. Make your report. I need to know all that has gone on here in my absence.'

Stiffener knocked on the Badger Lord's chamber door in the mid-afternoon. Entering, he found Brocktree hurling incense burners from the window. Wiping dust and cobwebs from his paws, the badger looked round.

'That's better. I'm sure this chamber wasn't full of muck and spiders in my father's day, eh?'

The boxing hare went to the window and stared down at the vermin crowded on the beach. There were even more than before.

'Yore right, sire, 'twas always neat'n'clean, but that's not wot I've come 'ere t'talk about.'

Brocktree sat down on the edge of the bed. 'I can see that you've got something on your mind, friend. I'm always ready to listen. Speak on, Stiffener.'

The boxing hare banged his paws down on the sill impatiently. 'We've been here most o' the night an' the best part o' the day . . . When does the fightin' start?'

Brocktree joined him at the window and placed a paw about Stiffener's shoulders. 'You're a brave beast, Stiffener Medick, a truly perilous hare, one of the true sons of Salamandastron! But you've only got to look out of this window to see that the foe still has far superior numbers to our small force. When we set out from Bucko's court I thought I had enough warriors at my back to face any army, but I was not prepared for anything like Trunn's Hordes. He must have every vermin on the face of the earth here. We have fought with him, wisely and with the aid of good planning. I could give the signal right now to continue the battle. I'm certain that my friends, brave friends like you, would hurl themselves on the foe, with no question or quarter given. Most of you would die, and that's no guess, it's a fact. Hear me. I refuse to sacrifice the lives of good and gallant creatures!'

Stiffener gnawed on his lip, troubled and puzzled. 'But if we stay 'ere an' don't fight, Trunn ain't about to turn an' march away. That murderin' wildcat wants Salamandastron as much as you, lord. What do we do?'

Brocktree tapped his head with one paw. 'We think, Stiffener, we use our brains. Listen, d'you hear?' Strains of music and merriment sounded faintly from the window spaces on the second level, growing louder by the moment.

Stiffener was scratching his ears as Brocktree showed him to the door. 'What's goin' on, sire?'

'Oh, sorry, didn't you know? Go and see young Dotti – she'll explain it all to you. Hurry now, or you'll miss a good feast. That should baffle the bluebottoms, eh?'

Dotti's scheme was simple, to show the starving vermin that there was no shortage of food on her side, nor of courage and good cheer. In short, to dishearten the Blue vermin Hordes. Lord Brocktree had given the plan his blessing. It gave him time to think of his own solution to the problem, in peace and relative quiet.

Down on the shore, the vermin could not help but stare pitifully up at the happy, well-fed defenders. Ungatt Trunn and Karangool were some distance away, behind the rocks, assessing their own force numbers and laying their own plans. Ripfang and Doomeye were behaving in a most undignified manner for two horde captains. Every time a pie crust or scrap of cheese was tossed from the second level windows, they joined in the wild scrabble for it.

Dotti and her friends gave the impression that there was a limitless amount of food at their disposal. In reality there was not, but they kept up the pretence perfectly, stuffing down goodies and glugging down cordials, cheerily waving to the gaunt-faced vermin packing the shore. Log a Log Grenn even sang a song about nice things to eat, which had the vermin drooling. Guosim cooks burned branches of aromatic herbs used in their cooking, and the scent drifted downward, adding to the foebeasts' distress as Grenn sang.

'I won't eat pie or pudden,
Filled with grass an' roots,
For me a tart's a good 'un,
With ripe plump juicy fruits.
Take some cherries an' blackberries,
Honey so thick an' sweet,
In golden crust, all fit to burst,
Aye that's the stuff to eat, mates,
That's the stuff to eat!
Say nay who can, to mushroom flan,
All baked with onion sauce,
Unless you think 'tis better than
A crisp green salad course,
Sup cider pale, or nutbrown ale,
Oh isn't lunch a dream,
Surrounded by an apple pie,
With lots of meadowcream, mates,
Lots of meadowcream!'

A hollow-cheeked rat gave a strangled sob. Fitting an arrow to his bow, he shouted insanely, 'Yahahaha! I can't stan' it no more, I tell yer. I'll stop 'em singin', just yew see if'n I don't!'

Doomeye grabbed the shaft from the crazed rat's bowstring and caught the unlucky vermin a hefty kick which sent him sprawling. 'Yew ain't been given no orders to attack! Don't dare go shootin' at those creatures, they're chuckin' vittles down to us!'

A bitter-faced ferret laughed mirthlessly. 'Vittles? Yew call those vittles? A few scraps o' cheese an' some crusts of pie an' bread. Tchah!'

Ripfang shoved a cutlass under the complainant's snout. 'Shut yer scringin' gob. Any vittles is good vittles when a beast's starvin'!'

Gurth threw down an apple with only one bite out of it. Ripfang went after it, flaunting his authority. 'Hoi, put that down. I saw it first. Gimme that apple. I'm yer cap'n, an' that's an order, y'hear?'

Towards evening Brocktree put in an appearance and called a halt to things. One or two of the hares, Dotti included, seemed puzzled by his decision. The Badger Lord ordered the second level openings to be closed.

'Come to the dining hall. I have an announcement to make.'

They completed blocking the window spaces with much speculation.

'Dorothea, whit d'ye think big Brock has tae say?'

'Dunno, old chap. Your guess is as good as mine, wot?'

'D'you think he's going to start the final battle?'

'Who knows? We're far too outnumbered I reckon.'

'True, but we're in the best position. We hold the mountain.'

'Aye, but think, we could end up in the same blinkin' boat as the vermin. Under siege an' starvin', if the war takes any time at all!'

'Burr, whoi doan't us'n's jus' go to ee hall an' lissen to wot zurr Brock be wanten to tell uz?'

Brogalaw led off, patting Gurth's back. 'Haharr, there speaks a wise cove, eh, Bucko?'

'Och aye, ye cannae argue wi' mole logic!'

Leaning on the hilt of his great sword, the Lord of Salamandastron waited until the hum of voices died away before explaining his plan.

'They say the only way to kill a snake is to cut off its head. Ungatt Trunn's blue vermin are the snake, he is its head. Without him they are leaderless. Tonight I am sending out a challenge to Trunn which should settle this conflict. I will meet him, face to face, claw to paw and tooth to fang in combat to the death!'

An immediate hubbub broke out. Dotti jumped up beside the badger, silencing them in her severest manner.

'Will you be quiet this instant, please! Such bad manners, behavin' like a horde of vermin, bad form!'

Baron Drucco's loud grumble echoed round the hall. 'Ain't we h'entitled to no 'pinion?'

The haremaid shot him a frosty glare. 'You certainly are, sah, but only after his lordship has had his say. Then we'll elect a spokesbeast to represent us all. I vote that'll jolly well be me!'

Amid the laughter which followed, the hare twins cried out, 'Well said, miss Dotti. Capital idea, wot!'

'I second that, old chap. Motion carried without argument!'

Drucco's response was a shout which all heard. 'Oh, awright, long as she don't start singin'!'

'Withdraw that remark, sah, or step outside with me!'

'Wot? Not before he's stepped outside with me. I'll box his ill-mannered spikes flat!'

Brocktree's booming voice silenced everybeast. 'Stop this silly quarrelling or I'll stop it for you!' An immediate hush fell. The Badger Lord continued, 'There will be no arguments or opinions about this; it is my decision as your leader. Tomorrow at noon I will meet Ungatt Trunn out on the shore in front of this mountain. There will be no quarter given or asked and a free choice of weapons. Having said that, I do not expect for one moment that the wildcat will obey any rules. He did not get as far as he has by being a fair-minded creature. So, to guard against any treachery I will make my own arrangements with you so that the proper precautions are taken. Dotti, will you and Stiffener see to the guard patrols for tonight. Ruff, Grenn, Brogalaw, Drucco and Gurth, come to my chamber. Those of you not on sentry, get a good rest. You will need it to stand you in good stead tomorrow.'

A blazing javelin whipped out of the mountain, cutting a fiery trail through the night. It buried its point in the damp sand below the tideline, extinguishing the flaming tip. Weasel Captain Bargut plucked the weapon from the sand and carried it to the rocks, where Ungatt Trunn was still in conference with Karangool.

'Mightiness, this came from the mountain. I think there is a message tied to it.'

Taking the javelin, Trunn dismissed Bargut. He slit the twine, holding the scroll to the weapon's middle, with one razor sharp claw. Karangool watched the wildcat as he scanned the parchment which had been rolled around the haft. Ungatt Trunn's shoulders began shaking. At first the fox thought his master was suffering an attack of ague, then he realised Ungatt Trunn was laughing, a sight no creature had ever beheld. The wildcat made no sound, but his eyes narrowed to slits and his mouth curved up at either end, his whole body quivering convulsively.

'Everything comes to the beast who waits, eh, Karangool?'

'Might'ness?'

'Here I am, trying to think of a way to accomplish my plan, when the stripedog unwittingly solves it all for me!'

'Good news, eh, Might'ness?'

'Better than you think, much better. Come, follow me!'

Ruff put his eye to a crack in the wood of a window shutter, peering at the approaching shapes.

'Well, they're comin', Brock, whole bunch o' the blue scum!'

'Can you see Trunn with them, Ruff?'

'Not so far, mate. 'Ang on. Aha, I sees the cat now, but just a glimpse. That 'un's takin' no chances. He's well shielded by three ranks o' guards, shields up too.'

The group halted within hailing distance. Trunn's shout rang out from between the ranks. 'I received your message, stripedog!'

Brocktree's sharp growl answered. 'Well, cat, do you agree to the terms?'

'How could I not agree? The one left standing takes all. But can I trust you to honour your word?'

'I am a Badger Lord. My word is my life and honour!'

'Good! I am Ungatt Trunn the Conqueror, I too will pledge you my word. I will respect your terms!'

'Tomorrow then, when the noon is high. We will meet there, where you stand upon the shore at this moment.'

'Then I will look upon your face, stripedog!'

'And I will look upon yours, cat!'

'Not for long. I will close your eyes for ever.'

'You waste your breath on idle threats. Go away, cat!'

There followed a moment's silence, broken once or twice by outraged growls from the wildcat. Ruff returned to his spyhole in the shutter and peered out.

'Looks like they're gone, Brock.'

Instinct guided Brocktree to the rift in the rock wall of his bedchamber. Moving the bed, he ran his paw along the crack. About halfway down he found the widening, where both his paws fitted. Only a beast with the strength of a badger could move the slab. Corded sinews stood out against bunched muscles beneath Brocktree's fur. Knowing that other badgers had done this before him, it gave Brocktree much pleasure to unleash his own raw power. The slab seemed to groan, then it moved inward, unable to resist his might. Though he had never been in the secret place of Badger Lords before, Brocktree felt at home there, his mind familiar with it. Fetching a lantern from his bedchamber he traced the lines of carving which told the mountain's history, the legacy left him by the mummified figures of past Badger Rulers. Urthrun the Gripper, Spearlady Gorse, Bluestripe the Wild, Ceteruler the Just. He stared sadly at the place which stood unoccupied. His father, Lord Stonepaw, had been denied the right of taking his place there.

From the bedchamber, he carried through the big chair. It was almost like a rough throne. This had been his father's, he could feel it. Placing it in the space, he sat down. There was a heap of dark powder on a ledge, and he reached for some. It smelled like strange herbs, dried and crushed. A faint memory of a scent like this came to him. Brocktree sprinkled some in the lantern's air vent. Leaning back in his father's chair, he closed his eyes and inhaled.

It was an ancient fragrance, autumnal woods, faded summers, a winter sea and soft spring evenings. Badgers came and went through the crossroads of his mind, some dim and spectral, like those who had gone before, others light and ethereal, as if yet unborn. There was even a strong fearless mouse, bearing a beautiful sword, every bit as great a warrior as the badgers who roamed through his dreams. Battles were fought beneath forgotten suns, ships ranged the heaving seas through lightning-torn skies. Armies marched dusty paths, comrades in arms singing lustily. Brocktree's dream world turned through seasons of famine and feast, maidens singing, babes playing happily, silent lakes, chuckling streams, flower-strewn bowers and fruit-laden orchards. Then the tableaux changed: deserted caves, burning dwellings, vermin driving enslaved creatures over the slain members of their friends and family. Blood, war, misery, suffering . . . and finally . . .

The face of a wildcat he had not yet looked upon. Ungatt Trunn! The once fragrant aroma became bitter in Lord Brocktree's nostrils, and he awoke, shouting, 'No, it shall not happen, do you hear me, cat? No!'

Smearing a flat rock with vegetable oil, the Badger Lord began to put an edge to either side of the broad blade. Never having been a singer, he recited the ancient lines of a badger's swordsong as he worked.

'My blade like winter's cold doth bite,
Come guide me, Badger Lord,
For truth and justice we must fight,
Wield me, your Battle Sword!
Defend the weak, protect the meek,

Take thy good comrades' part,
My point like lightning, send to seek
The foebeast's evil heart!
Eulalia loud like thunder cry,
Be thou mine eyes and brain,
We join in honour, thee and I,
To strike in war again!'

Ungatt Trunn had singled out his best ship and moored it at the fleet's south edge, close to shore. Closeted in the main cabin, with Karangool, Ripfang and Doomeye, he laid further plans. The wildcat was a beast who left nothing to chance, and now that the moment was close he took precautions by covering all angles.

'I need an archer, the very finest bowbeast, one who never misses. Is there such a creature in my Hordes?'

Brimming with confidence, Ripfang replied, 'Look ye no further, cap'n. My brother Doomeye can pick off a butterfly on the wing, an' I'd take me oath on that. Yew ain't never seen a beast livin' that kin fire off a shaft like ole Doomeye 'ere, ain't that right, mate?'

Doomeye tapped the bow and quiver he always carried. 'I'm the best, Mighty One, yer can count on me!'

Trunn's tail curled out and drew him close. Doomeye's paws quivered as he gazed into the wildcat's savage eyes.

'Fail me and I'll make sure you die bit by bit, searat! Now, here's what you must do. Climb the mountain tonight, letting nobeast see you. Find a spot where you can command a good view of the combat. If the fight is going against me, kill the badger. Go now. Take your brother with you, and make sure you find a good hiding place. Be certain none see you!'

When the pair had departed, Trunn gave Karangool his instructions.

'You are certain this is our fastest vessel?'

'Yah, Might'ness, she sail faster than wind.'

'Then crew this ship with your best creatures, and be

ready to make sail on the noon tide. If all goes wrong I will need to get away from here with all haste. Understand?'

'Might'ness, she be ready, waitin'!'

Karangool was trapped by the bulkhead. He could move no further back as the trident points prodded his chest. 'Make sure she is, my friend, or you will curse the mother who gave birth to you!'

Trunn left then, to go aboard his own ship and spend the remainder of the night in his more luxurious stateroom.

Hidden behind some hatch covers, Ripfang and Doomeye waited until the wildcat was gone. Karangool, still rubbing his chest, ushered them into the cabin. 'You 'ear what Trunn say?'

Ripfang's face was the picture of wicked indignation. 'Every word, mate, every word! So, 'Is Mightiness is feared that it might all go wrong? I never thought I'd 'ear Trunn talkin' like that. We don't wanna be sidin' wid nobeast who's got the idea 'e might be a loser!'

Doomeye's head bobbed up and down in agreement. 'Yore right, Rip. Let's up anchor an' get away from it all right now. Us three could sail this craft easily!'

Karangool preened his brush thoughtfully. 'No, best we stay, 'ear me. If Trunn be losin', you shoot the stripedog, yah. Then you kill Trunn also! Us three be lords then, we take all!'

'But wot if that stripedog slays Trunn right off? That'd knock all the fight out o' our 'Ordebeasts. Wot then, eh?'

Karangool produced two brass hoops from his cloak. He threaded them through the holes in his ears and smiled. 'Yah, then you get off mountain fast. I be waitin' crewed up for sail. We forget diss place, go piratin' again!'

Ripfang did a little jig of delight, rubbing his paws. 'Hohohoho, ain't yew the one, cap'n. We're with yer!'

*

Dotti and her friends were laying a few plans of their own at that very moment. Grenn had the floor.

'When our Badger Lord goes out there to face Trunn tomorrer, he'll have enough on his mind. Now I know Brock's given us our orders, but there ain't no reason why we shouldn't make double sure o' things. Trunn knows nothin' of honour. That cat can't be trusted, take my word for it, mates.'

Brog nodded his agreement wholeheartedly. 'Yore right, Grenn, so wot's the scheme?'

Grenn turned to Dotti. 'Tell them, miss.'

The haremaid outlined the plan she and the shrew had devised. 'Right, listen up, chaps. Grenn and Drucco will stay inside the mountain – they'll have the Guosim, the rabblehogs and Jukka's tribe with them. Slings and bows, cover every window an' arrow slit. I'll be outside with our force of hares an' otters. We'll push in close to the place of combat, make two rough circles, more or less back t'back, fully armed of course. That way we'll be able to watch the vermin an' keep an eye out for trickery. If Lord Brock gets hurt, we'll surround him an' drag him back into the mountain, where Grenn'll be waitin' to barricade the main entrance once we're inside. But if our badger slays the cat, this is the counterplan. Bucko will give out with a loud Eulalia to Grenn. She'll lead her forces outside an' try to circle the bluebottoms. With a bit o' luck we'll have 'em both ways, us in the middle, the rest at their backs. Not a word to Brocktree now – he thinks he's goin' to carry the day by whackin' Trunn alone.'

Gurth waved a digging claw airily. 'Hurr, an' so ee will. Thurr bain't no wurrier loik zurr Brocko, boi okey thurr bain't! But us'n's be keepin' watch on ee vurmints, wun way or t'other. Moi ole dad allus sez count ee diggen claws if'n you'm shaken paws with ee vurmint!'

Bucko Bigbones looked up from honing his javelin point. 'Och, yer auld faither's a braw rock o' sense, mah friend. Aff tae yer beds, mah bairns, 'tis after midnight, ye ken!'

Ruff shouldered a long-bladed sword. 'I'll take first watch with the night sentries. Goodnight to ye all, an' good victory tomorrow, mates!'

'Thankee, zurr, oi bidden ee gudd noight too!'

'Good night, miss Dotti, pleasant dreams, wot!'

'Don't drub too many vermin in your slumbers, it can be jolly tirin' y'know. G'night, Grandpa Stiff!'

'Night, you two. I'll give ye a call at dawn.'

'Aye, ye can call me'n'Drucco too, if ye please, an' bring us a wee tray o' brekkist, auld pal!'

'Anybeast not on the breakfast line by dawn will be fightin' on an empty stomach. Did ye hear that, mister Bigbones?'

'I say, Log a Log Grenn marm, can I have Bucko's scoff if he's not there, wot?'

'You'll get wot yore given, Trobee. There'll be liddle enough to go round as it is, after wot you put away this afternoon.'

Amid the good-humoured joshing they filed off, some to bed, others to guard posts, laughing and joking. However, everybeast knew that at noon of the next day the merriment would cease, temporarily for some, permanently for others.

36

Lord Brocktree of Brockhall unshouldered his great sword and strode into the sandy arena. Behind him the sea lay calm, like a glittering mirror. He breathed deep and stood ready, clad only in a loose green tunic, a broad woven belt circling his waist. Dotti and her friends jostled their way roughly through the blue-furred vermin. Trampling paws and knocking aside weapons, they pushed their way to the inner fringe of the wide sandy circle. It was hot; golden noon sun blazed down out of a cloudless blue sky.

Standing at the western edge of the ring, Dotti felt herself shoved to one side as Ungatt Trunn prowled into the place of combat. A tremor of apprehension ran through the haremaid; the wildcat was a barbarous sight. His pointed ears could be seen through the slits of a round steel helmet with a spike on top and a shoulder-length fringe of fine chain mail. He wore a purple tunic, topped by a copper breastplate. Above his paws were metal bracelets with spikes bristling from them. In one paw he carried the big trident, in the other a woven net edged with metal weights.

Silence fell upon the packed shore, a quietness that was almost unearthly in its intensity. Lord Brocktree came to the centre of the arena. Lifting the sword level with his face, he saluted his enemy in the traditional manner of a beast about to do combat. But salutes, rules and formalities did not figure in Ungatt Trunn's nature. A screeching growl ripped from his throat and he charged.

Krrraaaanggggg!

Metal struck metal as the badger met his rush. The sword slammed down between the tines of the trident, shock waves running through the paws of both beasts. Digging in their footpaws, they bent to the task of trying to push one another backwards. Both were huge male animals in their prime, well matched. Brocktree allowed himself to be thrust back a pace, then he retaliated with a roar, sending Trunn skidding across the ring, ploughing two furrows in the sand. Suddenly the wildcat whipped the net about his opponent's footpaws, catching the badger unawares and crashing him to the sand.

Rrrip!

The sword came thrusting and slicing through the net meshes, its point punching a hole in Trunn's breastplate. He let go of the net and danced backward. Brocktree tore the net from his body and came after his adversary whirling it. He flung the net and Trunn leapt to one side, the metal weights whacking his side painfully as it sailed by. He stabbed downward in an attempt to lame Brocktree, but the badger shifted swiftly, an outside prong tearing the side of his footpaw. Ignoring the wound, he stamped down on the trident, trapping it against the ground. Flicking up the huge sword, he laid Trunn's right paw bare to the bone. Trunn fell down, but only to grab the net. Whirling it about his paw he came up, battering the badger's face with the weights. They broke and circled, the trident probing, the sword seeking. Then the net shot up, enveloping Brocktree's head, followed by a pawful of sand which the wildcat flung into his eyes. Trunn had no time to stab, so he hit Brocktree hard on the side of his head with the trident butt. The badger fell heavily, blinking and trying to rip the meshes from his face. Trunn raised the trident for the kill, but the badger rolled over. Folding his body into a curled-up position, Brocktree hauled sharply on the net and Trunn stumbled forward, his back bent. As he fell towards Brocktree, the badger lashed out with his uninjured footpaw, smacking it into the wildcat's nose with a sickening thud. Trunn fell backwards. Brocktree struggled upright, tearing himself free of the net, and quickly pawed the sand from his eyes. From flat on his back Trunn beheld his foe bearing down on him, sword upraised. He shoved the trident out in front of him to counter the weapon's swing, and Brocktree's battle blade sheared right through one of the thick barbed copper prongs, which zinged off skyward.

Doomeye fitted the shaft to his bowstring. 'Time fer the stripedog t'die. Trunn's flat on 'is back!' He drew back the seasoned yew bow to its limit, and sighting expertly down the arrow he fired. The force of the blow which had severed Trunn's trident prong took Brocktree a staggering pace forward, but he whirled and straightened so quickly that the arrow, which would have pierced the base of the badger's skull from behind, thwacked through his left shoulder.

Ripfang clapped a paw to his brow. 'Idiot, y'missed!'

Doomeye's lip pouted sulkily as he laid another shaft on his bowstring. 'The stripedog cheated, 'e moved, but I still got 'im, Rip! Watch me finish 'im off wid this next arrer!'

But Ruff was already moving. Grabbing Bucko's javelin, he kept his eyes on the vermin head he had spotted, poking above the rocks, atop the second level. One paw out straight, the other wide outstretched, balancing the weapon, the big otter did a hop-skipping sideways run right across the arena. His footpaws pounded the sand as he gained momentum, one eye centred firmly on the high target, and he let out an almighty yell as he hurled the javelin with all his strength. It whistled up through the hot summer air, with almost every eye on it, up, up, with breathtaking speed. Doomeye had the arrow stretched tight on his bowstring. He stood up and placed his cheek against it, closing one eye to sight on Brocktree. Though he had not intended it, Ruff's javelin actually cut the bowstring. Doomeye could not lower his chin. He turned to show his brother the javelin, growing out of his neck on either side, and fell dead on top of him. With a sob of horror, Ripfang heaved the body off himself and fled.

Lord Brocktree towered over Trunn like a giant oak. As the wildcat tried to rise he kicked him flat again. The pandemonium which had rung through the arena when the arrow struck the Badger Lord fell hushed. Every eye was on Brocktree, standing over his enemy, the barbed shaft embedded in his shoulder, filled with the terrible Bloodwrath. Dragging the arrow out without the slightest sign of a flinch, the Badger Lord flung it into the wildcat's face. Kicking the net to one side, he stamped down hard on the trident shaft. It broke with a loud crack, leaving Trunn with a pawful of splinters. For the first time in his life, Ungatt Trunn felt cold fear. He tried to drag himself backwards, but Brocktree's powerful paws seized him and hauled him up until their faces were touching. Like a knell of doom the badger's voice rang in his ears.

'Now I see your face, Ungatt Trunn. Look upon me!'

Trunn finally looked into the eyes of his tormentor, but this time it was no vision – the terrifying nemesis of his dreams had at last become flesh and blood. One word escaped the wildcat's lips and echoed around the silent, crowded shore.

'Mercy!'

The next thing everybeast heard was the bone-jarring snap of Ungatt Trunn's spine as Brocktree caught him in a swift, deadly embrace. He picked up his sword, pointing with it at the huddled figure on the sand.

'Cast this thing into the sea!'

The second level barricades fell, and a hail of arrows and slingstones shot out over the crowd.

'Eulaliiiiiaaaaaa!'

Bumping, falling, scrambling and trampling over their comrades on the sand, vermin ran madly to the fleet of vessels moored in Salamandastron bay. Bucko Bigbones grabbed a sword and yelled, 'Yaylahaaaar, mah bairns, let's send 'em on their way!'

Guosim came pouring out of the mountain, Log a Log Grenn roaring the shrew battle cry.

'Logalogalogalooooog!'

Ripfang was already in the sea, half wading, half swimming after the stern of the lead vessel, which Karangool had already ordered to sail.

'Wait fer me, cap'n, 'tis Ripfang, wait fer me!'

He caught a rope trailing from the after end and hauled himself up, paw over paw. Karangool watched the exhausted searat climb wearily over the rail and spit out seawater.

'Trunn's dead, everythin's lost!'

The fox curled his lip contemptuously. 'I know that, fool, why you think I sail?'

Bucko was first to the sea. Dashing into the shallows after the fleeing vermin, he chanced to glance south at the vessel which was already crewed and under way. The mountain hare's eyes lit up with grim satisfaction. There leaning over the stern rail was the fox called Karangool. Bucko tore south, spray flying everywhere. Grasping his sword in his teeth he gave a wolfish grin and went after the ship.

Still sprawled by the stern, recovering his breath, Ripfang watched the crew trim the sails to let the breeze take her south. He turned his attention to Karangool, who was guiding the tiller.

'Huh, some mate yew are, fox. You was goin' t'sail off

an' leave me, after all the plans we made t'gether, eh?'

Karangool did not even bother to look at him. 'Stop you moanin'. Got aboard, didn't ye?'

Ripfang was facing away from Karangool, and now he could see Bucko swimming strongly after the ship. Suddenly the searat became philosophical.

'Yer right, mate, I did get aboard, an' well shut o' that lot too. Pore ole Doomeye's back there lyin' slain – shame, that was. Still, worse things 'appen at sea, eh, mate?'

Karangool aimed a sharp kick at Ripfang. 'You don't mate me, rat. I cap'n now!'

Ripfang continued appealing to the fox's better nature. 'You don't mean that, do yer? You said we was all goin' t'be cap'ns. I know Doomeye ain't around no more, but that's no reason why we can't be cap'ns together, is it, me ole cully?'

A sword appeared in Karangool's paw. He swung it upward, readying himself to take Ripfang's head off. 'Only room for one cap'n on diss ship!'

Ripfang leapt up and sprang to attention, saluting smartly. 'Yer right there, cap'n. I wishes to report a beast follerin' yer ship, one o' those longears, just aft of us there!'

Karangool went to the rail and leaned over. He felt a momentary wave of fear as he glimpsed Bucko, but it soon passed when he realised the hare was in the water, whilst he was aboard a fast ship, headed south. 'Yah, that longears come after me, I not know why.'

Ripfang sneaked up behind Karangool and suddenly heaved him overboard into the sea. 'Why don't yer go an' ask 'im wot 'e wants?'

Karangool wallowed in the vessel's wake, shouting at Ripfang, 'Ahoy, pull me up, mate!'

The searat tut-tutted severely. 'I ain't yore mate. 'Member wot yew said, only room fer one cap'n aboard this ship? Well, yer talkin' to 'im!' He tipped a broken mast spar over the side. 'You kin be cap'n o' that. Steer 'er careful, cap'n. Goodbye, an' the worst o' luck to ye!'

Karangool had lost his sword in the fall overboard. Bucko still had his. He sat on the spar facing the fox, with the sword pointed at his eyes.

'Och, 'tis a braw day for sailin', mah bonny wee foxy. Now, ye set still there an' ah'll tell ye a sad auld tale, aboot a puir young hare, whit wis left for dead by a wicked auld fox who beat him wi' a sword blade.' Bucko's chuckle was neither pleasant nor friendly. 'Weel now, ah see ye reckernise me at last. Tell me, mah friend, how does it feel t'be wi'out yer great horde o' vermin tae help ye out?'

Whup!

Karangool screamed in pain as the flat of Bucko's sword struck him smartly across his shoulder. The mountain hare bellowed in his face.

'Tell me!'

Evening sun was dipping low on the horizon. Dotti sat with all her friends and comrades in arms. From where they rested, on a broad terrace of rock slabs and vegetation, above the mountain's main entrance, the whole scene of that day's activities was spread before them. Like autumn leaves strewn by the wind, distant vessels ranged far and wide over the darkening sea, to the north and south and out to the west.

Shading his eyes from the sun's crimson glow, Stiffener watched them growing smaller. 'Lots o' those ships overladen with vermin, y'know. I'd say some of them'll sink afore the next dawn comes.'

Baron Drucco wrinkled his browspikes, in that manner hedgehogs adopt when they could not care less. 'Serves 'em right. Ain't our fault they wouldn't stand an' make a fight of it. Hah, ran like forficartickers they did!' Nobeast bothered enquiring what a forficarticker could be.

'Well I for one am jolly well glad they did run,' Dotti admitted. 'We never lost one creature in that little scrabble across the shore t'the shallows, what d'you say, Ruff old chap?'

'I'm with you, missie. There was more vermin drowned than slain in combat. A score or so of ours wounded, no great slaughter. Almost wot they call a bloodless victory.'

An iron arrowhead clinked on the rocks, and Lord Brocktree emerged from an open window space to sit with them. 'Anybeast want to keep that as a souvenir of the battle? Ruro dug it out of my shoulder – that squirrel's a marvel when it comes to patching a beast up!'

Gurth viewed the Badger Lord. He had compresses of herbs bandaged to shoulder, back, side and footpaw, plus one across his striped brow, which gave him a roguish air.

'Burr, you'm looken loik ee been in a gudd ole bartle, zurr!'

Brocktree took a sip from the tankard he was carrying. 'I suppose I do, but I'm feeling no pain at all. One of your cooks gave me this to drink, Drucco. What is it?'

The baron took a drink and winked knowingly. 'Special ole berry'n'pear wine wid some cowslip an' royal fern essence. That'll make ye sleep tonight, sire!'

Trobee took a mouthful and nodded approvingly. 'Tastes absolutely spiffin'. Wish I'd been wounded!'

Brogalaw tweaked the hungry hare's ear. 'Don't start talkin' about vittles an' drink again, y'great longeared stummick, we're flat out o' grub. But you won't need t'wait long. 'Ere comes my bird t'the rescue!'

Rulango soared gracefully in out of the evening sky. If it were at all possible for a heron to smile, Dotti would have said that the great bird tried his best. He was all over Brog, wafting him with both wings and knocking his beak against the sea otter's paws, as if checking he was unhurt. Brog stroked Rulango's neck to calm him down.

'Steady on there, ole mattressback, I'm all right. How's my mum an' the rest o' me mates? Snug'n'safe, are they?'

Rulango placed both wings over his eyes, letting his head bob up and down. Brogalaw roared laughing.

'Still weepin' an' cryin', eh? Good ole Mum. She an' 'er pals ain't 'appy if they can't 'ave a good blubber. Lissen, matey, you get back t'the cave an' tell 'em to whomp up vittles fer victors, lots of the stuff, as much as they can cook afore mornin'. I'm sendin' Southpaw an' Bobweave, Durvy an' Konul an' some Guosim over there, an' we'll get 'em moved lock, stock an' vittles back 'ere. I tell ye, mates, I feels a feast comin' on!'

Stiffener's eyes lit up, as did many others'. 'I say, splendid idea, old lad, wot!'

'Aye, a great feast at Salamandastron!'

'Wid enough scoff t'sink a gang of my rabble'ogs!'

'And singin' an' music, for days an' days!' Grenn added.

'Ho urr, an' darncin' too, oi loiks t'darnce!'

'An' when it goes dark we'll light big bonfires on the beach, so we can carry on all night!'

'Capital, an' miss Dotti can play the harecordion an' sing!'

'Why didn't I think of that, South? What a great wheeze!'

Ruff pulled a face. 'Don't yer think we suffered enough in battle?'

Dotti stared severely at the otter, then broke out giggling. 'Heeheehee, I'll sing an extra long ballad, just for you!'

Lord Brocktree laughed until the bandage on his brow slipped and fell over his eyes. 'Oh, look out, it's gone dark. Time for bed, you lot!'

Sounds of merriment rang out from the happy creatures on the mountain, so loud that a pair of seagulls, building a nest in the rocks, squawked complainingly. The birds had come back to the western shores.

37

It was lonely on the far reaches of shoreline to the north of Salamandastron. Night had fallen over the restless sea. A flood tide was rising, claiming back the flotsam and jetsam it had cast up on its previous visit. How long Ungatt Trunn had lain there, he could not tell. Salt water crusted the wildcat's eyes, slopping bitterly into his half-open mouth. He could not move his body. Most of it was numb, frozen solid, as if encased in a block of ice. But his chest, head and neck were on fire with unearthly pain. The last thing he could recall was the Badger Lord, crimson-eyed as they came face to face, snarling at him. 'Now I see your face, Ungatt Trunn. Look upon me!' Beyond that, everything was a blank and unknown void.

But the wildcat was not dead. He recovered consciousness slowly, sodden, freezing cold and grunting in agony every time a wave smashed over his helpless body, moving him down the slope of the shore. Damp seaweed and the sharp edge of a shell pressed against his cheek. Something small and spiny scuttled across his face. From the corner of one eye he could see a half-moon and the star-scattered skies. Another wave buffeted him. Now he could see the sand and a rocky outcrop. Realisation invaded his senses with a shock of terror as his awful position dawned upon him. He was lying at the mercy of the sea. Floodtide was drawing him back into the waves, where he would be swept out into the vast, unknown deeps.

Hissing like a huge reptile, another wave crashed over him, rolling his broken body into the shallows. The wildcat turned his gaze landward, and gave an agonised groan. Then he saw something. Two footpaws and a bushy tail. Somebeast, a fox, was sitting on the rocks, watching him. Karangool, it had to be Karangool! His own voice sounded distant, strange to him, as he croaked out, 'Please . . . 'elp . . . mmmee!'

The fox came down off the rocks and crouched before him. Trunn managed one word before the fox pushed him further into the water.

'Groddil?'

Then he was swept away on the current, drawn out to sea with rollers lifting him high on their crests and tossing him down into their troughs.

Groddil watched the bobbing object until it became a far-out speck amid the night sea. He was chanting aloud, though his former master was beyond hearing the crippled fox magician whom he had bullied and tormented for so long. None the less, Groddil chanted on.

'These are the days of Ungatt Trunn the Fearsome Beast! O Mighty One, he who makes the stars fall! Conqueror, Earth Shaker, son of King Mortspear, brother to Verdauga! Lord of all the Blue Hordes, who are as many as the leaves of autumn! O All Powerful Ungatt Trunn!'

Turning his back upon the sea, the crippled fox limped away and was never seen in those lands again.

38

Mornings were dawning in soft mist; the days grew shorter, sunsets earlier and more crimson. The earth was turning its season from summer to autumn.

Hares had come to the mountain, travelling from far corners to serve under the banner of Salamandastron's ruler, the fabled Lord Brocktree. Travellers carried abroad tales of his valour and the brave army who had defeated the evil might of Ungatt Trunn and his Blue Hordes. There was a fresh spirit of joy and freedom upon the lands; now anybeast could range the earth in peace. But there were also creatures leaving the mountain to return to their homes. Ten ships from the defeated fleet had been recovered and made good and seaworthy. Twoscore vermin captives, their coats scoured clean of blue dye, had worked on the vessels, making them ready for this special day.

Brogalaw took five of the ships. His crew of sea otters and their families boarded, laden with gifts, for their voyage south. Then he came ashore with Durvy, Konul and the heron, Rulango, to say farewell. Dotti was embracing them when she went into floods of tears. She fought to stem them, to no avail.

'Oh, I say, you chaps, sniff sniff, I feel absolutely

dreadful, boohoo! Can't help m'self, Brog, waahaah! Gettin' your tunic all wet, look. Boohoohaaah!'

The kindly sea otter Skipper gave her his kerchief. 'Haharr, you carry on, miss. I'm used t'this sort o' thing, y'know. Wot with my mum weepin' an' wailin', I'll wager we end up balin' out tears to stop us sinkin' afore we're back 'ome down southcoast!'

Lord Brocktree stood in the mountain's main entrance, waving with his sword as Brog and his friends returned aboard their ship. 'Farewell and fair winds, friends. Brog, you'll come back and visit, I trust?'

'Aye, lord. Keep the vittles a-cookin' – you never know wot season the ole Bark Crew'll come blowin' up the coast to eat you out o' 'ouse an' 'ome. Watch out for us, Ruff!'

Tears sprang into Ruff's eyes, and he looked at the badger. Brocktree nodded and clasped his paw fondly. 'Go on, get along with you. See you next spring mayhap.'

Kissing Dotti, Ruff bounded past her into the water. 'Ahoy, Brog, I'm comin' with ye! I always wanted t'learn 'ow t'be a sea otter. Lend a paw 'ere, mates!'

As he was hauled aboard, Bucko Bigbones came marching out of the main gate, followed by his mountain hares.

'Ach weel, Brock, there's mah ships an' here am ah. Ah won't stan' aroond weepin' like a wee bairn. 'Tis aff tae the North Mountains for me'n'mah clan. Mind, though, we'll be ever ready tae come ef ye call for us. Not that ye'll be needin' help, a braw beast like yersel', with all these fine young hares a-floodin' in by the day. Fare ye weel!'

Dotti held Bucko's paw before he boarded his vessel. 'I'm going to miss you pretty awfully, y'know, Bucko. Wouldn't you consider staying on a few seasons, help me to command the new Long Patrol that Lord Brock's forming? We'd have lots of super adventures, you'n'me, ranging the shores an' woodlands an' whatnot, wot wot?'

The mountain hare ruffled her ears affectionately. 'Och

no, lassie, ah'm yearnin' tae return tae mah mountains. But we'll be the highland branch o' yer Long Patrol if ye like, an' ah'll call mahsel' General Bucko. Fare ye weel, Dorothea, live lang an' happy. Yer a fatal beauty the noo!'

Biting her kerchief so as not to let Bucko see her weeping, Dotti hurried back to the main entrance. Ruro was waiting for her, wearing a silver medallion about her neck.

'Look at the honour thy Badger Lord bestowed upon me. I'm to be leader of my tribe. 'Tis called a Jukka medal!'

The haremaid inspected the beautiful insignia, a likeness of Jukka, twirling what else but a sling. 'It's lovely, Ruro. I won't say goodbye, 'cos your pine grove's not more than a couple o' days' walk from us. We'll call and see one another often, wot?'

Ruro signalled her tribe to move off. ''Tis a promise, Dotti!'

Dotti turned to Log a Log Grenn. 'An' you, Grenn marm – you and your Guosim will be on your way then, won't you, wot?'

The shrew Chieftain nodded, close to tears herself. 'If ever you need us, just send word.'

Mirklewort chased after Skittles. He came out of the mountain like a tiny boulder, knocking Dotti flat, a great smile plastered all over his cheeky face.

'We gonna stay onna mounting a few seasons, wiv you an' B'ock. I paggle every day inna water wiv ya, Dotti!' Mirklewort took a swipe at the hogbabe with a dish towel, but he scampered up on to the Badger Lord's sword hilt. 'Choppa you tail off if ya do dat again, Mummy!'

Gurth flicked Skittles's snout with his digging claw. 'You'm 'ave respecks for ee muther, likkle zurr. Oi'm stayin' yurr jus' to keep a h'eye on ee, villyun! An' as furr ee, miz Dott, you'm cumm with oi. Yurr h'aunt Blench sez ee got to lurn ee cooken!'

Dotti ducked beneath Brocktree's paw for protection. 'Oh I say, sah, bit much, isn't it? How in the name o' seasons is a gel supposed to be bossess of your blinkin' Long Patrol an' whomp around the bloomin' kitchens helpin' Aunt Blench? What am I, Patrol Bossess or flippin' cook?'

Brocktree hid a smile as he looked down at her. 'The title is Patrol General, miss, not Bossess, and there's a whole lifetime ahead of you, Dotti – you're still young enough to learn lots of new things. Now, is everybeast here? I see they've hauled anchors. Brog's bound south and Bucko's bound north.'

Striding out on the sands, Brocktree looked about at the legions of hares, sitting on the mountain terraces and perched on the shore rocks. 'Up on your paws now, my friends,' he called. 'Let's give our departing comrades a real Salamandastron farewell. Ready? One, two . . .'

Leaning over the sterns of their vessels, both Brogalaw and Bucko Bigbones could not help joining in with the thunderous roar from the shore. The ten ships sailed off into the golden afternoon, with the farewell war cry gladdening the hearts of all.

'Eulaliiiiiiiaaaaaaaaaaaaaaaa!'

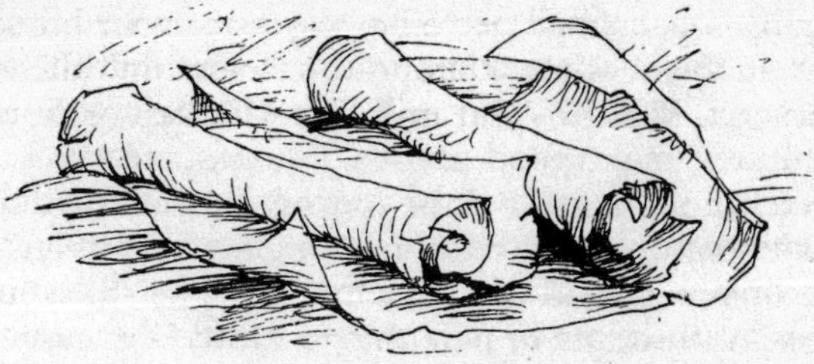

Epilogue

Lord Russano put aside the final piece of parchment. His pail was empty, the tabletop covered in bundles of scrolls. He looked around the crowded dining hall.

'So there you have it, my friends, how the great Lord Brocktree first came to our mountain, and the odd bond of comradeship which existed between him and a young haremaid. Dotti, as far as my researches show, became the first officer when our Long Patrol was formed. Thank you for listening to my account.'

The audience cheered him to the echo, standing to give the Badger Lord an appreciative ovation. There was only one creature not applauding, Russano's son Snowstripe. He was three seasons younger than his sister Melanius and still a Dibbun in many ways. Snowstripe had been sitting on his mother's lap, listening to the final episode of his father's narrative, when he had drifted off into a slumber. Rosalaun had covered him with her shawl and let him sleep on. It was the noisy volume of the cheering that woke him.

Snowstripe yawned, rubbing sleep from his eyes. Russano gathered his little son up, still wrapped in the shawl. 'Come on, matey, time you were in bed.'

Looking up at his father, the youngster murmured

drowsily, 'Is the story finished, Papa?'

The Badger Lord shook his head solemnly. 'Only a part of it, my son, a small part. One day you and your sister will rule this mountain and you will find that the story carries on. Both of you will live through your own adventures, make good friends of honest creatures. The defence of our coasts will be your responsibility, though fate and seasons forbid that you will have to face vermin invasion and war. Salamandastron's story will continue, as long as there are brave badgers to rule the mountain wisely. Your mother and I have often told you and Melanius the law of Badger Lords. Can you remember what we said?'

As they mounted the stairs, Snowstripe's eyelids began to droop, but he recited by heart the lessons he had been taught.

'Defend the weak, protect both young and old, never desert your friends. Give justice to all, be fearless in battle and always ready to defend the right.'

Snowstripe gave out with a yawn, and his eyelids fluttered, gradually closing.

'Anything more?' Russano whispered in his ear.

As sleep overcame the little badger, he nodded. 'Hmm, the Badger Lord of Salamandastron must always show a welcome an' good cheer to all of true heart who come to visit here in peace. Our gates will be ever open to them . . .'

Snowstripe's voice trailed off as slumber claimed him, and Russano completed the last line for his son.

'For this is the word of the Badger Lord and the law of Salamandastron, passed down to us from Lord Brocktree!'